Also by

VICTORIA JANSSEN

The MOONLIGHT MISTRESS

Also by

VICTORIA JANSSEN

**THE DUCHESS, HER MAID,
THE GROOM & THEIR LOVER**

VICTORIA JANSSEN

The MOONLIGHT MISTRESS

AN EROTIC NOVEL

THE MOONLIGHT MISTRESS

ISBN-13: 978-0-373-60536-1

Copyright © 2009 by Victoria Janssen.

www.Spice-Books.com

Printed in U.S.A.

For Charlotte, for more reasons than I can put into words.
Happy birthday!

1

THERE WERE NO TRAINS TO STRASBOURG.

The hand-lettered sign on the station wall might be wrong, or something might have changed. She would ask again. Lucilla Daglish clutched her single carpetbag more closely, to protect her scientific glassware from the anxious crowd, but also for reassurance. People jostled past her in every direction, all of them speaking in high-pitched, anxious tones that blurred into a babble conveying nothing but fear. Two different babies wailed, and a larger child screeched between gulping sobs. A fat man, reeking of stale pipe smoke, elbowed her sharply in the kidney as he pushed his way behind her.

Lucilla cursed herself mentally as she tried to explain her problem to the ticket agent. Had the man in the booth needed to know about titration or some other element of practicing chemistry, she could have explained it to him in great detail. However, her more basic conversational German was lacking. Perhaps she had misunderstood his meaning, or he had misunderstood hers. Perhaps her fear had led her to misspeak.

Summoning different German vocabulary, she phrased her question again. She was an Englishwoman. She wished to travel to Paris via Strasbourg. She had a ticket. Here was her ticket. Here were her papers, proving her nationality.

No, it was the *gnädige Frau* who did not understand. There were no trains to Strasbourg. There were no trains at all. Germany had declared war on Russia. There would be no trains until further orders were received.

"I am not at war!" Lucilla exclaimed in English, knowing the agent would not understand her frustrated outpourings. "Why can I not travel out of this country? Surely you have no use for me here?"

There were no trains today, the agent repeated in German. Perhaps tomorrow. Or the following week. The *gnädige Frau* would do well to find a room in the town, before they were all taken.

She could not smash her bag into the ticket agent's smug, condescending face because he would surely call the police. She turned sharply away. She would have to temporarily abandon her trunk here at the train station. She would return to the Institute. Perhaps she could sleep there. She had been a fool to give up her room. An utter fool. But she had not had the money to pay for an entire additional month, as her landlady had insisted, and she was leaving anyway. Or so she had thought.

She had no friends here whom she could approach for help. The other women in the boardinghouse had grouped together at meals, discussing their prospects of marriage or employment. Unlike them, Lucilla was well past the age of marriage, and she was already employed. She had never stayed longer than needed to quickly eat while perusing a journal article;

she did not have time for the pleasantries, when the laboratory called to her so passionately. One could not be a friend
to one's colleagues, either, when one was a woman, and they
were all men who viewed her more like a trained monkey
than a chemist. Some of the men would not speak to her at
all, even to exchange pleasantries. After six months in
Germany, she knew no one whom she might call, even to
meet her for a cup of tea.

The sun had set while she fought the crowds inside the
station. Even in the dark, the hot, dusty streets were mobbed,
three times as crowded as on a normal night. Compared to
that morning, the whole town felt alien to her. Boys hawked
newspapers on every corner. Men stood and read the papers
under streetlights and in the street itself, arguing vociferously,
blocking wagons, whose drivers cursed. Singing and pipe
smoke, drunken cheers and angry shouts billowed from the
open door of a beer garden. Some men walked purposefully,
carrying small bundles—soldiers, already? All the women she
saw were in a hurry, whether they hefted market baskets or
towed children. Their anxiety wormed its way into Lucilla's
stomach, and she found herself almost running as she drew
closer to the Institute.

The tall iron gates were closed and chained, and the gas
lanterns to either side flickered merrily, mocking her.

Lucilla ran forward and grabbed the bars with her free
hand. Someone would be within. She shouted. No one
answered; not a blade of grass stirred. The windows were all
dark. She was sweating in her sober wool suit, but her belly
contracted with cold terror. She shook the gate and shouted
again. "Let me in!"

"Mademoiselle Daglish?"

Lucilla whirled. A young man loomed behind her. She recalled seeing him at the Institute, marked by his height, his pronounced Gallic nose and a truly spectacular air of untidiness, currently exacerbated by his dusty clothing. Smears of dark grime marked his sleeve and his cheek, just to the left of his unostentatious brown mustache.

He was a visitor like herself, but she had never learned his specialty, or his name. He would know her name because she was the only woman ever to study at the Institute. She took a steadying breath. "Where have they all gone?" she asked in English.

"The entire faculty was summoned to a meeting at the gymnasium. My country being likely soon at war with their country, I fear I am not welcome there, nor are you," the young man said. He spoke English fluently, though with a French accent. From beneath the brim of his hat, he looked her up and down. She had an impression of grim displeasure, though nothing in his voice had revealed it. "You cannot stand here in the street, shouting."

"And I suppose you have a better idea?"

"I have retained an hotel room. I suppose you have not done the same?"

"Such deductive prowess," Lucilla muttered. Her hair was coming unpinned. She shoved the curling strands away from her face, one-handed, and glanced down the deserted street. She had to calm herself and think. "There must be another way out of the country."

"I do not wish to be shot in the dark as a spy because I am in the act of escaping," the Frenchman said. "You must accompany me. You will stay in my room tonight."

"I will do nothing of the sort. Mr....?"

"I am Fournier. Tomorrow we may consider our dilemma

further. Come, we should go." He turned and began walking, not offering to carry her bag. She didn't want to release her bag anyway; it held her precious laboratory notebook as well as her glassware.

She should not go with him. It was quite improper. True, Fournier was younger than she by at least a decade, so she did not fear he had designs upon her. Or not more than a basic level of caution would dictate. But it galled her to be ordered about like a lab assistant.

Lucilla scurried to catch up with him. "I will find my own room," she said. He could ruin her reputation, merely by being seen with her in a hotel.

Fournier snorted. "A woman alone, and a foreigner? Don't be foolish. No one will give you a room."

"A woman might," she pointed out.

"If she had a room to spare. Even early this morning, I had difficulty in procuring lodging for an additional period. You are not the only person who has just discovered there are no trains. Come, we should hurry."

He was correct. And after her long dusty walk to the train station, then her futile longer and dustier walk back to the Institute, Lucilla was in no mood to procure a newspaper, peruse its listings and then perhaps circumnavigate the entire town in the dark, alone and subject to male harassment, in search of a bed. "I wish you weren't right," she grumbled.

Fournier glanced over at her and smiled, a quick flash of white teeth beneath his mustache. For that moment, he looked no older than her baby brother, and twice as dangerous. Then he began walking even faster, and all her energy was consumed in keeping up. If she lost him, she would truly be in the soup.

Fournier ducked into a shop and she followed. He purchased cheese and biscuits, the only available choices. Lucilla realized she had forgotten all about food, but the need would soon become urgent. On the way out of the shop, she halted abruptly; a *Polizist* was demanding Fournier's papers.

She wasn't sure if approaching was the wisest idea, but Fournier was helping her, and she would not abandon him. She came up beside him just as the *Polizist* snarled an uncomplimentary phrase and tried to seize her arm. Fournier swiftly intervened, but the *Polizist* wouldn't release her. She struggled in his gloved grip, dropped her bag and heard the unmistakable shattering of glass.

Fournier shoved the *Polizist,* hard. "Run!" he said, so she grabbed her bag and ran, her heart pounding, hearing the scuffling behind her. She ran for perhaps a block, enough to soak her in sweat, then flung herself around a corner and peered back. Fournier was fleeing down the street toward her, still clutching the wrapped package of cheese and tin of biscuits. His tie was jerked askew, his hat nearly falling off the back of his head. The *Polizist* lay curled on the sidewalk. She could hear him cursing.

"This way!" she said, grabbing Fournier's arm. He shook her off but followed her down several alleys. She had no idea where she was leading him, but quick action was paramount. When she could run no more, she flung her back against a wall and gasped for breath. Fournier bent over his knees, panting.

"Are you hurt?" she asked. She felt light-headed and exhilarated at the same time.

He didn't answer her. Eventually, he straightened and said, "This way."

By the time they reached Fournier's lodging, the night

seemed even darker. He grabbed her hand and pulled her around the corner of the building, to the servants' entrance. His long fingers engulfed hers. He might be abrupt and over-bearing, but he'd rescued her, and defended her against the *Polizist*. She appreciated his warm and reassuring human touch in the midst of chaos. She was sorry when he let go, glanced around and pushed the door open. "The stairs," he murmured once she was inside. "Second floor."

Fournier's room was last in a poorly lit, narrow corridor. He unlocked the door briskly and pushed her inside before slipping in after her and throwing the bolt. She sighed in relief, then nearly laughed; never before had she considered that being locked in a room with a strange man could be a good thing.

Street noise, the rumble of wagons and voices mingling like a river, pushed in through an open window. Lucilla sought out the light switch with her hand, then was glad she hadn't tried to move farther. She saw scarcely two feet of bare floor, with perhaps another foot covered by an open rucksack and a scatter of notebooks. The room held one narrow bed with an overstuffed mattress, a small table supporting a jug and basin, and an upended steamer trunk. A hook above the trunk supported a single towel. She stood with the rucksack at her feet, near the wall. She could easily sag backward against that cool, comforting plaster and let it support her aching head. Her carpetbag felt as if it weighed a hundred pounds. Her elbows hurt from carrying it.

Fournier, the end of the bed at his back, was so close she could smell sweat and wool and the remnants of lime shaving lotion. He said nothing, instead dropping their dinner on the coverlet and futilely brushing at the dust on his charcoal jacket. He further loosened his navy tie and tossed his hat onto the steamer trunk.

Lucilla wanted to touch him again; an impulse, she was sure, caused by the close quarters and the sudden safety and intimacy implied by a closed and locked door. She was afraid. It had nothing to do with him personally. She worked closely with men every day, but she had never wanted to edge her body closer to any of them. A thought sprang from the depths of her mind. "Where will you sleep?" she asked.

Fournier snorted and shoved his hands into his pockets. "Better to ask, where will *you* sleep. I believe women are equal to men, and if that is so, then I should not have to yield my comfort to yours. It is hardly my fault you did not have the foresight to retain lodging. Besides, I cannot fold myself into this small patch of floor, and I cannot sleep in the corridor."

His tone was harsh, but he made sense, and there was no use arguing when she agreed with him. Beggars could not be choosers. Lucilla squeezed past him and set her bag atop his steamer trunk. "No, you can't sleep in the corridor," she said after a moment's thought. "Any foreigner is at risk at the moment, and if that *Polizist* finds us…" She could not deny the hostility and suspicion she'd felt in the air, steadily intensifying over the past few days.

"Many Germans still hate the French. I imagine they will find an excuse to declare war on us soon, and they know all Frenchmen have served their time in the army," he said. "Any one of us might be a soldier."

"Or a spy. This would be a wonderful opportunity to spy, if only I knew what to look for."

Fournier grinned, just as briefly and startlingly as before. He blew breath out his nose, and she decided he was nervous, too. She began to feel more kindly toward him. He said, "Perhaps we will spy on the kitchen later, if we grow weary of cheese and biscuits. There is a bath down the corridor. I will guard the door, if you will do the same for me."

"I have nothing clean to wear," Lucilla said. Thinking she would be leaving today, she'd sent her trunk ahead, and her carpetbag held only toiletries and a change of linen for emergencies. And, of course, broken glass. She supposed it didn't matter so much, not really, but she felt as if more had been broken than her glassware.

Fournier ducked his head. "A shirt," he suggested. As if in afterthought, he added, "I am quite tall enough for it to be decent. Pah! Though why we should be concerned with niceties eludes me. It is obvious we no longer live in a world that rewards us for cherishing such concerns."

Lucilla had no answer for him, not when her shoes chafed, her bust bodice chafed and the collar of her suit jacket chafed worst of all. "Thank you," she said. "Though perhaps you should bathe first. I don't want to guard you wearing only your shirt."

"You are very sensible," Fournier said, sounding surprised. Belatedly, he added, "And gracious." Lucilla very carefully did not respond with her true thoughts at his belated compliment, which were uncharitable. As he stripped off his jacket, she held up her skirts and hurdled the rucksack, to sit on the end of the bed. She didn't want to leave this room barefoot, so she would have to wait longer for the pleasure of removing her half boots, but simply being off her feet was lovely, and she sighed in relief. She unpinned her hat and set it aside.

Fournier reached for the towel, and it was then she saw his shirtsleeve was torn and stained with blood. "You're injured," she said, in case he'd planned to hide it from her.

"I was not quick enough to evade all injury," he said, draping the towel over that arm, concealing it. He rummaged in the rucksack and produced a shaving kit. "That was from a disagreement earlier this morning. It's a small price to pay for having later punched a rude *Polizist* in a tender place. You may borrow my soap. We must share the towel."

"Have you cleaned the wound?" she pressed. "I am trained as a nurse." At his incredulous look, she added, "One must earn one's living somehow."

Fournier shook his head. "You study chemistry at the Institute and go home to wipe runny noses."

"There aren't so many places that will hire a woman chemist," Lucilla said sharply. "Perhaps you haven't noticed, France being full of them. Or no, I'm sorry—those women are cooks, aren't they?"

Fournier snatched away the towel and held out his arm to her. Deciding to accept this as a peace offering, Lucilla extracted his cuff link and carefully folded up his sleeve, revealing a strong, flat wrist that appeared and felt sound except for bruising. That would be painful enough, and likely worse tomorrow. She could not push the sleeve above his elbow, but the rip helped her to expose a long, bloody scrape, deep enough to hold street grit. The dirt on his jacket sleeve, she realized, had actually been blood. He must have hit the ground forcefully to rip through a layer of tweed as well as his shirt. Or had there been a knife involved? He hissed sharply when she probed the wound. "Your hands are not clean," he snapped.

"They will be soon enough," she remarked. "Come along to the bath. I'll clean it for you properly. You're lucky I carry a kit with me."

Fournier smiled wryly. "If this is the first wound in a war, perhaps I can obtain compensation for your labors."

"Monsieur Fournier—"

"Yes?"

"Thank you. For rescuing me."

"It's nothing," he said, not looking at her. He hurried down the corridor.

Lucilla hadn't dealt with so simple an injury in a long time, as she specialized in nursing surgical recoveries. She'd forgotten how finicky a job it was to pick bits of grit from a wound. Tweezers helped. Her patient cursed freely each time she touched him, but seemed content to hold still when she pinned his hand beneath her arm. She could feel its warmth on the side of her breast, even through her clothing. The pressure felt good. She almost wished she could shift his hand a bit higher. She flicked her eyes to his. "This is not an invitation, young man."

He sighed. "A great pity, Mademoiselle Daglish." She could not tell if he was joking. She'd heard Frenchmen could be importunate. In her experience, all men could be importunate; but some could choose not to be. Emotion washed over her at this thought, almost lost as she concentrated on his wound. She realized she felt disappointed. A man bent on seduction would have been a welcome distraction just now.

After she'd finished her ministrations, she leaned against the wall outside the bathroom, plotting routes out of Germany. She did not have a good map in her head or in her bag. If she had to walk, she would be in sore trouble. Perhaps she could beg a ride from some other refugee. She need only reach a neutral country, such as Holland or Belgium. Would the market be open, to purchase supplies? Would she be able to take anything with her?

Much as she preferred to stand on her own feet, it would help to have a male companion such as Fournier on the journey. Any companion would be an advantage, but a man's presence often rendered the woman with him negligible to the view of other men, hiding her in plain sight in the established role of wife or dependent relative. A woman alone drew the attention of predators, and she felt sure predators would take advantage of the current chaos. It might be a very good thing indeed that she and Fournier had encountered one another. She would broach the topic with him in the morning.

He might refuse. It made more sense for them to escape together, but perhaps he wouldn't see that. Could she persuade him in some way? She thought of seduction and laughed into her hand, flushing up to her hairline. Before her fiancé's betrayal, all those years ago, she had definitely enjoyed being seduced.

When it was her turn for the bath, she almost wept when fresh hot water poured from the tap. She didn't dare soak too long—she feared encountering other guests, even with Fournier's protection—but she relished every moment of what the previous day had been a utilitarian activity. She had no idea when she might have a bath again. She might find herself walking to France before she could catch a boat home.

Fournier had given her his silk dressing gown as well as a clean white shirt. The shirt fell past her knees and the dressing gown, redolent of shaving soap and male skin, dragged the floor. She belted it to ankle length and cautiously stepped into the corridor. Fournier waited for her, leaning against the wall and scribbling in a notebook with a stub of pencil. Muffled voices emerged from other rooms, but she saw no one else. Perhaps everyone had gone to ground. She felt huddled inside her own mind, too tired right now to think and plan any longer. She envied Fournier, able to work even in the midst of dangerous upheaval.

Her mind circled back to the sleeping arrangements. She could share. She'd shared a bed with her little brother, Crispin, when he'd been small. Fournier would be no different. He scarcely seemed aware of her as a woman. She discounted the moment when she'd been working on his arm. He'd only been joking with her.

When they reached the room, she bolted the door. Having already placed a dry dressing on Fournier's arm, she put away her first-aid kit, then slipped out of her borrowed dressing gown. Its dubious protection would be too hot and awkward to wear for sleeping. The air from the window felt a little cooler than earlier; the voices on the street less frequent, but more strident. She shivered when one basso voice abruptly yelled invective, of which she caught only one word: *coward*.

Fournier straightened from tucking away his shaving kit. He seemed about to speak, then looked to the side. Lucilla waved to the bed. "You first. If we're to share, you needn't be overly concerned about modesty."

Fournier nodded once and stripped down to his combinations, which covered him from biceps to knees. He then knelt and reached into his rucksack once again. He produced a pistol and loaded it, quickly and efficiently. Lucilla had always avoided seeing Crispin handle his sidearm. She had never been so close to a deadly weapon before. Her heart went into her throat as he handled the gun, expecting it to go off at any moment. Fournier set it carefully on the upended steamer trunk before climbing into bed. "You can shoot?" he asked. "You could shoot a man?"

Slowly, numbly, Lucilla shook her head.

"If you must, aim for his body. Hold the gun with two hands. Squeeze the trigger, do not yank. Be gentle with it, and be prepared for it to—" He jerked his hand. "Do not let it fly from your grip. You have six shots."

Lucilla wasn't sure what to say. At last, she settled for "Thank you."

"Let's hope it will be of no consequence," Fournier said. He turned to face the wall and tugged the bedding over his shoulder. Lucilla loosed her hair, switched off the electric light and climbed into bed beside him. She could not lie flat without touching him. She did not mind the brush of his warmth against her hip and shoulder, for she lay awake, nerves thrumming, staring up at the ceiling in the faint light from the window. Gradually, the street noise quieted, and she could hear Fournier's steady breathing and the ticking of his wristwatch. She closed her eyes, but her heart raced and her leg muscles twitched as if they wanted to run. Where they touched, the heat spread and sank through her skin. She shifted restlessly.

At least an hour had passed when Fournier said in a low rumble, "You aren't sleeping."

"Nor are you," Lucilla replied as softly as she could manage.

Fournier turned over. He threw his uninjured arm over her ribs and pulled her to him. "Closer," he said. "If you please."

His arm was like a hot brand. Lucilla could no longer deny that she wanted to touch him. She eased against his body. She would definitely never sleep now. Cautiously, she rested her hands on his arm, which now wrapped snugly around her, beneath her breasts.

"Better," he pronounced. He nestled his face into her hair,

which was still damp from the bath. She could feel his breath fluttering on her scalp, and it flushed her entire body. He murmured, "This is better still."

She'd thought at first he'd meant to be seductive, but clearly she'd been wrong, for he made no further move. He was only comforting the dried-up spinster. It was crazed to feel disappointed that she was not being ravished. Still, the embrace was nice. More than nice. She pressed her back into his chest, heat soaking into her through two layers of thin cotton, sensation rushing out from even the slightest friction as they shifted against each other. She remembered the heat of a man's body, sweat springing into being and melting skin to skin; she remembered from her few nights with the man who would later betray her. She had never been held so closely since, and until now the memory of how it had felt, the safety of it, had been tainted for her.

Patience, Lucilla, she told herself. *You might taint this moment yet.*

She closed her eyes and inhaled scent and warmth, hers and his mingled. A decorous woman would protest even this, given their dishabille. She had passed decorous simply by being in this hotel, in this room, in this bed. She closed her eyes and felt their hearts beating, concentrating on the sense of well-being that cocooned her, trying to sear it into her memory against future need. She didn't dare move, for fear it would end.

Fournier's voice caressed the inner tunnel of her ear. "This is permissible?"

"Yes," she said. Her throat tightened. Foolish to want more. Foolish. She did not even know this man. This young man. Far too young for her.

"Is it polite among the English to ask if you have experience?"

Lucilla's breath stopped as the world flipped. She should

not have been surprised. The world had flipped more than once today already. She drew a deep breath. "I don't think so," she said. "That seems silly just now, doesn't it?"

"Well?"

He sounded as impatient as if he had demanded coffee from a recalcitrant waiter. Lucilla laughed a little. He was clumsier than she in these matters. "I was engaged to be married, once. It ended badly, very badly. Yes, I am *experienced*." She paused as a thought occurred to her. "And you?"

Fournier snorted, a ticklish sensation against her neck. "Somewhat."

A delicious sense of freedom flooded her to her bones. Lucilla rubbed her hand along his arm where it lay against her. She liked its heat and the contrast of soft skin over firm muscle, and the friction of hair beneath her palm. He must have liked it, too, for he shifted a little closer to her. She wondered how his skin tasted. "Have you asked me this for a reason?"

"You are toying with me."

"Teasing," she corrected giddily. She lifted his arm to her mouth and kissed the back of his hand. It didn't taste of anything in particular. She would need to taste some other spot, such as—her breath caught at the thought—the crease where his leg met his thigh. "I've never done this with a stranger. Or anyone, except the one."

"I do not make a habit of seducing women," Fournier said. "If that is what you wished to know. I have always wondered why numbers are considered to be a factor in these matters, if once is enough to be damning." He paused, rubbing his nose against the back of her neck. Lucilla shivered at the odd but pleasurable sensation. "It was not my plan to seduce you when I brought you here."

"Oh, surely not," she said. "You were so gallant. Why, when you offered to share your towel, I declare, my heart was all aflutter."

She couldn't help herself; she began to laugh at the absurdity of it all, at the circumstances that had led her, a spinster chemist, to find herself nearly naked in a bed in Germany with a French scientist. She didn't even know his field of specialization.

That thought sent her off again, and she laughed until her gut hurt. At some point, she gasped out a few words of explanation and Fournier laughed with her. Seemingly without transition, she was on her back and his face loomed above her. She lifted her hand and traced his mustache with her finger, then he was kissing her, first gentle brushing and nibbling, then deep kisses full of bristles and heat and wet swirling sensation, whirlpools sucking her down.

Lucilla clasped her hands behind his neck, stroking the close-cropped hair there, then tangling her fingers in the longer hair above and trying to drag him closer. Fournier pulled away from her mouth instead, and began nipping her throat, each scrape of his teeth like a lightning bolt across her skin and into her sex. He was working his way lower; she felt his fingers at her shirt buttons, slipping one free, then another. His hands circled her nipples and traced designs on the skin of her breasts before he settled in to suckle at her, the pulls of his mouth echoing in her womb. His right hand traveled slowly down her chest, then her belly, unbuttoning her shirt and smoothing the flesh beneath.

She turned to flame. She shifted desperately, lifting her hips to him, her hands roaming over his back, trying to feel every shift of muscle. This was better, so much better, than it had been with the despicable Clive. Already Fournier had spent more time pleasing her than her former fiancé. Of whom she had planned never to think again. She banished the fleeting thought of him easily, as she had an overwhelming distraction at hand and a hard, hot erection digging into her leg. She found the bottom of Fournier's vest and worked it upward. His skin sang to her palms.

He sucked in a breath when she lightly scratched the small of his back with her nails. "More," he demanded. She was willing to oblige him. She shoved his thin knitted vest higher on his back and dug her fingers into the straining muscles of his waist, then slid her hands lower, beneath the waist of his drawers, wrenching them down, glorying in his gasp and curse as his erection sprang free and slammed into her thigh. She gripped his buttocks firmly and yanked him to her, wanting his flesh melded to hers. He landed on his injured arm and made a sharp noise of pain. Before Lucilla could apologize, he stopped her words with a quick, hard kiss.

For a few moments, they lay together, panting, her hand circling in the soft hair on his chest. She swore she could feel his cock pulsing against her leg, straining to go higher and burrow deep within her body. Her thighs slid against each other, bathed in her own wetness. She shifted them apart, cradling his narrow hips, needing pressure against her sex more than she needed air to breathe.

Fournier abruptly sat up. "Prophylaxis," he said, as if it were a swearword. His chest heaved, and he yanked his vest the rest of the way off, throwing it onto the floor. Lucilla's hand, without her volition, floated toward the line of dark hair that bisected his belly, pointing the way to his cock.

She said, "I have prophylactics," and stroked the silky-soft hair all the way down to the tangled, coarser hair of his sex.

Fournier froze in place. She grasped his cock in her hand and dreamily stroked it in the ring of her thumb and forefinger. His skin there was the softest and most delicate skin in the world. With some effort, she summoned words to her lips. "I have condoms. In my medical kit. Sometimes they're useful. As bribes. If you get one, and put it on, we can—"

Panting, Fournier said, "What?" She repeated herself. He said, "Let go. Let go or in moments we will be fucking. Without prophylaxis."

Clive had never said the word, but that was what they had done. They had fucked. At least this stranger admitted to what they were doing. After Fournier tumbled off the bed and took a moment to finish removing his drawers, Lucilla might have found sanity or decorum. What use, though, were they? She wanted this, and she was old enough to choose for herself. She sat up and decisively stripped her shirt the rest of the way off. The breeze tickled her bare skin, and she shuddered, already needing his hands on her again.

"Fournier, hurry," she said.

"Pascal," he growled, then lifted a hand in triumph, holding a paper packet. "What is your name?"

"Lucilla," she said.

He gave a little bow. "Good. We are introduced," he said, snorting with laughter. After a moment he noted, "I fear you would enjoy this process too much," and applied the condom himself before rejoining her on the bed.

She liked the way he'd laughed. Lucilla reached for him as he lay down on his side, butting her forehead into his chest and wrapping one arm firmly around his waist. He was breathing hard; she felt light-headed. "We're going to do this, aren't we? We're really going to do this."

Pascal said, "It's my devout hope." His hands shaped her shoulder blades, her spine, the upper curve of her buttocks as his hips eased against her, flinched away, then shifted toward her again. "It is wondrous. Inexplicable that this mere act can make one forget all else. Not merely a matter of biology. Truly it makes me believe in the physical existence of souls, for they must meet somehow when—you are a scientist. You understand these things, that is why I can say them to you."

She'd heard Frenchmen were flatterers. She had to confess she liked being flattered—and the incongruity of his theorizing while naked and aroused. Lucilla cupped the head of his cock in her palm. He gasped, and said, "I…am sorry. I fear all the blood has left my brain."

Lucilla chortled and pressed a kiss to his chest. "A philosopher!" She hesitated, then said, "I think it's wondrous that our animal bodies can give us such pleasure, which I suppose is a form of transcendence."

Pascal said, "Do you think the body matters, when it is the soul that is immortal?"

She stroked her free hand over his rib cage. "How can we separate ourselves from our bodies?" she asked. "Would anyone desire that?"

She did not think she had ever met a man who would have had such a conversation, especially with a woman. It made her belly shiver, to think of souls mingling like two chemicals in a beaker. What would be the end product? *Apply heat*, she thought. *Distill.*

She said, "I want you inside me. I don't want to be alone."

Pascal kissed her, groaning deep in his throat when she squeezed the length of his cock. Lucilla needed his weight on her, enveloping her. She turned onto her back and he followed, bracing himself above her with his injured arm. "Closer," she said, spreading her thighs. Air tickled and cooled the hot folds of her sex, and she squirmed.

"Soon." Streetlights limned his tousled hair, the prominent bridge of his nose, the long line of his jaw. He traced his hand down her cheek, her neck, her breast, her hip. He ran his fingers through her pubic hair and thumbed apart her folds, slicking his hand and circling with his thumb until he brushed her clitoris. Lucilla had gone rigid with anticipation, and now a cry escaped her. Her awareness spiraled inward, down and in, as his thumb circled and pressed, circled and pressed, until the whole area was so sensitized she thought she could come from a puff of air. She was moaning, she knew that because she had to gasp in a breath. Pascal pressed the heel of his hand into her mound, slow and steady, imprinting her with pleasure. She couldn't breathe. She didn't want to breathe and make this stop. It built, and built still more. She cramped with pangs of ecstasy, and then it overflowed, spilling out of her, jerking her helplessly in its wake.

All her strings had been cut. She lay gasping while Pascal kissed her forehead, then her mouth. She could feel him smiling. "In me," she murmured. "We haven't finished this experiment."

She held him close as he guided his cock into her, both of them flinching at first from the intensity of the sensation. She laid her cheek against his chest, liking the slide of his flesh on her face as his cock pressed the walls of her vagina. She flung one arm over her head and he twined his fingers with hers as he thrust and withdrew. After a time, she found the strength to lift her hips to his, working with him toward climax. It all flowed into one sensation of lazy pleasure, an endless rocking and slapping like floating in the sea. She did not climax again, but she didn't mind. It was too fascinating to concentrate on Pascal, the feel and sound and musky salt scent of him as he lost himself to physical pleasure.

At last, he growled, his fingers tightening on hers as his hips rapidly jerked. She felt his cock twitching within her and kissed his chest lingeringly until his crisis passed and he sagged onto her, panting. A few moments later, he kissed her, withdrew with a sigh and disposed of the condom. Lucilla snuggled into his arms when he turned back to her, drifting in a lake of well-being. Their skins were slick with sweat in the summer air, but lying still, the breeze began to cool them. Her eyelids drooped. From the limp weight of Pascal's arm on her, he was already asleep.

After one of the worst days she could remember, and the most surprising evening, Lucilla slept the best sleep of her life, at least until an elbow dug painfully into her breast. She shoved Pascal's arm away. His eyes opened and he blinked at her, dazed. *"Quelle heure est-il?"* he asked.

"Go back to sleep," Lucilla mumbled. A loud noise from the street sent her bolt upright, clutching his forearm. "A gun?"

"Backfire, from an auto," he said.

"Are you sure?"

"I have had army training. I know the sound of a gun." He turned to her and smoothed her hair away from her face. "You must not be afraid. It will obscure your thinking."

"You aren't afraid?" She thought he must be, given that he had embraced her in the night for comfort before he had done so for sex. She wished, now, that she had been brave enough to draw nearer to him. The mere act of joining together had strengthened her, soothing the near panic that had buzzed along her nerves like bees.

She sensed him smile. "Were I an English gentleman, I would say I wasn't afraid. It would be a lie, of course."

"No, it's a way of pretending until the pretending feels real." Lucilla grabbed his wrist and turned it to see his wristwatch in the light from the window. Three o'clock. "It will be light soon," she said. "If there are no trains, I had thought we might find someone with a wagon who would be willing to take us closer to the border. Perhaps one of the men who brought deliveries to the Institute. They will recognize me, and I have some money."

"If we can reach my colleague at the Institute, perhaps we can borrow his motorcar," he said. "That is why I came here in the first place, to see him. Perhaps he will feel obligated."

"You sound doubtful." Lucilla drew up her knees and rested her chin on them.

Pascal turned to his side, facing her. "I was…dismayed, by Herr Doktor Professor Kauz. We had never met before last week, only corresponded. He requested I come here, insisted he must share a discovery of incalculable importance."

"Kauz," Lucilla said, remembering a paper-skinned old man with wild hair and a cane. "A biologist as well as a chemist, with a grant from the kaiser's special fund. He was rude to me." In truth, he'd said a woman who worked alongside men was no better than—she'd had to research the German word he'd used, which turned out to mean *whore*. From his vicious tone when he'd said it, and his frequent vituperative glances, she hadn't been surprised by the meaning.

Pascal hesitated then said in a rush, "I did not like his laboratory. He used animals in ways that were cruel, even for science. He said I was soft, and all Frenchmen doubly so."

"You study—"

"Everything," he said, with no trace of arrogance that she could detect. "I have a special fondness for maths and engineering, but my work now, it is to find the new things in biology, on behalf of an agency in the government. Since I am paid for that, and I prefer to eat and provide a home for my cats, I cannot practice engineering as I would like. Though I find biology is something like engineering."

"The new things?" Lucilla asked, still wrestling with the image of Pascal with pet cats.

"The things that will be of interest, that will reward further study. I report on these things to a board, and they decide who is to receive funding. I have met many…eccentrics, I suppose you would say, who believe their work is vital. None discomfited me like Herr Kauz."

"He's vicious," she said without thinking.

Pascal stared at her for a moment, in silence, then he touched her leg, petting it idly. "Yes," he said. "That is there, beneath the surface. Perhaps it is not a good idea to ask a favor of a man who is vicious, and who has a dislike of women and Frenchmen. But the others at the Institute do not know me, nor I them. I know where to find Kauz."

"We can only try," Lucilla said. "A motor would be much better than our other choices, and there are not many available in this town. He can only say no."

"He could do far worse than that, I am sure," Pascal said.

"It might be worth the risk," she said. "He need not know I am involved." She paused. "If I am."

"You are certainly involved *now*," Pascal said, sounding affronted. "I did not intend that we should fuck and part."

"I might swoon, that is so romantic," Lucilla said.

He glared at her. "I will see Herr Kauz alone. You will wait nearby. If he refuses us, then your plan will be next. Where will we begin?"

"I'll speak to Frau Greifen, at the coffeehouse across the road from the Institute. She must know someone who would be willing to help us. I saw enough deliverymen lounging there and smoking, every afternoon. If anyone could tell us how we could obtain a motor, or a wagon, surely they would know."

"Good," Pascal said. "We should sleep now."

Lucilla spoke before she could lose her courage. "I don't think I can." She cupped his cheek in her hand and brushed his mustache with the edge of her thumb. "Perhaps you would help me."

He grinned. "And you, me." He bore her down into the mattress.

INTERLUDE

CRISPIN DAGLISH LOOKED UP FROM THE STACK OF counterpoint exercises he was marking and froze. The new diction and deportment master held out a slip of yellow paper, a telegram. "Sorry, old chap," he said. "Didn't mean to read it."

Crispin snatched the paper from his hand and scanned it, then blew out his breath. It was not about his missing sister, Lucilla, at all. His hand shaking with relief, he laid down his pen and stood. "I've been called up," he said. "Could you let Miss Tremblay know, so she can take my classes? I've got to talk to the headmistress, then I'm to be on a train tomorrow morning."

Diction and Deportment was extraordinarily beautiful, and the girls were already swooning over him in battalions, but Crispin had quickly and sadly discerned that he was self-centered and not very bright. "We're at war? With whom?"

"Not yet," Crispin assured him. "Perhaps you could glance at a newspaper to learn more about what's happening in Europe. Your girls might have questions. Particularly the German ones."

At home, he spun his hat toward his bed, stripped off his suit jacket and tie, and unbuttoned his tweed waistcoat before ascending to the attic. He brought his trunk down and quickly threw together his kit. His uniforms had been laundered recently, and he regularly unpacked his pistol from its box for cleaning and oiling. Quickly, he polished his cap badge, which bore the device of a running wolf. All that was missing was his sister to give him a kiss goodbye.

He thought he would know if anything had happened to her, but confirmation of her safety would have been nice. Perhaps his company captain, Wilks, could put in a word for him with Whitehall or the German ambassadorial offices. Or he could make the journey himself. He'd met some of the other lieutenants in his battalion before, albeit briefly. He particularly remembered the charismatic redhead Noel Ashby. Also the band's leader, Lieutenant Meyer, a handsome blue-eyed blond whose regimentals were uncommonly finely tailored. He could ask Meyer to go with him to London, he thought, and blushed, then was promptly ashamed of himself for thinking what he'd been thinking while his sister was trapped in Germany.

He ought to be worrying about Lucilla, and of course he was, every minute, it had only been a silly fleeting thought.

Regardless, he would at least send a telegram to the British embassy in Berlin. No doubt they'd be inundated with similar pleas. He'd had a tutor at King's, though, who might be able to help. Still pondering, he assembled a duffel and pronounced himself ready.

Ready for *what,* he wasn't sure.

2

LUCILLA WOKE WHEN PINK LIGHT BEAMED THROUGH
the window. She was pinned beneath Pascal's arm and one of
his legs, her nose shoved into his shoulder. She'd had barely
any sleep and had gotten quite a bit of unexpected exercise.
Also, she was trapped in a country at war, with no easy way
home. She felt better than she had in weeks. There was something to be said for meeting the body's animal needs, when
one wasn't bound up with romance and love and guilt. And
when the man one chose paid attention to her needs as well
as his own.

Pascal snored very lightly. She drew one finger along the
prominent bridge of his nose. He ought to have been producing quite a bit more sound, she thought, and smiled. She
hadn't expected to like him at all after their first meeting.
Perhaps he'd blurred her mind with orgasms, because she felt
deeply fond of him now, mixed with tender exasperation
because she was awake and he was not.

She wanted to kiss him awake and entice him into one

more coupling, one last time before they left this temporary haven. She was apparently more of a sensual being than she'd thought. After so many years with no sexual contact at all, once she'd had a taste of how good it could be, she wanted more and more. Perhaps she would become depraved and have to be analyzed. She grinned, then her grin faded. They had no more time for indulgence. She had better accept that their idyll had ended.

Outside, wagons rattled along the street. She couldn't hear any movement within the hotel, at least not in their corridor. They both needed another bath before they set out. Reluctantly, she set to waking Pascal.

An hour later, the sun was fully up, and she was struggling back into her walking suit from the day before. She was cleaner than the suit, but she had washed her underthings, and they had dried overnight, or mostly dried in the case of her bust bodice. Pascal cautiously slipped into a clean shirt; his entire forearm had turned black with bruising overnight. He was lucky he hadn't fractured the bone.

"Let me help you," she said.

Pascal swore. Lucilla ignored this and buttoned the shirt for him. "The aspirin will help. Give it time."

He murmured a foul word in French and reached for his jacket, a clean and undamaged one he'd extracted from the steamer trunk. "Can you drive a motorcar?"

"Luckily for both of us, yes."

A slow smile stole across his face. "You are a paragon among women."

Lucilla patted his shoulder and handed him his hat. "Where does Herr Kauz live? In the town, I hope."

"It's not far."

Pascal carried the pistol in his jacket pocket, his uninjured hand tucked in on top of it. She'd suggested a sling for his other arm but he'd said it would be too conspicuous. He'd abandoned his trunk and stuffed a few items into his rucksack. Lucilla carried her carpetbag, with his rucksack slung over her back. Herr Kauz lived only two streets over from the Institute, in a brick house that looked far more pleasant than its owner, with fat red flowers growing in pots to either side of the front door. A plump woman in a servant's uniform pinned wet trousers to a line in the side garden. Lucilla could see the motor, an open two-seater model, parked just beyond.

"Wait here," Pascal said, stopping in the shade of an elm. It overhung the corner of a neighboring house's front garden, and would provide good concealment.

Lucilla desperately wanted to go with him, not because she felt it wise, but because she felt more exposed standing in the street than she had the night before in their bed. She set her carpetbag on the grass and crossed her arms, to prevent herself from reaching for him. She was a middle-aged woman who had traveled to a foreign country to perform research, not a green girl who couldn't let her lover out of her sight. "Go," she said.

She watched as Pascal strode off down the street. He followed a neat brick path to Kauz's door and rapped the knocker. She could not see who answered, but he was admitted. She bent and fiddled with the hooks on her shoes, feeling excessively visible again. She was sure many pairs of eyes burned through her back and could sense lace curtains being twitched aside all along the street.

She amused herself by imagining explanations for her presence. She was Pascal's mother, and he the illegitimate son of Kauz. She was a spy. She had been sent by the German government to check their readiness to deal with foreign spies. She was selling scientific glassware, door to door. She watched Kauz's housekeeper finish with the laundry, pick up a basket and go inside by a rear door, letting it slam behind her. Lucilla stared at the motor, thinking.

Pascal emerged. He did not turn toward the side garden, but walked quickly toward her, his shoulders rigid. He ducked behind the tree's trunk and swore.

"Stay calm," Lucilla said. She picked up her bag and handed him his rucksack. "The servant went inside. We'll walk to the motor now. There's no crank, it must have a self-starter."

"He refused."

"Then we commandeer his vehicle. Isn't that the word? You know how to start the engine, don't you? I can do it if you don't know how."

Pascal only hesitated a moment before seizing her arm and walking back toward Kauz's home.

"Not too quickly," Lucilla murmured. "We must behave as if we have every right."

"He will hear the engine."

"There's a clear path from his garden to the street. We must be quick. Do you know where he is in the house?"

"He returned to his library."

Laughter gurgled in the upper region of Lucilla's chest as she ducked beneath damp shirttails fluttering in the summer breeze. Pascal pushed his way through a sheet. She would never have dared this on her own, would never have entertained such desperate measures had the night not changed her entire idea of herself. She would never have imagined that stealing a motor could be such a thrill.

She laid her carpetbag gently in the rumble seat, took

Pascal's rucksack and laid it in, as well. Pascal quietly opened the door; he fiddled with the spark and throttle levers while she arranged herself to block him from view and kept a wary eye out. He looked at her beneath his arm. "When the engine catches, be ready. You must drive."

Lucilla nodded and gathered her skirts into her hands. The engine roared and Pascal threw himself onto the seat, sliding across. She followed, remembering to release the hand brake before she slammed the door and sent the motor into high gear. She hadn't driven in over a year. "It's like cycling," she said to herself, turning onto the street. Behind them, she heard banging doors and shouting. She gave the motor more petrol, and soon the shouting faded. It was satisfying to drive faster than Kauz could run. She hoped he'd seen her. He could add *thief* to *whore,* she thought with savage glee.

The Institute's gates were still shut. As they neared the more populous areas of the town, she tried to look as if the motor belonged to her. Surely someone would recognize it. But if they did, they were too concerned with their own business to take note of who occupied the seat. They passed the train station's brick facade. The shaded porch was even more crowded than the day before, and there was no sign of trains. She glanced at Pascal, who slouched in the seat next to her, cradling his arm. "Do you have a map?"

He shrugged. "In my head."

They motored past the town's medieval walls and were suddenly surrounded by countryside. The summery smell of grain blew in Lucilla's face. She would have to see if Kauz kept goggles in the glove box. For now, her hat would have to serve as protection. "Can you get us to France?"

"If no one shoots us, and we do not run out of petrol."

"I'd forgotten about petrol," she admitted. "It's a pity motors can't eat grass."

"Perhaps in the next town they will be willing to sell us some."

"I'll be helpless," Lucilla decided. "My children are waiting for me."

"You have children?" Pascal asked abruptly.

"Not a one, but I'll pretend if necessary. You?"

"Of course not! I am not married."

Lucilla laughed. Unless she had amnesia about the event, he was not married to her, but that had not stopped him from making love to her for most of the night.

He seemed to hear her thoughts. "That was different!"

Lucilla continued to laugh. He sounded younger with every protest. At last she said, "I'm laughing in relief, I think."

"We aren't safe yet."

"We'll proceed one step at a time," she said, thinking of chemistry experiments.

"Perhaps if we run out of petrol, we can sell the motor and buy a cart," he said.

"That's a good plan."

"I would sell this motor now for coffee and croissants."

Lucilla's stomach growled in agreement. "I forgot about that sort of fuel, too."

"You were fed by criminal instinct," Pascal suggested. She glanced at him, and he was grinning. "This could be easier if you stayed in France. With me."

Excitement leaped in her chest. She took a deep breath. "In the middle of a war."

"England will soon declare war. This may have happened already. We did not see the papers, as we did not have coffee and croissants."

Her empty stomach fluttered, and she felt short of breath. "I have to go home. My brother, Crispin, is a reservist. He might be called up. If there's fighting, they'll need nurses."

"You could nurse for France, if you desired. Or you could work as a chemist."

"I'm sure France would look on that as kindly as England does," she said. "I already don't like being a foreigner alone among foreigners in a country at war, and that's how it would be for me." When he said nothing, she added, "If I don't return now, I might not get the chance later. I don't want to be away from my family in a crisis."

"They cannot endure this crisis without you?"

"It's not a matter of—think of sheep huddling together."

"You are not a sheep. Not in the least."

"I am also not young and idealistic, like you," she said. "I would love to stay with you a bit longer, to see what might happen, but I can't. I have to go home. I feel I owe a duty toward my country." Also, she feared Pascal did not truly mean what he said, not deep in his heart. He might think he did, after their enjoyable sexual encounters, but she doubted he could have formed serious feelings for her in so short a time.

Pascal didn't speak for several kilometers. At last he said, "There's a sign. Perhaps we can find coffee in that town. That would immeasurably improve the quality of this day."

As Lucilla had suspected, croissants were not on offer in the village of Grobschmiedensberg, but she was able to obtain sausages, cheese, fresh bread, a thermos of strong coffee, and bottled beer and lemonade for a reasonable sum. Two cans of petrol cost an exorbitant price, but she was glad for it, having no idea how much remained in the motor's tank, and how much petrol would be required for the distance they must travel. The hazards of being an auto thief, she supposed. Three kilometers down the road, she stopped the motor and they ate ravenously, in silence.

Lucilla offered the last of the coffee to Pascal. He shook his head, so she drank it herself and shook the drops into the road. "Will you tell me about Herr Kauz?"

"Why do you wish to know?" Pascal looked wary. Even earlier, in the midst of danger, she hadn't seen that expression on his face.

"It's a long way to the border." He knew about her work—it was common knowledge that she experimented with pharmaceuticals to alleviate pain—but she knew little about his. Before she had to leave him, she wanted to know more of this man with whom she'd shared her body.

Pascal leaned over the seat back, rummaged in his rucksack one-handed, and emerged with a crumpled wax-paper packet. Lucilla tidied away the remains of their breakfast and tucked the brown paper parcels in among the beer and lemonade, so the bottles wouldn't clink together. When she settled back in her seat, Pascal pressed a small piece of chocolate between her lips.

Sweetness blossomed on her tongue, mingling with the saltiness of his fingertips. She suckled the tip of his thumb, closed her eyes and swept out her tongue, caressing its length. He cursed softly and kissed her, crushing their hats together.

Desire drenched her entire body. For a few moments, she didn't care that the motor sat beside an open field, many kilometers from safety. The sun heated her blood, and Pascal's hand on her cheek was even hotter. She dislodged his hat and grabbed the back of his head, holding him to her with a desperation she'd buried until this moment.

He pulled his mouth away and thudded his forehead to hers. His breath puffed unsteadily against her face. "Pardon," he said.

"Bugger," Lucilla said. She loosened her hands in his hair and let them drift down to his shoulders, stroking him absently as she tried to bring herself under control instead of nuzzling into his chest and tasting him with lips and tongue. She pulled away and clenched her hands in her lap, staring down at her whitened knuckles. Her desires fought her, and she had a difficult time remembering why she could not set them free. "I will miss you when this is over."

He reached for her again, then let his hand fall. "I will help you to get home," he said. "I have cousins who work in Le Havre."

"Thank you," she said. For the first time in years, she wanted to weep.

"We should go," he said.

Lucilla started the engine and released the hand brake. She concentrated on the road for several minutes, then said, "Tell me about Herr Kauz."

The noise of the motor and the wind necessitated he face her as he spoke. Lucilla focused on the road ahead rather than risk glancing at him. What did she think she would see in his eyes, anyway? They were brown. That was all. Her own were the same, and just as subject to bits of blown grit. She had sand in her eyes now. Her own fault, because she had not looked for Kauz's goggles. She blinked furiously.

Pascal said, "Kauz first wrote to me over a year ago."

"Why?" She swallowed, and gave the motor a bit more petrol.

"Long before I was born, he was married to my great-aunt."

In some families, like her own, a connection by marriage could be a close one, but Pascal's tone said otherwise. Lucilla looked away from the road for a moment, at Pascal. His expression was blank. She sensed some family trouble there. "You didn't know him well."

"At all," Pascal said. "My great-aunt never returned from Germany. She died shortly after her marriage. She bore no children. It was forever after a source of grief for my *grand-oncle,* Erard, who was her brother."

"Kauz presumed upon his distant relationship with you?"

"To try and obtain funds, yes. My superiors found items of interest in his work and thought I would be the best candidate to extract further information from him."

"Unpublished items of interest, I assume," Lucilla said. She cast her mind back to the library at Somerville and the welcoming odor of old books. She remembered pursuing strings of letters through a series of journals, trying to discover if any of the writers thought or felt as she did, back when she still imagined she had hope of a permanent academic position, somewhere other than a school for girls. The shifting rivalries and alliances had fascinated her. She'd corresponded with a few fellow chemists, never revealing her gender, but it was difficult to explain why she held no position, and never attended conferences. She had not wanted to lie and pretend to be infirm.

"Yes. He is very secretive—it is rumored he has other laboratories than those at the Institute and at his home, where he pursues bizarre interests in isolation from the scientific community. His public work is often privately funded, and no one knows how much remains unpublished. For instance, his work with the body's healing mechanisms ran parallel to that of an English biologist I knew from Cambridge, and there were hints of great advances he did not fully reveal. Also, disturbing implications about how the body could be harmed."

"What college at Cambridge?" she asked.

"Trinity." He paused. "My English is more respectable than my French."

She'd barely heard him speak his own language. She nodded. "So why did you come to Germany? What did he promise you?"

Pascal said, "You should understand, not all of the scientists with whom I speak are conventional. I am used to being told strange things. I didn't know when I traveled here what Kauz wished to reveal to me, though I had my suspicions. He gave only hints."

"Stop hedging," she said, annoyed. "I want the story." She risked a glance at his face, and was surprised by how disconcerted, almost fearful, he appeared. He looked away quickly. His next words were almost lost in the roar of the motor and the rush of the wind.

"Very well, I will tell you. Kauz claimed he had met a woman who could transform her body into that of a wolf."

"You mean a werewolf?"

His jaw dropped. "You don't sound surprised."

"If it weren't odd, you wouldn't be embarrassed to tell me about it," she pointed out. "I think such legends are interesting. My father used to terrify us with lurid tales of beasts who would eat us at the full moon. Well, lurid enough for children. I imagine Kauz's imagination outdid my father's. For instance, that he made his werewolf a woman. That doesn't surprise me at all." He'd acted as so virulent a misogynist, could perversion be far behind?

"The scope of Kauz's imaginings is impressive." His tone was flat.

"I take it you didn't believe him." Pascal didn't reply immediately. Lucilla glanced over. He was glaring at the innocent cows whom they were passing. "You did believe him," she said.

"I did not disbelieve. There are more things in heaven and earth," he growled.

"That's true," she said. "But?"

"He had no evidence, no photographs or film."

"Or a werewolf."

"No, not one of those, either," he confirmed with a hint of humor. "Though perhaps I should be grateful he did not present me with a corpse. Wolf or human."

Lucilla shuddered. "What evidence did he show you? He must have had something. You seem like a practical sort of chap." Except when blathering about human souls in the midst of sex, but she could forgive him that. "Did he have samples, of blood or fur?"

"No, only quantities of figures," he said. "Weights of the woman and of the woman-as-wolf. Lengths of time to shift from one to the other, and back again. A detailed description of the process, which was not limited to the full moon as legend suggests. An analysis of nutritional needs, and lack thereof." He paused. "Length of time to heal injuries. As woman and as wolf, and if the change from one form to the other took place while injured. Clean cuts, ragged cuts, cuts from a silver blade, bruises to soft tissue. Broken bones."

"I like Kauz less and less. That's monstrous." Electrifying a dead frog was nothing compared to deliberately injuring an intelligent creature. One was science, the other cruelty.

"His laboratory notebooks read as if he'd held a werewolf captive for months. The records did not appear to have been faked—he'd written them over a long period of time. His results were consistent with physical possibility. However, he could not produce this werewolf, though he repeatedly hinted that he would do so once he was sure he could trust me. But I do not think that day would ever have come. His werewolf may have existed only in his fevered mind. I am not sure if I am grateful or not, that he could produce nothing to support his statements. Then, I cannot help but worry that his captive was real, and that he might have killed her. As he kills his laboratory animals once they have served his purpose."

She glanced away from the road and saw Pascal looking back at her, his expression troubled. "Perhaps she escaped," Lucilla suggested.

"Perhaps," he said. "To survive so long, she must have been—*be* resilient."

Lucilla said, "I don't think anyone at the Institute knew of this."

"No. Perhaps I should have spoken of it to the trustees, but I didn't think they would take my word, a visitor and a foreigner, over his. I was preparing to visit him again, to see if I could gather more evidence. Then I heard that war had been declared. I am now obligated to return to France."

She drove for another kilometer in silence. Neither of them could do anything now about a situation that might be at least partly illusory. Best to distance herself from the troubling implications and concentrate on the most fascinating part of Pascal's revelations. "Both species are mammals," she said. "I wonder how different they are? Humans and wolves?"

"I'm afraid I can't tell you," Pascal said. "Do you think it possible?"

"Perhaps the wolf form isn't a true wolf. Perhaps it only looks like one. On the inside, it could be more human. It's an interesting exercise. Though I wonder how the change would initiate? Would the werewolf trigger a chemical reaction in her own body? It's a bizarre idea, but possible, I suppose."

"Like the duck-billed platypus."

Lucilla cast him a glance. He was smiling. She said, "If it could turn into a duck, as well."

"Have you ever traveled to the Antipodes?"

Lucilla considered his change of subject. She didn't want to talk about Kauz anymore, either. "Alas, no. You?"

"Once, with my *grand-oncle* Erard, who worked on a merchant ship. I was eleven. It was the greatest adventure of my life."

His tone sounded affectionate in a way she hadn't heard before. "Tell me about it, and him," Lucilla said.

"Perhaps later. First you will tell me how you became interested in chemistry," Pascal said.

"Done," she said.

INTERLUDE

LIEUTENANT GABRIEL MEYER WAS IN THE MIDST of testing his boy trumpeters on their fingering exercises when his fellow lieutenant and closest friend, Noel Ashby, entered the band room. Ashby, a lean man with cropped red hair and a slender mustache, leaned against a cabinet and crossed his legs at the ankles, outwardly casual, but Gabriel could read the tension in his normally relaxed posture, and he tensed, as well. Kern fumbled a pattern and stopped.

With a glance, Gabriel silenced the comment about to erupt from Wiley's mouth. Wiley was inclined to rivalry. "No, keep on with it," he said to Kern gently. "If you stop, you might stop there the next time, and make a habit of it."

"Sir," Kern squeaked, and lifted his trumpet again, aiming it at the regimental wolf banner that hung behind Gabriel's chair. This time, he played more slowly, but accurately.

"Good," Gabriel said. "Why don't you two run along. I hear there's cake for tea."

When the boys had gone, Noel ambled over to Gabriel's

podium and leaned on his wooden music stand. "Reserves have been called up," he said.

Gabriel rubbed his mustache with his forefinger. "So it's happened then."

"Soon," Noel said. "I came here because we're to be in the same company."

"The same—you mean, the band—"

Noel gripped his forearm and gave it a shake. "I'm sorry. When it comes to war, your boys are to be trained as regimental stretcher bearers. There won't be any band for you to lead."

"Bloody hell." Gabriel bowed his head, reeling from having his musicians snatched away from him. They'd be scattered across the regiment. Some of them weren't old enough for active duty, and would have to be left behind. Kern and Wiley would be someone else's responsibility now.

His stomach plummeted as another thought occurred. "Jemima," he said. "She won't be pleased."

"Now's a good time to break it off, then," Noel said.

Without rancor, Gabriel said, "You'd marry to have children, too. You've said it a thousand times."

"Yes, but I wouldn't marry *Jemima*."

"She's Jewish," Gabriel said with a shrug. "You know I can't marry a Gentile. Not unless I never want to hear the end of it."

"You don't really care about that," Noel said.

Gabriel wasn't up to resurrecting an old argument. "I'll run down to the office and telephone her."

Noel sighed, and cuffed his shoulder. "Good luck. I'm thinking I'd rather be shot at."

3

THE REST OF THE DAY'S DRIVE FELT LIKE AN OUTING. Lucilla had rarely had the opportunity to speak at such length, and with such freedom, to another scientist. She didn't think she ever had done, except once or twice at university with older alumnae, as her own crowd all studied literature or languages. The next village appeared, but the motor had plenty of petrol, and she and Pascal had plenty of food. They ate their tea while sitting on the grass, seen only by a few birds gleaning seeds from the roadside. She doffed her hat and let the afternoon sun glow on her face. Bees buzzed in the hedge.

Pascal drew an astonishingly detailed map in one of his notebooks, his lines strong and sure. Lucilla peered over his shoulder, noting that they would need to drive through the night. When he'd finished drawing, he tore the page free. "Take this, and keep it safe," he said.

Their fingers touched as she accepted the map. "Do you have an eidetic memory?" she asked.

"For some things," he said. "Why do you wish to know?"

"You needn't snap," she said. "I was only curious. It's a useful talent."

Pascal took her hand again, and kissed the back. "I am sorry. I tell no one."

"I won't tell anyone, either." It was a strange thing to be embarrassed about, but he was entitled to his secrets. She did not reclaim her hand, and soon he clasped it to his thigh, interlacing their fingers. She asked, "Have you told anyone before?"

"My mother knew," he said. "My father does not. He would tell the government."

Enlightenment struck. "I see. You would make a most excellent spy."

He smiled grimly. "I would make a terrible spy. I am not…diplomatic. Also, I doubt I could withstand torture, or die with patriotic dignity. I wish to do neither of those things. I am not a brave man. I want to live."

Lucilla tightened her fingers on his. In a rush of boldness, she said, "Kiss me."

Pascal studied her, then took off his hat. "Come and sit across my legs."

"Striving for efficiency?" Lucilla knelt, leaned over and kissed his mouth, awkwardly and sideways. Thoughtfully, she teased the corner of his mouth with her tongue. "Mind your arm," she said before climbing into his lap.

His uninjured arm closed around her so tightly that the boning of her bust bodice dug into her flesh. She hooked her arms around his neck and yanked his face to hers. The heat and slickness inside his mouth forcibly reminded her of how his cock had felt inside her, each slide hot and sweet. She shifted restlessly as their tongues darted and tangled. She dug her fingers into the back of his neck, then her nails, and he groaned and pulled away. "Off," he said.

Disentangling herself reluctantly, Lucilla sighed. "Of course we must stop. We're right beside the——"

She landed on her back in the fresh grass. "Road," he said. "We'll have to hurry." He shoved up her skirt, having to unfasten both sides to do so. It wasn't cut for such unconventional activity.

"Pascal!"

"You wear too many underthings," he said, flipping up her petticoat. He swooped down and kissed her through her drawers.

She couldn't get her breath. He hadn't done this the night before. His fingers shaped and massaged her thighs while he slowly and deliberately rasped his mustache against the cambric covering her sex. The hair on her arms prickled. He nuzzled deeper, and hot velvety sensation flooded over her rear and belly. "Christ almighty," she choked out.

He lifted his head. "Did I hurt you?"

She stared at him, dazed. She licked her swollen lips. "You don't have to hurry too much," she said. "If we drive through the night, this…this might be…"

"It will not be the last time." Pascal bent and firmly kissed her thigh. "I will go to England and find you."

"What if you're killed?"

"What if *you* are? Don't fret about that now. Have you no romance in your soul? You English," he said, fumbling with the drawstring of her drawers.

"It isn't romantic to be ravished beside a country lane?" Lucilla asked.

"Bees, flowers, I suppose so," he admitted. "Touch me."

She couldn't reach much of him, so tangled her fingers in

his hair. She didn't let go even when lifting up so he could drag off her drawers and her awkward skirt. Her petticoat made for admirable protection from the grass, which she quickly forgot about as his rough cheek brushed her thigh. He spread the lips of her sex with his fingers, and for a moment the air on her wet skin was like a chill up her spine. Then his hot breath gusted over her, and his tongue pressed her open with a long lick. She arched into his mouth, her eyes fluttering closed. Delicately, he searched out each fold and traced its path while she twitched in pleasure. She'd never experienced such a light, slick, exact touch; it was as if he found thousands of nerves too hidden for fingers to discover, nerves that tingled and sparked deep inside her belly and sent electrical currents coursing through her arms and legs.

Her belly twisted, coiling her ever tighter. "More," she said at last. "Please, Pascal. More."

He shifted her leg, and to her shock lifted her knee over his shoulder. A brief awkwardness, and he did the same with her left leg, wrapping his injured arm lightly around her thigh. She felt splayed open, yet secure because he held her. She tightened her calves against his back and he sighed before bending to kiss her again, his tongue flicking inside her with unbearable intimacy and lapping at each fold of flesh as if it were her mouth. Her body throbbed ceaselessly, and she writhed in his grip, panting for breath. She moaned when he slipped the very tip of his finger into her opening, the sound a momentary relief of the pressure building inside her, until his finger slid deeper and she was forced to moan again. She couldn't think. "Please," she said. "I can't—"

"Harder?" he asked.

"Yes—deeper—"

He slid two fingers inside her, massaging his thumb over her sensitized flesh and, after a moment, closing his mouth over her clitoris and sucking, a bolt of feeling that speared her to the ground. Her back arched; she both craved and winced away from the intensity of his fingers thrusting within her, his lips pulling at her. A brief climax shuddered over her skin without giving her relief. Her body continued to fight toward pleasure until she let her mouth open and screamed, short and satisfying.

Pascal froze and withdrew. "You aren't hurt?"

Lucilla panted. "Needed air," she said. "More."

Lubriciously, his fingers slid into her again, reaching up and in, rotating on withdrawal. He laid his cheek against her thigh, watching his hand move, his expression intent upon her. Lucilla watched his face until she had to close her eyes from the intimacy of it. She laid her head back on the grass and drew deep breaths. The pressure inside built inexorably now, as if her first climax had been only the first road sign on the way to fulfillment. She could feel the tightening within her beginning again, from a different place than before. "It's so good," she said, then moaned when he touched his mouth to her again. "Pascal—"

He didn't withdraw this time, suckling harder, thrusting faster with his fingers. Lucilla lost count of how many times her skin shuddered, flutters of climax teasing her toward some unknown peak. When she crested, at first she expected another small spasm, but it built and built, and then the heavens ripped open and golden sunlight spilled through her and over her, racking her with pleasure in its wake.

She fell into sleep almost immediately after, aware of Pascal kissing her mouth, covering her with her skirt and easing his jacket beneath her head, then no more. She woke, and it was dusk. A dog howled, then another and another, like a pack of foxhounds baying—she realized that was what had woken her. She blinked at the emerging stars, too few as yet to pick out the summer constellations. Pascal was watching her.

"You needed to sleep," he said, his tone brusque. His finger gently traced the shape of her upper lip. "I don't think we should stop again."

Lucilla lifted her arm, which seemed to weigh ten stone, and closed her fingers over Pascal's wrist. "I will miss you," she said.

He leaned down and kissed her, a quick hard pressure. Then he took her hand and helped her to her feet. They didn't speak as they stowed the remains of their meal, lit the motor's lamps and set out again.

INTERLUDE

IN THE UNDERGROUND LABORATORY, TANNEKEN did not change form, so as she had expected, her wounds took three days to heal. She no longer regarded the pain. She refused to think of it. She had long ago given up imagining herself free; now she imagined the hot salt of the old man's blood coursing across her tongue. She ran pattern after pattern in her head that might lead her to this goal.

During those three days, the old man did not come to the room where she lay on concrete, beneath a bare bulb. Neither did either of the men in uniform, who stank of tobacco. This was unusual, but not unheard of. She would much rather forgo food than suffer their odoriferous presence.

On the third day, she began to wonder if their absence was part of some new test. She paid more attention to the sounds of the laboratory, dim and muffled by this room's thick walls: water in pipes, the roar of a generator for electricity, the occasional distant rumble of a train rushing over her head. Nothing else. The motorcar did not arrive or depart.

When she'd been in the room with cages, she'd heard wolves whine or growl, but could not smell them to discern whether they were like her or true wolves, or perhaps even dogs. Sometimes she'd seen them, the gleam of their eyes across a room as they watched her, and heard their breath, but the stench of the laboratory blurred all scents, even her own, and she could not identify them at all. Perhaps they were merely dogs. They did not seem large enough to be wolves.

Their presence now, whatever they were, would have been welcome as a diversion as the third day moved into a fourth. Had the old man taken them elsewhere? Was she to be left here to die? Surely he would not waste the opportunity to see how long it took for her to die from his torture.

She was hungry, and glad she had become accustomed to rationing her water. If not for that necessity, she could have gone into her wolf mind and ignored the dull passage of time, but then she would have no water, and though she could live for a few more days without food, water was another matter. She'd been wise not to change form. Her weak human body could not last so long.

On the fifth day, she found a new corner to pace, then lay with her head on her paws, drowsing. It was difficult to remember how long she had been in this room. She had not been entirely conscious when dumped here. Perhaps it had been longer than she thought. She might not have drunk water each day. She might have been forgotten here—

Above, she heard a shallow roar. Not the motorcar, but perhaps a motorbike? She'd heard this one before, or one very like it. It heralded the taller of the uniformed guards, who held her down after she had been drugged, and broke her bones upon request. That one often brought food.

She rose slowly and stretched, careful to loosen each muscle. She might have one chance. The guard might not know she had been alone so long. He might not know that she was fully recovered from her injuries. She might, this time, be able to escape.

She always thought these things, and was always driven back from the door by the old man and his electrical prod. This time he was not there. She had not heard him or his motorcar in days. She stalked over to the door, her legs weak from lack of exercise and hunger, and leaned against the concrete wall, trying to ignore its pervasive chemical stench. She waited.

The door opened, tobacco and wool and engine oil. She sprang. A gun went off. Her teeth met in flesh. Blood spilled into her mouth. She thrashed. The gun went off again, spitting bits of concrete over them. He was down! She released her bite and breathed in his face. He stared back, trapped, eyes wide, lost in terror. Good. Let him see what it was like.

She trotted out of the room, following his distinctive scent through twisting corridors. The fool had left open a door leading to the surface. She ran.

4

THE MOTOR RUMBLED IN THE SILENCE OF A RURAL night. Lucilla wished she'd saved some of the coffee from earlier. To her relief, Pascal eventually asked, "Do you know your primes?"

"Choose something more difficult," she said. "That won't keep me awake, it's only recitation."

He thought for a moment. "What is the pattern? Eighteen, fifty, one hundred fourteen, two hundred forty-two."

Lucilla pondered as she drove. Working backward, she arrived at the solution. "N plus seven multiplied by two. Another."

"Create one for me," Pascal said. They passed an hour in this fashion, their patterns growing quickly more complex as they tried to outdo each other, laughing and cursing when they failed. After an hour, they switched to word games, which became games of association and thus reminiscences.

"We lived on the outskirts of London, so we could play outside. When I was small, I liked playing with boys more than with girls. Dolls bored me, unless I could send them flying from trees or floating downstream on a raft. I played with Anthony, who lived in the house next door. My brother, Crispin, was too small, really, but he followed Tony everywhere, and me, as well, and I liked having a follower. He was the sweetest little boy."

"I didn't like other children," Pascal said. "They never wanted to speak of interesting things, only run about like a pack of rabid, howling animals."

"I doubt they appreciated being called rabid," Lucilla noted with some humor. "I assume you did not restrain yourself?"

"No, I did not," he said. "Tact is foreign to me. It's a waste of time. We have so little on this earth."

"So how did you amuse yourself?"

"My *grand-oncle* Erard, the one who took me to the Antipodes, taught me accounting, and navigation, and a number of card games. He was a most satisfactory companion," Pascal said, and when she glanced at him, he was looking at her. "It's always pleasant to meet someone agreeable."

Lucilla refrained from pointing out that if he made himself agreeable to more people, this might happen more often. She was beginning to understand his priorities, and to wish she could share his indifference to societal rules of politeness. A woman didn't have as much freedom in these matters as a man, but she could think of some cases in which she might have been better off to say what she thought. In the future, she decided, she would do better. She said, "When Anthony grew up, he married our neighbor, Lizzy."

"Should I be sorry that he married her and not you? You would not be here if he had. Or would he have allowed his wife to travel abroad to study derivatives of phenacetin? If not for those things, I might still be negotiating for a way home to France, instead of motoring along with a woman of considerable intellectual attainments."

Intellectual attainments, and willing to have sex with him, as well, Lucilla thought, amused. "You can be insufferably smug when you're right," she said. "My life would have been very different had I married Tony. He and I grew apart when he became interested in girls, as I apparently was not one." She could not imagine ever allowing Tony to kiss her as intimately as Pascal had done. Perhaps unfamiliarity had some advantages. One did not know what to expect, so one was more open to new things.

Pascal said, "I scorned girls long past the point of most boys."

"You must have had a change of heart at some point."

"I will tell you, if you wish to hear."

In the easy intimacy of the long dark ride, it was easy to say "I do want to know." She paused. "I'd rather not speak of my broken engagement, if that's all right with you."

A brief pause. "My curiosity was so obvious?"

Lucilla admitted, "I don't want to spoil this by thinking of him. In fact, I don't think I shall think of him ever again."

"Will you think of me, instead?"

"I will," she said. Pascal would be difficult to forget. "Now, tell me of your amorous adventures."

He hesitated. "I have never spoken of this to anyone else. You understand?"

"Yes," she said.

"Very well. My father worked at shipbuilding, and my grandfather, as well. We lived near the docks. I saw prostitutes ply their trade, and at home we children slept in an open loft above my parents' bed, where we could hear what went on. I saw no mystery in sexual congress."

For all his English education, he'd grown up among the

working class. Lucilla found it didn't matter to her. "My upbringing was very different," Lucilla said, though it was obvious he did not need her to tell him this. It was the best she could say to acknowledge their differences. "My mother would have summoned up the wherewithal to give me the basics if I'd gone through with my marriage, I suppose, but I had to go to all sorts of lengths to find out what I wanted to know." She paused as an idea slid into place in her mind, like a puzzle piece. "Women are easier to control if they are not allowed to know their own desires." After pondering this for a moment, she asked, "Did you know your desires?"

"I felt desire, but it caused me to be angry with myself. I had thought I was different from other males," Pascal said ruefully. "It was a sad day for me when I found myself loitering for a glimpse of women's ankles. I was not prepossessing. I was healthy enough, but very small until I reached my seventeenth year. Like a plucked chicken." Lucilla laughed at this image. He would not yet have grown into his nose. He continued, "I had no idea how I should speak to women, or how to entice them into an alliance."

"Surely you'd seen others courting." In her world, once one reached a certain age, courting had taken up ninety percent of everyone's energy.

"Their conversations had no point, and even seemed duplicitous at times, as surely no one could truly believe all the things men said to women, and vice versa. I watched, and eventually deciphered the language of their bodies, which was often quite different from their spoken language. Communication on both levels was required. Mastering both was the solution. I then experimented."

"With some success?"

"None at all."

Lucilla laughed. "I was expecting the triumph of the scientific method."

"I continued to have faith in it for some time, though my academic studies took more and more of my time once I began to prepare for university and work toward various scholarships," he admitted. "I had given up when a woman chose to seduce me, just before I left for Cambridge."

He fell silent for a moment, drinking from his bottle of lemonade.

Lucilla said, "Will you tell me what it was like?"

"How would you like me to tell you?" He spoke quietly, barely loud enough to be heard over the rumble of the engine.

Lucilla swallowed. She kept her eyes on the packed dirt of the road, winding away before the motor's lamps. "Tell me as if we were lying together. After." She pictured it in her mind, their bodies close and warm, the sound of their breathing, the scent of their effort lying on their skins, and shuddered inside.

She heard him take a deep breath. "I was sixteen."

"So young!"

"Ancient, compared to my compatriots in the neighborhood. One could have a prostitute for a single coin, if one were not afraid of one's mother finding out."

"Who was the woman?"

"The widow Jacques. She owned her late husband's bakery. She was not so old, but had been a widow as long as I could remember—perhaps ten years or more. She had no children. I recall my *oncle* Marius wasted a year in courting her at one time, but she did not wish for a partner in her business."

"Her name?" Lucilla felt this was important.

"Marie-Beatrice. I did not call her this, you understand. I was not so brave."

Lucilla wanted to know more; she wanted to know everything about how Pascal's experience had differed from hers. Women weren't supposed to want to know these things, but if she did know—it felt as vital to her now, to know his experience, as when she had learned the first workings of chemistry. "How did she——"

"She was a woman much to be admired. One afternoon, I had extra francs from my *grand-oncle*. I was hungry—I was always hungry, no matter how much I ate, or how often—and as I walked past her shop, I smelled the bread baking. I went inside, but no one was there to sell me bread. So I slipped past the counter and went in search of her in the kitchen."

"What did she look like?" Lucilla asked.

Pascal offered her the bottle of warm lemonade, and she drank, one-handed, as she drove, then handed the bottle back. Their fingers brushed. He said, "She was very small, even compared to my height then, but with a prodigious bosom." He added wryly, "You understand that this was of the greatest interest to me."

So far as Lucilla had been able to determine, his interest was for all parts of the female body, but perhaps he'd been less catholic in his tastes as a young man. "Was she alone?" she asked.

"Yes." Pascal paused, as if remembering. "She stood behind a table that was dusted with flour. She wore an apron, decorated with flowers, and a cap over her hair, of the same fabric. She didn't wear these things in the front of the bakery. It is hard to explain. It was as if I saw her in a negligee, to see her in these items that she wore for baking in her own place, where none saw her."

"I understand," Lucilla said, remembering the first time she'd seen a man other than her father or brother in shirtsleeves.

"She asked after my studies, and told me that she herself had left her home in Picardy to marry Monsieur Jacques when she was just sixteen, and she had never regretted this decision. She did not think I would regret it, either."

"Did you?"

"No. She was the first person who had told me this. All my family, they left France to travel, but they always returned home, to the same two streets. I did not plan to return there, and to this day I never have, except to visit. You went away, to Somerville College?"

She didn't want to talk about herself just now. "I did," Lucilla said. "My father thought I would meet a man and marry before I'd been there a year. Tell me what happened next."

"She asked me for help in removing her apron. The knot was too tight."

"You believed her?"

"I did," Pascal said. "I did not see myself as she did. I went to help her." He paused. "She smelled of baking bread. Her nape was bare. I wanted to lean closer and lick it, perhaps even bite. I could see myself bent over her. I had never had such a desire before. I had to look away, but I could still smell her. When I touched the knot of her apron, I also touched her skin. It was hot and damp, from the heat of the ovens. As I untied the knot, I could not help but touch her with my fingertips, again and again."

Caught up in the story, Lucilla was surprised to find that his description aroused her; whether the cause was imagining herself as Marie-Beatrice, or putting herself in Pascal's place, or both, she didn't know. "Did she touch you?"

"She removed her cap. Her hair fell onto my hands and across my wrists. It smelled of bread and vanilla. Then I did lean closer, and she told me I could go home if I wished."

"But you didn't."

"No. I realized her intent as soon as she released her hair. I asked her why she had chosen me."

Lucilla had guessed. "Because you were leaving."

"Yes."

When he didn't continue, she asked, "How did she—"

"She lived above the bakery. She closed for the afternoon, and took me up the stairs, to her bedroom. The drapes were drawn, but sun beamed through gaps and laid bars of light on her bed. It was the largest bed I had ever seen, with many pillows."

Lucilla's pulse beat between her thighs. She was not Marie-Beatrice; she was Pascal, about to experience the hot wet pain of sexual congress for the first time. Her throat felt thick. "Were you ready?"

Pascal snorted. "In those days, there was no time when I was *not* ready. Or I thought I was. I sat on the bed, and I grew harder still while she undressed me. She explained that she did not want this encounter to be over too quickly, as we would not have the opportunity for another. I agreed, of course. She took off my cap and ran her fingers through my hair, as my mother and sisters had sometimes done, but her touch was utterly different. It went through me like electricity."

"I would like to undress you," Lucilla said.

"I will permit that, when time allows," he said with some humor. "The widow Jacques, she undressed me down to the skin and laid my clothing on a chair. I had never considered before what happened to one's clothing, as the couples I had seen all wore their clothing while coupling. When she bent to tuck my boots beneath, I could see into her dress."

"Did you undress her?"

"No. She stood before me and disrobed. Her corset unhooked in the front and she—" He swallowed. "Beneath it, she was bountiful. She did not wear drawers beneath her shift. I thought I would choke for lack of air, when I realized I could see the hair on her cunt through the cloth. I had never before had a close view of the hidden places of a woman's body, and I felt balanced above a fall into some great understanding. She touched her breasts, stroking her nipples. She told me she liked to have them suckled gently, and that later she would like me to take her from behind, as that was the best for her."

Pictures flashed through Lucilla's mind, and she nearly lost control of the motor. "Pascal," she said, her voice shaking. "We need to stop soon. I need you to fuck me one last time."

He drew a long breath. "Perhaps we could stop now. It need not be the last time."

If only that could be true. Lucilla drew a matching breath, remembering where they were. "I would prefer to be safely in France first. Finish your story."

"After asking me to fuck you, you still wish me to tell you of Marie-Beatrice Jacques?"

"Yes."

"It's difficult to think of her when I would rather think of sinking between your soft thighs."

Lucilla's heart pounded in her ears. "Finish the story."

Pascal breathed deeply again. "Very well. We stood beside her bed and I explored her body through her shift. She explained that she liked the fabric to rub against her skin."

"Especially when your skin is damp," Lucilla said. She felt strangled, though she was breathing deeply; her nipples had drawn tight, and rubbed painfully against her bust bodice.

"I suckled her nipples and also her cunt, then she removed her shift. Her skin was like cream, except on her breasts, where the skin had stretched and left shiny lines. I licked each one, trying to forget my cock, but this was difficult, you understand."

"No doubt. What did she do for you?"

"She held my shoulders or arms, but that was all. I think if she had done more, I would have spent myself immediately."

She would have done more, had she been in the widow's place. She wouldn't have been able to restrain herself from stroking every inch of him, for wasn't that part of the pleasure? The freedom to touch as one willed? Perhaps for Madame Jacques, the freedom had been in allowing another to borrow the control she held over her body. "And then?"

"When she was ready for me to fuck her, she knelt on the bed with pillows to support her, and I knelt behind her. I rubbed myself along her back and on her rear, which was soft as a pillow, and could easily have done nothing else, but she spread her thighs and cried out for me to fuck her. It was…"

"Powerful," Lucilla said, imagining that she could order someone else's pleasure.

"Yes. But as soon as I was inside her, I felt an obliteration of the self, of the self that thinks. It was not only my cock that she squeezed inside her passage, but my whole being, shrunk into one fine point. It was extraordinary. All-consuming." He paused. "Is it like this for you?"

Lucilla had to think to understand the question he'd asked. He'd been honest with her, so she would do her best to be so with him. "It's like…holding my breath, and reaching, and… No. That doesn't explain it." She swallowed. "There's wetness, and tension, and it's close, so very close… I'm no good at explaining this."

If there were a formula, perhaps, and a predictable outcome. A protocol of physical actions leading to replicable results, easily described in terms of weight and color and viscosity. It ought to work that way, if the world were just. But she knew it didn't. Though her first experiences with sex had only felt more than physical at the beginning, her later solitary experiments had been harder to quantify and more varied in result. And what she'd shared with Pascal had been different than that; she hadn't always been aware of herself, or of her own body, in her fascination with him and his. Yet at the same time she felt fulfilled. Happy. Why? Did her body need sex, like a vitamin? If that was it, why was sex better with Pascal than alone? She shouldn't notice a difference. She drove another kilometer in silence.

Pascal interrupted her thoughts. "Perhaps next time, I will ask you what you feel at the appropriate moment."

"If I can form sentences, you're welcome to try." She took a deep breath. "What happened next? With Madame Jacques."

The motor purred. "It progressed in the usual way," he said.

Lucilla cast him a glance. "That's vague. I thought you remembered everything."

"I don't think I can speak on this anymore, unless my hands are on you," Pascal said.

Her stomach twisted a little, as if hungry for him. "Finish the story, at least."

"The smell of baking bread is, to this day, a reminder."

"So if I brought you a baguette, you would—" Imagining

the lewd appearance of a baguette, Lucilla began to laugh. Pascal joined her. To her surprise, the rest of their journey, all through the night, became a blur of laughter and shared memories, but now only memories of safe things, such as her childhood experiments with vinegar and bicarbonate of soda, and his first dish of ice cream, which had been strawberry.

She told him of when she'd been a girl, and imagined that she could easily dress in boys' clothes and run off to have adventures, just like the boys in the illustrated stories that Tony and Crispin pored over. She'd had to read those stories in secret, sneaking them into the garden shed to avoid her mother's lecturing on what was appropriate for a young girl and, at much greater length, what was not. "But now," she said with great satisfaction, "I am on an adventure of my own."

"Am I required to be your assistant in this endeavor? Or may I be the intrepid scientist?"

Lucilla grinned at him and deftly swerved around a hole in the road. "I stole the motor. I think you'd better be the girl. Only no swooning, I beg you."

"Only if you ravish me at the end," he said hopefully.

INTERLUDE

BOB HAILEY'S SISTER WAS NOT IMPRESSED WHEN told the regiment was mustering.

"You can't leave," Agnes said. "The water closet's got a leak. It makes a terrible drip all night, and keeps Mother awake."

"I'll have a look before I go," Bob said. "Captain Wilks is expecting me early."

"You care more about that old man than about your own family!"

"It's my duty."

"We're your duty! And what do you think will become of us if you get sent who-knows-where to be killed?"

"Haven't I done enough already? You'll get my pay, same as you've been getting," Bob said. "I've asked Mrs. Tollis upstairs to look in every few days. She's happy to do it."

"She doesn't care two pins for me, she just likes to gossip with Mother."

"You're able to take care of yourself," Bob said. "You had a factory job before I went into the service. If you need to, you can do it again."

"And then who'll take care of Mother, I ask you? She can't stay by herself any longer, and you know it. Yet I don't see you here but once in a fortnight."

Agnes was convinced the army was like a holiday camp, enlisted in for the adventure of it, much as their father had signed on with the merchant marine. Though of course he'd never been seen again.

"If I'm killed, will you still blame me for not mending the leaks?" Bob asked wearily. "I'm off." *To my other life.*

5

LUCILLA DID NOT REALIZE THEY HAD CROSSED
the border into France until she stopped the motor so they
could relieve themselves. The night sounded unusually quiet;
she'd grown used to the motor's vibration and the mournful
baying of dogs, and she stood for a moment, listening to the
engine tick. She heard Pascal's returning footsteps, then a
curse. He'd stumbled into a stone milepost. She backed the
motor enough for the headlamps to illuminate it. The distance
it marked was worn illegible, but it sheltered a gaily painted
plaster Madonna, her feet pinning at least twenty scraps of
paper, their penciled prayers inscribed in French. Lucilla was
tempted to leave an offering of her own, she was so glad to
be free of Germany, but at the same time, she realized her
journey's end would mean the end of her affair with Pascal.
She restrained herself from snarling at the statue's serenely
smiling face.

She stepped out of the headlamps' glare and said, "If we keep
going, we might find a village in time for coffee and croissants."

"We could stop here and rest," Pascal said.

"And sleep on the ground with no blankets? If we push on, we might find a nice, comfortable bed."

The wavering headlamp turned Pascal's grin more devilish than he might have intended.

"I intend to have a good day's sleep, at least!"

"I intend to make sure of it," he said. "Come. You're right. This road should lead us toward Verdun and Reims. There will be towns along the way if we run out of petrol."

Lucilla planned never to forget that dawn, pink and orange like a dish of sweets, the light gently washing over fields of summer hay. She glanced at Pascal to share it with him, but in the few moments since they'd last spoken, he'd fallen asleep.

She yawned, and considered pulling to the side of the road for a small nap herself, but she wanted a bed. More than that, she wanted one last time to make love with Pascal, so the sooner they reached a place where she could have that wish, the better.

This adventure was drawing to an end. She could feel it like a doom advancing. They would be separated, by her own choice before it could be his, and she would go home, and if England went to war, she would go, as well, who knew where—she might be sent anywhere. For all she knew, she would be sent back to Germany—that would be ironic. And Pascal had been in the army, like all Frenchmen. He would not be able to escape some form of service, no matter how he felt about it. And he could easily be killed, or be wounded or so changed by a war that he would forget about her completely. And that would be that. She would spend the rest of her life alone.

She berated herself for being melodramatic. It would

matter to her if he were killed, but so far as her life went, it would not matter, as she knew already she would not see him again. Clinging together in the midst of chaos was no solid basis for anything long-lasting. He was a young man, with a future ahead of him, whereas she was already past forty and had no wish for children or housewifery. If she planned, hoped, to see him again, she would be building castles in the air, as she had when she'd envisioned marriage with Clive, long and comfortable and filled with hours of quiet study, when she should have known what he really wanted was a helpmeet and someone to bear his children. He'd only wanted an educated wife so he could show her off to his fellow dons as she served them tea.

She had even less idea of what Pascal wanted. She'd only known him for…she was too tired to calculate the hours, and too dispirited to think on the future any longer. Oh, for a thermos of coffee. And now they were in France. She could really have croissants, with thick creamy butter and clots of strawberry jam.

Pascal woke when she slowed the motor on the outskirts of a sizable town. He squinted at the sunlight and growled in French. His stubbled face and shadowed eyes made him look particularly villainous and bad-tempered. Lucilla grinned because she felt much the same. "We'll have coffee soon."

"And a bath," he said, scrubbing at his face with one hand. "And a bed. If such are to be had."

They soon discovered that hotel lodging was difficult to come by here, as well, but a concierge directed them to a lodging house that still had a few rooms. Posing as a married couple, by afternoon they were ensconced in a large attic room, a bit warm from the sunlight that poured through a skylight, but clean and smelling of lavender and old wood, and enlivened by bouquets of bright poppies. Best of all, there was a shower, the prettiest Lucilla had ever seen, with brass fittings on three walls in the shape of lily blossoms, and tiled in green-and-white patterns like lacework.

Lucilla was nearly asleep in a borrowed linen nightgown when Pascal returned from his shower. He didn't speak, but smoothed his hand over her wet hair, and stroked her face. She murmured, pleased, and reached her arms for him. He went into her embrace, tucking her close against him, before he said, "Lucilla. Please wake up."

She blinked, her hand lazily curling on his shoulder. "Be quick about it."

"The German army has crossed into Belgium. Your country and mine are now both at war with Germany and Austria."

Lucilla closed her eyes again. She might not have forgiven him, had he spared her this news. They had little time left together now. She didn't want to waste it in sleep. "Kiss me. And help me remove this gown."

They woke in the wee hours of the morning and coupled once more, in a feverish and sweaty tangle of limbs that, in her fatigued haze, felt like a dream, even when their bodies struck together with enough force to shake the heavy iron bedstead. It was the sort of dream that is brighter and more vivid than reality, and that upon waking is so engraved in memory that it feels as if it were real. If only it were a dream, then she would not suffer the inevitable grief of their parting. Lucilla clamped her thighs on Pascal's hips and locked her arms about his torso, hiding her face in his shoulder as she silently urged him on with her hips and fingernails; his fingers and cock, meanwhile, drove her higher and higher until she screamed her pleasure into his skin. After, he turned onto his side and kissed her for an interminable interval, his hands tracing over her skin as if to imprint her body on his perfect memory. They broke apart only to gasp for breath before joining their mouths again. Lucilla thought that was to be the end, but hadn't reckoned with Pascal's vigor. In a quarter of an hour, he rose to the occasion again, and this time she took him from above, silent and fierce and angry that this had to end.

It was less than an hour until dawn when she dragged herself from his arms and tugged him down the hall into the bathroom, luckily deserted at this hour. She inspected his injured arm once more, then pulled him into the shower with her, where they soberly soaped each other, and washed each other's hair. When her gentle, soapy handling brought Pascal erect again, Lucilla backed him against the shower door and took his cock in her mouth. She'd never done such a thing before, but they had no condoms with them, and she feared, besides, that coupling would be unsafe on the slippery floor. He tasted of clean flesh and his cries, even muffled by his teeth in his arm, were the sounds of someone torn apart with pleasure. The hard pressure of his cock's head against her palate reminded her of having him deeply inside her sex, except that she was more in control of this and could lick and scrape and tease and pull on his cock and scrotum to such an extent that his knees failed him and they sank to the floor of the shower in a heap.

They'd intended to leave at dawn, but her vision blurred with exhaustion. She wouldn't allow Pascal to reciprocate the pleasure she'd given him when they returned to their room. Together they made up the bed with fresh sheets she'd found in a closet, and tumbled into an exhausted heap, her head pillowed on his chest.

She slept until the afternoon. This time, Pascal woke her with aromatic coffee and rolls and an omelette on a tray. Unshaven, wearing a severely crumpled shirt with the sleeves pushed up, and with his bruised arm all the colors of the rainbow, he still looked delicious enough to make her mouth water. She tasted raspberry jam on his lips.

"Café au lait," he said, placing a cup into her hand. He ripped a roll apart and buttered it for her. "The trains are running. Not often, but perhaps the train would be better than the motorcar. We can get to Le Havre by way of Rouen."

Lucilla swallowed coffee and closed her eyes for a moment, in bliss at the smooth sweet milkiness. "You don't have to go with me," she said. "I could leave from Brest, or Dieppe."

"With a great deal more trouble, and knowing no one at those ports," he said, putting down her roll and picking up another for himself. He paused, with the bread held in one long-fingered hand. "You don't want my help?"

"I don't want you to feel you have to take care of me," she said.

"We have had this discussion before," he noted. "We have fucked, and now you wish to part? Have you considered my faults and taken me in dislike? Because I know you aren't in the least foolish, and I can think of no other reason. What is the point of, of rabbiting across France alone—"

"Haring off," she said. "Not rabbiting. I can take care of myself."

He flicked his hand dismissively. "You do not need to prove to me that you are capable of taking care of yourself. Truly, do you want me to go away?"

His jaw was tight, and his brows drawn. Lucilla remembered tracing her fingers along the lines of his eyebrows in the night. "No." She looked down into her coffee cup.

"Good, then we will stop this pointless arguing. We go to Le Havre, and my *oncle* Marius will find a berth for you. Yes?"

"Yes."

"Good," he said, ripping apart his buttered roll and stuffing half of it into his mouth.

Lucilla drained her coffee and cut herself a bit of omelette. It was dense with soft cheese and thin ham and fine herbs. For the next several minutes, they ate in silence. When she emerged from her troubled thoughts and glanced at Pascal, he was watching her, his fork lax in his hand.

She said, "It's very good of you to offer your help, and your family's."

"You are welcome," he said. He poked at the omelette with his fork. "I am not at all gracious. I do this because I'm selfish. I wish you to be safe. I would be unhappy if you were not."

Lucilla swallowed the lump in her throat. His gaze burned straight through her. "When does the train depart for Rouen?"

The posted train schedule was overly optimistic, but the trains were running. One had only to be patient amid the tense, unusually large crowds. They bought tickets and drank coffee at the station as the sun set. Lucilla bought a pack of cards from an enterprising vendor and taught Pascal to play All Fives while they sat crammed onto a bench near the departures board. The snap of their cards vanished in the noisy clack of numbers being constantly changed on the board and the low roar of hundreds of conversations.

On the crowded train, Pascal used his long legs to secure seats for both of them, and for all the ride to Rouen, though she'd intended to converse, Lucilla dozed with her head on his shoulder, waking only when he waved a sandwich beneath her nose sometime after midnight. The paper-thin slices of ham and dark mustard might as well have been paper, for all she tasted; the fizzy lemonade burned in her stomach, which was uneasy with nerves.

Pascal poked the crumpled sandwich paper into a pocket on the outside of his rucksack. "Sleep," he said, his voice rough. "I will wake you at Le Havre."

"It's your turn to sleep," she said. "I can play Patience."

"I'm not tired," he said. A moment passed, then he touched her cheek, tracing the shape of her cheekbone. Lucilla shivered. He said, sounding angry, "I would go with you if I could."

"I know you must stay here."

"I could leave. I have lived in England before."

"You will go back to the army," she said. "I understand that you must. Just as I will do what I must."

Scowling, he turned his head toward the window. Lucilla slipped her arm into his and laced their fingers together, not caring if anyone saw. She would never see these people again. His hand tightened painfully. He did not speak again. Lucilla closed her eyes and fell into shallow, chaotic dreams.

Despite the early hour of their arrival, Le Havre was even more overwhelmed with travelers than the train station had been. She heard English spoken more than once, fragments carried to her on waves of the crowd's ocean. *Have the tickets?…Where's Teddy? I told you to watch…leaves on the hour, but I don't believe…what shall we do…hold the bags…*

Lucilla was glad enough to cling to Pascal with one hand and to her carpetbag with the other. She was gladder still when he led her away from the mobbed station and through a series of small side streets to his uncle's house, a white two-story cottage wedged tightly in a row of similar homes, each one featuring a different array of flowers in front. Pascal introduced her as a chemist and colleague, which garnered baffled looks from his uncle, aunt and three female cousins, but she was still offered kisses on both cheeks and fresh coffee and croissants and a chance to freshen up. She scrubbed her face and the back of her neck roughly with a cloth, hoping to wake up before she had to be polite to strangers.

Lucilla spoke French with some facility and understood it better, but their accents baffled her unless they spoke very slowly, so she smiled and nodded as often as she could. Pascal's accent was the same, she noted, as he explained her needs to his uncle with a number of expressive hand gestures. His uncle departed soon after reassuring her that a berth would be easy to obtain, for him at least. Lucilla would have given him money for bribes, but he assured her it was not necessary; he was calling in favors.

Her lack of proper sleep had left her in a hazy, numb state. When one of the cousins took her by the arm and led her upstairs to a cramped loft, she was only barely aware of having her shoes unhooked for her as she drifted off to sleep, fully clothed and atop the coverlet.

"Lucilla," Pascal said.

She patted the mattress next to her, but he wasn't there. She rolled over and reached for him; he captured her hand and brought it to his lips. She shivered all through the center of her body, waking into a rush of sensual awareness. What was she to do without him?

He said, "You must get up. Your ship leaves in an hour."

"What time is it?"

"Nearly six." Pascal tugged, and she sat up, swinging her

legs over the edge of the bed in a tangle of crumpled skirt and petticoats. She spotted her stockings draped tidily over the fireplace screen, her shoes set beneath. "I'll go with you to the dock," he said in a tone that permitted no argument. "My aunt has made you sandwiches. She is sorry she could not brush out your clothing for you."

"It's too late for mere brushing to do any good. Please thank her for me," Lucilla said. "I need to wash my face."

Pascal bent and kissed her, briefly but not chastely. "Come downstairs when you're ready to go."

Lucilla barely had time to thank her hosts before, smiling, they bustled her and Pascal out the door. He walked quickly, this time carrying her carpetbag for her while she kept her hand around his biceps, careful not to stray toward his bruises, which he had not shown to his family.

"You'll see your father, won't you?" she asked.

"After you've gone," he said. He led her past a boatbuilder's shed and toward a row of ships, their railings crowded with passengers. "This one," he said, and stopped at the foot of the gangway.

"Already," she said, foolishly.

He set down her carpetbag, took off his hat and dug in his jacket pocket. He held up three wrapped chocolates, then slipped them into her skirt pocket with a stealthy caress. "I will find you when this war is ended."

Lucilla tipped up her chin, trying to send her sudden impending tears back into her head. She wasn't so brave when it came down to it. She wanted to fling herself into his arms and beg him never to leave her, like someone in a cheap novel. "I've enjoyed our time together. I'll miss you."

"Don't speak as if you'll never see me again." Pascal ducked beneath her hat brim and kissed her, long and lusciously. Her knees turned to water, and she clutched at his jacket until he pulled away and slapped his hat back on his head. *"Au revoir."*

"Goodbye," she said. She picked up her carpetbag and turned away. All the long walk up the gangplank, she did not look back.

6

ON THE FIFTH DAY AFTER HER ESCAPE FROM THE cage, the wolf decided she had finally outrun all pursuit. She stopped to lick at the dried blood on her wounded shoulder before she slept, to allow herself to heal. She waited for twilight that evening before she moved on, and did the same on many subsequent nights, covering perhaps twenty kilometers without ceasing her steady lope, unless she found water; then she would stop to drink and clean herself. Traveling as she did through fields of grain and vegetables, devouring field mice, only clean dirt clung to her pelage's stiff hair, but she had become fastidious since her escape.

She not only swam in any suitable water she encountered, but rolled vigorously in sand or against rough rocks, whatever she could find. The stench of him lingered, no matter what she did, and to the wolf an illusory stink was as real as the ground beneath her paws. She took to scrubbing her muzzle in the grass when the taint overpowered her. That helped, or at least provided a distraction from her mother's never-ceasing voice in her mind: "You must not attack a human. It's forbidden. Forbidden. Forbidden."

The weather grew steadily warmer and the days longer. The farther she ran, the more her mother's voice faded, submerged in the wolf's mundane concerns. The air of freedom smelled sweet as a fresh kill.

Only once did memory return. Weary of hunting mouthfuls of mouse, one evening she hunted hare, successfully predicting its zigzag dash and seizing its quivering body in her jaws. Blood spurted into her mouth, over her tongue, and it was a man's blood flowing down, soaking her ruff as she gripped his hip in panic and anger, too weak and fearful to let go and rip instead at his tender belly. The shock of memory almost forced her to change. When she came back to herself, she found the hare's mangled corpse lying at her feet, but could not summon any appetite for it. She left it for the smaller predators of the fields and went hungry that night, running until she forgot all but the raw-rubbed skin on the bottom of her paws.

After dawn each day, she denned in hedges or ditches, nuzzling her way beneath brush and leaves or whatever cover she could locate. This might have been easier with human hands, but she was reluctant to change, lest anyone see her. And…she did not want to see her human form again. Not yet. It didn't matter that she bore no scars. That form was bizarre to her, unlikely, and, oddly, she felt as if it had betrayed her. Absurd, when as a human she was also herself; but as a wolf she had never cowered in quite the same way, or yielded to dominance. Her human form was small, pale, weak. It had nothing to offer her today, or tomorrow, or any day after that. Besides, when in wolf form, it was difficult to think too many days ahead. As far as she was concerned, she might remain on four legs forever. So long as she reached home, what did it matter which form she held? This one was as good as any other.

When the full moon came, she dared not run. She heard her mother's voice again, sensed her mother's human hands on her puppy fur as she gently told tales of the wolves who'd gone out in the light of the moon, been seen, and been killed.

"You must hide, little one. Hide when the light is too bright. We are only safe here, on our own lands."

She denned on the edges of a forest, too skittish to go deeper into the dense, cagelike trees and too afraid to lie in the open without concealment. She tried to sleep the night through, to pass the time, but sleep came only in shallow snatches, her legs twitching as if to continue running, so she woke even more weary than she'd been before. At dawn, she found water, then fell truly asleep.

Perhaps her body sensed the trees close around her. She dreamed of being held immobile in a wooden chute, claws scrabbling frantically at the floor while bullets slammed into her haunches, bursts of numbness blossoming into hot, ripping agony. She snarled and yelped, trying to curl in on herself, but there was no refuge, and her blood slowly soaked through the layers of her golden pelage, her strangled whimpers of pain erupting into howls that wrenched and tore into human screams. In her dreams, the change was pain like snapping bones and she jolted into another place, another time. She heard her leg bone creak and twist and pop while she fought uselessly against crisscrossing, pinching leather straps, growling through her bound, bleeding muzzle, while her captor cursed her and smacked her nose, annoyed that she would not hold still. Across the room, the others watched and growled.

She could not bear to sleep among the trees after that endless night. She trusted cornfields, open and predictable, to hide her from view, but sometimes even the spaced green rows seemed to whisper behind her and close in over her head, leaving her no escape but a panicked burst of speed under the white light of the revealing moon.

She had traveled forever. One evening, when she'd slept next to a road, she woke to the stench of tobacco and man. The wise course would be to remain hidden. Instead, she sprang free of concealment and into the road, hackles raised.

He stopped. He spoke.

Her upper lip quivered and lifted, a growl tremoring forth from her belly. *Run,* she thought. If he ran, she would chase. If he ran, he would be prey. Rage and revulsion fought each other in her belly. She imagined hot blood gushing into her mouth and the slick tenderness of meat beneath his hide.

He spoke again, a question. His voice trembled, but he didn't move. He smelled old, like—

He would be easy prey if he ran. She could bring him down alone. She did not need to bite. She need only protect herself. But if he tried to bind her...

Hesitantly, he took one step toward her, muttering non-sense. "Good dog... My, you're large. Where do you live? Good dog, good dog..."

She would not hunt prey that approached her. Also, he stank, but his words weren't what she'd expected. A thread of famil-iarity crept into her ears and gradually she identified the feeling.

He spoke Flemish.

She cringed. She was home, might have been home for

days. She should be overjoyed, but she cringed. She had almost attacked a fellow Belgian.

The man stopped speaking. He wore sandals. She could smell the mud on his trousers, the wine he'd drunk and the pipe he'd smoked. She smelled no weapon and sensed no bitter tang of contempt. A farmer, probably. Not a threat. Slowly, she backed away, strained whimpers replacing her growl. As soon as she could control herself, she turned tail and fled.

Almost full, the moon glowed fat and brilliant, illuminating her path and clearly marking her retreat to any observers, but she could not stop herself from running, not even retreating to the edge of the road for many kilometers.

Thirst eventually brought her up short. She yawned nervously from a queer sense of pursuit, though the road was deserted. She could smell a village nearby. She could smell bricks and thatch, stoves and fireplaces, and the bodies of humans and horses, dogs and cats, chickens and goats and pigs. Like a promise, she also smelled the first hints of baking bread. Soon it would be dawn.

She staggered to the ditch and there, without quite willing it, she changed form. It must have been a long time since she'd been human. Her muscles wrenched painfully as she thrashed, her head slamming into the dirt. She felt as if her spine was being ripped from her back and her yelp twisted to a strangled cry. She fell naked in the ditch, panting, her hair tangled around her, her face streaked with tears of agony.

Growling, she dug her fingers into the dirt and ripped loose handfuls of grass and flowers, flinging them from her with all her strength. That was not enough. She clawed at her own skin, her weak pale flesh, but her ripped nails could not damage enough to release her rage. She tried to change form again, but exhaustion and her disordered feelings prevented her. That final effort sucked the last of her strength and she collapsed to the ground, shaking with a roil of human and animal rage. She could not stop weeping until after the sun rose.

In the gray light of dawn, she crept toward the village, slinking in and out of any cover she found. Dogs silenced and retreated from her at a single commanding look, and a farmer headed for the nearby tobacco fields did not notice a single unmoving shadow behind a rosebush. She crept on bare, callused feet into a laundry shed and there found two dresses, still redolent of their human owner and too large for her slight form. She took one anyway and struggled into it, wrinkling her nose at the human stench, then crept out again. She stole bread from a windowsill, tore off half the loaf, then returned the other half, driven by some distant impulse of human behavior.

Inside the house, people were talking with great vehemence. She had to concentrate to make sense of the human speech at first. They were outraged, and fearful. Some terrible event had taken place.

She didn't piece everything together until she heard the word *war*. German soldiers had invaded Belgium without cause?

She fled with her breakfast, walking down the dirt road in the yellow light of day.

First, she would go home—the desire to hide in her own forest was so overwhelming it frightened her. If she did that, she feared, she might never emerge. It would not be a bad life, except that then Kauz would have won. That, she would not allow. And now there was this other problem, of the invasion. How dare they? And what could she do about it?

Who knew what power Kauz would gain if his country succeeded in their conquest?

She would go home, and recover her strength. Then she would find Kauz again. And she would rip out his throat.

7

LUCILLA ARRIVED HOME IN KENT TO THE FERVENT embraces of her mother, and a more formal though no less heartfelt embrace from her father, who'd thought her trip to Germany a bad idea in the first place. Her brother had been called up to his regiment already, though no one yet knew when or if Crispin would be shipped to France. It was likely he'd have a brief leave before that happened, but no one was sure of anything.

Her house was strewn with dismembered newspapers as her family attempted to piece together scraps of information about the war—everything from the text of threatening diplomatic letters to the movement of men and ships—into a logical whole. Neighbors went in and out, sharing news and gossip and speculation, littering every table with teacups and saucers covered in crumbs. Finding out what was happening was the crux of every conversation. Lucilla felt no urgency on this point, as she was now sure war would happen. Her discussions with others on the ship from Le Havre and on the train to Kent had made that clear to her. Europe was a powder keg, and fuses had been lit all over. It was only a matter of time. She went to the hospital where she normally worked and inquired about the requirements for nurses willing to travel to France. With her surgical experience and maturity, she was told, she would be accepted with alacrity.

She informed her family that she was traveling to London as soon as possible to see Clara Lockie, a friend from university who now served as an administrator for the Red Cross. Ignoring her mother's increasingly loud demands for further details, she climbed upstairs to her room and shut the door. She would need her carpetbag, which she had never unpacked after her journey from Germany. It sat on the corner rug. She drew a decisive breath and popped it open. On top lay the map Pascal had drawn, and her medical kit in its own case. She didn't need to unbuckle the leather straps to know that she would need to replace her bandages and refill the jar of wound salve before she traveled again. And she remembered that she had no more condoms. She and Pascal had seen to that. She contemplated acquiring a new stock of them. They were still valuable bribes, and perhaps she would meet some other man, a doctor or army officer, who took her fancy. She closed her eyes but would not allow herself to shy away from considering the idea. The rest of her life might stretch very long, and she was losing her fortitude against loneliness. Even as a paragon of moral rectitude, she would never be allowed to freely work and study as men did. With the world bent on destruction, she had little reason to stick to propriety.

The remnants of her glassware were padded with dirty laundry about which she had forgotten. She swore and carefully unwrapped each piece, setting it on her writing desk.

She found the remains of a tin of acid drops that had gone sticky, and cut her finger on a bit of broken glass she'd missed. Her laboratory notebooks lay in the bottom of the carpet-bag; she stacked them neatly on a shelf, as her mind was too turbulent for that sort of work. It looked as if a page had come loose, she realized as she lifted the bag to set it on her bed. She drew out the single sheet, at first thinking it blank, but then saw the penciled, back-slanted words: *16 Rue du Canotage*. An address. She'd never seen the handwriting before, but knew it for Pascal's. Had he dropped this slip of paper? A memory tugged at her of walking along a pier in Le Havre, and a warehouse with its address painted on the wall in flaking white letters. He'd told her that his father lived on that street, and two of his brothers. Pascal had no need to write down an address on the Rue du Canotage for himself. He'd written it down for her.

Lucilla wept. It was, she thought afterward as she lay emptied atop her bed, a reaction to everything that had happened to her in the past weeks. It had nothing to do with her momentary desire to seize notepaper and write to Pascal. His family lived at that address. He did not. Anything sent there might never reach him. He would not really want her to write. He might have met someone else already. She was a fool.

No, she was doubly a fool. She shouldn't lie to herself to make this easier. She and Pascal had shared true companion-ship, not just sex, and if she saw him again, he wouldn't turn her away. But that was the difficult part. She couldn't count on seeing him again, and aim her whole life toward that goal, for who knew what would come of it? She was no longer a young girl to moon over imaginary futures that would solve all her problems. Having a man would not give her the deep, sustaining happiness that intellectual fulfillment provided her. Chemistry was a lover who would never forsake nor destroy her.

Still, she would miss the sex, and even more so, the physical intimacy. Her body ached for Pascal, even now.

Crispin returned home the following day. Lucilla met him at the door, and at first she could only stare. He wore crisp khaki service dress, and his curly hair was cropped and nearly hidden beneath his uniform cap. His usually open and pleasant face was tense and worried, but he relaxed when he saw her.

"Hello, Luce. I'm so glad you made it home."

She flung herself into his arms, holding him so tightly he was forced to drop his rucksack. After a time, she broke free, kissed him and said, "I thought I might not get to see you again."

"I've twenty-four hours," he said, chucking her lightly beneath the chin, then smoothing back her hair, which had become mussed in their embrace. "Is Mum home?"

"Gone to the Osbournes'. She'll be back in a few hours. The pater's upstairs."

"I'll do the pretty, then we'll go down the pub, all right? I'm starving."

Half a dozen friends stopped them on their walk to the pub, but Crispin put them all off with a few words. Lucilla's heart went into her throat each time she looked at him. He was so young, only twenty-three. She could still easily remember rocking him in his cradle as a baby.

The publican wouldn't let him pay for his pint, nor Lucilla's decorous bottle of fizzy lemonade. They sat outside, at their favorite outdoor table under the oak tree, and drank for a few minutes in silence, watching a pair of mongrels chase each other beside the dusty lane. At last, Crispin took off his cap and tossed it onto the table before wiping his forehead on his sleeve. "Bloody uniforms are too hot," he said. "I don't like these new boots, either. They'll take weeks to break in."

"Do you think you'll have weeks?" she asked.

After a small pause, he shook his head.

"Right, then. I'm going to find work as a nurse. They'll be in need of them."

Crispin's cheeks colored. "I don't need a nursemaid."

"I don't expect we'll be able to see each other very often," she said, "but I'd rather be there than trapped here at home. And I certainly can't return to the Institute. I fear I can never return there again."

"Perhaps after the war's over—"

"And when will that be?" she asked. "No, I've burned my bridges there."

Crispin sipped his pint, then wiped the foam from his lip. "So…I haven't really time to cajole the story from you. I was expecting I'd have to go to Whitehall and beg them to send someone after you. My captain even said he would give me leave, and find some business to send Lieutenant Meyer with me."

Lucilla said, "I thought I'd be trapped there, as well, once the trains stopped running. But I found help." To her horror, she felt heat rising in her cheeks.

"What sort of help?"

Perhaps it would do her good to speak of it, as an event long over and gone. Taking another fortifying sip of lemonade, Lucilla began with "There was another foreigner at the Institute, a Frenchman," and went all the way through to "and he put me on a ship across the channel." By the time she'd finished, the sun had moved halfway across the pub's yard, and Crispin had munched his way through an enormous plate of fish and chips.

"I can see why he didn't go with you," Crispin said. "He'll be called up soon enough. Do you have his address?"

"I don't plan to use it," she said. "He might have been Lizzy's age, no more. That's only thirty. I'm forty-two. We live in different countries, speak different languages."

"You said he spoke English."

"Well, he does, but—"

"And you're going back to France."

"Well, yes, but not to see—" She drank more lemonade. "I have a career, Crispin."

Grimly, he said, "Sure, but no one will hire you. You said Monsieur Fournier works for the French government. Things might be better in France. Maybe he can get you a position. Sometimes all it takes is a sponsor."

"He won't want to see me again."

"That might be true, but…" He took another sip of his pint. Tentatively, he said, "You sounded happy when you talked about him. Very happy. That isn't something to ignore."

She looked down at her hands. "It was pleasant to converse with another scientist who didn't consider me the equivalent of a trained circus dog."

"Isn't that worth searching out?"

"Oh, Crispin. I don't know. I just don't know."

The ship carrying the regiment to France was at least cooler than the troop train had been. Crispin settled his men and wandered the deck, trying to pretend he wasn't watching Lieutenant Meyer, who sat by the railing scribbling in a notebook and humming to himself, writing music as he always did. When Meyer didn't look up, Crispin leaned his back on the railing, a few feet down, and alternated staring out to sea with keeping an eye on the men, so it wasn't so much like standing alone. He could review their names while he was at it.

Mason was easy; he was half Negro, and the most accurate shot in the company. Lyton was the oldest, already going gray. Private Figgis always had a cigarette hanging out of his mouth, whether it was lit or not; luckily, he also had a mole next to his nose, in case he ever lost the cigarette. Evans had curly dark hair much like Crispin's own, and the remnants of a Welsh accent; Woods, the same age as Evans and usually in his company, looked at least five years younger. Cawley had hairy knuckles but was already going bald; Lincoln was also balding and generally wore a sour expression. Skuce was the best card player, aside from Hailey. After Meyer, Corporal Joyce was the best looking, though too muscular for Crispin's taste, and Southey was another easy one, his hair the palest blond, with a graceful walk that reminded Crispin of the first boy who'd ever fucked him at school, Tobin Major.

Crispin shook himself. Dangerous to think of such things now. All that was past, gone. He might watch Meyer a bit, but he wasn't going to *do* anything about it. He had no desire to end up jailed, or worse.

Pale and pudgy, and much tougher than he appeared, Lieutenant Smith of the fourth platoon was curled up asleep by the wheelhouse. Lieutenant Ashby crept over and ever so carefully placed a couple of empty wine bottles and a biscuit tin by his hand, so Figgis could take an incriminating photograph. Ashby could do that sort of thing and not lose the men's respect over it; they'd only love him more for his pranks. Ashby was friends with Meyer, Crispin had learned. Ashby and Meyer had been neighbors since boyhood. That probably explained the odd intuition he'd felt when he'd first seen them, standing together, Ashby's grin seemingly telling Meyer secrets.

Crispin really needed to stop imposing his own preferences on other men.

Private Hailey's appreciative eye on Meyer, for example, was likely the normal admiration of a young man for a well-dressed officer, particularly one much younger and hand-somer than the captain whom Hailey served as batman. The only thing different about it was that, because Meyer was a Jew, most of the men focused their admiration on Ashby instead, even though he was far less handsome. Crispin admitted that Ashby did have an appealing energy about him, and a compelling presence, but to Crispin, he just wasn't as…involved. Ashby was always just a little distant, as though he was thinking of two things at once. Meyer really cared about the men he commanded, and to Crispin that said a con-siderable amount about his personality.

Captain Wilks strode into sight then, and Hailey bounded to his feet like a pup sighting its master. Wilks was an enor-mous man in both height and girth, who often told the story of how he'd been unable to find a decent-size polo pony in all of Peshawar, until he'd befriended a Pathan horse trader through winning at jackstraws, and from then on had never suffered. He always avoided explaining why they'd been play-ing jackstraws instead of a more usual soldiers' amusement; Crispin suspected the game had been more risqué. Hailey never seemed to tire of this story, no matter how the rest of the company rolled their eyes.

Wilks, in turn, clearly loved having someone to listen to him, far more than he cared about the state of his boots and buckles, and would regale them at any opportunity with tales of hot plains and snowy mountains, of tigers and tame elephants and cows that freely wandered the city streets, and how he and three old men had hauled a cannon up a mountain with ropes, and how he'd once saved a child from a snake as big around as his thigh. Crispin wasn't sure he believed that last one, but he wasn't going to spoil it for anyone else by questioning it.

Hailey stepped over a few sleeping soldiers and saluted, and Captain Wilks handed him a sandwich. "Better eat that, son," he said. "Never miss a chance to eat, sleep or piss."

"Yes, sir," Hailey said, grinning. "Do you need anything, sir? I altered that second jacket for you, and mended your shirts."

"Maybe when the bullets start flying I'll need some assistance," Wilks said. "Until then, you just keep yourself out of trouble. When I was your age, you can't imagine the hell I raised. Though you're a good boy, I'll give you that."

Crispin didn't have to imagine; Wilks had told everyone in the company, relishing every detail. It didn't hurt that Wilks had grown up in India as well as later serving there, so even his boyhood scrapes involved monkeys and tigers and mongooses. Hailey said, "Thank you, sir."

"Be off with you now."

"Sir—" Hailey didn't have to say anything else. Wilks clapped his shoulder with a huge, weathered hand.

"You'll do fine, my brave lad," he said. "But only if you eat your sandwich. If you can nick me a bottle of port from the colonel later on, there's a crown in it for you. And check on old Hammerhead down in the hold, make sure he has a carrot."

"Sir," Hailey said. He ate the sandwich standing up, saving a bit of the crust, which he tore into small bits, flinging them over the railing for the swooping, screaming gulls. When he dusted off his hands, he noticed Crispin watching him. "Sir?" he asked.

"Nothing." Crispin pushed his hands into his pockets and leaned back against the railing. He wished he didn't feel jealous of the obvious affection between the captain and his batman. It had just been so long since he'd trusted anyone as much as that.

"All right, sir?"

The boy could be a mother hen. Crispin tried to smile. "Of course." He paused. "If you're still hungry, I have another sandwich. I couldn't stomach it. The sea, you know."

"Better eat it anyway, sir."

"Never miss a chance to eat, right?" He dug the packet out of his tunic pocket, then dug farther and offered Hailey a handful of nut-milk choc. "Maybe you could hand this around. And some for you, of course. No need to say it came from me. My sister gave it to me before I left."

"Of course, sir." Hailey smiled back at him, a surprisingly sweet smile. "If you need any mending done, you come to me."

"I will," Crispin said, feeling a bit better at the genuine offer. "Thank you." He glanced at Meyer, felt himself flush and focused on unwrapping his sandwich. "That's kind of you."

"My duty, sir."

"Not really," he said, "but I appreciate it all the same."

"I'll be on my way then, got some things to take care of for the captain," Hailey said.

Crispin mentally shook himself and joined a group of the men lounging on the deck, some of them smoking in tense silence, some talking with nervous energy, some alternating both activities. Corporal Joyce pored over a first-aid text. Meyer was still scribbling and humming over by the railing; Ashby loitered near a group playing cards, and Smith slept on, oblivious to the noise. Eventually, Hailey returned, smelling of horse, having presumably been to check on Hammerhead, Wilks's ugly chestnut gelding. Crispin was surprised when Hailey sat beside him, pulling out a sock to darn; they sat together in silence, listening to the men talk.

Evans said, "My girl and I are getting married as soon as I get home." He unbuttoned his tunic collar to display an impossibly delicate gold ring on a chain. "If I get killed, someone send this back to her, will you?"

"Do we inherit the girl?" Lincoln chaffed. "Cover your tender ears, Hailey."

Hailey looked up. "You got a girl, Lincoln?"

Lincoln leered. "Anytime I want."

"What about what they want?"

General laughter erupted.

Mason said, "I've got my eye on a nice plump French girl."

"Which one?"

"Any one that'll have me!" More laughter.

"Make sure she can cook, lad," said Lyton, scrubbing at his gray mustache. "My wife can make roast turnips taste like the food of heaven."

Cawley countered, "My sister's bread is so light it could float away, but she couldn't keep a husband."

"He's the fool, then," said Lyton. "Hearth and home, lad, hearth and home."

"Who wants a home when your wife's screeching at you all the day long?"

"I like screeching," Lincoln said, raising a significant eyebrow.

Southey sneered. "For Christ's sake, man, give it a rest. Your mum wouldn't like to hear that spilling out of her baby boy's mouth."

"Not here, is she? War's no place for a woman."

"We'll be sure and get a nice husky fellow to mop your manly brow in hospital, then. Me, I'll settle for a pretty young thing with soft hands."

Woods said, "You'd let a lady nurse you? She'd see—you know—"

More laughter. Hailey turned to Crispin. "You got a sister, you said?" he asked quietly.

Surprised, Crispin answered, "Yes. Always set me right when I needed it. You?"

"Yes," Hailey admitted. "Doesn't like me much."

Crispin said, "Lucilla's so much older, it's like…she's my friend."

"Not Agnes. She's stuck home caring for Mum while I—" Hailey didn't finish.

Crispin said, not really asking, "You're caring for them, too, aren't you? I mean, with your pay?"

"That's why I joined up," Hailey admitted. "Mum's often ill, and Dad left us—"

"I'm sorry." And he was truly sorry.

"Oh, it was years back," Hailey said. "I took a factory job, then I apprenticed at tailoring."

Crispin had never heard Hailey say so much, all at one time, so he wasn't surprised when the boy handed him the last of the nut-milk choc and retreated from the conversation. They sat together in companionable silence. When Southey came over a little later to tell Hailey the captain was looking for him, Crispin patted him on the shoulder once and then turned again to look out to sea, trying to reconcile himself to living in close company, but always alone.

8

TO MEMORIALIZE HIS BROKEN ENGAGEMENT TO
the gorgeous and well-off Miss Jemima Ruthven, Gabriel
Meyer began a viola concerto on the British Expeditionary
Force's voyage from Southampton to Le Havre. Having
expected to brood upon his dismissal from an arrangement
of nearly a year's standing, one that would have benefited
both her family and his, he was disconcerted by how quickly
his melodies drove out thoughts of her and her glorious legs.

Perhaps Ashby had been right. He *knew* Ashby had been
right about Jemima, but he had decided to at least give her a
chance. People married all the time with less in common that
they'd had. At least they'd been physically attracted to one
another. Perhaps he ought to have tried harder to understand
her sometimes rigid opinions on social issues. But the
regiment still would have been mustered, and Jemima still
would have handed back his grandmother's ring.

He was relieved she'd done it. He tried not to think he
might be relieved because he didn't really want to be married

at all. It wasn't true. He liked women. He liked sex with them. After this war ended, he would meet another woman, nicer than Jemima, and they would marry, and he would give his mother grandchildren.

He worked at the concerto's *largo* while on the train that carried them toward the potential line of battle at Maubeuge, scribbling notes with a pencil in a hardbound staff notebook propped on his knee, striving to hear music in his head rather than snoring. He might have ridden in the first-class car with the other officers, where he was sure the food would be better than biscuits and Bully Beef, but his major had nothing but contempt for Jews and for Gabriel in particular. So rather than combine a grand case of nervous jitters at the thought of being killed with constant animosity, he'd chosen to stay here with his men. He thought they might take comfort in his presence, anyway. His platoon included the youngest men in the company; only fitting, as he was—at twenty-six—the eldest of the lieutenants, and likely to remain so, given his religion.

He'd never expected to command anyone other than his bandsmen. Sergeant Pittfield had been a great help, but he'd been sure his lack of combat experience would diminish him in the eyes of his company. So far, they'd shown remarkable respect toward him, more than he'd received since his enlistment. He suspected Ashby's hand, passing some of his charismatic glow in Gabriel's direction, or at the very least reassuring the boys that Gabriel could be trusted. Or perhaps they had no choice other than to trust their officer. They came to him often enough, with the smallest of problems. The youngest lieutenant of their company, Daglish, often came to him, as well; like him, Daglish had taught music, but at a girls' school. He suspected Daglish was homesick.

"Sir," said Private Evans, his tall and gawky form rocking slightly with the motion of the train. "Sir, this is a cattle car. It smells like cows."

"So it does," Gabriel said. He grinned up at the boy. "Be glad the cows aren't riding with us."

"Yes, sir," Evans said, and retreated to the cluster of men at the car's opposite end. The murmur of their voices resumed. Sergeant Pittfield continued to snore. Gabriel pondered the difficulty of fingering a particular passage on the viola as opposed to on his cello. He wasn't yet familiar enough with the viola to feel it in his memory. He left the passage as it was. Likely no one would ever play the piece, anyway.

The train stopped briefly for a sanitary break and he met up with Ashby, who slipped him a fat packet of roast-beef sandwiches, two boiled eggs and a bottle of wine. "Your rations," he explained.

Gabriel studied the bottle's label, which bore hand-painted floral designs in gold ink. "You stole this from Major Harvey, didn't you?"

Ashby grinned. "Captain Wilks provided a distraction, and I took advantage of it. Harvey was complaining his port was agitated on the crossing. I simply spared him additional discomfort. And he can't blame you, you're riding with the men."

"He'll find a way," Gabriel said, and sighed. He didn't normally deal with the major directly, so perhaps things would improve later, when he found someone else upon whom to express his displeasure. "All's well?"

"We've had some pretty *mademoiselles* trading kisses for badges. A couple of them tried to pluck Daglish's buttons at the last stop. I didn't hear what he said to them, but their faces were a picture! Watch none of your boys get left behind, accidentally-a-purpose."

"Watch *you* don't get left behind," he said. "I seem to recall you can be counted on to take advantage of free kisses, yourself."

Ashby wiggled his eyebrows. "Ah, but you know I won't stay behind with them. They all lack that certain something."

"That's never stopped you before. Hold on to your badge." Like the rest of his family, Ashby had always been free with his physical affection, though with Ashby, it went a bit further than that. Gabriel had a disconcerting mental flash of an afternoon, a decade past, they'd spent together in a gazebo on the Ashby lands, their last summer together before Gabriel went abroad to stay with his uncle and attend conservatory. Their kisses had been practiced by then, and once they'd finished their first urgent coupling, they'd teased each other for hours, kissing, caressing and talking about girls, in particular strategies for meeting girls they could marry, a subject on which Ashby obsessed, as he was the last male of his line, and never allowed to forget it. Gabriel had never told Ashby that he'd been perfectly happy at the time without thinking of girls at all.

Sometimes he thought Ashby suspected what he'd felt, but neither of them ever brought it up. Perhaps he'd grown out of the feelings he'd had for his friend. He liked women, after all. He'd been with three different women, and it wasn't as if he hadn't been attracted to Jemima, even if he'd lusted more for her body than for her mind.

He and Ashby had been two against the world once, the only two families in the district who didn't belong to the Church of England, and Ashby with that other difference, as well, the secret Gabriel had kept for him since they'd been children. He'd thought, back then, that Ashby's future chances at marriage were more limited even than his own, but he'd failed to account for his friend growing into even more charm than he'd possessed as a boy. Ashby never lacked for sex, and surely he would find the right woman someday.

Ashby lifted a heavily callused finger and reverently touched the lacquered *wolf courant* adorning his field service cap. "No fear I'll be led astray. The Germans will have to carve this off my corpse," he said, and waved cheerfully as he loped back up the line to the first-class carriages.

Gabriel wasn't devout, but he said a prayer anyway, hoping Ashby hadn't been tempting fate. Tucking the wine beneath his arm and the boiled eggs in his pockets, he carried the sandwiches and returned to his platoon. Sergeant Pittfield had awakened at last, and was leading the men in a singsong:

The Bells of Hell go ting-a-ling-a-ling
For you but not for me:
And the little devils all sing-a-ling-a-ling
For you but not for me.
Oh! Death where is thy sting-a-ling-a-ling
Oh, grave thy victory?
The Bells of Hell go ting-a-ling-a-ling
For you but not for me.

Gabriel guiltily glanced down at his sandwiches as the train's whistle blew again. He was hungry, but he ought to share; he had a feeling rations were going to be somewhat irregular until they arrived at their destination. He stopped at the boxcar's door, juggling his packages. Woods stuck his head out. "Sir! Grab on, sir!"

"Essentials first," Gabriel said, tossing up the sandwiches, then handed up the bottle of wine. Woods hauled him up into the car just as the steam whistle blew a third time and the train jolted into ponderous movement.

"Here's your rations, sir," Woods said, giving him his sandwiches.

"There's plenty to share," he said. "Ashby seems to think I need fattening up."

"Oh, no, sir. Skuce trotted up to the engine and got us a dixie of hot water so we've even got proper tea. Look, we've given you that corner over there, so you can have a kip after."

The corner in question was now clearly officers' country, in that it boasted a folded tarp for a seat and another, rolled up, for a pillow. Clearly, he was not allowed to fraternize with his subordinates. Gabriel hoped to God he wouldn't spend the entire war in glorified isolation. At least in England, he'd had the constant supervision of the boy trumpeters. He found himself missing their mischief, though he was glad they hadn't been allowed to accompany the regiment and wouldn't be in danger.

As the train picked up momentum, Skuce leaned halfway out the door and shouted. Gabriel cast a glance around the car, the head count as automatic as breathing. No one was missing. Some other platoon's soldier, then. Evans joined Skuce, then Pittfield, as well, laughing and encouraging. "Help him in," Gabriel called. "We can't leave anyone behind."

"Jump!" yelled Evans. "Be quick about it!"

Gabriel stepped away from the surge of movement around the doorway as the runner hurtled inside, sending his rescuers careening into their fellows, just as the train picked up speed. The newcomer stood and brushed himself off. "Thanks," he said, a cheerful grin on his round face. His dark curls had fallen onto his forehead; he pulled his field service cap from a pocket and slapped it on. "Meyer," he said.

It was Lieutenant Daglish. He was lucky he'd ended up with Gabriel and not a more rigid officer. "Found yourself a *mademoiselle* back there?" Gabriel asked.

Daglish looked puzzled, then flushed. "Looking for you, actually. I brought you some sandwiches."

Gabriel held up the package Ashby had given him.

"Oh," Daglish said, looking at the floor. "I was worried you might not—"

It had been a foolish act, but kindly meant. "We'll need them sooner or later," Gabriel said. "Come on, sit over here with me. Now if only we had some coffee!"

He and Daglish talked easily, wandering from subject to subject in a way that reminded him a bit of his conversations with Ashby. By the end of the train journey, Gabriel had decided Daglish would make a good friend. Daglish understood music; he'd collected folk songs all over Britain, taught theory and directed the choirs at the girls' school where he'd worked before being called up from the army reserves, and sung in the choir himself at King's. Gabriel had never been able to avoid the extensive repertoire of the Anglican church, and eventually had arrived at an appreciation that his family found inexplicable.

After Gabriel requested, and the men begged, Daglish sang snatches of his favorites, Joseph Barnby and Charles Villiers Stanford and even the Roman Catholic composer Edward Elgar, in a tenor voice that rended the heart with its clarity. Daglish must have been the most cherubic boy soprano ever to grace a church, all the more so because he sang without self-consciousness, but Daglish assured him that no, his singing voice as a child had been unremarkable, and it was lucky he'd grown into a tenor, as every choir he'd ever sung in was short of them. One might expect such a voice to emanate from an androgynous pale wisp of a creature, not a man as sturdy and muscular as Daglish, though the more he thought about it, the more Daglish and his voice fit together. Daglish seemed to take joy in singing, be lost in a rich physical pleasure that reminded Gabriel, inappropriately, of moments of sexual transcendence.

Deliberately, he set to opening the bottle of wine, which put an end to the singing.

Gabriel never learned the name of the town where they disembarked to a small but enthusiastic crowd of cheering French. He clapped Daglish on the shoulder and sent him back to his platoon, then assessed his own men. He'd just instructed them to fill their canteens at a decorative fountain when Hailey, the captain's batman, ran up, looking scrawnier than usual in a field uniform that was slightly too large. Hailey saluted quickly and announced, "Fourth Dragoons've met the enemy already. We're to hold the line."

This entailed reaching the line. Mustering the men into fours, checking over their Enfield rifles and webbing equipment, and marching them to their destination, mostly uphill and over slippery cobblestones, took the rest of the afternoon and half the following night. Gabriel was glad his men had water, as there was no time to stop for more than a bite or two of iron rations. The British had been intended to protect the French army's left flank as the Germans advanced through Belgium to breach the French border. However, if they did not arrive in time, that exposed left flank would provide an easy entrance point to the country, and allow the Germans to trap the French in pincers.

The men were by turns grimly professional and youthfully exuberant. As the miles wound away beneath their boots, Gabriel heard music from down the column. Daglish's platoon was singing, not very well, *Mary Mack's mother's makin' Mary Mack marry me,* gradually growing faster, stumbling over words, laughing and starting again. Gabriel found himself smiling when he heard Daglish's clear voice riding the waves of semituneful rumbling, and gave Pittfield a meaningful glance. "We can do better than that, can't we?" The hours passed more quickly once a friendly competition began, the song only fading as the long still twilight grayed the fields of corn and beets and fragrant clover.

After midnight, Hailey ran back again, carrying more orders. "We're to bivvy here and dig in, then head out to Mons Canal in the morning."

Digging shallow trenches for protection took another hour, then Gabriel and his platoon collapsed where they could and plunged instantly into sleep, only to be roused two hours later by the roar of a wild thunderstorm. Weary, dirty, unshaven and now soaked to the skin, Gabriel found the other officers. Daglish's draggled curls were plastered to his forehead, his cheeks rosy with chill. Smith's pale moon face was even paler than normal; he looked as if he'd been dragged out of the Thames. Ashby was in the same soggy state as the rest of them, but still managed to look insouciant, even with water dripping off the end of his long nose. Gabriel took off his rain-spattered spectacles and tried to wipe them on his uniform tunic. When he put them back on, all he could see was a grayish smear. He sighed and took them off.

Captain Wilks, tall and ruddy and looking perfectly rested, joined them. He asked Ashby, "Shall we stick it out, or advance?"

Ashby, whose weather sense was nearly infallible, sniffed the air and said, "I'd say pack up. We've carved some nice canals of our own, unfortunately, and it's going to rain for a bit longer."

Wilks grinned, barely visible under the dense brush of his mustache. "Hoped you'd say that. Got no taste for drowning in a hole. Meyer, roust out the men, will you? Smith, see what you can round up in the way of provisions."

In the dead of night, as their regiment advanced toward Mons, the rain slowed and stopped. They were forced to a halt by other soldiers passing through the edges of their line of march, obscured by trees, fog and darkness, trudging silently as ghosts. Gabriel hurried up the column and found Ashby again; he had better night vision. "Who are they?" he asked quietly.

"French."

"Advancing, do you think?" It didn't seem likely, given what Gabriel knew of the situation.

"I don't think so," Ashby said. "They smell of gunpowder."

Gabriel took a deep breath, trying to slow the nervous action of his heart. "You have my letter?"

Ashby snorted. "You're not going to die, Gabriel. I won't let you."

"Noel. Do you have it?"

"Yes. Do you have mine?"

"Of course!"

"Good, now that's done. No more of that." Ashby clapped him on the back, then squeezed his shoulder, his hand big and rough and comforting.

For a long moment, Gabriel let himself enjoy it. In the guise of removing Ashby's hand, Gabriel squeezed it in return. He said, "I'm a bloody cellist. What am I doing about to march into battle?"

"Just keep your wits about you," Ashby said. "That's what Wilky always says, and he managed to survive half a dozen skirmishes in India."

"And tigers and elephants and troops of baboons, as well, to hear him tell it."

No one sang on this night march. The column spread into a moving line, Enfields constantly at the ready, waiting for word from their cavalry scouts. Gabriel couldn't watch for the enemy as much as he would have liked; he was too busy scanning his own men, trying to gauge their endurance and alertness in the darkness while incongruous music, a series of minuets he'd never liked, twinkled through his mind like the stars above. He tried to think of other things—Jemima, the women he'd known in Berlin, even Ashby, but nerves prevented him from reverie.

His only distraction was a growing desire for a cup of coffee, and occasionally reporting to Wilks when the captain rode down the column on Hammerhead. The horse looked in better fettle than Gabriel felt. Besides the drag of his wet uniform, his socks were soaked with sweat and beginning to rub his feet raw. The horses he and the other lieutenants had been promised were still on the other side of the channel.

Just when he thought he might crumple to the side of the road, Daglish appeared and hooked his arm through Gabriel's. "I'll teach you a song," he said.

Gabriel groaned. "And someone will shoot us when they hear us singing." He wasn't sure he could take listening to Daglish sing right now. It affected him too strongly. Though they marched amid hundreds of other men, the darkness and quiet lent a strange intimacy to their conversation.

"You can carry a tune, so at least I won't die in agony," Daglish quipped. "Here, listen."

"Quietly," Gabriel insisted.

Daglish leaned close to Gabriel's ear as they walked, his breath stirring the fine hairs at the back of Gabriel's neck, his mouth close enough to nearly brush his skin. Gabriel shuddered inwardly with the unexpected sensuality of it, then Daglish sang, softly,

'Twas on the good ship Venus,
By Christ you should have seen us:
the figurehead
was a whore in bed,
And the mast a throbbing penis.

The words grew more obscene immediately after that.

Gabriel choked and stopped. "What the hell kind of song is that?"

Daglish stopped, too, and chortled. "Sea shanty, very historical. It gets filthier. You can share it with your tune-murdering platoon tomorrow."

Gabriel was overcome with a sudden urge to press his lips to Daglish's smiling mouth. Shaken, he looked away and started walking again. Daglish caught him up and proceeded to teach him the rest of the song. *The captain of that lugger, he was a dirty bugger...* Gabriel tried not to think of the implications of the words, and managed it by concentrating on memorization, though one verse shook him out of his distance:

Each sailor lad's a brother to each and every other
We take great pains at our daisy chains
Whilst writing home to mother.

He'd never been to public school, but he'd certainly heard the rumors of what went on among the boys there.

Had Daglish—was he trying to say—no. Of course not. Another thought chilled him: did Daglish suspect?

No, that wasn't right, either. Not after how friendly Daglish had been. Not when he held Gabriel's arm so snugly.

The men would definitely appreciate the song.

At daybreak, they approached a village, deserted except for a growling stray dog and a distrustful boar rooting in someone's flower garden. Gabriel saw no people or other animals. The weird, unexpected silence made the hair stand straight up on the back of Gabriel's neck, and his stomach felt as if he'd swallowed a bucket of ice. The houses and gardens offered too many hiding places. The men spoke in weary murmurs. Gabriel could see most of them were near collapsing under the weight of their heavy packs.

Perhaps they might have stopped and dug in hours ago, except they'd received no orders to do so. They'd received no orders at all. It was clear that messages had gone awry in the lines of communication. Gabriel wondered if the reason had been interference from the enemy, or simple disorganization.

Hailey brought word from Captain Wilks that their company was to fan out and search for the enemy, should any be waiting in ambush, then form up to protect the bridge that lay just beyond. This was marginally better than marching down the single street, waiting to be shot by stray Germans. The rest of the battalion would proceed, and their company would wait here to cover any necessary retirement.

Gabriel's platoon clustered around their heap of packs, munching whatever scraps of rations they had left. Southey was sharing out a tin of acid drops, Lyton passing around cigarettes. Pittfield, he noted, was already checking ammunition. Gabriel captured them with his eyes and relayed their instructions. "At the bridge, I want you to pair up, take whatever cover you can find and be ready for rapid fire as soon as the enemy's in sight. There might be no enemy, not for some time, so find a way to stay alert as long as you can. If your attention starts to wander—I know that's not supposed to happen, but it will—switch out with your partner. Oh, and be careful not to shoot any of your mates. We're the ones in khaki."

As he'd hoped, his last statement got a laugh. "Any questions?" he asked.

There were no questions, only a few ribald comments directed at the shooting skills of their comrades. Gabriel took a deep breath and unholstered his pistol, checking it swiftly and keeping it in his hand. He glanced down the street and saw Daglish listening intently to Hailey's message. When Hailey ran off to find Smith, Daglish unbuttoned his holster, much more slowly than Gabriel had, withdrew his pistol and stared at it for long seconds as if he'd forgotten its purpose.

Had he frozen? Gabriel took a step toward him, then stopped when he saw Ashby loping over. Ashby clapped Daglish's shoulder, then held on to it while he spoke urgently to him. Ashby always knew what to say. Gabriel sighed and returned to his men. He'd long ago given up being envious of Asbhy's innate charisma; instead, he was glad Daglish had benefited. They could, he reminded himself, talk later. He needed something to which he could look forward.

Sergeant Pittfield, who'd transferred in from an Indian regiment along with Captain Wilks, had more field experience than the rest of the platoon combined. Gabriel set him on point, with the rest of the platoon fanned out behind, then casually took up his own position between Woods and Evans, to keep an eye on them. He wasn't worried about their nerve, exactly; it was only that they were the youngest of the entire company, not even twenty, either of them. He didn't relish the idea of writing letters of condolence to their mothers, particularly Mrs. Woods, who'd visited them in barracks on more than one occasion, bearing fresh-baked sugar biscuits.

He'd spent a good hour talking to the both of them on the ship, warning them against visiting the prostitutes who always flocked to an army on the move. It wouldn't have done any good to appeal to their better natures, so he'd stuck with the tried-and-true method of explaining how easy it was to contract gonorrhea or, worse, syphilis, with its inevitable horrible results, from sores on the cock to naked screaming and throwing excrement in a madhouse. He'd learned it was best to be graphic, and the boys had been properly impressed, but also reveled in the horrific details. When he'd explained that venereal diseases could cause penis rot or permanent impotence, they'd immediately sobered, and Woods had tentatively offered the information that something of the sort must have happened to the major, as his wife was known to entertain the colonel quite frequently. Gabriel wished he'd been able to let the rumor stand.

Hot as it was, he was perishing for want of a cup of coffee, both to wake him up and to soothe his nerves. The empty village was worse than the open fields, perhaps because it was clear that all was not business as normal. Gabriel's hand sweated on his pistol's grip. The first house was the largest on the street, built of brick with a fine wooden door and a knocker. No Germans lurked among the trellised roses, or in the garden shed, or in the shelter that looked and smelled as if it had housed goats.

Woods said, "Sir? Is it true the German lancers'll bugger their prisoners?"

Gabriel gently closed the door of the goat shelter. "Who told you that? Bloody Lincoln?"

"Yes, sir."

Evans said, "He also said the kaiser has a harem that's all boys, and he likes the young ones best, like us—"

"Lincoln was having you on," Gabriel said shortly. "Let's check the house now."

Both of the house's doors were shut tight, but not locked. Gabriel and Woods and Evans entered at the front door, Gabriel's pulse pounding like a drum, his boot heels even louder on the polished wooden floors. The house was deserted, the red brocade curtains drawn, though it bore signs of being abandoned in haste, a scattered pile of papers here and a fallen knickknack there. The air felt stale and close, as if it had been vacant for decades. He startled when Evans said, "Sir? Are we allowed to provision here?"

The inhabitants had fled, so there was no asking them for permission. It was also true that there'd been quite a bit of freely given hospitality on the long march. And his men were not only hungry, but working far too hard to go without food. He nodded. "After we search, we'll see what we can find."

He mounted the stairs, leading the two boys, and investigated a workroom for sewing, a dusty parlor and a messy bedroom. The large bed bore distinctive stains on its sheets, and the smell of sex and sweat lingered like a memory in the air. Woods lifted the bedskirts with his rifle barrel, then poked the coverlet that lay in a heap on the floor. Evans peered into the wardrobe and behind the curtains, Enfield at the ready. Nothing but dust.

Gabriel scooped up a discarded doll with an impassive porcelain face and laid it gently on the unmade trundle bed. Its human hair brushed disconcertingly against his bare wrist, and he yanked his hand away, feeling as if he'd touched a corpse. If he'd married Jemima, he might have had a child with a doll—what would he have done, forced to flee his home, with his family in tow? He tried to think of the real family that lived here, but could only focus on the empty bed. He and Jemima had been together in her bedroom, more than once. They'd never fucked, not quite, but near enough, and just the memory of her silky skin beneath his tongue, her fingers in his hair, the scent of her arousal, made him ache.

He was glad to go outside again. Evans reminded him about provisions, but a quick search of the house's kitchen and pantry turned up little beyond a tin of biscuits.

The rest of their house-to-house search was also uneventful, though Evans found a coop of chickens who'd been left to fend for themselves, and tossed them a bucket of feed. Gabriel suspected the chickens would go into a pot today, if the company lingered long enough to cook. Woods nearly shot a scarred marmalade tomcat, who yowled disdainfully before vanishing into the woodpile from whence it had come.

Gabriel met Daglish at the end of the street, which led straight to a bridge over Mons Canal. Willows shaded the bridge; red and purple wildflowers tumbled down the grassy banks and spilled onto rocks that looked perfect as seats for fishermen. A few rowboats were tied up at a dock on the far side, and on this bank, someone had abandoned a cartful of furniture, turned and stained chair legs protruding from its sides like broken bones.

Daglish removed his cap and wiped sweaty dark curls off his brow. He appeared to have recovered from his earlier distraction. He pointed to the cart. "Could that be cover, you think? For a marksman or two. Cawley and Lyton."

"Let Wilks know. I'd be happier if the rest of us could dig in a little," Gabriel said, rubbing his gritty eyes and stiff forehead. "Those trees won't be worth tuppence once bullets start flying."

"If the supply wagons ever catch up, we'll have picks and shovels," Daglish said wistfully. "Oh, well, I guess a rousing song or two will resign them to the entrenching tools."

By the time Gabriel had gathered his men, Captain Wilks himself was outsinging the men in his favorite tune, "Riding Down from Bangor": *Maiden seen all blushes, for then and there appeared, a tiny little earring in that horrid student's beard.* It was more difficult for the men to sing as they dug lying flat on their backs to avoid exposure, but they made a valiant effort for the hour it took to dig down a foot or so, just enough to protect them from rifle fire.

Gabriel glanced longingly at the muddy canal water—it would feel amazingly good on his swollen feet—and instead sent three men off to scavenge for food and for any shovels they could find that were larger than their entrenching tools. Ashby wandered over, cap in one hand, scrubbing his cropped red hair with the other. "It's bloody hot," he said.

"At least our uniforms are drying."

"Speak for yourself. My drawers have been trying to circumcise me for the last five miles. You think I'd be able to marry your sister, then?"

Gabriel choked on a laugh and punched Ashby's arm. "Idiot," he said. "What did Wilks say to you just now?"

"Last word he had from staff was that the French can't close the gap between our flank and theirs."

"Oh."

"There seem to be more Germans than anyone thought," Ashby said, his voice unusually flat. "So the longer we can hold out here, and all those other companies spreading out up the road, the better. We're trying to hold a salient, though how we're to manage that with roads blocked all up and down the line, I don't know. Maybe the Germans won't be able to move, either. I think it's just prettying up what's going to be a strategic readjustment."

"Retreat, you mean," Gabriel said.

Ashby grinned. "We're not beaten. This is only the beginning." He touched the wolf badge on his cap, as if for luck. His face eased. "I showed Hailey how to make a smokeless fire, and he's brewing us some coffee."

"I think I heard a siren's song," Gabriel said, though actually his mind had given him the trumpet solo from Handel's *Messiah*. "If we had milk, I think I would die of pleasure."

"And you call *me* easy," Ashby said, grinning. "Hailey found a sow eating her way through a garden. It's too bad no one left a cow behind, instead."

"I'll settle for the coffee. Where in the world did you come by it?"

"Daglish had a packet hidden away—he begged it from the major's aide sometime before we split off, bless his big innocent eyes. He insisted I share it with you. I think you owe him a kiss, at least."

"Very funny," Gabriel said, glancing around to make sure no one had heard.

A long, hot afternoon ensued, made worse because the sunshine and pastoral setting sang of naps to Gabriel's fogged mind. The coffee, gulped scalding from a metal cup, had given him energy for directing perhaps an hour of trench digging before his mind again sank into lethargy and a sawing Baroque bass line he could not even identify. By that time, Skuce had found two shovels; Gabriel took one and joined in the digging.

Their shallow earthworks, augmented by mattresses and horsehair sofas dragged from the village houses, were complete enough for shelter by the hottest part of the afternoon. Pittfield and the ever-resourceful Southey had scavenged empty wine bottles and petrol. With the aid of those items and some scraps of cloth, they set the rowboats on fire by dint of tossing their homemade explosives across the canal. The columns of rising smoke made Gabriel uneasy, but as Captain Wilks pointed out, there was only one road. The Germans would come this way no matter what lay in their path. Better to have removed one more method of getting across the canal, since they hadn't explosives to blow the bridge. Wilks then sent Mason and Southey into the nearby Christian church's small spire, to keep watch and to sharpshoot if necessary.

Wilks had the rest of them count off, and Gabriel was relieved when a coin toss gave his group first rest period, though ironically for him, they were to sleep in the church, large, nearby and defensible. Daglish wandered over as Gabriel directed the men to gather their kit. After a quick, nervous glance at the ground, Daglish handed him a suspiciously large sack, saying, "Looks like you'll get to use this before I do."

Gabriel peeked inside at a feather pillow, covered in an embroidered slip. He was surprised enough to laugh. "I'll make good use of it, no fear," he said. The inside of the church was dim and cool, and once the men had settled, quiet. Doing his best to ignore the graphically carved crucifix hanging above the altar, he lay down on a wooden bench and tucked the pillow beneath his head. He fell asleep before his head made contact.

Gabriel bolted upright, cold and alert. He'd heard a shot. He slid silently to the floor, crouching beside his discarded gear while he slipped out his pistol. Soft rustlings let him know he needn't wake the men. Another shot came, not too close, then another, then a crackling chorus like fierce iron-throated birds. Gabriel glanced across the aisle at Smith, who held his pistol in one hand and was rubbing his face with the other. A single round window, high above, sent down a shaft of orange light, a hot circle in the middle of the foyer. Gabriel guessed it must be sunset, or close to it. Once he'd caught Smith's eye, he gestured to the front door, then toward the other exit they'd found near the confessionals.

Smith took the front with a decisive point, so Gabriel gathered his boys as quietly as he could and led them down the aisle, up a step, and through a narrow door into a room crowded with candlesticks, books, priestly vestments and miscellaneous serving dishes. Pittfield braced his shoulder against the heavy wooden door, then eased it open. The shooting crescendoed, percussive raps ricocheting from bricks and stones and rooftops. Gabriel led the men into the churchyard; there were some bent trees, and though most of the headstones had sunk some distance into the earth, they also provided some cover. The cover would be more effective as the light failed. If necessary, they could retreat into the church and hold it.

Gabriel slid from tree to tree until he reached the low wall bordering the cemetery. He stepped over, then wriggled to the road on his belly. The terrain dropped toward the canal just in front of him, and he could see. Smoke scummed the air. He smelled acrid burnt powder. Gray-uniformed men crowded the width of the bridge, firing as they advanced, struggling to climb past fallen comrades who blocked their way to the bank. He tried to count, to estimate their numbers, but kept losing track at the middle of the bridge. He couldn't see how far the crowd of Germans stretched on the other bank. Two companies? Three? A cluster of willows on the opposite bank blocked his view. Where were Ashby and Daglish? Were they safe? He sighed in relief when he spotted Daglish's stocky torso on the right flank. He looked to be under adequate cover, training a pair of binoculars at the opposite bank.

The men were doing well. He estimated twelve to fifteen rounds a minute, at the least, and considerably more accurate with their aim than their German opponents, even given that the Germans were exposed and moving. He crushed the thought that he, too, might have to shoot soon. He'd never killed a man. He'd never intended to. He only hoped he could manage it if the need arose.

As Gabriel watched, Cawley and Lyton each fired a final round from their advance placement, then abandoned the wagon's inadequate cover and retreated for the barricades. Cawley went down, his body jerking with the impact of two, then three bullets.

Gabriel closed his eyes for a moment, but the picture was the same when he opened them, Cawley sprawled amid the lush grass and wildflowers like a painting, bright and unreal. He didn't move again. Lyton didn't see, and a moment later was dragged behind a heap of sofas and thrust into a trench.

Smith and his platoon edged their way along the other side of the road. He could see Smith's fevered grin even at this distance, Figgis close by his shoulder with an unlit cigarette hanging from the corner of his mouth. Gabriel eased himself onto his elbows and tried to spot Wilks or Hailey, to let them know they had somewhere to retreat. Someone touched his elbow, and he rolled, pistol ready. Ashby halted his movement with a hand on his wrist, and Gabriel let his breath free in a rush. Trust Ashby to move like a ghost. Ashby said, loudly enough to be heard over the rifles, "You're to hold this position."

Ashby's usually insouciant expression had tightened, his mouth drawn into a thin line, his face caked with dust and sweat beneath the brim of his cap. A red line streaked across his neck, the blood already crusting. He'd come within inches of being killed already. His throat too tight for words, Gabriel could only nod.

Ashby grinned at him and gripped the back of his neck for a moment, a comforting squeeze that conveyed fresh energy. Then he scrambled down the road. Gabriel worked his way back to the cemetery wall and relayed their orders, then returned to his vantage point. A couple of Germans had fought free of the chaos at the foot of the bridge and were advancing at a run, bayonets leveled. Gabriel couldn't hear individual shots amid the percussive storm of them, but the two interlopers jerked to a halt and landed short of Cawley's body. Southey and Mason, he realized, peering up at the spire. Sure enough, he could just see the tip of a rifle protruding from the narrow arras.

He spotted Hailey, small and slender, darting across a small stretch of open ground to speak urgently to Smith. Smith and his platoon fanned out behind the barricades as three more Germans clambered over corpses and hit the bank. Someone behind them had the bright idea to drag the bodies out of the way and shove them into the cover afforded by the bridge's arch. Two of those men were shot, then another, who collapsed into the water and thrashed amid a further spatter of bullets. Hailey dashed back to a clump of willows, and Gabriel finally glimpsed a hint of Hammerhead's coppery flank and swishing tail through the greenery. Wilks was too close to the action; he ought to fall back to Gabriel's position, at the least. He hoped Ashby had presented this advice. Wilks liked to be in the midst of everything, but sometimes he would listen to Ashby.

As if he'd heard Gabriel's thoughts, Wilks's wide shoulders poked free of cover, then he set off at a jog for the rear area. Gabriel's relieved breath caught when Wilks's hunched-over form froze. An endless moment later, he collapsed to his knees, then forward.

Hailey burst from the trees, heedless of danger, still grasping Hammerhead's reins. He fell to his knees beside Wilks, struggling to turn him over. Even from this distance, Gabriel could see bright blood rapidly soaking the front of Wilks's tunic as his heart pumped too much, too fast, like one of those horrid dreams in which one could see and see but not touch or interfere. Hailey struggled to lift the captain's immense form onto Hammerhead, but wasn't nearly strong enough, and Gabriel could tell it wouldn't matter anyway. Ashby skidded into sight then, grabbing Hailey and heaving his small form onto the horse instead, then dragging the horse and running for cover, back toward Gabriel and the church.

Gabriel yelled for someone to provide cover. Ashby sprinted toward them while Hailey scrambled for a grip on Hammerhead's saddle and neck. Gabriel waved them toward the cemetery; Ashby vaulted the low wall and Hammerhead neatly popped over it behind him, narrowly missing a headstone.

Hailey yelled incoherently as he tumbled to the ground; his arms were stained red to the elbows. Ashby swept him into a tight embrace, Hailey's flailing hand leaving a smear of blood down his cheek. Ashby firmly kissed the top of the boy's head and looked over him at Gabriel, and the anxious cluster of his platoon. "Wilks is dead," he said. Hailey burst into sobs, and Ashby clutched him more tightly, rubbing a hand up and down his back, but otherwise continuing as if nothing had happened. "We're going to be overrun shortly. I'm going to have Daglish take his platoon and fade back to this position. Smith will follow. We'll pick off as many as we can, to make it look like we've still men behind the barricades. Then we're getting the hell down the road as soon as it's dark, quick as we can."

The next hours were a blur of action, retreat and more action. Skuce was killed. Pittfield, Mason and Evans were all wounded but still mobile, and Figgis shot through both legs. Corporal Joyce rigged a sling between two men so he could be carried. Later, if they could find poles and had the leisure, they could build a stretcher for Hammerhead to pull behind him.

Once darkness fell, the shooting slowed to an occasional crack. Gabriel was shocked that the Germans seemed to be halting for the night, though if they'd had as little rest and food as his own men, he shouldn't be surprised. As soon as he judged it safest, Ashby got them moving, chivying them along like sheep until they reached the cover of the next hamlet down the road. Wisely, its inhabitants had already fled before the German onslaught.

Gabriel entered another church, a much smaller and humbler one than before, when he and Lieutenant Daglish were assigned to fortify the building as best they could. They worked in companionable silence, then split the abandoned communion loaves among the men and allowed them to sleep, some for the first time in nearly twenty hours.

A bicycle messenger found them four hours later with new orders. This line of defense was being strategically readjusted. They must make all speed. Again.

Gabriel spent the next hours running and rerunning the melody line of his adagio in the back of his mind, while at the same time periodically counting his platoon to make sure no one had fallen behind. He had to continually remind himself not to look for Cawley. Ten hours later, as they dug yet another hasty line of scratch trenches for the rearguard to occupy, he was too hungry and exhausted to create. His mind disconcerted him by playing through an obscure work by Salamone Rossi he'd learned in his conservatory days. Twenty hours after that, even his vast musical memory had failed him, and he was reduced to hearing an endless repetition of a single phrase of a cello exercise. He thought he might claw his own skull open to make it stop.

He lost count of the trenches they dug, both his platoon and Daglish's switching off with Ashby's and Smith's. His service dress was stiff with dirt all down the back, and he blistered his hands helping dig, because no man's hands could be wasted when the aim was to get the army away from the German onslaught intact. No one had any rations left, and there was no one left in the army's path to sell them any.

Ashby sent the company, a few men at a time, foraging into every field of corn or orchard they passed, but an apple wasn't much to sustain a man through a day of marching in full kit, stopping only to dig and snatch brief naps while sitting upright. Worse, they had to be sparing with their canteens, for without the cavalry scouts who were otherwise occupied, no one knew where water could be found, and when they could be refilled. Gabriel could only imagine what all this was like for the men, who carried considerably more kit than he did, and some of them wearing stiff new boots.

To top it all off, after forty-eight hours their progress slowed to a hobble when their portion of the battalion caught up to the army of refugees, the former inhabitants of villages and hamlets who'd originally welcomed them as saviors. Now they were less happy. The British, their words and gestures indicated, belonged between them and the advancing Germans. Else what good were they? Daglish tried to explain *strategic retirement* to one vituperative old woman via sign language; Gabriel had to drag him away by the elbow, and then haul him off the road and out of sight when the younger man argued, then briefly wept in exhausted frustration.

Gabriel kept hold of Daglish's forearm with one hand and fished for his handkerchief with the other. "Here, wipe your face," he said. "You can't let the men see you like this."

"Bloody Goddamn fucking hell," Daglish said, pressing the linen to his eyes. He blew his nose, leaving a smear of sweaty dust on the cloth, then sucked in a breath and blew it out. "My feet are bleeding."

Gabriel patted his shoulder, wishing he had someone to pat his, or better still, massage his aching lower back and swollen feet. He took his hand away before manly comfort changed into something else. "Mine, too. At least we're not carrying sixty-odd pounds of kit. All right now?"

Daglish looked over his shoulder at a field of turnips, currently being trampled by fleeing refugees and their assorted wagons and prams and dogcarts. "No, but I'll keep on." His eyes met Gabriel's. "Thank you. I mean it."

"Good man." Meyer clapped his shoulder, as Ashby would have done. "Let's catch them up."

The British Expeditionary Force might have prevented the Germans from invading France, but Gabriel did not consider it a promising beginning to the war.

INTERLUDE

THE BILLET WASN'T BAD. NOEL, AS THE NEW COM-
manding officer, and Hailey were assigned what had once
been the master bedroom of a prosperous banker, with more
of the men bedding down in the parlor, study, garage and
emptied wine cellar. Hailey set down three small kits atop a
polished bureau and began fussing with their contents, his
back to Noel. One of the kits had belonged to Captain Wilks.

The bed linens smelt overwhelmingly of cedar, mingling
with the rich lemon oil–beeswax odor of furniture polish, in-
congruously clean and fresh layered upon the thick layers of
their own sweat and horse and dust and gunpowder. Noel
could also still smell blood, Wilks's blood, soaked and dried
into Hailey's uniform tunic. He could practically smell the
miasmic grief hanging over Hailey's small form, as well. Left
to his own devices, he would have crossed the room and once
again taken Hailey into his arms, as if he were a relative.

Such things were frowned upon in His Majesty's army.
Instead, he wandered over to the long window and thrust

aside the heavy drapes, letting the last sunbeams filter into the room. He could at least give Hailey some privacy, usually in short supply. Hailey might appreciate that more than anything else. "Does this place have modern plumbing?" he asked.

"Yes, sir. Do you want a bath, sir?"

Noel gazed out the window, at a rolling green lawn now scored by military boots. His Majesty's officers did not run outside and roll in the grass, either. "I think you'd better go first. Get that blood off you. Take your time, I won't be back until you're done. Requisition some kit out of these wardrobes to wear until your tunic dries."

"Sir." The word was choked.

"I've got to have the standard chat with the rest of the men downstairs. You can come down when you're ready."

"Sir."

"And leave me some hot water, will you? Go on, now. Leave all that for later. I'll help you decide what we should keep of Wilks's things." Without waiting for an answer, Noel left the room and trotted down the carpeted staircase. Men sprawled everywhere, packs for pillows, several snoring, Lieutenant Smith among them. Seeing him, Sergeant Pittfield scrambled to his feet, but Noel waved him back down. "Just wake them up for me. Gently, now."

He hadn't planned on being a captain, or even acting as one, quite so soon. His mother would be impressed. His father would be convinced Noel had moved up through superior innate ability instead of Wilks's being caught by a bullet.

Pipes groaned and gurgled. Hailey was being sensible. Noel said to the array of filthy, unshaven, exhausted faces, "We'll have a watch, two and two. The rest of you, sleep. You've more than earned it."

Meyer found him afterward and glanced at the ceiling, their private code for outside. They walked a short distance in silence before he said, "Is Hailey all right?"

"Will be," Noel said. He considered saying something else about Hailey, then changed his mind. "Anyone else? You?"

"Fine. Daglish had a moment or two. He's fine now. Smith's enjoying himself."

"Vicious little bastard," Noel said without heat. "A vicar's son, too."

"I wanted to say…" Meyer's pale skin had always flushed easily. "You were right about Jemima."

Hearing her name here, after all they'd experienced, was surreal. "I shouldn't have said the things I did."

Meyer clasped his hands behind his back. "You never said an untrue word about her, not once."

That was true, but it wasn't what mattered, not really. What mattered was that he'd been secretly jealous, not of Jemima, but of the children she would eventually give to her husband, and that had led him to be cruel to his closest friend. Noel asked, "Did you love her, Gabriel?"

He didn't look away when he said, "No."

It wasn't fair that Meyer should be so alone. Noel tried not to put himself in Meyer's place, and failed miserably. "I'm sorry. Truly I am."

Meyer looked uncomfortable. "Thanks. I—I felt a bit guilty sometimes. Knowing I'd found someone, when it was you who really wanted to marry."

"You'll find someone else. Someone who loves you." *I will find someone. Someone like me, who will stay with me and bear my children.*

"Enough, all right?" Meyer cuffed him. Noel feinted in

return, tried to grab his shoulder and failed when Meyer took off running. Noel brought him down in a tackle and they wrestled viciously but companionably, growing ever muddier, until Hailey appeared to summon them inside.

Noel felt much better for the exercise.

9

THE DAY AFTER CRISPIN LEFT FOR FRANCE, LUCILLA boarded a train for London. Though she and Clara Lockie had once been close, she had not seen her in three years, since before Clara's employment with the Red Cross. However, the wire she'd sent had been answered with all the gleeful enthusiasm typical of her friend. Remembering the teas they'd shared as undergraduates, she'd packed tins of ginger biscuits and Bovril in the bottom of her carpetbag, along with a couple of the romantic novels Clara had always loved to mock.

She successfully maneuvered the chaos of Victoria Station, though she was shocked to notice how many of the passengers were men in khaki uniforms, or in civilian clothing and carrying military haversacks. It was one thing to know there was a war, and quite another to see the evidence in such a familiar environment. On the streets, she passed a line of men outside a recruitment office, and a small but vigorous demonstration against becoming involved in the affairs of Europe. She caught herself stopping at the end of the block and glancing back at the extraordinarily handsome man who led the demonstrators; he didn't wear a hat, and his strong features and leonine gray-streaked hair made him look like a king in a portrait. Though he would likely be horrified to know it. Lucilla looked away, and her gaze collided with a man in a dark City suit, who touched his hat brim and smiled at her with a bit more warmth than she would normally have expected. She pretended she hadn't seen, and hurried on her way. Where had all these men come from? Or was it that her recent experiences had opened her eyes?

Clara worked in an office building overrun by men in dark suits and bowler hats. Lucilla took the lift up to the appropriate floor and was impressed to find that she had a room to herself, overlooking a street crammed with vendors of flowers and fruit. Clara rose to greet her, enfolding her in an enthusiastic embrace and kissing both her cheeks. "You are a godsend!" she exclaimed. "Have a seat. Would you like some tea? I have fresh in the pot."

Once her gifts to Clara were laughed over, and Lucilla settled in an old armchair, teacup in hand, she said, "Why am I a godsend? Surely you're not lacking for volunteers."

"My dear, it's not a volunteer that's wanted here. Tell me, you're still working with the surgery cases, aren't you?" She referred to a sheet of notepaper on her battered desk. "You've worked with abdominal surgeries?"

"Yes," Lucilla said. "It pays the best, frankly. Are you saying that this is a paying position?"

Clara beamed. "Yes! You see, there is to be a women's hospital in France."

"For women?"

"No, no. Staffed by women. Run by women. Women

doctors! Only, of the ones we have, they haven't had much experience with the sorts of wounds one encounters in war. Miss Fitzclarence qualified in obstetrics, and Miss Rivers in osteopathic surgery, so that's a bit better. Miss Gould is to be chief of anesthesiology, and she's quite experienced. But they're in want of a surgical nurse, someone experienced who's willing to work with women and teach them, as well. That's why your wire made me dance, Lucilla, dance about my tiny room here, and then immediately dash off a reply to you."

Lucilla could barely speak for wonder. A hospital staffed by women? And Clara offered her money to do this? Of course, women doctors might be just as awful as the male variety, but somehow she doubted it. "How many beds?" she asked.

"One hundred to start, perhaps one hundred twenty. We're hoping to have two hundred eventually. The site is found— it's to be a casino building, made over. Local workmen are putting in extra wood stoves for heat, and more electrical lines for the surgeries. We're hoping to send the first staff over within the week. So, will you go? Please say you will." Clara leaned across the desk and gripped her forearm. "I wish I could go myself. Perhaps later, if there are funds. Such an adventure!"

Adventure always proved to be more tiresome and dirty than one wished, but Lucilla couldn't bear to stay at home any longer. Now that her studies in Germany had been termi- nated, she needed a purpose. Once she began to assemble her supplies, a tentative excitement began to wake her early in the mornings and keep her up at night as she paged through her medical books, finding the most useful to bring with her.

Two weeks later, she found herself again in Le Havre, about to board a train, only this time with a trunk for luggage and a group of cheerful nurses and women orderlies for companions. She was tempted only briefly to visit the Rue du Canotage; after all, what would she say? Pascal would not be there. And she couldn't wander off; they might miss their train, and trains for civilians were currently few and far between. She would be back where she'd been at the beginning, and she intended to go forward, not backward. She was making a life for herself.

The first days were all hard work, such hard work that she fell into her bed each night already nearly asleep from exhaustion. Bedsteads had arrived, mattresses had accidentally gone to Rouen and had to be retrieved by lorry. Twenty roulette wheels had to be carried up to the attics and stacked atop card tables covered in green baize. Tanks of nitrous oxide were procured, but some of the tanks of oxygen needed to mix with it had leaked and arrived empty, and had to be replaced. Only boys and men over fifty years of age were available to work as orderlies, so Lucilla and even some of the doctors pitched in to carry immense piles of bedding and cases of bandages up the casino's grand staircases and into the wards. The official inspectors arrived, and declared one of the rooms they'd chosen for surgeries to be unacceptable, so another had to be prepared, all its carpeting ripped out and every surface scrubbed and painted.

At last, however, Lucilla gazed around a makeshift ward in satisfaction. The variously colored brocaded coverlets and lap rugs, all donations, made the room look cheerful. She'd successfully directed her cadre of six French volunteers in making the beds and laying out the requisite kit in the lockers beside: pajamas, flannel, towel and soap, and a bag to hold the patient's uniform once it had been labeled and laundered out in the paved courtyard. She doubted this perfection would last beyond the first influx of wounded, but she let her volunteers enjoy their success while they could, and for a break requested they stock the entertainment cabinet at the far end of the ward. Lucilla set the *mademoiselles* free to roam the casino's every room and closet to obtain sufficient decks of cards and cups of dice, secretly gleeful that such a male bastion was now the domain of women.

She looked out the glass doors at a crew of local workers struggling with electrical wiring for the temporary buildings that would house the X-ray department and laboratories. The white-haired man who directed them looked ready to strangle his helpers. Several more aged Frenchmen, aided by a crew of youngsters, were building paths out of boards, so trolleys could be wheeled directly from the hospital. One of those small buildings would be Lucilla's own kingdom, where she would perform double duty compounding disinfectant and irrigation solutions. The extra work would be worth it for the attendant privacy.

Matron swept through the elaborately carved doorway, studying the watch she wore clipped to her uniform cape. "Daglish, I'm afraid I'll have to move you over to the east wing. It's not quite ready, and I've heard we might be receiving casualties sooner than we'd expected."

So it begins, Lucilla thought. "Yes, Matron. Someone will look after the *mademoiselles?*"

"I'll send Sister Inkson."

Most of the rooms designated for the isolation cases were smaller than the grand salons they'd taken over for the general wards. The gorgeous burgundy-and-gold-flocked wallpaper had not survived its first encounter with antisepsis procedures, nor had the beautifully oiled wooden floor, but at least the painted ceilings, rich with flowering vines and imaginatively draped and undraped nymphs, would give the patients something to stare at while lying on their backs. The beds, she noted with approval, had brass head and footboards that would be easy to keep clean, and the furniture, though heavy and antique, was all well stocked with bandages and other materials for dressings.

She found another volunteer and set her to folding back the bedcovers, in preparation for slipping patients in with little fuss. Then she hurried to the large surgical ward, formerly a long room set up for mingling and drinking before the night's gaming began. Its minimal furnishings had been dragged away, and once the carpets had been removed, they'd set up portable beds the length of the room. She checked that supplies were laid to hand at each bed, then moved into the operating theater itself. Quickly, she counted the trays of sterilized and wrapped scalpels and retracting tools, then the readily accessible disinfectants. Another nurse and Miss Gould examined the supplies of anesthesia and made sure each unit of equipment was operational. Lucilla went on to the pharmacy.

Sister Loudon welcomed her with a brief smile and pointed to a stack of crates. Most of the straw-swaddled bottles had not yet been unloaded. Lucilla set to the task with a will, the clink of bottles bringing sweet memories of her tiny, quiet lab at the Institute. Suddenly, she remembered seeing Pascal for the first time. She'd been washing glass tubing, and had turned at his quiet *"Pardon, mademoiselle."* She wasn't sure how long he'd stood there, waiting for her to be finished with the delicate glassware. She'd quickly given him directions to an office upstairs, Kauz's office as it happened, then returned to her work, having no idea what was to come. Did all change begin so simply?

She would give anything to talk to him now. She felt the phantom brush of his mustache beside her mouth.

No wounded had arrived by the afternoon, but mail did, a brimming sack hauled between the two strongest ambulance drivers, college girls who looked so much alike in their bobbed hair and squarish faces that Lucilla had at first assumed them sisters. Lucilla had a cheerful letter from Clara, and a small tin of biscuits from her mother, but nothing at all from Crispin. She worried where he was, and what he was doing. Surely he had not gone into action already.

She couldn't think of him, not when she had work to do. She would be seeing entirely too much in the days to come, and she wouldn't have the energy to do her work, keep up the spirits of the wounded and keep herself healthy if she worried endlessly over things she could not control. She took copies of the London papers, only two days old, and carried them off to the tea room. And she wondered where Pascal was now.

10

PASCAL HATED BEING INTERRUPTED WHEN HE was thinking, so he ignored the thumping at his door and the polite calls of "Major? Major?" and continued drawing his diagram in strong black lines over the pages of *Le Petit Parisien*. His adjustments would have implications for the future. He glanced at the list he'd tacked to the wall. The Marne would be a problem in this area, he could see it already. The Meuse would also be a problem, though less immediately. He would need maps to record his ideas, but that could wait, as a crew waited for his figures in the minor matter before him. An adjustment of the gun *here* would necessitate another adjustment *here* of another fraction. Perhaps that would help to compensate for the gun's engineering flaw.

He needed another color of ink. He tunneled among the desk's litter and emerged with a glass bottle. It held only a dried stain of blue. He cursed and searched again.

The polite calls had increased in volume. Really, they were quite distracting. Pascal bellowed, "I am busy!" and resumed his search for colored ink. The army had promised to supply him with all he required. Well, he required colored ink. If they wished to have results, they must feed the beast that would provide them. His work would progress much faster with the proper supplies.

He could find no more ink, and in his agitation he'd spilled the open bottle of black. Pascal cursed in English, short and blunt, and shoved the papers onto the floor. He rose, straightened his blue uniform coat and flung open the door.

A scrawny lieutenant fell into the room. Behind him, in the corridor, huddled a tiny woman with huge, rage-filled eyes. She wore widow's weeds, and a small pin depicting the Belgian flag instead of the more common cameo or crucifix. Pascal raised his brows at her. Her dress was too ragged for her to be an officer's wife. She was not part of the domestic staff, or she would be wearing an apron. She was not a prostitute; her expression was in no way enticing, and besides, such indiscretions were utterly frowned upon in the Rue Deuxième. She had been brought to his office. She was, therefore, either a scientist or a spy.

Lucilla's face flashed across his memory, and her scent, and the scar of an acid burn that marred the soft flesh at the base of her left thumb. He carried a letter to her, in his pocket, which he touched ten times a day. He could not mail it, now he was a spy in truth. Who knew what could happen to her if that came to light?

He needed to keep his mind on business. "Out," he said to the lieutenant, whose expression, he now noted, looked desperate. Apparently, they'd sent the woman to him because no one else could discern what to do with her. It was the story of his life. *"Madame?"* He waved the widow into his office. "Would you like coffee? A pastry?"

The woman pushed by the exiting lieutenant and placed her back against the wall, near to the open door. When the door began to fall closed, she pushed it open again with her foot, and this time it stayed. Pascal noted she wore no corset, and only sandals below the hem of her dress. Her feet were dirty, with ragged nails; a strange contrast to her dress, which looked to be of fine material. Perhaps she had fallen on hard times, or she disliked shoes, or had received the dress from a previous owner. She did not at all have the air of a rich woman. She had not demanded anything of him, not even a chair. Unless she was the sort who was so abominably rich that eccentricity was allowed.

The woman had not spoken. Her eyes flicked around the room, not meeting his gaze, but repeatedly passing over him as if she waited for him to spring. At last she said, "You are the major of whom they all speak?"

Her French was tinged with Flemish but was pure and liquid and upper-class. Given her appearance, he had expected an accent more crude, more like his own uncouth vowels. He nodded. "I am Fournier." He was careful not to ask her name. "You have information for me?" he asked, sitting on the very edge of his desk, to avoid the spreading pool of ink.

She glanced at the open door, then the window, its sill cluttered with books and two sleeping calico queens. "We will go outside," she said, and ducked into the corridor, graceful as one of his cats. Pascal followed.

Outside, soldiers hurried up and down the town's winding narrow streets, most of them as old or older than Pascal's father. All the young men had been rushed to the front, and many of the men of middle age, as well. A few boys remained at this headquarters, a few younger officers on detached duty, and Pascal, whose brains were far too valuable to be blown out. Women could be seen on the street, local women carrying baskets and trailed by children. Pascal saw a khaki-clad British officer, as well, climbing into a motor driven by an elderly Frenchman. The officer took off his cap and wiped his forehead. He had red hair, uncommon enough for Pascal to give him a second look. A dusty terrier ran to the officer's feet and barked imperatively. Pascal had seen the dog hanging about in the street all week, probably abandoned. The officer swung back to the ground, scooped up the animal, inspected it and tucked it beneath one arm before hopping gracefully back into the motor.

The spy stared at the British officer, stiff as a dog who'd spotted ducks, until the motor pulled away. Pascal thought of taking her arm to gain her attention, but decided against it. She might be violent. *"Madame?"* he said.

She began walking. Pascal, taller by three heads, caught up to her easily and then moderated his stride. "We should appear casual," he suggested. "How shall I address you?"

"I am Tanneken Claes," she said. "It is my name and I need no other."

"Madame Claes," he said. He rummaged in his uniform tunic. "Cigarette?"

"They are foul," she said. "The enemy can smell the stale tobacco on your person. You would be wise to abstain."

Pascal had no intention of getting close enough to the enemy that he could be smelled. Also, he did not particularly care for tobacco, but he'd found it to be a good icebreaker and bribe. He clasped his hands behind his back. "What have you brought me?"

"Numbers," she said. "I am told you like numbers."

"They are useful," he said, a profound understatement.

"I bring, also, measurements. These are not so clear. You will have to interpret them."

"Measurements of distance? If you will permit me, *madame,* I can teach you methods to more accurately ascertain such matters as distance while in the field. That is, if you wish to continue to help us."

"Can you teach these methods to a wolf?" she asked.

Pascal blinked. Perhaps he'd misheard, as he often mused on Kauz and his notebooks at inopportune moments. "Pardon?"

"I am a werewolf," Madame Claes said, as if she discussed making soup. "I visited beyond the Boche lines in the form of a wolf. It is difficult for me to translate this knowledge into a form that will be useful to you."

Pascal drew a slow breath. If true, this was the luckiest coincidence of his life, after finding Lucilla, of course. He could think of no reason Madame Claes would have to lie about such a thing. He must first ascertain if she had any useful information at all, then he could question her further on the matter of being a werewolf, and what she might know. A chill raced down his chest and settled in his belly. Had she been the werewolf Kauz held captive? "How did this come about?" he asked.

"I have a hatred of the country that invaded mine, particularly since their uncouth soldiers have encamped all over my estate, so I changed my form and went to spy on them," she explained patiently.

"No, no, *madame.* Tell me about being a werewolf."

"Do you want my information or not? I obtained it the night before last. It is still fresh."

"I want it," Pascal said. "I am simply curious."

"Your interest is prurient," she said scornfully.

"Indeed not, *madame!*"

"You all wonder—is she nude when she changes? Is she nude when she changes back? Where is her body hairy? Where—"

"Madame!" Pascal had not in fact been considering those questions, but now the images surged through his mind with the inevitability of the sea. He could not now help himself from looking at her as a woman: the elegance of her mobile, delicate hands; the shape of her bosom beneath her dress; the tendrils of hair curling against her neck, caressing skin that looked smooth as porcelain.

She smiled, slow and feral, then sniffed. "I can smell your desire," she purred, those patrician vowels suddenly sensual beyond bearing. "And something else, as well." She lifted a single eyebrow.

Pascal had always been annoyed with people who had mastered that trick. "Do you have information for me or not?" he asked, aware and irked that she had sidestepped his question.

"I suppose you are no worse than any other man," she said, suddenly dismissive, as if his reaction reduced his conse-quence. "Very well. Would you like to hear of the artillery batteries first, or the experimental chemicals?"

"How did you discover the experiments?"

"From the stink," she said. "My nose was blinded by it. I was forced to retreat."

"And this was—"

"Near Nimy."

Pascal nodded. "I would like to hear more of this. But first, if you can tell me the numbers of guns and their sizes as you saw them."

"You don't wish to write down my information?"

He snorted. "If you would like every person on the street to see me writing your words, I would be glad to do so. I am not a fool, Madame Claes. I can hold the information in my memory."

She looked him over, clearly assessing. "You have not asked anything further about the matter of werewolves. You know about us. And I know why."

Pascal met her gaze. "Give me the artillery information first."

"Very well," she said at last, and began to recite what she had seen.

Pascal filed it all away in his memory, even the things that seemed useless or that confused him. One never knew what might make sense later. The chemical odors she spoke of disturbed him profoundly, all the more because he did not know the aim of the research, assuming it had been research and not accidental. Perhaps he could bring her to a laboratory, and ask her to smell various chemicals in the hope of identifying them and their uses. It was a pity Lucilla was not here. She could be useful.

All the while as Madame Claes talked, they continued to stroll down the street, occasionally pretending to look in shop windows. Toward the end of the street, he glanced into a tea shop and found it empty but for the shopgirl. "Would you like tea, Madame Claes?"

If she had not been so much smaller than he, she would have been looking down her nose. "I am not hungry," she said.

Pascal was. His stomach reminded him he had eaten nothing since his coffee and croissant at dawn. "Then perhaps you will accompany me. You will have to pretend, at least, so we are not conspicuous."

She sniffed, and he had the feeling that she did so functionally, to discern his intentions. After a moment, she nodded. "I will sit with you."

Pascal held out his arm, and she laid her hand on it, just barely touching his sleeve. The gesture matched her accent. He decided the dress was hers. Odd as it seemed, her feet were also a part of her, or perhaps a visible sign of her werewolf nature. Were shoes too much trouble when she changed form? And, no doubt, a corset would be impossible.

The shop was tiny, with equally tiny tables and spindly chairs that forced him to hunch like a crane. The shop did not sell coffee. He ordered a pot of their strongest tea and a plate of madeleines and little flaky pastries filled with sweetened cream. Madame Claes sat stiffly atop her chair, hands folded on the table. She wore no rings. Her fingernails were not dirty, but just as ragged as her toenails. A man's wristwatch clasped her bony wrist, just visible beyond the edge of her sleeve.

She said, "You are very rude to stare."

"I am rude," Pascal acknowledged. He poured tea for both of them, adding copious amounts of sugar to his. She looked as if she could use a good meal. Her fingers looked as if they could be snapped like twigs. He remembered Kauz's laboratory notebooks and felt sick. He held out the bowl to her. "Do you take sugar?"

"I do not want any tea."

"Pretend as if you do. It will give you something to do with your hands."

She said abruptly, "You would like my hands on you." She didn't sound as certain as before.

"If I did, we would not be sitting in this lovely shop." He glanced toward the counter. The waitress had retreated to the rear and begun washing dishes. The noise easily covered their low-voiced conversation. "Tell me about being a werewolf."

She gave him a pitying look and ate a madeleine in one bite, then picked up another. She chewed, swallowed, and said, "You will not lock me up. I would kill you first." She took a third cream pastry and studied it a moment before popping it into her mouth. Despite himself, Pascal watched the movement of her lips as she chewed. It wasn't entirely his scientific interest that led him to do so. He felt an incongruous curl of arousal simply from watching her eat.

He had not told Lucilla he had met a werewolf before, so he already knew Madame Claes's magnetism was not inherent in her species, or at least not entirely; he had only met male werewolves. Perhaps what he sensed was her focus and concentration, so like Lucilla when she pondered a problem.

Deliberately, he looked down at his tea and poured in some milk, then wrapped his fingers around the cup. He imagined Lucilla sitting next to him, her expression alert with scientific interest. She would have so many questions. "Where did you come from?"

"I did not arise from the earth like a plant. My mother gave birth to me."

"I meant, where is your home?" he asked, and sipped his tea. "Were both your parents werewolves?"

"I am a Belgian. It is not always necessary," she said, drinking down her tea. She did not expand on this answer. Pascal poured her another cup, and again offered the china bowl that held lumps of sugar. This time, she took two lumps and dropped them in.

Pascal raised a hand and called for the waitress, ordering a plate of sandwiches. "You are few, in Belgium?"

"Do you see us making armies and defending our land from the Boche?" The waitress set down their plate of small sandwiches. Madame Claes took one and ate it in a single bite. She did not appear to take any pleasure in the food, Pascal noted. She simply ate it for fuel, like a soldier too long in the field. "Why are you asking these questions?"

"I am curious. It is the besetting sin of the scientist."

"What do you hope to gain?"

Pascal shrugged. He ate a sandwich, and wished it was bigger. He had another. "Have you thought of all the ways in which an intelligent wolf might be useful to the war effort? Your spying was most effective, but at times bearing a simple message is even more valuable. The Boche have dogs which serve this purpose."

One corner of her mouth twisted. "I am not a dog. If I had a compassionate soul, I might consider this. But I told you, I have a hatred of the Boche. I prefer to strike directly whenever I am able, since my government will not allow me to be a soldier. Even though I can rip out a man's throat in less than a heartbeat." She picked up the last remaining madeleine and nibbled on it delicately.

Pascal felt short of breath. Her teeth were very fine and white, her canines slightly sharp. She had spoken with calm certainty. He did not doubt she could do as she said. "If you are not willing to be guided, your efforts may be of little use to us," he pointed out. "Some information is more valuable for when it is obtained, and how. One cannot simply blunder in and out."

"And who makes these decisions? You?" She sounded scornful.

"Not I," he confirmed. "These subtleties are not for me.

However, I do believe there is a place for them when dealing in such delicate matters as acquiring illicit information. Sometimes, one's labors are even made less dangerous when one has outside help."

Madame Claes picked up the last sandwich and ate it in quick, neat bites, leaving not even a scrap of crust. "Surely you do not intend assigning me a partner, and convincing him that I am a werewolf."

"You have convinced me."

"Yes. I can smell it on you. But I warn you, any attempt to constrain my activities will result in…let us say, that you will not be happy. Or perhaps even alive."

"And what of your life?" Pascal asked, lifting his hand for more sandwiches. He was still hungry. "I have heard that your kind is in particular danger if captured."

She stilled. He could not even see her breathe. "Who told you?" she asked.

"I obtained this knowledge before the war. And I received further information from a German scientist."

A low rumbling arose from her throat. "And this scientist, he was your friend?"

"Not in the least. My friend and I stole his motorcar."

She laughed, then looked astonished at the sound she'd made. Her gaze narrowed, grew savage and intent. "Tell me where to find him. The chemical experiments of which I spoke, they are his, but he was not there, and has not returned for many days."

"Alas, I cannot tell you. He is gone to ground somewhere. However, I suspect that you might be able to help us to find him."

"Gladly," she growled.

11

CRISPIN HADN'T FELT ANY FEAR AT ALL AS HE'D led his platoon into battle, only a strange feeling of intense concentration and heightened senses. Now that the worst of the fighting was over, though, chance had left him stranded far from his company, his twisted ankle swelling inside his boot, each beat of his pulse throbbing up his whole leg. He lay surrounded by mud and metal fragments, corpses and incomplete corpses, and the shattered skeletons of trees. That was a very different thing, and he'd had to work to keep from panicking.

Meyer had arrived after about an hour, and now Crispin couldn't stop shaking. He'd been holding together rather well when he lay in the mud alone, waiting for death. A blanket of acceptance had eventually settled over his mind: someone else would take care of his men, and either another shell would land on his head and blow him to bits, or it wouldn't, and he would worry about survival later. Dying that way would be quick. If his legs were blown off, or an arm, he still had his pistol. He could always shoot himself before he bled to death. He thought God would forgive him suicide, if he was dying already and in terrible pain. He needn't fear the worst, being ripped open by a bayonet, as no German would be insane enough to venture out of his trench during this kind of assault. Being trapped in a shell hole hadn't been nearly as bad as he'd feared.

Now, though, Meyer was with him, and if he was killed, Meyer would likely be killed, too. Crispin carefully unhooked his pistol from its lanyard, reholstered it and buttoned the flap. His hands were shaking too badly for it to be any good. "Why did you come after me? Where's your platoon?" He heard the sound of a train rushing overhead and pressed himself deeper into the mud, his arms protecting his face. The shell exploded some distance behind them. Smoke from previous impacts drifted by, like ghosts. Crispin shuddered.

Meyer lifted his head. His spectacles were spattered with mud, his mouth wry. "I thought it was over. My boys headed back. I came to look for you."

Probably, he'd gone looking for Crispin's corpse. "I can take care of myself," Crispin growled, though it wasn't entirely true. No one could take care of themselves in the midst of a battle. You couldn't protect yourself from a shell, not really. Crispin wasn't sure why he was so angry. He'd never been happier in his life, at least for a few moments, than when Meyer had slipped and skidded his way down into this god-forsaken hole. Perhaps it was that he'd been ready to die, finally calm about it, and then Meyer's arrival had reminded him that he'd left something unfinished, and he would regret it for eternity.

"Goddamn it," he said. Another shell whistled and he ducked again. That one had been closer. He stole a glance at

Meyer, and unexpectedly met his steady blue gaze, or what he could see of it through the mud. His heart stopped. Meyer looked down, fumbled off his filthy specs with an equally filthy hand and slid them carefully into the breast pocket of his uniform tunic. His slight squint when he looked at Crispin now bore a disturbing resemblance to a look of lustful contemplation.

Meyer said, "I'd give a hundred guineas for a hot bath right now."

Crispin's mind presented him with an image of Meyer's naked form ensconced in a porcelain bath, one leg flung over the side, his cock bobbing in the water. He closed his eyes. That made it worse. He opened them again and reflected wryly that at least it was better than contemplating his own dismemberment. "I'd give two hundred guineas for any bath," he said. "There's a puddle down at the bottom of this hole."

"Let me guess. You found it with your boots."

"My arse," Crispin said. "Good thing my coat took most of the damp." He rested his cheek on his arm and tried to slow down his breathing. Sometimes that helped. This time it helped for two breaths, until a Screaming Minnie tore through the air, then another, then a whole host of them, smaller shells ripping their way toward inevitable destruction. Terror washed over him like cold rain, then a vast numbness that he dived into gladly. He wasn't entirely sure what happened immediately after that, but when he could see again, the shelling had stopped and Meyer was touching his face.

He'd imagined this, lying wrapped in his blankets. Meyer would touch his face softly after they'd made passionate love such as he'd never known; he had foolish dreams like a teenage girl might have, that he would never, ever share. But now Meyer's hand, chilled and caked with dried mud, cupped his cheek with the tenderness he'd imagined. Meyer said, "Crispin?"

He couldn't form words; he was shaking too hard. He turned his face into the other man's touch.

"We're safe," Meyer said. Crispin tried to believe him, but couldn't, quite.

"Night will come," Meyer said. He kept his hand on Crispin's face, so he couldn't look away.

"That won't stop the shelling," Crispin said as best he could through his chattering teeth.

"But we won't have to worry about snipers. We can head back."

"To another bloody hole in the ground."

"It's full of luxuries," Meyer said, his tone enticing. Crispin shivered inside, this time not from fear. Meyer might sound like that if he was trying to seduce someone. His next words dispelled that impression a bit. "We have our own latrine pit. And every size tin of Bully Beef."

Crispin struggled to smile because he knew that was Meyer's aim. He couldn't quite manage. He turned his face to the mud. Meyer's hand slid to the back of his head and ruffled through his hair. Crispin suddenly had trouble breathing.

"Think of music," Meyer said.

"It's too loud," Crispin whispered.

"Maybe you could sing for me a little."

"Someone will hear." And his throat felt tight as a twisted rope. He could barely push his breath through it, much less his voice. He turned his head a bit more and concentrated on where his forehead touched Meyer's forearm. He smelled wet wool and mud and sweat, but there was still the barest hint of shaving lotion. He would recognize the scent of Meyer's bay and lime shaving lotion from the other side of a room.

"I don't sing nearly as well as you, so I won't try." A pause. "Do you want me to keep talking?"

"Please."

His hand tightened on the back of Crispin's neck. "Right, then. Breathe easy, Crispin. Imagine you're getting ready to sing."

Crispin's heart stuttered with the grateful words he wanted to say and couldn't. He let go his fistful of mud and seized Meyer's coat instead.

Without ceasing his steady flow of words, most of which Crispin couldn't hear, Meyer looped his arm over Crispin's back and pulled him closer, until his voice and warm breath fanned over Crispin's throat. Gradually, that warmth melted invisible ice, and Crispin's breathing slowed and deepened. He shifted closer, his body easing and stretching against Meyer's until they lay with only the thickness of a notebook between them. Crispin's cock was straining at the seam of his trousers, both from fear and from being so close to the man he lusted for. He shifted his hips back a bit and hoped Meyer wouldn't notice. If he had noticed, Meyer didn't thrust him away.

Crispin flinched when another Minnie screamed overhead, but this time he flinched into Meyer, who seemed to absorb the fear and send comfort back. "Talk to me," Meyer said when a brief silence fell and Crispin shuddered in relief. "We haven't had a chance to chat lately."

After a moment's stunned silence, Crispin said, "What the hell are you talking about? We're in a bloody shell hole. Got any biscuits on you? Sugar tongs? We could have tea."

Meyer chuckled; Crispin could feel Meyer's belly move, feel

his breath on his neck. His hand rubbed soothingly on the back of Crispin's neck. "A nice social afternoon," he agreed. "What was tea like at home, when you were a boy? Cucumber sandwiches and little cream Napoleons? Or beans on toast?"

"Depends," Crispin said, trying to let the massaging hand distract him from the roar of the guns and the cold mud in which he lay. "Mum does the sandwiches with no crusts and iced cakes and all that. She likes to be posh. But I would go round the neighbors' a lot, the Osbournes. They would have eggs and toast sometimes, or little mince pies, different things. They were a lot more jolly than we were, but not as much fun as my sister, Lucilla. She didn't mind things like digging and catching frogs and the like." He realized he'd been rambling, and said, "What about you?"

"Oh, I was always at Ashby's house. His mum laid out a spread that would feed a pack of starving wolves, she said."

"I could eat a pack of wolves right now," Crispin said.

Gabriel laughed, then drew Crispin more tightly to him. "Sorry I forgot the biscuits."

"Tell me something else," Crispin said. "About you."

Meyer hesitated, but only for a moment or two, while Crispin's stomach surged and plunged with nerves and arousal. "We had a nice house," he said.

"You lived near Ashby, didn't you?"

"Next to him." Meyer paused. "We used to joke about all the outcasts in the neighborhood being made to live together."

"I thought Ashby's family was rich."

"They are, but they're also Roman Catholic."

Crispin blinked, for a moment forgetting they lay in the mud. "Papists, eh? That's funny."

"Not really. One of the other boys used to throw stones at

Ashby's sisters, and mine, as well, until we found out and did something about it."

"I'm sorry."

"What's to be sorry for? I don't want to be a Christian, and Noel says, if anybody doesn't like what his mother gave him, then fuck 'em."

He'd never heard Meyer use that word. He didn't say anything for a while. He wondered, feared, if Meyer would let go of him, but he didn't. A big Coal Box went over, and after the shell went off, somewhere to the west, his ears rang and he realized he had both hands tangled up in Meyer's tunic. No, not his uniform tunic; that was partly unbuttoned, and he had his fingers full of linen shirt.

Meyer was murmuring to him, and petting his hair like he was a boy. Except he didn't feel like a boy. His nose was full of grown man and he wanted to nuzzle that shirt aside and taste his chest. He might die if he couldn't do it. He didn't care anymore what Meyer thought. He might die anyway, and if he did die, he didn't want to do it before he'd kissed Gabriel Meyer with all that was in him. Crispin sucked in a breath, then another and another. It took him almost a minute to get his courage up, then he lifted his head and simply lunged.

Their teeth banged together, and his lips stung and burned from impact. He turned his head, just a bit, and suddenly their mouths slanted across each other at just the right angle, warm and smooth, sending a shock of pleasure through him pure as a hot mouth on his cock. Meyer's mouth shifted and opened, and then he was fairly sure he was being kissed back.

Crispin whimpered, and then Meyer's tongue teased at his, gentle and soft as a summer breeze. He whimpered again. It was so sweet he wanted to cry. He'd never been kissed like this, never kissed anyone like this, delicate, slow, move in and retreat, try a new angle and start again. He'd kissed, of course. A few times. But mostly the men he knew didn't kiss, at least not on the mouth. Spectacular as it felt to have someone kiss his cock, this moved him a thousand times more, and at the same time pulsed through his cock until he felt stiff and protuberant as a rifle barrel.

Meyer started kissing his throat and his whole chest grew warm with it, shudders rippling over his skin. Now he could die happy. His muscles melted under those kisses, his neck wilting like a flower to give Meyer more access. Meyer bit along the tendons leading down to his shoulder and Crispin thought he *would* die from the pleasure that punctured him like bullets. He wanted to reciprocate, but his whole body trembled and he couldn't move or do anything except press into Meyer's mouth. He kept his eyes closed, savoring every minute lick and suction, plunging into sensation and far away from smoke and unbearable noise.

Time went away, and memory and the future with it. Crispin felt as if he were floating, having left his exhausted, battered, dirty body somewhere below. *Don't stop*, he thought. *Never stop.* He couldn't summon the words to his lips. Meyer might have heard his thoughts, they were pressed so close. His mouth came back up to Crispin's and he kissed him softly again, his tongue's caress like strokes down Crispin's belly. He nibbled at Crispin's lower lip and thrust in his tongue a bit harder, and there came a terrible *thump*. Sounds and smells rushed in: ragged breathing, a rattle of sliding dirt and stones, fetid slippery mud and smoke. Time jolted forward, seizing his muscles with fear, and with the fear a rush of blood to his cock.

The ground shuddered again. Another impact, a nearer

one, vibrating his bones in his body. Crispin could smell the smoke already. Fear flushed through him, chilling his skin. "Hush," Meyer murmured, "hush, I've got you—"

Crispin tried to crawl inside Meyer's body, scrabbling for a hold, any hold. Meyer's arms wrapped him, confined him, but that wasn't enough. Crispin dug with his knee until his leg was clasped tightly between Meyer's, then threw his other leg on top, pinning them both to the ground. His erection slammed against hardness, hipbone or a twin erection, he wasn't sure and didn't care, because for a moment it felt so good that it took him away from this place and back to the other place where only their two bodies existed.

Meyer would pull away any second now, he would, and Crispin would die. Frantic to keep this contact, he tightened his grip, arms and legs both. Meyer couldn't leave him until this was finished. Then they could die, he didn't care. His cock felt swollen to twice its size and so tender he couldn't imagine touching it. His trousers' grip on it was torture. At the same time, he ground it against wool, buttons, hard flesh, anything to ease his torment.

Please. Please. Please. Almost. Almost there. Almost. He thrust up, sawing against hardness and gasping for breath now. Meyer panted in his ear. He was speaking in between gasps, words Crispin couldn't make out; he could only feel damp hot breath and imagine it on his straining cock. He thrust desperately, again, again—he could feel the end barreling through him, from the soles of his feet up to the top of his skull, and he couldn't breathe until he came, harder than he could ever remember coming in his life, his cock still trapped against the buttoned flap of his trousers and pulsing there like an animal trying to escape, spurting everything out of him, terror and strength all together. And then even the scream of Minnies over his head couldn't budge his muscles, and the world went black.

Crispin actually slept through the next half hour, missing it when the noise stopped. He only woke when, impossibly, Ashby's voice called out Meyer's name, then Crispin's, and he bounded blithely down into the shell hole as if he were on a country ramble. It wasn't so dark Crispin couldn't see the look that passed between the other two men. Ashby knew, or guessed, what had happened between them, but wasn't going to speak of it. And Meyer, it seemed, wasn't going to speak of it even to Crispin.

He knew this game well, and hated it with every ounce of his being. If he'd had the slightest excuse he would have picked a fight with Ashby, just to vent his rage at the other man's untimely interference. If Ashby hadn't come along, he and Meyer might be talking right now, in the dark, under the stars and the distant light of occasional shells. For once, he might have been able to have a conversation with a man *after* he'd had his tongue in his mouth. But no. Ashby had decided to come along and rescue them, and then look innocently ignorant of any criminal activity while gently binding up Crispin's ankle. Crispin felt a creeping jealousy to realize that Ashby probably only realized what had happened because he was so close to Meyer. And he cared for him enough to protect him.

Crispin had to accept Ashby's support as he limped back to the company; Meyer trailed behind, carrying the rifle Ashby had brought. Crispin didn't speak. After an attempt or two at conversation, Ashby gave up, and led them back through a pocked hell of splintered trees to a newish trench, never once stumbling—and saving Meyer from skidding into a nasty puddle that contained half of a corpse. Once Crispin was ensconced on a crate of canned peaches, with Joyce looking after his ankle and the new company terrier solicitously licking his hand, Meyer spoke to Ashby and then scrambled out of the trench, presumably to look for more of the men. It was a great pity, Crispin reflected, that he hadn't fallen for Ashby instead. At least Ashby might not have pretended nothing had happened.

Hailey skidded to his knees, sheltering behind a shattered cottage wall while a few Minnies winged overhead. This hamlet reminded him of the ones they'd seen on their way into France, full of cheering people who gave them cigarettes and flowers and loaves of bread. Now it was devastated, all the people gone, gardens trampled, animal corpses bloating in the streets, houses and churches shot to pieces by the guns. His company and several others, their numbers sadly reduced in the last couple of weeks, had been fortifying the place as best they could and taking potshots at the Germans who were holed up on the banks of the river Marne. But after today's bombardment, it was strategic retirement once again.

Lieutenant Smith was missing. Hailey had to find him and pass on Captain Ashby's orders; if it were Daglish missing, he would be smart enough to come in on his own, but Smith was more likely to hare off so he could bag another souvenir of the enemy. Pittfield was with Smith, or had been earlier, and he was a canny sort, so maybe it would be all right, but unlike everyone else, Smith didn't always listen to Pittfield. And there was Lincoln to consider; no one had found Lincoln yet when Hailey had set out.

Because he was terrible at cards, Lincoln owed Hailey a

guinea sixpence, enough for a new overcoat. Hailey was damned if he would allow that debt to go unpaid, with winter coming on and no sign of going home anytime soon. He hoped Lincoln was with Smith and Pittfield, because he didn't relish staying out much longer. It was already dusk, and the idea of tramping across broken ground in the dark alone sent chills right down to his feet.

The Minnies died off and, cautiously, Hailey quartered the village, peering into any sheltered spot just in case anyone lay there wounded. He didn't fear finding the enemy, at least not yet. They wouldn't be stupid enough to march forward under their own guns. He found one dead man, a Frenchman in red trousers, now stained brown with dried blood. He took a few moments to extract the man's identity papers, or what looked like them, and stack some fallen bricks over the top half of the body. He didn't have the courage to look at the man's face. He didn't want to see it in his memory as it disappeared under rubble, brick by brick.

A rattle like a sewing machine split the air and Hailey dropped onto the remains of someone's kitchen garden before he realized the sound hadn't been that loud, just confusing in the way it had bounced off walls and rubble. The machine gun had to be down the road, and probably belonged to the enemy, and they had to be shooting at someone. Possibly Lincoln, who owed him a guinea sixpence, or maybe even sevenpence. Lincoln would have stuck to Pittfield like glue if he'd found him, and Pittfield wouldn't have abandoned Smith to blunder around on his own. Hailey took a couple of good deep breaths and dropped into the ditch running alongside the road. He'd have a look.

A rifle popped, then another and another. Hailey lay in the

ditch. He heard shouting in English and equipment clanking before there were more shots, then a motor groaning, the familiar protests of a lorry stuck in the mud. Were the enemy shooting at the lorry?

The shouting sounded ordinary now, not battle yelling. Cautiously, Hailey scrambled out of the ditch. He'd barely taken a single step when a bee whined past, then another, and he half spun round, his arm going numb. "Bugger," he gasped, staggered and fell to his knees.

Noel felt a bit like a sheepdog as the men of the company trickled in. Daglish was eyeing him worriedly, so Noel gave him a bright smile and a clap on the shoulder, then paced up and down in the guise of keeping an eye out. He was practically jumping out of his skin with the desire to search out more of his men, circle them and shepherd them back to safety, especially the younger ones, especially Hailey, who was running around without even a rifle for protection. Not that this trench was entirely safe; a single shell could wipe them all out. But Noel couldn't do anything about that.

The company terrier barked at him and rolled onto his back. Noel crouched and caressed the animal's wiry coat, his every sense alert for the sound of approaching footsteps.

He managed not to show any reaction when Gabriel arrived, leading Lyton, Mason, Southey and Woods. Woods's arm was bound up close to his chest, but wasn't bleeding any longer. Noel sent Joyce to have a look at the wound and took Gabriel aside. "Any sign of Smith? Or Hailey?"

Gabriel shook his head. "No one's seen Hailey. I'm a bit worried. He knows where to meet us?"

"He was carrying the word."

Pittfield arrived next, using his Enfield as a makeshift crutch, and bearing ill news. "Smith's dead," he said, not wasting time softening the blow. "Hailey went after him, couldn't manage it, he's such a little thing. Took a bullet in the shoulder."

"Where is he?" Noel demanded, suddenly short of breath. "And why aren't you with him?"

"Stretcher bearer helped him. He was on his way to a truck. Lincoln is wounded, too, and went with him. I'm not hurt so bad—"

"The fucking hell you're not, that's why you're abusing your weapon. Get that leg taken care of." Pittfield stared at him.

"I can bloody well curse if I want to," Noel growled. "Joyce! Come and help Pittfield." He turned to Gabriel. "You're in charge. I'll be back."

Gabriel stared at him.

"I've got to go after Hailey."

Gabriel stared some more. Daglish had caught some hint, and was looking in their direction.

Noel touched Gabriel's arm. "Go and tell Daglish about Smith. I'll be back before morning."

"If you get yourself killed on some idiotic stunt, I will fucking kill you a second time," Gabriel said.

"Hailey needs me," Noel said. He grasped Gabriel's shoulder and gave him a little shake. "This is important."

Gabriel sighed. "That boy is more competent than a lot of the older men. He'll manage a ride to hospital on his own."

"I have to make sure."

Gabriel sighed. "Fine. But you'd better be back before I have to explain your absence."

"Done." Noel winked and grinned, then turned and sprinted off. He had to find Hailey, and quickly.

12

"SISTER, IT REALLY IS RATHER URGENT THAT I find Hailey."

Lucilla barely glanced at the officer, who was filthy but un-wounded. "I'm busy, Captain. Perhaps one of the porters can help you." She checked beneath a bandage, sniffing discreetly, then patted the man's shoulder. "You'll do." She moved to the next in line.

"He's not very large. Brown hair, brown eyes."

She ignored this. Unless Matron told her otherwise, she refused to ignore new patients in favor of a single officer with a ridiculous request. He could easily find someone else to help him. That was the purpose of porters and orderlies and VADs—Voluntary Aid Detachments—to handle simple tasks so she could get on with nursing.

"I'll wait," said the voice behind her. "Hailey's wounded, you see. He's my batman."

"This is the right place for him, then. Someone will see to him," Lucilla said absently as she scribbled a note and tucked it into the next soldier's tunic pocket, reassuring him when he looked alarmed.

Ten minutes later, she'd forgotten about the captain. The current batch of VADs was efficient in cleaning the men up and, with the help of orderlies, getting them into beds, but there simply weren't enough of them, leaving more work for the nurses. Lucilla took charge of the abdominal wounds. When a khaki-clad soldier appeared at her shoulder to hold basins, she was able to move more quickly, and finished before midnight.

She closed her eyes and stretched, careful not to touch her uniform with her dirty hands. At last she could apply some lanolin to her cracked skin.

"Sister, I hate to bother you, but—"

Lucilla turned and stared. "You're still here?" she asked. Her helper was the captain from earlier in the evening, whom she'd been too distracted to speak to. He must truly be desperate, to help her with some of her nastier tasks. She said, "One of the porters could probably have told you where to find the boy. Aren't you due back at your battalion?" She peered more closely at his cap badge. He was from Crispin's regiment. A momentary rush of cold fear took her breath, until she realized that if the captain had brought bad news, he would have said so immediately upon arrival.

"Sister, may I speak to you privately? Briefly," he added. "Very briefly."

He'd helped her when he didn't have to do so. Most wouldn't have bothered; they would have gone to Matron and demanded. Lucilla sighed. She ought to reinforce good behavior. "Outside," she said. "Only for a moment. But I have to wash first. You'd better wash, too."

Chill had descended with the night. The air outside smelled

clean, though, which improved her mood immeasurably. She pressed her hands in the small of her back and stretched, looking up at the stars. If not for the shelling, and her importunate visitor, it might have been a lovely night.

"I wasn't able to find Hailey in any of the wards," the captain said. "It's important that I locate him."

He'd washed his face as well as his hands. His cropped coppery hair looked as if he'd run wet fingers through it. Outside in the clean air, she was more aware of the scents that clung to him: dirt and sweat and gunpowder, all layered beneath the strong soap they used in the hospital. She noticed sharply angled eyebrows, freckles, a long nose, a lush mouth that looked as if it belonged on a woman but wasn't the least bit feminine. His stance and facial expression made her imagine he didn't have much trouble obtaining the loyalty of his men. Perhaps that loyalty went both ways.

"You're sure he was sent here?" she asked.

"Absolutely. He was wounded this morning, in the arm, and my sergeant saw him on a truck heading here. Sister—I didn't catch your name—"

"Daglish," she said. "And you?"

He looked at her strangely for a moment, his nostrils flaring, then said, "Ashby, Noel Ashby." He stuck out his hand. She shook it, and he didn't let go as he continued to speak. "You're Lieutenant Crispin Daglish's sister, aren't you? That must be why I chose you. Your brother's fine, just a twisted ankle today."

Lucilla reclaimed her hand. Captain Ashby had heavily callused palms, which she rarely encountered in an officer; they'd sent a warm shock up her arm.

He said, "I'm afraid Hailey might not have entered the

hospital. I was hoping someone could help me look for him. Discreetly."

A thought occurred to her. She asked, "You think he's deserted?" That offense earned a penalty of death. She could understand him wanting to prevent a young man's death.

Ashby shook his head vigorously. "I think he's hiding from the doctors. But he can't do that, even if he's not much wounded. He could die of gangrene."

"I think you have a little time before you need fear that," Lucilla noted. "Still, it's not good to wander about bleeding."

"Can you keep a secret, Miss Daglish?"

She blinked, trying to keep up with Ashby's lightning shift of topic. "What sort of secret?"

"Hailey is, well…he has a reason to hide. Hailey's not a man. He's a young woman."

Lucilla blinked again. "Don't tell me no one noticed. Not least the recruiting office."

"I noticed," Ashby said. "He's good, though. I only noticed because…because we're in such close quarters. He doesn't know I know."

Lucilla stared. So far as she could tell he appeared perfectly serious. "And you did nothing? Is this some sort of joke?"

"He's an excellent batman," Ashby said.

She folded her arms across her chest. "This had better not be a joke, or I will cause you to be very, very sorry."

"I wouldn't joke about one of my men!"

Unless he could control the color rising in his cheeks, Ashby was genuinely outraged. Or embarrassed at being caught out in his game. "Prove it. How did you find out this batman of yours was a girl?" If there even was a batman. But then, if not, why spend this entire evening holding noxious, heavy basins?

Ashby straightened. Until that moment, she had not noticed he only topped her height by a few inches. "Please help me to find her." His face glowed with sincerity and an almost feral attraction. She felt the urge to reach out and touch him, to see if he was real, and shook it off. She'd obviously been on her feet too long.

"I doubt she even exists," she said. "Come now, Captain. Your joke is over. Go back to your battalion. I would think you would have a little respect for the medical staff. If you go now, I won't report you."

"I'm already in trouble if anyone finds Meyer in charge instead of me. Now, for the last time, will you help me find Hailey?"

"How did you know he was a girl?" she countered.

For a split second, she thought he might leap at her, and she tensed. Then he grinned, loose and friendly, as if he'd been presented with a plate of his favorite dinner. She wasn't sure if his smile was forced or not, but she felt its impact as a slow caress on her skin. She'd been right about the magnetism. He said, "I knew Hailey was a girl because she smelled like a girl."

"Hailey wears violet toilet water?"

Still smiling, he shook his head. "No, she smells like a girl. I have a very good sense of smell. For instance, I can tell that before the trucks came in with the wounded, you were having naughty fun in your bed. Alone, alas."

Lucilla's eyes widened before she realized she'd confirmed his supposition by her reaction. Denial seemed pointless. "I suppose Lord Kitchener forbids such goings-on?" she asked sweetly. "Go home, Captain."

"You still don't believe me!"

"This grows tiresome. Crispin wouldn't put you up to this—who was it? If you're trying to cause him trouble, I swear I will—"

"Wait." He grabbed her arm, then let go immediately when she whirled on him. "I'll prove it to you. About my nose, and all that. Just wait here, and I'll go behind that shed, and—"

"You're not going out of my sight," she said. "Unless it is to leave."

He shrugged. "Don't complain, then." He set his cap on the ground, loosened his tie and began unbuttoning his uniform tunic.

"What the hell are you doing?"

"Taking off my damn clothes," he said. "It's chilly out here, too." He tossed his tunic on the ground, then his tie, and started in on his shirt.

"You're insane."

He bounced on one foot while wrestling off his boot. "Hailey usually helps me with the boots."

Lucilla sighed and pressed the heels of her hands into her eyes. "Oh, Lord, if you're insane I'll have to bring you in for hysteria, and we haven't any proper facilities. I can't just leave you out here."

He didn't seem to be in the grip of a compulsion, but she wasn't an expert, either. She'd seen some strange reactions to combat already, everything from constant tremors to sleep-walking. This could be another manifestation. She'd need to find help in case he became violent. She wouldn't win a physical fight. But if she left him, he might disappear, or harm himself. She stayed, keeping a close eye on him.

Ashby's trousers hit the ground, and he blithely shucked out of his long shirt and drawers, turning away from her as he did so. She didn't note any signs of physical injury, and she would have easily seen any in that expanse of smooth, pale skin. His skin wavered, or was it her vision? Was she truly that tired? Another ripple passed over him, like a full-body spasm, only smooth and controlled. Then he hit the ground.

Lucilla dashed forward. He fended her off with one hand. "Wait!" he said.

She would need an orderly, or perhaps two, to help her deal with this. But she couldn't leave him alone in mid fit to fetch anyone. "I'll stay with you," she said as calmly as she could. She'd need something ready to thrust beneath his teeth if necessary; she reached into her pocket and found a handkerchief, swiftly twisting and knotting it.

"All over—in a few seconds—"

He spoke coherently. His eyes did not lose awareness, and he focused on her face until she felt trapped by his golden gaze. This was the strangest fit she'd ever seen. She could only watch as his body twisted and shifted and arched and...shifted, muscles elongating beneath his pale skin, his skin darkening, coarsening... No. He'd sprouted fur, thick and rufous. His face was gone, and his hands. No, she had to be hallucinating, from fatigue perhaps. She blinked slowly, and saw a very large red dog. No, not a dog. Not with that thick brush of a tail, that ruff, those quizzical dark lines above amber-colored eyes. Except for color, he might have been an illustration in a Jack London novel. This was a wolf. A wolf. In France. In the middle of the hospital grounds. Staring at her, its head tipped to one side, ears pricked.

The wolf sprang to its feet and shoved its nose between her legs. She slapped it away. It backed up a step and grinned at her, tongue lolling. Slowly, she sank to her knees in the dirt.

Her knees protested. The wolf butted its head into her breasts and she saw the flicker of its tongue near a very inappropriate place. She grabbed his ruff and yanked him to arm's length. "Ashby," she said. The wolf licked her bare wrist.

"Bugger me," she breathed.

The wolf grinned at her again. He sat in the heap of his clothing. She had watched the entire process. A man had turned into a wolf. Kauz had been telling the truth. She couldn't wait to tell Pascal.

Her longing to see Pascal again momentarily swamped her wonder at the miracle she'd just seen. The wolf—Ashby—whined and licked her face. His ruff was soft beneath its coarse outer layer. She burrowed into it and held on for a moment. Ashby wouldn't be able to speak. At least she didn't think he would. "You can't speak like this, can you?"

He produced another whine, different from the first. Wolf language, she supposed. "I didn't think so," she said wearily. "All right. Because you've astonished me beyond..." Beyond anything except for Pascal Fournier. "Beyond...oh, never mind." A thought occurred to her. "Why couldn't you track Hailey as a wolf? By scent, if you're so proud of your sense of smell?"

She could have sworn the wolf lifted an eyebrow. At least, the dark line over his eye gave that effect.

"A bit conspicuous, yes. As we're going to be, shortly. Perhaps you'd better change back, and I'll help you look for him. Her."

Once he'd reverted to human form and dressed, behind a shed this time, Lucilla led Ashby to the temporary buildings housing the X-ray unit, the photographic laboratory and storage for the medical-supply kits that were assembled for the ambulances. Vehicles constantly passed to and fro, both motor driven and animal drawn, carrying ill and wounded. It would be easy to hide there amid the chaos, and a sharp eye could soon discern where bandages were stored, and could be stolen. Lucilla halted on the edges of the stretch of mud where sleepy orderlies and female drivers were washing down the motor ambulances, inside and out. She said to Ashby, "You might have a sniff round here."

He lifted his head and sniffed, the barest flare of his nostrils. His eyes drifted closed. "Petrol," he said in a disgusted tone. "Worse than the carbolic." He scrubbed above his mustache with his finger and sniffed again, wandering an aimless path around the outskirts of the electric lights dangling from every available roof.

She supposed she could leave him to it; he was in uniform, and could no doubt come up with an acceptable reason for his presence. But she was curious to meet Hailey, to see with her own eyes a woman who lived as a man, in her own way as much a shape-changer as Ashby. Hailey, apparently, had no idea of how much she had in common with her superior officer. Lucilla didn't plan to tell her. For all she knew, Ashby told everyone he met, but it wasn't her secret to divulge.

Ashby circled a particular patch of air and then headed toward a storage shed, no longer scenting, at least not obviously. Lucilla trotted over, her knees protesting, the boots she wore beneath her skirt squelching in mud. Ashby gently pushed open the shed's door and poked his head inside. "Bob?" he said.

Lucilla heard a scrabble of motion and hurried to catch up. She followed Ashby into the shed. A young man sat on a crate next to a soldier, a Gurkha; there'd been a group of them earlier in the evening, she remembered now, most of them with barely a lick of English. The doctors had depended on one of the ambulatory Sikh patients to translate, and none of them had liked it much. This Gurkha wasn't much bigger than Hailey, though much more muscular and cheerfully danger-ous looking; he had a dirty bandage around his thigh. Lucilla almost reached for him, then held back as Ashby went to one knee in front of the two of them.

"Goddamn it, you terrified the bloody living hell out of me, you little bastard," he said, his tone tender. Hailey stared at him, wide-eyed. Ashby reached out and the Gurkha blocked his hand. Ashby glanced at him; the Gurkha lowered his hand but put his arm firmly around Hailey's shoulders, not quite touching the bandage poking out of her ripped sleeve. Ashby completed his gesture and touched Hailey's face, brushing her cheek with his thumb. "You need to have that wound seen to."

Hailey spoke, for the first time. "Jemadar Thapa knew Captain Wilks, in India."

"Perhaps he can tell us more about it later. Bob, this is Sister Daglish. The lieutenant's her brother."

"Don't need nursing, sir."

"Thapa does, doesn't he, Sister?" He pointed at the Gurkha's bandage. "Bob, it's all right. There's nothing you need to worry about with Sister Daglish. In fact, she's going to set you up in a private room for now."

Lucilla stepped forward. "I am."

She managed a greeting in Hindustani; her phrases were limited, but efficient, and Jemadar Thapa grinned at her. In a thick accent, he said, "You take care of the boy," and patted Hailey's arm. "Wilky-sahib taught me to play at jackstraws."

"Sir—" Hailey said.

"It's all right," Ashby said. He ruffled his hand through her hair. "I know, Bob. And it's no one's business."

"Sir!"

"I've got to get back before someone notices I'm gone," he said, squeezing Hailey's shoulder before rising to his feet. "Sister, you'll be all right?"

"Perfectly," she assured him.

"I'll return when I can. I owe you more than thanks." He patted Hailey's arm once more, exchanged salutes with Thapa and departed.

Lucilla stared at her two new charges. A jemadar was a lieutenant, and he spoke English. At least one of her problems was temporarily solved. If she set him to translating as soon as his wound had been cared for, she'd be able to spirit Hailey away. Assuming Hailey was really his—her—name.

Luckily, she was able to catch a couple of orderlies to help support her new patients into the ward. Jemadar Thapa immediately took charge of the wounded Gurkha riflemen, insisting on limping to each bed for a word or two before being settled into his own. Lucilla took advantage of the distraction to lead Hailey into Dr. Fitzclarence's office and bolt the door. "Have a seat," she said, seizing some supplies from a cabinet. "I'll help you with your tunic and shirt."

Cautiously, Hailey sat on the edge of a wooden chair that stood across from Dr. Fitzclarence's desk. Lucilla saw a boy perhaps as old as his late teens, slightly built, with large hands and feet he might grow into later. Too-long hair flopped into his angular face, which, along with his cap, obscured his eyes. He had a strong jawline and a snub nose and a wide mouth. Then she touched the boy, who winced back, and she somehow knew more than intellectually that Hailey was not male. Her face seemed to change before Lucilla's eyes, and she was a gamine young woman with a boyish form.

Abruptly, Lucilla felt less maternal and more as if she was caring for a comrade. "I'm Lucilla Daglish. You're Hailey?" she asked.

Hailey nodded. She lifted her hands to her jacket buttons, winced and let them fall. "Don't cut my sleeve on the bias," she whispered. "I can mend it."

"I'll see if I can manage." Lucilla undid the buttons and carefully peeled the jacket off her arms, first the uninjured arm and then the bandaged one. She laid the jacket aside. "Where is your coat?"

"Gave it to a bloke on the truck," Hailey said. Her voice was low, hoarse. Lucilla wasn't sure if she naturally sounded like that, or if the effect was cultivated. Lucilla had known a few women at university who'd affected men's clothing and mannerisms, some of them lesbians and some not, but they'd all been wealthy women, and not really hiding themselves, at least not from other women. Hailey's accent placed her as lower class, from somewhere south of London. Lucilla wondered if her family knew of her masquerade, and what they thought of it.

"Give me your cap," she said, and when Hailey obeyed, studied the running-wolf badge. Her memory flashed up an image of Ashby, a grinning wolf with lolling tongue. She couldn't ponder that properly now. She had work to do. "Once I've seen to your wound, we'll get you tidied up," she said. "No one will come around trying to bathe you if you're already clean."

"Thank you, Sister," Hailey said, her voice a mere breath, her eyes fixed on Lucilla's hands as she unbuttoned her shirt.

Lucilla very deliberately did not react to the breast bindings she found beneath, nor try to unfasten them. She could get at Hailey's wound well enough like this. She spread her supplies over the scarred surface of the wooden desk, ready to hand.

To distract the girl, she asked, "Do you know Lieutenant Daglish?"

She looked up; Lucilla swiftly untied the bandage over her wound and explained, "I don't get much news."

"He was all right, last I saw," Hailey said.

"Thank you."

"Was pretty rough out there, though."

Lucilla was sorry she'd asked. She said, "When you return to your regiment, would you carry some letters to him, for me?"

"Yes, ma'am."

"You needn't call me *ma'am,*" she said more sharply than she'd intended. "Do you have a brother, Hailey?"

"Just a sister."

"And how long have you been—" She covered her moment of hesitation with an injection of morphia. Hailey winced as the needle entered, then relaxed almost immediately. "When did you join the army?"

"Five years ago."

"Why—" She was suddenly embarrassed to have asked. "Never mind."

"For the money," Hailey said. "Army pays better than being a seamstress." She grinned a little drunkenly.

"It's an interesting change of career," Lucilla noted, cleaning the wound more ruthlessly now that her patient didn't notice the pain of it. She wiped the whole thing with Lysol, then doused a handful of gauze in tincture of iodine, ready to slap on once the stitches were in.

"First I wanted to be a tailor. Pays better than being a seamstress. So I learned all about men's clothes. But nobody would hire a woman to make a man's clothes, not unless they didn't have the money to pay for a man. I did some uniforms, though, for young lads just starting out. So I got the idea to make a uniform for myself, and a suit, and all that. I figured out all the best ways to hide that I was a woman, and then I went right up and enlisted. Never looked back."

"Worked out well for you, has it?"

Hailey's head was twisted around as she tried to watch the needle going into her skin. Suddenly, she closed her eyes. Her head drooped. "It's moving. Like a boat."

"Deep breaths," Lucilla advised. "How's the army been?"

"Not bad, 'cept for the war coming along, bollixing it all up." She paused. "Still, I'm learning all kinds of things. All kinds."

Lucilla tied off her thread and slapped on the dressing with one hand, scooping up a rolled bandage with the other. "Will you stay in the army once the war ends?"

"Have to, don't I? I've got my family to care for. You're lucky to have a brother like him, ma'am. He's a good one, Daglish is. Don't let anyone tell you different."

"He's the best brother in the world."

After Hailey was safe and cared for, Lucilla walked down the muddy path back to her quarters in one of the slapdash rear huts. She was dizzy from lack of sleep and reliving, in a near trance, the moments when Ashby had shifted from one form to the other. If only she could tell Pascal. For a few wild moments, she considered ways of sending him a letter— through the French command, perhaps, or to his relatives in Le Havre—before laughing at herself. He would not be pleased to hear from her, she was sure. He no doubt had quite a few pretty *mademoiselles* trying to catch his eye. No, that was unfair; there was work to be done, and she felt sure the French army had not overlooked his usefulness. It made her feel a bit better to think of him occupied with engineering problems. She could even consider him with nostalgia.

He would love knowing that werewolves truly existed. She could encode that information in a letter, perhaps; it would not be like sending a letter simply because she wanted to do so. He would wish to discuss her discovery with her, and they could—no. She really had nothing to do with all this. She was neither an officer in the army nor a person with any scientific standing that an army would recognize. She should let Ashby know about Kauz, and leave it to him to speak to Pascal, if it could be managed. She would betray no one's confidences that way. If she hadn't been so tired and overwhelmed, she would have done it already.

Perhaps Hailey could carry a message to her captain. Lucilla could give her a letter for Crispin, as well, and some tea or his favorite nut-milk choc. It made Lucilla weary to think of turning and going back to ask. Hailey would be asleep by now, she hoped. She could speak to her tomorrow. Oh, she would give anything right now for a cup of tea, heavily dosed with Irish whiskey.

When she pushed open the door to her hut and saw the light on, Pascal standing there beside her bed, at first she thought she was dreaming. In one stride, he held her by the arms. A moment later, his mouth swept down upon hers. His mustache tickled her nose. That felt real. He drew back, looked down at her as if to confirm his welcome, then kissed her again before lifting her off the dirt floor and holding her tightly against him.

Lucilla stroked her hands up and down his back. Was he thinner than he'd been? She'd never before seen him in his uniform. The pale blue didn't really suit him, nor did the loose cut of his jacket. Of course, her own uniform added at least ten years to her, and included a silly hat and cape besides, so she supposed she couldn't criticize.

"Lucilla," he said. He kissed her cheek and set her on her feet. "I thought I would have to search you out."

"How did you—"

He shrugged. "I am a spy. Not in the field," he added hastily. "I persuaded them that would be unwise. I have been working with data that others provide."

"But, here—"

"I missed you," he said with devastating simplicity. He cupped her cheek in his palm. "I had hoped you might miss me, as well."

Exhaustion and shock shattered over Lucilla's head like a shell exploding. Before she could burst into tears, she buried her face against Pascal's chest. She wrapped her arms around his waist and held on. "Yes," she said, muffled against his uniform.

His hands, so large and ludicrously familiar and comforting, rubbed her back as she had just rubbed his, then gradually pressed harder, crushing some of the ache out of her muscles. "You're wearied."

Lucilla could only nod.

"I must leave sometime tomorrow. I was not... I am supposed to be in Paris before I return to headquarters. Are you well?"

"I had some patients at the last minute—Pascal!" Stunned that she'd temporarily forgotten about what she'd just seen, Lucilla pulled away and grabbed fistfuls of Pascal's uniform jacket. She couldn't think what to say.

"You're not well?" he asked, sounding worried.

"No, no, that's not it. Hell! You just missed him!"

"Missed whom?" He scowled. "You have another lover?"

Lucilla laughed. "This is a hospital operated by women, did you discover that, as well? No, of course I have no lover. This is—not two hours ago, I met a werewolf."

"She was here?"

Lucilla was gratified he had no doubt of her truthfulness. "She? Oh, Kauz's werewolf. No! This was another. A British officer, of all things. Pascal, *I saw him change form.*"

His eyes widened. "Why did he do this? Why did you not tell me immediately?"

"You were kissing me," she pointed out. "I was glad to see you. I forgot."

Pascal leaned down and kissed her again. "And I you. So your werewolf, he's gone?"

"Back to his unit, I'm afraid. He came because of his batman—oh, it's a long story," she said. She didn't think Pascal would betray Hailey's secret, but she didn't have the right to share that secret, so it was better to avoid the subject. Of course, she'd just betrayed Captain Ashby's secret, but that didn't feel the same; she hadn't given his name or identifying information, after all. And she was sure Captain Ashby could take care of himself. Pascal had suspected about werewolves and had been searching for proof. Keeping that proof from him would be a greater betrayal by far.

Pascal said, "You need not tell it to me now. Please, tell him I would like to speak with him. I will give you a way he can send a message to me."

She said, "I'll do it as soon as I can." Weariness settled on her head, pressing her down. "I haven't slept in…I don't know. We can talk about it tomorrow."

"Very well," Pascal said. "I have news for you, though, which should not wait. I, also, have met a werewolf, or someone who claims to be so. I have not seen her change form. She is a spy, a Belgian who is working against the Germans, and I fear she is a bit mad. That is the other reason I came to see you. I wanted to speak to you about this."

"She," Lucilla said. "Is she Kauz's werewolf?"

He hesitated. "I think she might be. She is not very forthcoming. I was not as charming as I might have been."

Lucilla couldn't stop herself from smiling. She cupped his cheek in her hand. He turned his face and kissed her palm, softly from his lips and prickly from his mustache, then slipped his arms around her. She said, "May we talk about it more tomorrow?" She pressed closer to him. "I've missed talking with you."

"I think of you every day. Sometimes, I imagine what you would say. My imagination is not satisfactory, however." His hands slid lower, cupping her rear and squeezing lightly.

"We have to bolt the door," she said. "I can't be caught with a man in here." For the first time, she blessed the exigencies that had led to her sleeping far from the wards. She might not be getting any chemistry done, but at least she could have this benefit.

"Allow me," he said.

Lucilla followed him with her eyes as he threw the bolt and secured the loop of string she'd added for additional privacy. "I suppose we'll have to share the bed," she said. "Only this time it's mine."

How wicked, to invite a man into her bed. She could not think of anything she wanted more. Though if she pondered practicalities, she was sure his feet would freeze. Her bed wasn't long enough for him, and she doubted her blankets were much better. Perhaps he would wake in the night, freezing, and want to find warmer quarters.

Pascal touched her cheek. "I've dreamed of sleeping next to you. I was sorely disappointed each time to wake and find it untrue."

Lucilla couldn't find words to respond to this statement, which held the ring of truth. She turned away from him, dragged her cap from her head amid a spatter of hairpins and tossed it atop a crate. Her short cape was next, then her bloodstained apron. Pascal's hands closed over her shoulders and massaged them for a few moments, occasionally leaning down to kiss the back of her neck. She moaned in relief. "Thank you," she whispered. He helped her with the rest of her clothing, then stripped off his own uniform, heedlessly letting it fall to the dirt floor. Within a few moments, they were crammed together in her narrow bed, one of Pascal's long legs crooked over her hip and his chest hot against her back. He felt so good that she shuddered; she'd forgotten what it was like to be touched so fully, with such intimate intent. He squeezed his arm around her belly, curling his fingers into her waist, circling his thumb on her skin.

He murmured in French, so close to her skin she couldn't discern his words, then kissed her ear. "Sleep."

"Pascal," she whispered, already half drowning in slumber. She remembered nothing more until deep in the night, when she woke, gritty eyed, to his hands gently shaping her breasts.

"Dreaming," she mumbled, turning her face partially toward his nuzzling. His mustache pricked her cheek, then she felt the satiny brush of his tongue at the corner of her mouth.

She turned in his arms and pressed her cold nose into his chest. When he didn't flinch away, she clutched him more tightly.

He eased his arms around her and kissed her behind the ear. "You smell delicious," he said.

"I'm so tired," she said.

His hands stilled, then moved in a long, soothing stroke down her spine. "Go back to sleep, then," he said.

"No," she said. "You came all this way."

"It's enough to lie here with you in my arms."

"That's tosh," she said. "I can feel your cock on my leg."

Pascal chuckled against her hair. "It can remain there. I've not died of it yet."

She took a deep, steadying breath. "If you leave without fucking me, I shall be very angry," Lucilla said.

His arms crushed her close. He didn't say anything.

"That is why you came here, isn't it?" she asked, shifting against him for the pleasurable sensation of their skin stroking across one another. The thin stream of cold air that always worked its way into her hut from one crack or another blew across her bare shoulder, but the rest of her was warming deliciously. A male body provided a sovereign cure against cold weather.

Pascal tucked the blanket back over her shoulder, from where it had fallen. "You didn't want me to see you again," he said. His voice gave nothing away, and his chin blocked her view of his facial expression, dimly lit by electric light shining in the window.

"You're in my bed now, aren't you?"

"I was already here. You could hardly push me out into the night."

Lucilla sighed. "I could have. I do want you."

"If I happen to be present. You would not have sought me out."

He had no right to be angry at her. She'd made no promises. Lucilla sat up and shoved at his chest with her hand. "I didn't think *you* wanted to see *me* again!"

Pascal captured her hand in his and kissed it, hard enough that she felt the pressure of his teeth through his lips. "I did not lie to you at Le Havre! Why did you doubt me?"

His tone was angry, but his expression pained. Lucilla found she couldn't meet his gaze. It wouldn't be wise to tell him that she'd given up trusting men's words long ago. Clearly, he felt he should be an exception. So far, he had proven himself to be an exception. Everything he had done since his arrival spoke of a deeper attachment than Lucilla had dared imagine or hope for. "I'm sorry," she said, and she was. She hadn't meant to hurt him. She'd only worried about being hurt herself.

Pascal still held her hand. He kissed it again, gently this time, his mustache tickling between her knuckles. "If I misread your interest, I'm sorry," he said. "I will leave if you ask me to do so. Even now."

Lucilla snorted and squeezed his fingers. "You don't want to stride nobly out into the night. I appreciate that you offered, though."

"I would do it!" he protested.

"I don't want you to go," she said, took back her hand and lay down again, close enough to feel the warmth radiating from his bare skin. "I was afraid," she muttered. "Afraid I would never see you again."

"Because you want me to fuck with?" he asked, but his tone now was soft, teasing.

She replied, "I could've had any number of dashing young men in my bed if I'd wanted."

Pascal ran his big hand down her arm, raising fine hairs in its wake. "Perhaps one of them would not be so inconvenient as to arrive in the middle of the night, unannounced, and then to discomfit you with talk of affection."

Lucilla laid her head on his shoulder. "One of those men would be a poor bargain, then." She chuckled. "How silly you are. No one else wants me."

"They're incredibly foolish, then." Pascal ducked his head and kissed her, closemouthed but lingering. "I obtained two English journals and read your work. You are worth any five of the men I knew at Cambridge."

Lucilla blinked. "What?"

"The Journal of Palliative Care," he said. "And the other, *Pharmacopia.*"

"You read—"

"I am not entirely sure I understood the implications of your report in *Pharmacopia.* My knowledge of chemistry was not sufficient. Perhaps later, you can—"

"Pascal!"

He kissed her ear. "Pardon. I became distracted."

He'd read her work. He'd gone to the trouble to find what she had written, to seek out journals in a foreign tongue and then to both read them and strive for understanding. No one, not even her own mother and father, had ever done so much, cared so much about the work she'd spent years producing. A glow expanded to fill her chest and belly, a deep joy such as she'd never felt before. Lucilla captured Pascal's cheeks between her palms and kissed him softly. "Enough talking," she said.

She pushed him flat, arching herself over him, letting her

nipples tease his chest, teasing herself at the same time, staring into his eyes and watching them crinkle at the corners. He would have creases there when he grew older. Propping herself on one arm, she smoothed her hand over his tousled brown hair, then pressed his mouth open with her fingers. His tongue swept out, encircling, sucking. She closed her eyes, swaying. She collapsed against him slowly, nestling herself into each hollow of his long body, stroking his lips and mustache with her damp fingers, then letting him suck them again.

After a while, he dragged her up along him until they could kiss mouth to mouth. Lucilla experimented, brushing her lips so lightly against his that it felt as if a breeze blew over her skin. She licked her lips, then his, and did it again, pressing in slowly until their mouths slid slickly one across the other. Pascal made a sound, and she knew he'd made the same mental connection she had, of his cock sliding wetly in her vagina. She couldn't keep up her teasing long. After a quick taste of his inner lip, she plunged her tongue into his mouth for a long, deep kiss, and slid her hand down to mimic the action on his cock. When she drew back from his mouth, Pascal laughed unsteadily. His hands moved restlessly over her back. "You are ravishing me," he whispered. "Please continue."

"Hmm," she said. "Anything I like?"

"I would be pleased to discover what pleases you," Pascal said. "Then may we converse?"

"About?" Lucilla teased the tip of her finger beneath his foreskin and watched him arch and shudder.

"What—what we will do."

"I thought that was quite clear," she said, giving his cock a firm stroke.

"After. What we will do when the war ends." Pascal's eyes

squeezed shut, then he opened them and stared directly at her. "I don't wish to lose you."

She didn't want to spoil this moment. "Later," she said. "We'll speak of it later."

"Very well." His hand closed over hers, stopping her movement. "We have many things to talk about, together."

Lucilla smiled. "That's true." Still smiling, she bent and kissed him, then slid down upon his cock.

Afterward, she lay half on, half beside him in the narrow bed, petting his chest hair with one hand and cupping his jutting hipbone with the other, her thumb circling lightly on the thin skin there. "I would like to read some of your writing," she said. "Is any in English, or German? I'm afraid my technical vocabulary in French is nonexistent, outside of chemistry."

"I—" His hand shifted on her back. "I would like to, but I fear I cannot."

"I see." She asked, "Have you reported on research like Kauz's experiments? With people or animals?"

"No!"

"But he's part of it, isn't he? Kauz, and what he did. Does."

Warily, Pascal said, "Perhaps."

"Why?"

"I cannot tell you." He turned and looked closely at her. "They are not my secrets to share."

His expression pled for understanding. She said reluctantly, "I don't want to put you in danger."

"Others, more than me," he said. "I will tell you later, if I can obtain permission. I want to tell you more."

He was keeping secrets from her, yet she still trusted him. She said, "I'll hold you to it."

13

PASCAL USED THE SERVANTS' ENTRANCE TO SLIP
into the house at Rue Deuxième. He'd been hoping no one
would notice he'd been gone for two days longer than his
errand had warranted. The entrance was guarded, of course,
but only by old Armand, who knew where he'd gone and
why, and had cared for Pascal's cats in his absence. Pascal set
a bottle of wine on the kitchen table, and Armand turned it
to see the vintage. "I hear that Antwerp has surrendered to
the Boche," he said. "Did our people escape?"

"There is no word yet." Armand shook his head, as if to fling
off worry, and said, "And your errand? It was successful?"

Pascal broke into a smile.

Armand cackled. "If only I were twenty years younger, I
would have accompanied you, and found myself a pretty
English nurse." He tapped out his pipe and added, "You're a
good boy, bringing me wine that I cannot afford on my
pension. If you stay here and watch the door, I will make you
coffee and an omelette."

He hadn't eaten in almost nine hours. "Gladly." He took over Armand's chair, checked the pistol that lay to hand and propped his aching feet on a crate of turnips. "My informant—the blond woman—was to return this week. Did you see her?" Armand knew everything that went on in the Rue Deuxième.

Armand looked up from the basket of onions. "The skinny one? Who is mad?"

"She's not—"

Armand shook his head sadly. "Mad. She would cut a man's balls off, that one, should he cross her. My second cousin's third wife—"

Pascal interrupted; Armand's stories could stretch indefinitely. "Have you seen Madame Claes at all this week? Or had any word of her here?"

"None at all. She went to Antwerp, you know."

Pascal's stomach plunged to his feet. "She did not."

"She did. The colonel had a message, and she said she would take it, and no one else. We do not know if she was successful. We will not know until Piron and Verhelst return, if they return."

Pascal cursed, long and fluently, while Armand broke eggs into a bowl, added a little milk and beat them to a froth. As he wound down, Armand said, "I thought the English nurse was your woman. You are after the mad Belgian, too?"

"It is imperative she stay alive," he growled. "She is the most excellent spy we have."

"Not if she cannot obey orders," Armand said. "In my day, men were shot for less." He folded the omelette.

"She is not a soldier," Pascal said. "She has signed no papers. Our only hold on her is her hatred of the Boche."

"Ah," said Armand. "That hold can be powerful."

"Not if her own hatred is stronger than is useful. I fear she will do something foolish, and be killed, and then where shall we be?" Pascal stared down at the omelette Armand slid in front of him and remembered one of his first meetings with Madame Claes.

He'd sat across a table from her, and pushed papers across its surface. "If you memorize these maps now, as a human, it should help you as a wolf."

Her lip curled. "Do you think me a fool? I have already studied maps of the terrain."

"Unless you can fly, these maps are better. They show the lines of entrenchment from the air."

She spread the maps and peered at them, silently tracing lines with her finger. She said at last, in a distant tone, "It should not be, but it is true. From above, the lines look exactly the same. Never mind. I will know them by their scent."

Pascal wondered if she could truly tell friend from enemy by scent. If she could, would she have been taken captive by Kauz? And what if she was taken captive in Antwerp?

Many duties awaited him, many more pressing than the fate of one woman, but he felt more responsible for her fate than for any other's. She'd come to him first, with information, but she might not have continued had he not encouraged her and tried to channel her abilities for the good of France and, ultimately, Belgium. Had he been wrong to do so? He wasn't used to doubting and rethinking his decisions in this way. He tried to remain scrupulously logical in these matters, but this time he had followed his emotions, as he did too often with women. Perhaps it had been unwise to trust that Madame Claes would know when the danger she courted was too much.

Also, she was more than just a woman. She had survived the cruelest torments in both her forms, and had gone on to bravely fight her enemy with all her strength. He admired that. He did not think he would have been so brave, himself. He admired her, and he liked her, for her bravery and for her cutting sarcasm and cold humor that met his every verbal sally in kind. He refused to believe that she was dead. He would first discover if indeed Kauz had taken her, rather than some more mundane authority, and second where she was being held. He could not let her be held captive again.

He took heart when he remembered Lucilla. He would be able to enlist her help, and perhaps that of the werewolf captain. If he could find Madame Claes, the rest would be possible. Pascal took a glass of wine from Armand, sipped and began to eat his omelette. He could set the search in motion as soon as he'd eaten.

He could begin with Kauz's laboratory; perhaps this time he could locate its secret counterpart where once Kauz had held a werewolf captive. His superiors might not be happy with him for diverting resources in such a way, but he could see no alternative. He had once sworn he would aid the survival of werewolves as best he could. He could do no less than make this effort, and if Kauz was involved, then all the better. He could eliminate a threat to werewolves and a threat to his country with one blow.

"Miss Daglish?"

Lucilla jerked in surprise, her hand to her chest. She'd been rushing from her hut to X-ray to pick up the most recent films on behalf of Miss Rivers. It had rained all night, and the paths were awash in soupy mud. Her hands ached from the damp cold. She tucked them beneath her arms as she turned slowly, and confronted Captain Ashby. "Where did you come from?"

"Hailey told me you wanted to see me. Thank you for the chocolate."

"It was meant for my brother."

He laughed. His cheeks were ruddy from the wind, his eyes alive with humor. "Daglish was kind enough to share it." He cocked an eyebrow. "You can send more whenever you like. My favorite is the Belgian sort."

"Cheeky," she said. "I'm on my way to the ward just now. Can you wait a few moments?"

"I'll wait in Hailey's storage shed, how's that?"

"Don't let anyone see you," she said, and hurried on. As she delivered the films, she pondered what to tell Captain Ashby, and how to tell it to him. She had broken his confidence by telling Pascal of his existence, but stood by her decision. It was too late to do otherwise. She would have to go forward without shirking, as she had when she and Pascal had stolen Kauz's motor.

It wasn't so easy to sneak away from Sister Inkson, the latest crop of earnest young *mademoiselles,* and one or two of her mobile patients, but she managed it with the help of a preoccupied expression, a purposeful walk and an armful of linens. She dumped the linens on an orderly and escaped out a side door. It had begun to rain, the chilly sort of downpour that made her bones twinge. Disregarding uniform protocol, she draped her cape over her head and dashed for the storage sheds.

Captain Ashby crouched in a rear corner next to crates of knitted scarves that had been donated from women's organizations all over the empire. He rose gracefully when she entered and shoved his cap onto the back of his head, revealing some of his cropped gingery hair. Lucilla envied his ease of movement; she herself felt as if she'd been trampled by cavalry. She said, "Thank you for waiting."

"I never mind waiting for a woman," he said. "Why did you need to speak with me?"

"Have a seat," she suggested, taking one herself atop a crate of disinfectant. The bottles within clanked as she shifted uneasily. When Ashby was seated across from her, she said, "I know a man who works for the French government, and he would like to consult with you." She hesitated. "I didn't tell him your name, or anything like that. But I'm afraid he knows you are a werewolf."

Ashby was silent for a long time. After a few moments, Lucilla asked, "Are you *smelling* me?"

More solemnly than she'd ever heard him speak, he said, "Yes. Sometimes truth has its own scent. This man—he is French?—he knew about werewolves already, didn't he?"

"He suspected."

"He probably knew," Ashby said. "It isn't something most people think about. Is he a werewolf himself?"

"No!" She paused. "At least, I don't think so—" Wouldn't he have said so? Would Pascal have told such a thing to her? Why hadn't it occurred to her that he might have more than his stated motive for investigating Kauz? He *had* been evasive when she'd asked about his work.

Ashby continued, "Or perhaps he's related to one. We don't always breed true, you know, at least not with humans. It's not that uncommon to find a human with a trace of the blood. You can smell it on them. Sometimes they have hints of it—a better sense of smell, or hearing, or extra strength or endurance." He paused. "And sometimes there are humans who know of us, and intend us harm."

Lucilla's mind swam with possibilities. She forced them from her mind for later contemplation. She could not remain here long, and she had to give Ashby her message. "I don't know, but he does not intend you harm. I would stake my reputation on it," she said. "If you decide to speak to him, perhaps you will find out." She produced a sealed envelope from her apron pocket. "He gave me this. It has instructions for how to send him a letter, and, also, a telephone number, which he would appreciate you destroying as soon as possible. We have a telephone here, in the main hospital building. I might be able to get you in to use it."

Ashby took the envelope, his callused fingers brushing hers. "I'll have to come back for that, or find another telephone. I'm due at my regiment soon, we're to meet with a German officer about a burial truce. It wouldn't do for me to be late." He paused, then said, "I have a friend. Lieutenant Gabriel Meyer. He knows what I am. If you can't get through to me for some reason, try to contact him, instead. He will know how to find me."

"Captain—Major Fournier is an ally. I am sure of it." She *was* sure. She knew Pascal was not like Kauz. She paused. Pascal might have lied to her for other reasons, however. Some of those reasons, she might understand. "If he is…not quite human…will you keep his secret, if he keeps yours?"

"Don't worry about that, Miss Daglish. It's a matter of honor among my kind. If you're not sure I can be trusted, bite my neck and I'll have to obey your orders, whatever they might be. It's a dominance ritual. Wolves do it all the time."

Lucilla made a face. "You are ridiculous, Captain."

Ashby smiled at her, guileless as a babe. "No, it's true. Why can't you believe such a simple thing? You believe I'm a werewolf—"

"I *saw* that," Lucilla pointed out. "How do I know you're telling the truth about this?"

"Only one way to find out," Ashby said. He unbuttoned the collar of his uniform tunic and tugged it aside. His neck looked startlingly pale and vulnerable. "Would I let you do this if I didn't trust you?"

"Would you give me power over you?" Lucilla countered. "I wouldn't."

"I want your trust. You won't give it to me unless you feel confident I won't…well, do whatever you're worried I'll do. I only eat rabbits and rats and such, but if you won't believe me, then…" He tipped his head to the side. "Go on."

Lucilla already couldn't believe she was hiding in a storeroom with a handsome young man. The fact that he could turn into a giant, hairy wolf was only a little stranger than that. But the idea of her teeth touching his skin seemed more unbelievable than anything else. She couldn't imagine doing such a thing, here in the hospital, in a world where she only touched the ill and wounded.

Best to get on with it, then, as with any disturbing task. She leaned forward. Ashby smelled of bergamot cologne and gun oil. Before she could lose her courage, she pressed her mouth to his throat. The bristly rasp beneath his chin startled her, and she jerked back. He didn't taste like Pascal. "Well?" she said.

Ashby's breathing had sped up. "You didn't bite me."

"You moved," she said.

"I didn't—" He shut his mouth and lifted his chin. Lucilla leaned forward and, as gently as she could, pinched his skin between her teeth. He didn't move. She put her hand on his shoulder, to steady herself, but her fingers must have curled in too hard, because Ashby shuddered beneath her touch. "Harder," he said.

Lucilla drew back and licked her lips. She could taste him. His eyes looked huge in the dim light, and she could feel a flush building in her cheeks. She bit the rigid cord where neck met shoulder and slowly, slowly increased the pressure. It reminded her too much of sex. Pascal had liked it when she bit his neck. She liked it, too. Ashby tasted... Did it have to do with him being a werewolf? She wanted to lick Ashby's skin and imprint him on her taste buds. She wanted to bite him more softly, and then suck at his flesh. Ashby moaned.

Lucilla jerked back. If she'd hurt him, it was his own fault, but she didn't want to continue hurting him. She tried to step away and Ashby caught her around the waist. "Stop!" she commanded.

He froze.

She laid one hand flat on his chest. His heart raced, and his breath caught. Suspicion blossomed. "You enjoyed that," she said.

Ashby grinned slowly. "I didn't say I *wouldn't*."

Lucilla pulled out of his grip and stepped back. "You cad! You lied to me!"

"I did not!" He was laughing now.

"*Dominance ritual.* What complete and utter tosh. You were trying to seduce me!"

"You don't like being seduced? I like it. I wish you'd do it again."

"Wolves don't really do those things," Lucilla said.

"They do!" Ashby looked at her hopefully, then sighed and

buttoned up his collar again. "It's true that they're very hier-archical. It's only that the hierarchy changes at need." He paused. "For me, it's important that you were willing to do that. I'm more than willing to do your bidding." The tone of his voice made it clear what sort of bidding he would like.

Lucilla smacked his arm. "If only that were true."

He grinned at her. "I *am* willing to do your bidding. Truly. I will speak to your Frenchman."

Lucilla blew out an exasperated breath. "Thank you."

Ashby leaned in and kissed her, lightly, on the mouth. "Thank *you*. Just let me know if you change your mind about future biting, all right?" Then he was gone.

Noel crawled forward a few more inches. He and his two companions were now fifty yards into this wide stretch of no-man's-land, the closest they were likely to get to the enemy without being seen. He lifted his field glasses again, wedging them beneath the brim of his uniform cap. Sharp bits of rock dug into his hip, where the fabric of his trousers was not quite thick enough for protection, and newly deployed coils of wire atop the German trench obscured his view. Forcing himself to ignore the distractions, he murmured his estimates of the enemy manpower in the trenches a hundred yards away, doing so more by smell than sight. To his left, Lincoln scribbled the numbers in a dirty notebook. To his right, Denham's beefy hands restlessly caressed his rifle.

If one's nose could ache, his did, from too long spent crammed together with too many men, all of them in des-perate need of a bath and a good night's sleep; the sour tang of exhaustion exuding from their skin was worse than the stench of sweat. The Germans, from what he could gather on the wind, were in a similar state, their individual scents muddled together with layered masks of weariness and fear. Only their food smells differed. If all humans could smell with the acuity of wolves, he pondered for the millionth occasion, would they be able to go to war with each other?

He was thankful for the burial details that had gone out earlier in the day, under a flag of truce. Otherwise, this duty would be unbearable.

"Sir," Denham rumbled. "I could pick a couple off from here. Just give me leave."

"And we'd be peppered before we drew another breath," Ashby said. He encouraged his men to think and always be ready for the main chance, but some of them were idiots. He scrubbed beneath his nose with a gloved finger, trying to take advantage of his momentary freedom from confinement to enjoy a few clear breaths. Or as clear as he was likely to get—the dirt here between the trenches was impregnated with sharp reminders of metal and old blood. He handed the field glasses to his left and said, "Lincoln, start back. Denham, you follow."

"I'm supposed to cover you, sir. I should go last."

"Nobody's shooting anybody, so you may as well go. I want a closer look."

"Not safe, sir."

"From you, Denham, that is quite amusing." Noel reached over and patted the larger man's elbow. "Keep an eye on Lincoln. I'll be along shortly."

"Sir."

The rustling of uniforms and soft breathing retreated. Noel closed his eyes and rested his chin on his forearms, making himself a smaller target. He wished he could change and go for a run. Broad daylight was not safe for that, and at night the trench became a beehive of activity that he was required to direct. The brief shift he'd made for Lucilla Daglish was the last time he'd been a wolf.

He wondered if the Frenchman, Pascal Fournier, was a werewolf, as well. Nothing of his scent had clung to the folded paper; the carbolic stench of Miss Daglish's apron pocket had obliterated every trace. Once they met, Noel would know for sure. If he could manage it. He wouldn't have the opportunity to use a telephone capable of reaching Paris for another three days. Obtaining leave would take at least another day, probably more if Major Harvey was feeling particularly obnoxious.

Perhaps if Fournier was a werewolf, he would also have an unmarried sister. Or know a wolf who did. Noel had decided Miss Daglish didn't need to know that portion of his motivation for meeting with Fournier. His desire for a wife and children was frivolous in his current setting. A child or two would not be much of a return for the wanton destruction of several nations at war.

Time to return to the crowded trench. Perhaps he would spend a little time inspecting the advance trench before returning to the company, and exchange small talk with Southey, who would be on sniper duty there. He gathered himself to crawl backward and stiffened.

The wind changed, and brought a new scent, thick and chemical. Noel lifted his nose to the breeze and inhaled. Immediately, he sputtered and coughed, his nostrils throbbing hotly. It didn't smell like the residue of explosives. He couldn't identify it at all.

His curiosity warred with a keen sense of danger. If he was in danger, so, too, were his men. He needed to investigate;

no one else would have detected such a scent at this distance, or be able to find its source.

He crept forward instead of back, his nose half-tucked into the collar of his woolen tunic in a futile attempt at protection from the invisible thread of painful scent. The ground dipped and surged with shell holes, and his progress was slow. Denham and Lincoln would be wondering why he hadn't returned yet.

Noel was halfway up the side of a hole when he heard the distant whistle of the first shell and, closer, a murmur of voices speaking German. He wasn't going to make it back in time. If he made it back at all.

14

DARKNESS WAS FALLING LIKE A CURTAIN OVER bare and broken trees, and Crispin knew they had to get back, whether they'd found Ashby or not. His whistle was muddy. He grimaced and stuck it between his lips anyway, breathing out lightly. Pittfield's head lifted cautiously. Crispin signaled him toward the trench, noting that Denham followed Pittfield, and Lincoln was on their heels. Crispin hesitated before scrambling to follow them. He didn't want to see Meyer's face when he returned with no news.

Perhaps no news was better than dragging Ashby's corpse. Though the cap in his pocket might be worse. He could feel the wolf badge digging into his chest as he scrambled through clods of mud and scraps of metal.

All too soon, the twists and turns became familiar. With half his attention, he took note of fallen revetments, the sacks leaking chalk; sunken, rotting duckboards awash in soupy mud; a wall melting around its wooden supports, all of it needing repair. He passed tight clumps of men, pressing to the sides of the trench to allow him passage, and could not bring himself to look at them or speak. Meyer waited for him in front of the dugout. What could he say? What should he say? All he wanted to do was fling himself into Meyer's arms to hold him and ease the blow of the news he brought.

By the time he'd drawn close enough to speak, he didn't need to. Meyer must have seen it in his face. His blue eyes widened behind his spectacles, then squeezed shut. He turned abruptly and shoved past the curtain blocking off the dugout. Crispin was left standing, one boot in the mud, throat too tight to breathe.

Bob handed Daglish his mail. He'd received a letter from his mother, and several from teachers at the school where he'd worked, and even more from his former students; she recognized all the names, now, after so many months. It was a good haul, the best in the company. He only looked at her forlornly.

Bending close to him, she whispered, "Buck up. You'll get some choc next time."

She surprised a brief, sweet smile out of him. "Thanks," he said.

On her way to Meyer, she detoured around the fire step, currently occupied by Mason with a pair of binoculars and his rifle, and then trotted along the duckboards laid in the bottom of the trench, her boot heels no louder than the rattle of the chilly November rain. Lyton and Southey and Lincoln, hunched over a pail of burning coke, chaffed her as she passed; she tossed remarks back, but didn't stop to chat. The mud beneath the walkway was already thin as soup and considerably less appetizing. The men shoring up a wall with sacks of chalk were standing in slop to their calves, and cursing it dully every other breath. She could only imagine what the muck would be like in a day or two, especially if the rain kept up. Though perhaps the rain would stop. She could smell snow in the air.

She thanked Providence that she would be sleeping in a dugout, not in one of the makeshift holes the other enlisted men had scraped out of the trench's walls. She couldn't imagine that mud wouldn't seep into their blankets, no matter the oilcloth tarps or how much scrap wood and paper they crammed in for insulation, and the winter cold would only grow worse. There would be chilblains aplenty, if not frostbite. If they were lucky, the war would end soon, and they wouldn't have to worry about spending winter in holes in the ground.

The officers' dugout didn't have a door yet, only several overlapping layers of heavy canvas. She ducked through, startling Lieutenant Meyer, who hunched over a makeshift table studying a heap of miscellany in the light given by a single stub of candle. She brushed past the coats hung on the dugout's central support pole and said, "Sir."

Glancing down at the table, she realized the miscellany had belonged to Ashby—his cap still bore a stain of mud from where Daglish had plucked it from the battlefield. She recognized his penknife, with its silver plate engraved with the regiment's running-wolf device, and his favorite deck of cards, the ones with photographs of buxom women on the backs. Some of the women wore ribbons in their hair, or perhaps a single garter or a necklace, but nothing else. A hard way to make a living. At least soldiering wasn't as bad as posing naked in front of a camera, or maybe they didn't think so. At least a photography studio would be warm. And less likely to explode.

Meyer looked away from her. He rubbed the side of his

hand beneath his nose and sniffed. "Is there anything else I should send to his mother? I think—I think he was wearing his wristwatch."

His voice sounded thick. Lord. He'd been crying. She shouldn't feel so surprised. Ashby had been Meyer's friend since boyhood, after all, and today's incident with a shell had probably reminded him that they would never find Ashby's body, would never really know how he'd died. Bob couldn't blame him; after she'd heard Ashby had been killed, she had cried a bit herself, first making sure no one could find her. He'd been so kind and funny, and she'd spent so much time taking care of him, that it was a hard loss to bear, especially when she first saw his things lying about, the little framed photograph of his parents and their dogs, and his shaving kit and such as that. But for her it was not as hard as it would be for someone who'd known him for a lifetime. She wasn't sure quite what to do. Did she excuse herself, and leave Meyer to his grief? Did she pretend she hadn't noticed? Or did she offer comfort?

Ashby would have offered comfort. She remembered the hard pressure of his arms around her after Captain Wilks had been killed, his palm holding her face to his chest so she wouldn't look at the captain's bloodied corpse anymore. She'd briefly felt his lips against her hair. At the time, she didn't think he could have guessed she was female; he was simply doing his best for her. One really couldn't ask for more than that.

She'd been trying not to think about Ashby's bloodied corpse, or what was probably left of it by now. Having not seen his body, she was free to imagine the worst, as if all the horrors she'd seen up close weren't enough. It wasn't fair that someone like Ashby, so full of movement and grace, should be still, that someone so full of life should be dead. It was war, and they knew when they took the king's shilling that they might be going to their deaths, but she'd never signed anything that said she had to like it. And Meyer, he was a soldier now, but really he was only a bandsman.

Before she could lose courage, she moved in close to Meyer and put her arms around his shoulders, pulling him back so his head rested on her belly, and then held him as tightly as she could.

His breath hitched, and his eyes closed behind his specs. She could see the wet tracks on his cheeks, and his nose looked red. He sucked in a ragged breath, then another. "Sorry," he said.

"S'all right," she said. His golden hair looked like sunshine in the flickering light of the oil lamp, warm and honey-sweet summer sunshine. She couldn't resist touching her cheek to it, and once touching it, didn't want to pull away. She wanted to rub her face against his hair, then against his skin. Her hands were big for a woman's, but they would fit nicely into his open collar, and she bet herself that his skin was a lot warmer than hers.

It had been years since she'd touched a man's skin, outside of the ordinary ways relating to her duties. She'd thought she was done with all that when she went into the army, had put it off like her skirts and her long hair. She'd thought about sex sometimes, mostly remembering the men whom she'd loved before she'd taken on men's clothing: Johnny, who worked down at the pub, and Johnny's soldier cousin that one time, and Ted, who'd wanted her to marry him though he spent eight months of the year at sea, and dear Rob, who'd died in India. It didn't seem proper, or safe, to think that way about the men with whom she worked every day. It was better not to remember that she didn't have a cock between her legs as they did. It was just that Meyer smelled so good, bay and lime overlaying his skin, his skin that she knew would be warm and alive beneath her fingertips, the exact opposite of the cold mud that surrounded them on all sides. Knowing she couldn't touch him twisted her chest with pain.

Then she thought, *Why not?*

All her thoughts had taken only a moment. Before she could stop herself, she slipped her hand past the opened top button of his uniform tunic, past the loosened knot of his tie. The linen of his shirt was soft from many washings; she twitched it aside and eased her hand beneath his wool vest, laying her hand flat against his pectoral muscle. She'd been right, his skin was hot. She could feel his intake of breath. He didn't thrust her away, though, which surprised her. Had Ashby told him her true sex? She hadn't thought he would break a promise like that, after he'd risked his own life and career to protect her secret. Had Meyer somehow discovered it for himself?

Meyer reached up and covered her hand with his. Though his shirt separated them, she could feel his hand's warmth through the cloth. He drew breath as if to speak, hesitated, and then said, "Noel told you, then."

"Told me?" She flattened her hand just slightly, enough so her palm curved against his skin. She felt only the barest hint of chest hair. Blond men didn't usually have much. Perhaps he had more, closer to the center of his chest. Or lower. She swallowed, trying to remember if she'd ever seen him with his shirt off. He was one of the most physically reticent men in the company. She'd never been sure if that was part of his religion or just part of him.

She'd lost track of what he'd been saying. She startled when he spoke again, his voice vibrating beneath her hand. "About when we were boys. About—what he and I did together."

His meaning took a few moments to sink in. "Oh!" she said. "No, sir." She felt a blush heating her cheeks. She hadn't thought Ashby interested in that sort of thing, nor Meyer, either; then again, boys would fuck anything, given the chance. It ought to have disturbed her, but it didn't. If she thought about it a little more, Ashby and Meyer together, it wasn't distasteful to her. She felt more curious than anything else. They'd been so fond and sweet with each other, as much as men showed such things. What had they been like as lovers?

Meyer sighed. "He didn't tell you. It's me, isn't it? It's something I do."

"What is?"

"Perhaps I just imagine that I like women. It seems real at the time, but maybe I'm wrong." As he spoke, his hand idly caressed hers through his vest. She wished he was touching her skin, perhaps lacing his fingers with hers. "Or is it that men like me?" He chuckled softly. "It's not as if I turn them away. What, nothing to say, Hailey?"

She considered. He would find out soon enough that she wasn't what she appeared, and in truth his concerns seemed a bit silly to her. She leaned over and kissed his mouth, upside down, a strange sensation given his mustache and the awkwardness of their positions, but sparking with electricity all the same. She flicked out her tongue to taste just inside his lips, and straightened, seeing spots from the awkward way she'd bent her neck. "'S good," she said.

Meyer took a quick breath. "It's not really permissible," he said. "I'm an officer."

She considered logistics, and nuzzled his temple, briefly tasting his skin. "You going to tell?"

"I would never do that to you."

"Knew you wouldn't. Me, neither." She slid her hand a little farther down into his shirt, leaning against his back to do so. He did have a bit more hair toward the center. She circled her hand around once and found a nipple, hard as a fingertip. Her own nipples were well hidden beneath the layers of her tunic, her shirt, her vest and her cloth breast bindings, but she fancied she could feel his back muscles against them a bit. She'd like to have her breasts bare and rasping against that little scruff of hair on his chest. The very thought made her wet between her legs. It had been absolutely forever. Her body was yelling at her to get closer to him, and quickly. She tried a little persuasion with her fingertips. "You'll feel better, after."

Meyer breathed unsteadily. He said, "You mustn't feel obligated to improve my morale. I've dealt with grief before. I'll survive Noel's death, and so will you. We can talk about it."

"Don't like talking," she said. Talking too much was a fast way to betray far too much.

"You don't know what you're doing."

"Not a virgin," she said. She kissed his ear. "C'mon. Where's the harm?"

"Fraternization?" he said. "Court martial?"

"Good way to get sent home," she pointed out, grazing her teeth against the fine skin behind his ear. She was pleased when he shivered, tipping his neck toward her mouth.

"There's another thing I should tell you—"

"After." She didn't like letting go of him, but it looked as though he wouldn't move on his own. She grabbed his arm and towed him toward the cot shoved against the far wall.

"Wait!" Meyer tugged free of her grip and grabbed a

wooden sign from atop a crate. Daglish had made it. It read, Maestro at Work. Please Do Not Disturb. Meyer hung the sign from a loop of twine on the makeshift canvas door, then shoved his chair and a crate against it to make a flimsy barricade.

Bob nodded, approving. "Come on, then," she said. She began to unwrap her puttees. She was damned if she would fuck a man while wearing boots.

Meyer halted in front of her. "You're sure about this." He paused as she sat on the cot, untied her boots and yanked them off. It felt wonderful to have her boots off. He said, "You look sure. You really want this?"

She tipped her head back and examined him. He looked befuddled. He reached out one hand slowly, and brushed her hair back from her forehead. He asked, "How old are you?"

"Twenty-four."

"You look a lot younger than that. Tell me the truth now." His finger trailed down her cheek, which she knew was downy as a child's.

"Twenty-four, sir," she said. "Record says nineteen, though."

Meyer didn't ask why; usually, boys gave a false age older than their real one. Maybe he was starting to figure it out. He touched the corner of her eye. "I believe you," he said. Bob grabbed his wrist and put his hand behind her neck. While his fingers played in her hair, she unbuttoned her tunic and the flap of her trousers.

She needed to stand to properly undress. She didn't want to fuck with clothes on. She might be blown to bits tomorrow. Today, she was going to enjoy being alive. She jerked her chin at Meyer. "Get your kit off."

"You're not at all worried about being caught, are you?"

She shook her head. Meyer's hands went to his buttons. His

knuckles were scraped, from when they'd dug out the collapsed wall near the firestep. He always pitched in if there was work to be done, if his duties allowed. She liked that about him. She'd loved Wilks like an uncle, but he'd never gotten his hands dirty if he could help it. Meyer shed his uniform tunic and stopped, noticing her watching him. "What about you? Are you going to stop there?" he asked, challenging but not really. He was, she realized, giving her yet another chance to withdraw.

She stood up and flipped her braces off her shoulders, then shoved her trousers down. It didn't make much difference, as her gray-back shirt hung down to her knees, and she had a layer of woolen long underwear. She went to Meyer, the dirt floor cold beneath her bare feet, and pulled him down to her for a proper kiss, which he gave without reluctance. His mouth tasted sweet, and she liked the rough brush of his mustache as he nibbled at her lips. She pulled away first. "More later," she said. She started in on her buttons. Out of the corner of her eye, she saw Meyer do the same. When she'd draped her shirt over a crate, he yanked his vest over his head. As his chest was revealed, the hair there caught the candlelight, sparking gold. She did like a man who looked like a man. His torso narrowed down nicely toward his waist, and when he turned she had a fine glimpse of his high, tight rear. She could just imagine her hands on it, his muscles flexing, her fingers digging deep.

Bob hurriedly stripped off her vest and shoved down her drawers, her stuffed sock with them; she quickly tucked that out of sight in the folds of her discarded clothing. The cold air made her scarred shoulder ache, and she rubbed it. She still had to unwind her breast wrappings, and step out of the cropped drawers, her own invention, that she wore to keep her sock from chafing her thigh.

Meyer was struggling out of his boots, hopping on one foot. It was the first time she'd ever seen him be the least bit awkward, and she laughed. Meyer looked up, and stopped, one foot swinging in the air. Gently he put his foot down on the floor again and held out his hand.

She took his hand and placed it on her breast. He swore in a foreign language. She grinned. "Hurry up," she said.

He looked as if he wanted to say something else, then shook his head, grinned back at her and took his socks off. He looked happier than he had a few minutes before. More than shocked, he'd been relieved she was really a woman. She watched, expectant, as he shoved off his trousers. He wasn't all the way erect yet, but she could see the shape of him through his drawers, and her mouth and cunt both watered a little, wanting him to fill her up.

He stopped with his hands on the string of his drawers and said, "I want to see, too."

Abruptly, she felt strange. Since she'd first put on men's clothes, she'd never unbound her breasts in front of anyone, not even Sister Daglish when she'd cared for her wound. It scared her to think of doing it now. She forced her feet to move, one step closer to Meyer, then another. She took his hand and brought it to the little flat hooks in the middle of her chest.

He seemed to understand. He kissed her softly, and then worked the hooks loose, one at a time. She watched his hands, slender and graceful, with those odd calluses he'd told her came from playing the cello. She hadn't thought of music as work until she'd known that. She liked that his hands had worked. She could understand the hours he'd spent, mastering a skill as she'd once mastered tailoring jackets.

The last hook slid loose, and he met her eyes, steady and reassuring. "What next?"

"Like this," she said, unwinding the wrapping beneath her arm, around her back and beneath her other arm. Meyer took the fabric from her hand and continued to unwind it himself. Bob lifted her arms and, after a moment, rested her hands on his bare shoulders, letting him free her. His skin felt hot and smooth. She circled her fingertips on him and his breath caught.

His face was intent as the cloth loosened. She drew a grateful breath and rolled her shoulders; the binding slipped loose, and Meyer caught it in his hand, preventing it from landing on the dirty floor. Without moving his eyes from her chest, he wadded the cloth and tossed it accurately to the crate with her shirt. His hands slid up her ribs and cupped her breasts, so delicately her vision blurred.

She moved her hands atop his and pressed in. He made a small noise of appreciation and his grip shifted and tightened, his thumbs circling on her nipples, stirring them to prickling life after their long captivity. She hummed in appreciation. She put her arms around his neck again and pulled him down for a kiss, slick and exploring.

Meyer pulled back first. "Your name isn't really Robert, is it?"

She thought about teasing him, then decided it could wait. "Isobel," she said. The name felt strange in her mouth. She hadn't said it aloud, or had it said to her, in five years at least.

Meyer's face blossomed into a smile. "That's lovely."

She couldn't quite bring herself to call him *Gabriel*. She'd heard Ashby call him that once or twice, his voice rich with affection. She wouldn't remind him of that right now. This was for feeling, not talking. "There's a cot," she pointed out, and stripped off her last layer of underthings.

"What about protection?"

Bob sighed. "I got a tonic. So I won't bleed. All right?"

He cast a nervous glance at the doorway. She grabbed another crate, this one crammed with cookware, and laid it atop the first one in their barricade, shivering when a cold gust blew in under the canvas. She turned back to face him, hands on her hips. Cold air teased her ankles, and her nipples tightened with cold, a sensation she hadn't felt in a long time. "That better?" she asked.

"Not really," he said. "Come here."

This time they made it to the cot, and she got his drawers off, only to be stopped again when Meyer wouldn't let her yank him down to join her. His cock was interesting, dense and smooth with the veins showing; he'd been cut, his cock didn't have a sleeve. So that was true, about Jewish men. She liked the way it looked. She was getting impatient to have him inside her; she didn't want to risk being interrupted before that. The niceties could wait until they were done. She thought about the narrow space, and said, "I'll bend over."

"In a few minutes," he said. "Lie back."

"But—"

For all his reluctance at the beginning, he certainly liked being in charge. His hands pressed her hips into the blankets, soft blankets that smelled like him, and then rearranged her a little to the side. "Hush, you'll like this." He slid his thumbs down the crease of her cunt and her breath hitched at the delicate sensation.

She had to think a minute to make a sentence. "Not if somebody comes."

"I'm hoping that will be you." She blinked, not having expected ribald humor from him, and while she was distracted, he gently blew on her cunt, warm air as shocking as the cold had been a few moments before. He really meant to do it, then. He was going to kiss her cunt, and she was going to let him.

It was just as good as she'd heard. No, better. She stopped worrying about the time passing, except for the time he made her wait between delicate probes of his tongue and gentle shifts of his fingertips where he held her lower lips open. She seized a handful of blanket and pulled it to her mouth, biting down on it. Meyer looked up at her movement and grinned, then ducked down between her thighs and laid licking kisses along the tender creases where her thigh met her leg, and the soft skin between her pubic hair and navel, and the jut of her hipbone. She squirmed toward his mouth and he pinned her with one firm hand on her belly while he continued to tease, both letting her recover from his original intensity and stoking her desire higher. Then she felt his callused fingertips nudging at her, stroking back and forth until they slid easily, then sliding inside her cunt, only the tips at first. His mouth fastened over her clit and sucked hard, once; she arched and bit down on the blanket. Then his lips pulled softly at her while his fingers slid deeper inside her and his thumb rubbed her hair against her tender flesh.

She was gasping now. "Hurry up, Goddamn you!"

He pulled away enough to say, "I like this." He reached up his free hand and caressed her breast. "Perhaps you'd like to rub these. I haven't enough hands."

Bob meant to tell him where he should stuff his orders, except that her hands had moved as he'd commanded, cupping her own breasts, trapping his hand beneath one of hers. His palm shifted, abrading her nipple, and she gasped, then writhed the other direction when his fingers twisted inside her, sliding deeper. Meyer's mouth moved back to her clit and, as she rubbed and pulled at her own nipples, he flicked her repeatedly with his tongue, harder and harder. She'd been building to a climax for so long that the actual moment took her by surprise. She was about to curse him, then she was coming, frozen and vibrating with the force of it, her hand clenched upon his.

She was too limp after that to complain he'd taken too long, and in too forgiving a mood. When he joined her on the cot, carefully wriggling on his side and putting his arm around her, she snugged her arse up against his cock, so the weight of him pressed into the crease between her buttocks. He made a noise and she pushed back harder, shifting up and down a bit. "Come on," she said, reaching back over her hip and patting him, maybe his flank.

Meyer's hand cupped her breast, fondling her softly. He blew in her ear and said, "Are you sure you don't need a minute?" He reached over her and found a blanket, then tugged it over them. That was nice. She'd been getting a little chilled, once she was no longer in the thick of things.

"Had one." She followed the line of his hip toward his cock, trying to get hold of him. He nuzzled her neck and shifted her hips himself, then slid his cock into her, right then and there, still lying sideways. He didn't go in as deeply as she would have liked, but it had been so long since she'd had a cock in her that that little bit was more than enough to make her breath seize and stutter. She breathed and pushed back against him, so he went in a bit farther.

He rested his hand on her hip and squeezed. "Let me," he said.

"I would, if you'd get on with it."

He chuckled against her shoulder. "This cot isn't that sturdy. We'll have to do it this way." Gently, he rocked his hips forward and back. The cot's metal legs creaked, and it rocked, as well, just a little.

Bob laughed, which felt odd with him inside her. "Jolts like a Jack Johnson hit," she said, then wished she hadn't, because a big shell like that might have killed Ashby.

Meyer kissed her cheek and rocked into her again, soon easing into a steady rhythm. She curved her back into him, liking the soft rub of his chest hair on her skin, and his hot breath, growing ragged now, in her ear. He lifted her thigh up over his leg, and after that was able to work his way in deeper, the head of his cock brushing that sweet spot inside with each push. She also liked the way his arm encircled her rib cage, sometimes pulling her back against him even more tightly, sometimes sliding up to caress her nipples, sometimes sliding down and toying with her clit, circling and pressing in rhythm with the stroking of his cock in her cunt. She hadn't had sex this sweet in a long time, maybe only once or twice before, and she didn't ask him to hurry again.

She closed her eyes, paying attention to the tight slide of him in her and his lips playing in the prickly hair at her nape, breathing and nipping and licking a little, as if she were a sweet. The only thing she missed was being able to have her arms around him, which was a lot easier when one person was on top. This way, he was holding her, but she could only hold on to his arm or the top of his thigh. When his thrusting sped up a bit, though, she forgot all that and grabbed on to the edge of the cot, using it to brace herself as she pushed back onto him. Gradually, she turned more onto her belly, pulling him with her until he was almost straddling her arse, and his cock suddenly sank deeper than it had yet. "Oh, Goddamn it, yes," she said, having lost her grip on the blanket at some point. She arched up toward him, managing to shove a wad of blanket under her like a pillow, and he had to readjust, but then he was in her again, this time from above and behind, fucking her faster and deeper, his hands gripping the sides of the cot as it shivered beneath them.

She buried her face in the edge of his pillow and let herself moan as his thrusting rubbed her clit against the blankets, rubbing her raw, but at the moment it was what she needed. His balls slapped on her arse now, and his breath sawed in and out of him like sobs. The sound of him, his bitten-off groans each time she clamped down on his cock with her cunt, pushed her into wild spasms of pleasure and she screamed into the pillow, pouring out all the tension and fear and grief at once. Minutes later, she was still quivering from the force of her release when Meyer thrust once more, as deep as he could get, and she felt his seed gushing hot into her cunt and down her thighs.

Afterward, she wouldn't let him cuddle too long, as someone would need something soon and come barging in regardless. Regretfully, she had a wash over in the corner, where she wouldn't easily be seen from the door, then hurried into her clothes. Her cunt felt tender, and she didn't enjoy tying down her breasts, but it had to be done. Meyer had only half dressed by the time she looked up, the flap of his trousers hanging loose and his braces down. He'd wiped the sweat from his chest, but sat on the cot still, the wet cloth dangling listlessly from his fingers.

She took it from him. "You'll get cold."

He looked up at her, his eyes a bit vague without his specs. "Noel's still dead."

"We're not."

"No. I suppose not." He picked up his shirt and slipped his arms into it, but kept looking at her.

She fidgeted with her top button and said, "That was good."

One corner of his mouth lifted. "Thanks. Likewise."

"Why so glum?" She turned away after she'd asked, picking up his tie to hand to him.

Still watching her, he began to button up his shirt. "My best friend is—" he hesitated a split second, then continued "—dead, and you ask me what else?"

She flipped up his collar, looped his tie around his neck and touched his chin so he'd lift up. It was easier to talk to him while she fussed with the knot. "You've been funny," she said. "Since before that."

He cleared his throat. "So now I get the traditional advice of the officer's servant?"

"Maybe."

Meyer gently grasped her wrist and lowered it. He looked up at her solemnly for a long time, his eyes searching her face. He didn't do anything else, but she felt as if he was touching her delicately all over. "Thank you," he said.

"What for?"

He grinned again, briefly. "Persuading me. I do feel much better."

He obviously had more to say. She took her hand back from him and tightened the knot of his tie a bit more.

"You don't even have to say *anything,* do you?"

She shook her head.

"All right, then. I fucked Crispin Daglish."

She might have been more surprised about that before she'd known about him and Ashby. She wondered what he meant by fucked, if it meant sodomy or something less serious. It was clear they hadn't been caught, and she hadn't seen Daglish trying to eat his pistol or poke his head into a sniper's rifle, so it didn't make much of a difference, did it? She shrugged. "Where?" she asked.

"Where?"

"Yes, sir." The logistics stymied her. Whose idea had it been? Daglish had been smitten with Meyer since he'd joined the regiment, but hadn't made any kind of advances that she'd seen, or that any of the men had seen, and that kind of thing got around, fast. The men would have been on Daglish like a pack of wolves if they'd suspected him of anything sexually untoward. Even if no one else would have noticed, she would have; she was used to keeping a closer eye on men, simply for her own safety. What had changed? And why was Meyer upset, if men fucking men didn't shock him?

"I shouldn't have done it."

Bob handed him his uniform tunic. He laid it on the cot beside him, stood and began to shove his long shirttails into his trousers. He should have done it the other way around; he was going to have lumps. She watched him and tried to figure out how to explain. She said, "He's got a passion for you."

"What? Now?"

"Since the first." She thought back to when she'd noticed. "Before Southampton."

Meyer strode forward and grasped her shoulders. "Did he tell you that?"

She shrugged. "Saw it. He's a sodomite."

"I'm a bloody sodomite and I couldn't see it."

"No, you're not. Not like him," she said, lifting her chin to indicate the cot. He'd enjoyed fucking her, enough so he'd gone on for longer than she would have dared. "Daglish'd watch you. I watched him. Wanted to make sure he wasn't a wrong'un." Meyer wouldn't have noticed that on his own, not in a thousand years. She'd practically had to bludgeon him to get him to notice her.

Meyer covered his face with his hands. Should she do his trousers up for him, or yank them off and start over again, since he'd made such a mess of it? She found her cap and slapped it on. Meyer said, "I thought I terrified him."

Bob laughed. "I was proper terrified, sir, just now. If you want to terrify me again sometime—"

"I'm not fit to be let out on my own, am I?"

She grinned, patted his shoulder and yanked his shirttails back out of his trousers. "I say that about all the officers, sir."

15

LUCILLA PLACED A FEW MORE BEAKERS INTO THE sterilizer and closed the lid, then put a brick on top in case ground shudders from distant artillery triggered the faulty latch. She straightened slowly, hand pressed to her lower back, and yawned before she saw Matron standing in the doorway.

"Your brother is here," she said.

Lucilla's insides went cold, and she felt short of breath. "He's not hurt, is he?"

"No, no. I'm sorry I frightened you. He only just arrived. I put him in the front parlor."

"Let me wash my hands," Lucilla said. "May I have an hour with him?"

Matron smiled. "Take the afternoon, Daglish. I know you're on duty most of the night."

The casino's former front parlor had been the smallest room, no use for a ward, but its brocaded couches had proved an ideal place to stash visiting officials and the occasional newspaper reporter until someone could see to them. Crispin looked both as if he belonged in such a setting—he'd taken off his cap, and his curls tumbled onto his forehead, giving him a vaguely romantic, vaguely dissolute look—and as if he'd never been inside so elegant a building before, his boots and puttees caked with drying mud, and his uniform showing the signs of some hasty stain removal. He smelled distinctly of one who'd been living in a trench.

Joy spread out from her heart and into her face. He was someone she loved, and he was alive. She dashed across the room and kissed him warmly on the cheek, holding him close to her, not caring that he had come to see her before having a bath. "Crispin, love," she said. "Is everything all right?" She sat next to him on the couch and clasped his hands in hers.

"I'm fine," he said. "But…Hailey told me you knew Captain Ashby."

Her stomach plummeted. "Oh, no," she said. "How?"

"We don't know. We haven't recovered…him yet." Crispin looked down at his hands, twisting his cap between them. "We don't always find—"

"Oh, Crispin," she said, and embraced him again. "I'm sorry. I liked him very much." She could barely believe that he was dead. He'd been more alive than anyone she'd ever met. Belatedly, she realized she would have to tell Pascal.

"We all liked him," Crispin said. "Everyone's pretty broken up about it. Especially Gab—Lieutenant Meyer. They were best friends. Known each other since they were lads." He turned his face away from her and swallowed. "I actually came to talk to you about something else, if that's all right. If you have time. I know you're very busy here, and if you haven't time, I can come back some other day. I'm afraid I have to go back this evening."

"Don't be ridiculous," she said, tucking her grief away for another time. "I know you can't just pop over for tea whenever you like. Did you have any tea?" He shook his head. "Would you like some? We have a nook in the kitchen we use sometimes for chats."

"Please, if it's more private," Crispin said.

Lucilla fetched her personal tin and slipped a lump of her hoarded sugar into Crispin's cup while he warmed the pot. As the tea steeped, she sat across from him at the tiny corner table and grasped his hands. "It's so good to see you."

He stared at their joined hands. "I hope you'll still think so after I've told you."

Lucilla squeezed his hands. "You're a soldier. I know it's your duty—"

"Not that." He pulled his hands from hers. "I think the tea's ready."

"You'll have to tell me sooner or later," Lucilla said. "Else why come all this way?"

Crispin took his tea and turned the cup around and around between his palms. She noticed anew how square and masculine his hands were, his nails perpetually cropped short and the first joints of his fingers dark with curling hair. "Lucilla, I don't think there's another person in the world I trust more than you."

"Thank you." She caressed the top of his head before she sat.

Crispin lifted his cup, then lowered it without drinking. "I'm a sodomite," he said.

Lucilla blinked. She'd expected a bit more general conversation first. Still, he'd accomplished his purpose. He'd unburdened himself to her. And she found she was not shocked or even very surprised. A missing puzzle piece had slid into place. "That makes sense," she said. Something else occurred to her; this wasn't merely a matter of Crispin, but of laws, and presumably army regulations, as well. "You'll be careful?"

"I doubt he'll ever know," Crispin said dourly. "The man I want…we did some things, but not the real thing, you see, and now he hardly speaks to me. So I don't think I'll be caught doing anything I shouldn't."

"Oh, Crispin," she said. "I'm sorry." It had to be terrible, wanting someone he could not have. "Are you sure that he—"

He lifted a hand, and she stopped speaking. "You're not going to say anything else?"

"What is there to say? I don't imagine there's anything I can do to change you, if you're sure. You're still Crispin, and I still love you."

He clasped her hands in his and lowered his head. "Thanks. You can't know how much. I'm still getting used to this, myself. Not knowing—I've always known, I think—but deciding it's no good to pretend otherwise."

"Drink your tea," Lucilla said. "We'll have a nice long chat about it."

After, Lucilla knew far too much about Lieutenant Gabriel Meyer, and not enough about what had happened to Ashby. Would Meyer, who knew Ashby's secret, know anything more than Crispin did? Or perhaps she could obtain more news from Hailey. In the meantime, she passed on the news that she'd met up with Pascal again, fed Crispin all the fresh food he could eat, tucked a deck of cards into each pocket of his uniform tunic for his men and fixed up a tidy packet of sandwiches and chocolate biscuits for him to take back with him.

Crispin stood straighter than when he'd arrived. Perhaps it was the tea; perhaps it was because he'd unburdened himself to her, of a weight he'd been carrying for a lifetime. He didn't look exactly like the Crispin whom she'd known all her life. He looked like a soldier, entirely too much like the men whom she helped sew back together.

"Do be careful," she said, stroking his lapel, straightening his tie. "I couldn't bear to lose you."

Crispin grinned and embraced her. She'd forgotten how strong he was; he squeezed her hard enough to hurt for a moment. "Thanks, Luce. For the cards, too. And don't forget to let me know what happens with your Frenchman."

Lucilla was so sodden with sleep that at first she thought she was dreaming the soft mustache brushing her cheekbone. She turned onto her back, stretching up her arms, and met a solid chest clad in scratchy wool. In her dream, Pascal would be naked or she would know the reason why. She squinted open one eye, feeling as if she stripped off a layer of skin to do so. "What."

"Mon coeur," he said, grinning crookedly. In the light of a single candle, he looked monstrous, indeed a creature out of her dreams. "Rush to my arms and we shall make sweet love until the dawn."

"Bed."

His teeth flashed. "I love your practical nature."

Lucilla closed her eyes, dimly aware of movement and small noises. She must have drifted off again, for her next awareness was of her legs awkwardly bumping Pascal's as he arranged himself comfortably next to her. He wasn't naked, which disappointed her. Then he kissed the corner of her mouth and curled his fingers firmly over her breast, and she didn't mind so much anymore. If she'd had the energy to lift her head, she would have kissed him. She drew in a deep breath and as she let it out, subsided back into sleep.

She woke in time for her shift, before realizing she was off duty for the next twenty-four hours. Sleepily, she cursed until she remembered Pascal had come. She rolled her head to one side and saw his tall form bent, shirtless, over her washstand, attempting to shave in a tiny mirror. She lay still and watched his intent expression, so like when he was focused on her; then her gaze wandered down his shoulders to the sleek muscles of his back until she reached the high waist of his uniform trousers. The cut of them did little for his long legs.

She was still angry with him for not sharing his work with her, but the anger had dulled over time as she contemplated the fact that he had no real reason to trust her with his secrets, other than their physical bond. She might wish it to be otherwise, but wishing brought nothing. In the meantime, he was here, and she was already lonely for his touch.

"Come here," she said once he'd put down his rinsed razor. "Did you come here to see me, or is there news of some kind?"

"The news can wait a little longer," he said. He knelt next to the bed and kissed her, tasting strongly of tooth powder.

"I have news for you, also. It can wait for me to brush my teeth, and for us to fuck," Lucilla said, savoring the word anew, the word she could speak to no one else. She liked the sound of it so much that she considered saying it again, and again, and again, as she pressed her hot skin to his and forced away the bad news she would soon have to share.

"Hurry with the first, so we may be slow with the second," Pascal said, grinning into her eyes.

Lucilla brushed her teeth in the nude, her feet growing icy against the floor as she watched Pascal shuck off his drawers. His legs were long and strong and cleanly muscled, his skin dense with soft hair. His cock thickened and rose as she watched; after she'd rinsed her mouth, she grasped it firmly between her thumb and forefinger.

Pascal steadied himself with a hot hand on her shoulder. He kissed her neck and made humming sounds as she delicately touched the head of his cock and slid his velvety-soft foreskin over the firm flesh within. She laid her free hand on his chest, rubbing her palm against hair. "I want you inside me as soon as possible," she said.

"How?" he asked, pressing his lips behind her ear and sucking gently.

"Every way," she said, closing her eyes and tipping her forehead into his. She stroked his cock languidly and looped her other arm around his neck. His palm cupped her cheek and his mouth met hers, sucking her breath into his own lungs as if he couldn't live without it. She kissed his throat, caressing her own lips with his stubbled roughness, and remembered Ashby's skin beneath her lips and teeth. Sudden, sharp grief stabbed her, that Ashby would never feel such a thing again, so she kissed Pascal with desperate fervor, her fingers sifting through his hair, trying to find a grip. She released his cock and used those fingers to dig into his sharp hipbone, dragging him closer, trapping his erection between them, all the while kissing him and kissing him, afraid to stop.

Soon merely kissing wasn't enough. She dragged him toward her bed, stumbling over discarded boots and gasping as his fingers slid from her rear down between her legs, the tip of one long finger piercing her with sharp ecstasy.

"Turn around," Pascal breathed hotly in her ear. "Turn around and I will fill you so deeply our very souls will touch."

She fell toward the bed and caught herself on her hands, drawing her legs up behind her. She could easily feel the wooden slats with her knees, even through the thin mattress; she grabbed more blanket and wedged it beneath herself, for padding. "This will never work. You're far too tall."

"I am clever," he reminded her. He applied a condom and crawled onto the bed behind her, fitting himself to her back. "Also, I have great motivation. Here, sit up on your knees and lean back into me—"

His rigid cock thumped against her back, hot and smooth. He grasped her waist and lifted her, just enough to wedge his cock at the entrance to her sex. She reached and helped to guide him inside her as he eased her down, both of them breathless from the new sensations. And at last, she was too full of pleasure to think any longer.

"Hold still," Pascal murmured into her ear. He wrapped his arms snugly around her waist and curled himself over her shoulders, until there was scarcely any air between them. His heartbeat reverberated through her chest as well as his own.

"Tighter," she said. His arms tightened, and she layered her arms atop his. She swore she could feel his pulse beating inside her sex. She tightened her inner muscles on his cock and felt his groan throughout her body.

"Perhaps you've held still long enough," he said, loosening his arms and rearranging his hands on her hips.

Lucilla knelt up, tugging herself off his cock fraction by fraction. Pascal's ragged breathing and the pressure of his hands cued her when to slide back onto him, and soon they'd established a rhythm that kept them both hovering on an invisible edge, at least until her memory of reality began to intrude. She eased onto her hands and knees and said, "Please, Pascal. Faster now. Deep as you can."

He braced one hand on the bed and placed the other so

each jerk of his hips rubbed her clitoris hard against the heel of his hand, sharp stabs that quickly drove her to a peak. She came gasping, then rode out Pascal's last few thrusts in a blissful daze.

Afterward, they lay in a tangled heap, Pascal's shins dangling off the side of the bed but his arms firmly holding her to his chest. He said drowsily, "Did you hear that Antwerp has been lost?"

"Yes."

"Madame Claes is missing. She is stronger than a human, and quite capable, but I fear she may have attempted something unwise because of Antwerp's fall."

"I'm sorry," she said.

"I had hoped your British werewolf might be of help in locating her."

Lucilla closed her eyes. "My brother came to see me. He said that Captain Ashby was killed."

Pascal stiffened and cursed softly in French. "Bad luck. Very bad luck."

"That both should go missing at the same time..." She looked at him over her shoulder. "Crispin said they weren't able to find Ashby's body."

Thoughtfully, Pascal said, "There's no proof, then, that he's dead. Do you know where he was last seen?"

She shook her head. "I can give you the date, as close as I can estimate it from what Crispin said."

"And I can inquire of his regiment." He quickly kissed the back of her neck, then sighed. "Madame Claes—all her hatred of the Boche centers on Herr Doktor Kauz, or perhaps it is the reverse. We had a general idea of his whereabouts. My men were investigating laboratories as best they could, in enemy territory. There is at least one location where we know Kauz is working, on a government grant, and one more remote site that is a possibility. She could easily have obtained the information. If Ashby went missing in the same general area as either, then it is possible Herr Doktor Kauz has captured them both."

"You mean, Ashby might be alive."

"It is possible. Kauz did not kill Madame Claes when she was his captive. I think they are more use to him alive."

Lucilla stared into space. "If you can find them…" She laced her fingers with his. "We can't reveal their secret. We must rescue them ourselves."

"We?"

"We. I'll help you."

He said very quietly, "This could be a dangerous under-taking. Men with guns. Not like stealing a motorcar."

"Every day, I see men who've been shot, stabbed, blown to pieces. Do you think I don't know?"

Pascal drew a breath, then let it out. "I fear for you," he said in a low voice.

"But you will accept my help."

"Of course I will." His arms tightened around her, almost painfully.

"Pascal—" She rubbed his forearm.

"Yes?"

"Are you a werewolf?"

He hesitated. "No."

Lucilla could feel his heartbeat, and it had remained steady, though his breathing came a fraction faster. She asked, "Are you related to a werewolf?"

"Why do you ask?"

"I want to know."

"Will it make a difference to you?"

"I…don't think so." She paused and thought about it. "I would like you to tell me, anyway."

"Very well. My *grand-oncle,* Erard, he was a werewolf. But he had no children of his own. He could find no one to be his wife. And so I became his child, in a way, until he died."

"I'm sorry," she said.

"That my *grand-oncle* was a werewolf?"

"That he's dead." Lucilla turned in his arms and held on to him fiercely. "Thank you for telling me."

"You had guessed already."

"What's important is that you told me." She kissed his shoulder, then rubbed her nose against his skin.

"I trust that you will not share this secret." Pascal smoothed his hand over her hair.

"I won't," she said.

He kissed her. "I have never told anyone else. Not even my father."

16

NOT DEAD. THE PLACE HE OCCUPIED WAS PITCH-black and cold and silent. Noel had never quite believed in the afterlife described to him by Father Michael, since there were no wolves there, but he was also pretty sure that even hell did not include metal pressing against his face and the sensation of blood coagulating and drying on bare skin. He was bare all over, in fact, except for metal at his wrists, ankles, waist and throat, the latter extending over the lower half of his face, digging into the soft tissue beneath his jawbone and cutting into his lips. It was worse than being dead, because he had expected either death, injury or safety, not a combination of injury and continuing danger. Perhaps he should have.

The tang of iron in the steel, so much like blood, burned in his nose and throat, and he coughed. He would have spat if he'd been able to sit up, and if he hadn't been muzzled. As he lay flat on his back, he had to swallow carefully or he would choke. He sniffed again, cautiously, trying to discern clues beneath the heavy reek of carbolic and ammonia. His nose flinched from the combined stink and grew numb.

Losing his sense of smell was like going blind. In the darkness, he was already blind, of course, but this was worse, and for a few moments he panicked, thrashing against his bonds, only ceasing when he realized he could smell his own fresh blood and scraped flesh.

All right. It's all right. Just don't breathe it in so deeply, you idiot. Concentrate.

Noel was not bound in any sort of German prison. He didn't have to think about where he might be. His parents had told him horrible stories of werewolves who'd been captured by those who hoped to gain some advantage from it, such as being changed themselves, and no matter how one explained it was impossible to change a human into a werewolf, one would never be believed. Others had been caught by the self-righteous, who fought to rid the world of unholy beasts, or by those with personal grudges, true or not. His current bonds, his nakedness and his injuries all indicated his captor's purpose wasn't immediate death, but something more insidious.

He needed to know more about his captor's plans. To do that, he had to remain calm. He tried picturing the fields and forests of home, but that only made him want to run. He settled for disassembling and assembling his Enfield rifle in his mind, then a Maxim gun, then a bicycle, then the motorbike he'd been working on in his mother's garden shed.

A long, vague time later, he wondered if his captor's purpose was to drive him insane. He heard only occasional, very distant rumbles—the impact of shells? Thunder? Someone banging on a wall?—and saw nothing. His nose periodically gave up the ghost, and bound as he was, he could touch nothing but the metal table on which he lay. His muscles ached from confinement, and his cut lip throbbed and burned with his pulse. How long had it been? An hour? Two? How long had he been here? Who had won the battle?

Something hissed steadily, like an engine releasing steam. The space echoed, and he'd become disoriented enough that he couldn't tell how far away the sound was, or where it came from. He caught a scent and promptly gagged as a cloud of ether settled over his face. Eventually, he had to breathe, and despite his desperate thrashing, even his mental sight went dark.

A woman crouched before him, naked, her long blond hair trailing to the chalky stone floor. She had a round face with large eyes, a delicate snub nose and a cherubic pink mouth. "Wake up," she said, slapping his cheek. The blow was not gentle.

"Christ, my head hurts." The inside of his skull felt as if it had been burned, and the inside of his nose, as well.

"If you vomit again, I will make you wish you had never been born," the woman said.

Again? Noel tensed his arm and realized he could move. He drew up his legs to guard his belly and cradled his throbbing head in his palms. "Fucking hell."

"Yes," she said, as if agreeing. She slid something across the floor to him. He smelled water. He squinted open one eye. The water was in a shallow bowl. The woman's lip curled. "We are animals to him," she said.

We? Pain tore through him as he moved, snaring her arm and bringing it close to his face. She flinched, then froze as he pressed his nose to her skin and inhaled, deeply, the unmistakable scent of werewolf. His smile hurt.

She snatched back her arm. "You have nothing to smile about, Englishman."

Noel grinned. He had to squint, but he grinned. "I'm extremely pleased to meet you."

"Soon, you will not be. Are you going to drink?"

"Are you going to help me up?"

The room was small, perhaps ten feet square, and looked as if it had been carved out of the rock, then poorly whitewashed with lime. It smelled overwhelmingly of carbolic. A dim bulb hung from a wire strung across the low ceiling; he followed the wire with his eyes and noticed it exited through a hole next to a reinforced wooden door, with its locks on the outside, of course.

Noel felt fractionally better after drinking his fill, though he would have been happy for a handful of aspirin, as well. He sat on the floor across the narrow cell from the woman, his back to cool white stone, and contemplated changing form, to see if that would help alleviate the pain. The woman was watching him narrowly, then her eyes flicked toward the door, and again to a corner near the ceiling. His eyes following hers, he saw a port in the door, currently closed, and what looked like another opening higher up. They were watched.

Well, it could hardly be a surprise to their observer, or observers, that he would be curious about his situation. "Where are we?" Her accent was either Belgian or Dutch, with the former more likely. He didn't feel as if a long enough time had passed for him to reach Holland.

"I don't know." She rested her crossed arms on her updrawn knees, eyeing him through a thick swath of blond hair. Her scent tantalized him. He wanted to crawl across the floor and lay his head in her lap until he felt better, then he wanted to nuzzle her all over. It was too bad he couldn't. First, he didn't plan to let his wolf self dictate his actions. Second, she did not look as if she would be amenable to him getting any closer, though he didn't sense any dislike of him personally. Perhaps she felt a generalized wariness. In the circumstances, it was completely warranted. She was imprisoned, and not only imprisoned, but trapped with a man whom she'd never before met.

"How long have you been here?"

"Several days. I was wise and did not fight as you did."

"I find that difficult to believe."

"This is not the first time for me." The tightness in her voice made the hair raise on his arms; had he been in wolf form, his hackles would have flared. If she was afraid, her fear was well submerged beneath several layers of rage.

"Will you enlighten me on what's to happen to us?"

Her lip rose in a snarl, then she visibly calmed herself to a level of quivering tension that Noel recognized from soldiers who'd been in action about an hour past good judgment. "We are experimental subjects."

"Whose experiments?"

"Kauz," she said, almost spitting the name.

"German? Austrian?"

"German."

"Doubly my enemy, then." Noel rolled his shoulders, trying to loosen his cramped muscles. He would need not only to protect himself and the woman, but also prevent the German from gaining any information useful to the war effort.

The woman eyed him without blinking for a long time. At last, she said, "We could rip out each other's throats. It would not take so very long."

Noel caught her gaze with his own. "I'm Noel Ashby," he said. "What's your name?"

"Tanneken Claes," she said. "You are pretending there is a better way."

"We can escape. You escaped before."

"Are you willing to tear out the throat of a feeble old man?" she said, her voice dripping with irony.

"It needn't come to that. I'm lacking my uniform just now, but I'm a professional soldier in His Majesty's army."

"I am hardly a weakling," she snarled.

"That's unlikely, given you're a werewolf. But you were alone that other time, of course you had difficulty escaping. Now you're not alone. It's much easier to escape with two."

"I am together with a fatuous optimist."

"Your English is very good," Noel noted. "*Fatuous optimist.* If I wasn't an optimist, I'd be curled up on the floor right now, and useless to you."

"Or perhaps you have foolish thoughts of heroism," she said. "I told you, I have been held captive by this Kauz before. He has guards at his command, more than we can fight." She paused and added, "Unless you would prefer to die fighting them. I would be willing to attempt that, though I would prefer not to have their filthy hands touch me. And there are other creatures. Sometimes they are watching."

"Other wolves?" Noel asked. "German wolves?"

"I don't know," she said. "I never saw any of them change form, nor smelled their human forms on them. They stink of… I cannot describe it."

"Do they smell of wolf, or not?"

"I don't know so many wolves," she said. Her expression turned abstracted, her brows tipping together in a way that he found endearing. At last she said, "They did not smell like wild creatures. The stink of the laboratory clung to them. Like an apothecary's storeroom."

"Could they be like us, and concealing their natural scents in some way?"

"Perhaps—" she grinned, flashing sharp canines "—they would not want me to know them for who they really were."

"Could they also have been prisoners?"

"No. They wandered the corridors freely. I heard them pacing in the night, back and forth in front of my cell. When I was caged, they stood outside the bars, watching."

"How many?"

She shrugged. "Three? Four? They stayed in the shadows, and when one's nose is blinded, also, it is difficult to tell."

"Do you know if any of them are guarding us now?"

"I do not think any of them were guards, or there would be no need for human guards, as well. You don't need to worry. Kauz will not leave us unguarded." She lifted her head defiantly. "Or unwatched." She paused. "You realize why he has caged us together."

"Convenience?"

She laughed bitterly. "In addition to his foul experiments, he wishes to have more werewolves. And he expects us to produce them."

THREE DAYS AFTER PASCAL'S BRIEF VISIT TO THE hospital, Lucilla received a letter from him, carefully encoded using a volume of Dumas that he'd left for her, and sent by courier to avoid the censors. She pored over the letter into the early-morning hours, painstakingly counting letters with a sharp pencil and extracting his message, letter by letter.

His spies had discovered and reconnoitered the remote laboratory where several guards were employed, and where they suspected prisoners might be held. The spies assigned to Kauz's more visible lab heard rumors of experiments that would change the face of the war. Lucilla knew that rumors of this kind ran rampant in every sector of society, even when there was no basis for them, but she believed Pascal would not waste his time telling her of mere rumors.

A day later, she received by courier a small vial of volatile powder, with a request that she discover its use. Lucilla worked into the night testing the sample until it was all gone, but most of her tests were for her own curiosity, not necessity; she'd found immediately that the powder was poison, or would be as soon as the proper reagent was applied. She tested a small amount inside a beaker because she had no safe hood, and watched a thick, yellowish-green gas form. It burned the paper she'd put inside like acid. She'd never seen anything quite like it. The implications were chilling.

Not only would they need to rescue the werewolves, the laboratory where this horror was manufactured had to be destroyed, as well.

17

TANNEKEN COULD STILL FEEL THE IMPRINT OF Ashby's warm fingers on her skin. She resisted the urge to lift her wrist to her nose and sniff. His scent was deeply intriguing. She had never met a full-blooded male werewolf before, and had not realized how…delicious…such a scent could be. She wanted to rub her face all over his skin, and push her nose into his throat and beneath his arm, and nuzzle him lower still.

Mentally, she shook herself. She refused to give in to such desires, not when it would give Kauz what he wanted. How ironic, that the one thing she'd never denied herself should be the one thing in which she could not indulge! She tried to convince herself it didn't matter if Ashby was one of her kind or not. All that mattered was that he help her escape, in one way or another. She could deal with the rest later.

She said, "I will not attempt to gain time by pretending to acquiesce to Kauz's demands."

Ashby continued to stretch his arms and back. He was lean and rangy, but nicely muscular. He moved with grace. It would not be a hardship to engage in sex with him, if their situation had been different; if the choice had been hers alone. He said, "I wasn't going to suggest it."

"I could see the interest in your eyes."

He leaned back, propping himself insouciantly on his elbows. "You're the first female werewolf I've met in my life, excluding my mother and sisters. Of course I'm interested. So are you."

"You overestimate your charms."

"Do I?" He grinned, and she had to admit, it was a charming grin. She had a regrettable weakness for men, particularly confident men, if they were not obnoxious. He said, "I think you should consider me as a reason to escape this place instead of giving up and dying."

He was foolish to reject the escape of death so easily. He had no idea what Kauz would do to him, or even more foolishly, did not care. Did he think his army would come to rescue him? They likely thought him dead. Fournier would not know where she had gone—or he might know by now that she'd gone to Antwerp, and would thus assume her beyond his reach.

She said, the words bitter in her mouth, "Our only other choice is to endure what sufferings Kauz will unleash upon us. I once thought a werewolf could withstand any tortures and emerge triumphant. However, I learned otherwise. Given sufficient resources, an evil man can break the strongest of creatures."

Ashby smiled crookedly. "You don't seem broken to me."

"Not yet, perhaps," she said. "If you let me kill you, I will be quick. I have hunted often, on my estate."

"We hunt in England, as well," he said. "Tanneken, I don't think I'm able to kill you."

"Because I'm a woman?" She decided not to protest his use of her given name. There was no point.

He shrugged. "Since I can't, it wouldn't be fair to take the easy way out and let you kill me. So perhaps we'd better both stay alive."

After some hours, Tanneken still could not convince Ashby that her plan was the most viable. He continued to insist upon their survival as a necessary outcome for every plan. At least he agreed that, if necessary, humans other than the two of them could be killed. But even then, he thought having Kauz alive would be preferable, so they could extract information from him, perhaps handing him over to the military authorities. He knew of a man with the French army, he said. Tanneken eventually discovered that Ashby knew of Major Fournier. Fournier would appreciate the chance to question Kauz, she knew, but she would not put herself out for Kauz's survival. If he needed to die, she would kill him without compunction. Besides, in wolf form she was not as logical as in human form, not when it came to matters of survival.

She was in the midst of arguing this point with him— they'd moved closer and closer to each other in the course of their conversation, until she could sense the heat of his skin on hers—when she saw a wisp of gas curling through a vent near the ceiling. She pointed to it just as the wisp changed to a spray, clouding the ceiling and sinking down upon them.

She had no time to change. If only she could smell properly, she might be alerted sooner to the gassings, but Kauz knew this and prevented it. He wanted full control of which form they took, and now he seemed to want them human.

She woke in a cage, together with Ashby. Crouched next to her, both of them still naked, he looked more alert than she felt, probably because his larger form lent him more resistance to the gas. A hot electric light illuminated them alone, throwing the rest of the room into deepest shadow. Just at the edge of the shadow, Kauz sat on a plain wooden chair, rolling a rattan cane between his palms.

Her urge to snarl stopped before it reached her throat as fear slammed into her, unexpected and vicious as a blow. She had thought she'd forgotten, crushed her memories, but his unexpected appearance, her helpless at his will, was too much like it had been before, and her carefully built defenses crumbled.

Ashby laid a hand on the middle of her back, spreading his fingers wide over her spine. The touch was hotter than the light, tingling out to the ends of her fingers and toes. She sat up quickly, throwing off his hand, and summoned her most arrogant stare to aim at the old man outside the cage.

"Cowardly son of pox-ridden incest," she said. "Come closer, and I will give you all that you deserve."

Ashby said nothing. She could sense him near her, tension singing through his limbs. When she glanced at him, he settled back onto his heels, his hands loose at his sides rather than concealing his genitals. He smiled. "Like what you see, Herr Kauz?"

Kauz used his cane to lever himself from the chair, then stalked a step closer, then another. Tanneken willed herself not to cringe. Suddenly, he whipped the cane against the bars with a mighty rattling *clang*.

When she came to herself again, Ashby was gripping the back of her neck, holding her in place, and saying, "We won't do it. There's no profit in it for us. Would you sire children just to give them up?"

"These are not children, but subjects," Kauz said, his voice oozing charm that nevertheless stank of falsity. "Think of the advances to the werewolf race. Think how few you are."

"Fewer still, when you kill us," Tanneken spat.

"I did not kill you," Kauz said. "I tested you. I tested your fitness to be a new mother to a new race. It's hardly my fault if you are too stupid to see the value in it." He smiled, and she wanted to bash in his teeth with her hands. "It's lucky that I will be able to pass my intelligence on through your children. They'll be full werewolf, and thus able to breed successfully with one like me."

Tanneken could not speak for rage. How dare he speak of defiling her children? She would die first—but of course, she would die. There was no doubt of that once Kauz had what he wanted. Ashby touched her lower back, light and fleeting, a signal of some kind. She clenched her jaw on her angry words.

She could feel Ashby's anger, but his voice was calm as he said, "Surely, with the war, it's a poor time for such a complex experiment."

Kauz sneered. "You think only in the moment, wolf. Now is the perfect time. All of Europe will be turned up like soil ready for new seed. I will provide that seed, trained in the ways of science and logic, free at last of petty human politics." He lifted his cane and lightly rapped it against the bars. "You are both flawed, but with sufficient attention to detail, my breeding program will bring out what's needed to put the world to rights. In the meantime, my chemical experiments will bring in the government money I need to carry out my ultimate aims. And the immunity, as well. Once I've won their war for them, I'll have all the resources I could possibly need."

Tanneken said, "You won't live so long."

"On the contrary, though I cannot take a beast's form, my body is quite strong. You would find me a formidable opponent, were I to give you the chance." He smiled slowly, revealing teeth stained from tobacco. "Alas, I shan't give you the chance. How sad."

"We won't do as you ask," Ashby repeated.

"Oh, but you will." Kauz trailed his cane along the bars of the cage, his smile not fading. "And until then, you can serve as subjects for my research. It is so rare that I can test an adult werewolf. I will need those statistics one day, so even if you fall dead before you provide me with future subjects, I will have that. And this war offers many opportunities. Perhaps if you expire untimely, I will find others who won't be missed in the chaos of battle." He dragged his cane along the bars, a sound that shook inside her bones. "Until then, alas, I must make do."

"I will kill you," Tanneken said.

Kauz walked back to his chair and settled into it with every evidence of relaxation. "You may say it as often as you wish. It won't happen. Now, female, when you ran away, I lost track of your cycles, so we'd best take every opportunity."

Tanneken couldn't get to him; gradually, she became aware that the cage's bars prevented her, and Ashby's hard grip on her arms prevented her, as well. She tried to speak and could only howl. She couldn't understand what Ashby was saying into her ear. Another moment and she would begin to change.

She couldn't change. If she changed, Ashby might change, and their wolf selves would find it much harder to remember why they couldn't breed with each other. Such a mating wouldn't be fertile, but Kauz might not know it, and she refused to give him the satisfaction. Breathing heavily, she let go the bars and leaned back into Ashby, whose grip became a loose embrace. She concentrated, and managed to form words. "He won't force me, and I won't have him without force. How sad for you."

Warmth pressed behind her ear. Ashby had kissed her there, a caress so completely unexpected she almost laughed. He said, "I suppose you'd better get on with your so-called *testing,* then."

Noel probably shouldn't have refused Kauz's demands quite so vehemently. The epithet *pus-eaten syphilitic corpse-fucker* had possibly been unwise, as well.

He and Tanneken had been moved to an underground cell. He had no idea where exactly it was in relation to the surface; the corridors leading to this room were many, narrow and twisted, perhaps once intended as sapper tunnels. He couldn't bring himself to care too much just now. If he didn't move, and breathed steadily, he could almost ignore the pain of his fractured leg, so much more intense than that of his broken forearm. He tipped his head back against the wall and panted. He couldn't breathe too hard, or that would jostle his arm and leg, and strain his fractured ribs. If he didn't breathe deeply enough, the pain pooled inside him and built, as if his marrow turned to lava and burned its way out through his muscles, held taut against movement. "Tanneken," he said. Her name emerged in a hoarse whisper, but she heard him, and turned to face him instead of the door. "Talk to me. Tell me a story."

"I have none."

"Tell me *your* story, then." He'd been too vehement, and jolted his leg. He gasped and fought against the jagged pain until he remembered to breathe it out. "Please. Like a story, not you, not real. Unless you'd rather listen to me whimper."

A long pause. Noel shifted and whimpered. Hastily,

Tanneken said, "Before the summer of 1914, the life of a werewolf in the Belgian countryside was pleasant and gracious. I— Tanneken Claes grew up on a vast estate near Bruges, traveling into the city with her mother to visit the cathedral, care for her investments and to have clothing made for the social season. She would accompany her mother to dances and to salons where they would listen to overwrought poetry in Walloon and French, as well as their own Flemish, and fend off the suitors who flocked both to her and to her widowed mother. Tanneken never beckoned the suitors closer. When she wished to indulge in the pleasures of the flesh, she sought out heartier fare, men who knew little of her wealth and saw her only as a night's entertainment, not realizing it was they who were entertainment for her. After a few months, they would return to the estate, shed their fine gowns along with their human skins and run wild in their ancestral forest, hunting the deer fostered for this very purpose."

She paused. Noel said, "I liked the part about *heartier fare.*" When she didn't respond, he said, "Please, go on."

"Her mother maintained that running as a wolf was all the sweeter for having been trapped in corsets and skirts, besides the practical concerns of living in a human world that were made much easier if one could conform and maintain a high level of financial security. Tanneken would prefer to do without those human trappings altogether, not being fond of poetry, except that she'd discovered early on that she liked sexual congress and required it on a regular basis. Thus it was necessary, as a human woman, to hunt for men as she hunted for deer, though with a much better outcome for her prey. A long-term partner might have been better, for the sake of convenience, but she didn't see any way to effectively conceal her wolf nature from someone who lived with her. And though there were other werewolves in the world, they were few and far between, and like she and her mother, tended to keep to themselves for safety's sake. Finding an appropriate unattached male might be the work of years. So she continued with her occasional partners, trying not to think of the day when she would want a child, and the difficulty werewolves often had in conceiving from solitary encounters, and what she would do then. She did not even allow herself to think of love, as her mother and father had shared when she was small. Such a thing was as rare as a comet in the sky."

"Maybe it is," Noel said. "But you were leading up to something."

"Her mother's powerful werewolf constitution at last failed her in 1908, and she died soon after of a devouring cancer. Tanneken inherited all, of course. She was the last of their line, and her mother had trained her for this."

"I'm sorry," Noel said.

Another pause. "Thank you," she said, then continued her story. "She was well able to care for herself and her family's money and secrets. However, she had not realized how lonely she would be, running the forests alone, wandering their fine manor alone, visiting Bruges and Antwerp and Paris and sometimes Berlin alone. It was the loneliness that drove her, after two years of isolation, to the foolish action of marrying a liaison officer of the kaiser's Uhlans."

"Now you've surprised me," Noel said. "I'd have thought you'd go for a nice sturdy woodcutter, or perhaps a fireman."

"I am ignoring your fatuous remarks," Tanneken said. "Do you wish me to continue, or not?"

"Go on, please."

"At the time, the marriage seemed eminently sensible. He had a smell of wolf, but never spoke of it, so she thought he did not know of his ancestry. She would try, she decided, to get herself with child, and then perhaps be unfaithful to him so that he would divorce her, and she would have her child for companion, as her mother had done. She would settle money on her husband, so he would be satisfied. That was the chief reason he'd married her anyway. It was expensive to keep one's self in fine horses and cavalry gear suitable for display in a foreign country. She might not even have to divorce him and be rid of him—his duties often took him abroad, and she had the time to herself which she required."

To Noel, it sounded a sad excuse for a marriage, but perhaps he was wrong. Perhaps it was better than being alone.

"At first, she felt she'd made a good bargain. Edel was a superior lover, with whom she enjoyed many stimulating conflicts. She did not love him, but she did love what they did with each other in the bedroom and elsewhere. A year passed, then another. She did not become pregnant, despite a great deal of effort devoted to that end. And Edel wished to return to Germany, bringing her with him. They had plenty of money. They could buy a fine house, and entertain. It would help his career. She could hire managers for her estate."

"You didn't do it, did you?"

"I—Tanneken refused. This was her ancestral land. If Edel did not like living in a foreign land, then she would like it even less. She had never lived anywhere other than the countryside of Belgium. She would not go. If he wished to go, he could go alone."

"There's more to this, isn't there?"

"She did not yet know that he'd discovered her secret."

"Fucking hell."

Tanneken paused, then went on. "She did not learn until too late that he had known her secret all along, had sought her out for that very reason, had been attached to the embassy in Bruges solely to create a liaison with her. She did not know it until he convinced her to visit his family in a remote hamlet in Germany."

"How?"

"She did not want to go. By then, she was growing disenchanted with his pronouncements of what she should do and what he would do. He at last persuaded her by saying that perhaps a vacation would be beneficial to his efforts at impregnating her—she had told him by now of her desire for a child. She left her home behind in the care of agents, and traveled to Germany, and there Edel handed her into the care of Herr Doktor Professor Kauz and a squad of soldiers, who promptly dragged Edel outside and shot him. No one was to know of the true experiments to happen here." She paused. "That is all. You know the rest."

"You escaped? You must have escaped. How did you do it?"

"There was an opportunity when Kauz was not at the laboratory for several days. I was a wolf, and I attacked a guard."

Noel sucked in his breath, and promptly doubled over with pain, which bumped his arm against his belly and sent another explosion of pain from his head to his toes. His stomach roiled with nausea; the only thing that kept him from retching was knowing exactly how badly it would hurt.

"Look at me!"

Noel hissed through his teeth. Tanneken's fingers didn't let go of his chin.

She said, "You must change."

That would hurt even worse than retching. True, he would heal much more quickly, but then Kauz would see it happen. He couldn't speak. Grimly, he closed his eyes and tried a small shake of his head.

"You have no choice. He is clever. He knows how long we can bear it."

She had borne it.

"I changed. I changed every time. You must change. He is enjoying watching your suffering."

"Fuck," he said.

She leaned close and murmured into his ear, "If you are injured so badly, there is no escape. Tell me, and I will end it for you." She softly caressed his cheek with her lips.

"Fucking hell."

"Idiot! I should leave you behind."

"Not so much an idiot as that," he whispered, and changed. It was worse than he'd imagined; if he'd imagined this much pain, he would not have dared. He bit his tongue, then gave up and screamed, to see if that would help. He smelled Tanneken near to him, and focused on her through the most terrible, ripping agony he'd ever experienced.

His scream distorted to a yowl, more like a cat than a wolf, when he aligned in a new shape, his bones returning to their normal state. He sighed in relief as his head flopped to the floor. He thumped his tail, once. The pain receded, leaving him stiff and sore.

Tanneken laid her hand on his side and burrowed her fingers deeply into his pelage. Noel closed his eyes. He lacked the strength to thump his tail again, but she would understand. She shifted position, lying down on her side and resting her cheek on his shoulder, still digging her fingers through his pelage, tender comfort she would not give him in words. Noel sighed deeply and let himself sleep. When he awoke, perhaps they could play for time, lead Kauz to believe he might succeed in his demands.

Near dawn, the guards arrived and flooded the cell with anesthetic gas. He woke just enough to feel Tanneken being dragged from him; she struggled and yipped, but she was already losing consciousness. His own body wouldn't obey him, his growls and snaps existing only in his mind, his claws scrabbling helplessly on the concrete floor. He couldn't even force his body into a change, to shout his protests.

When he awoke again, he was alone. He threw his head back and howled.

18

PARIS WAS THRONGED WITH SOLDIERS, MOST OF them in French blue or British khaki, but Crispin saw Russians, as well, and even a group of French colonials, tall black men in red caps who came from Senegal, a country that to him was only a place on a map, but to these men was home. The Africans did not look happy with the gray sky and the damp chill in the air; some were so swathed in layers of scarves that their faces could hardly be distinguished. Crispin was grateful for the wool lining of his trench coat, and the woolen scarf Hailey had given him, but he would have been happy with none of it, he was so glad to be out of the trenches, and so glad that Meyer walked beside him. Meyer looked elegant in his wool overcoat until one noticed that the tip of his nose had gone scarlet with cold. He would need to be warmed up. Crispin would be happy to take on the task, if only he could find their hotel. They'd been walking uphill, so he knew it had to be near.

Meyer stopped outside a little café. "Let's have some coffee," he suggested. Obviously, he suspected Crispin was lost.

Luckily, at that moment Crispin spied a familiar facade halfway down the block. "Let's drop off our kit first," he said, daring to touch Meyer's elbow before he pointed to the Hotel Lutetia. He had stayed here once on a trip with his choir while at university, when they'd gone to sing at the British embassy.

The concierge did not look twice at them, nor did he read their scrawled signatures. The hotel had suffered in recent months; perhaps staff had been lost to the army. The lift was broken. Crispin and Meyer climbed two flights of stairs while a boy took their rucksacks and bag of food before bounding up the staircase like a goat, peppering them with questions about the front, the battles in which they'd taken part, and a whole series of gory inquiries that Crispin ignored but Meyer answered patiently. At the door to their room, Meyer gave the boy a coin and sent him on his way while Crispin fumbled with the key.

Meyer's gloved hand closed over his. "Gently," he suggested, and of course the doorknob turned. Meyer let go of his hand and went in. From within the small room, he said, sounding relieved, "Steam heat. It's warm. Come in quick and close the door."

Meyer quickly shed his scarf and coat, hanging them in the wardrobe. He tossed his hat onto the top shelf. Crispin stood in the doorway, unable to move yet.

Surely Meyer was aware of Crispin's intentions, even though he hadn't stated them explicitly. Trembling, Crispin fingered the tin of salve in his pocket, discreetly wrapped in brown paper and tied with twine. He slipped through the door. The room was indeed warm, enough so that he shivered, his toes prickling with returning feeling. He dared to tug down his scarf and sighed deeply as the warmth began to soak in. He didn't have to say anything just yet.

The lodgings weren't luxurious, but they were private and clean. He couldn't look away from the double-size bed and its inviting goose-down coverlets and pillows. Meyer sat on the only chair, rummaging in his rucksack, emerging with a hoot of triumph. He held a bottle aloft. "Brandy," he said. "Just the thing for a cup of tea."

Crispin took a deep breath. "I'd like a bath first, really."

"Hell, yes," Meyer said, grinning. "It's worth coming to Paris just for a bath and to have someone else take care of the laundry."

"I remember there was a tub and a shower bath both," Crispin said.

"Even better." Meyer paused, looked down at his hands, then up at Crispin again. "Hailey told me that you…were fond of me."

He couldn't breathe, but he had to, because he'd decided he was not going to lie, even by omission. "Yes, I am."

"I thought I'd done something to shock you."

At first, Crispin wasn't sure what he meant, then he began to laugh. "I thought I'd died and gone to heaven."

Meyer let out his breath in a whoosh. "That's all right, then. Let's have our baths, then we'll see what's to be done with the evening. If that's what you had in mind?"

Crispin sagged back against the door. "That's all? You're not shocked? Horrified? Planning to turn me in?"

Meyer stood, shoving his spectacles up his nose from where they'd slid. "No."

"You haven't read the regulations, then."

"Does it matter what the regulations say, or what we do in this room, where no one else can see, and where only we will know?"

Crispin shook his head slowly. "I've been defying the law all my life. But I didn't expect *you* would just—"

"I've done it before," Meyer admitted softly.

"Gabriel," Crispin said, then almost stopped, he was so surprised the familiar name had come out of his mouth. "What we did, back in that shell hole—that's not what I—"

"Noel Ashby and I were lovers."

Crispin could have been knocked over with a wisp of straw. "How did you manage that?" He felt, oddly, betrayed.

Gabriel grinned. "Not recently. We were boys. It all stopped when I went off to conservatory, but until then, we tried everything we could think of. And I...I like women, but I wasn't averse to any of that, either."

So Gabriel probably had more experience with making love to a man than Crispin did. It wasn't fair.

When he didn't answer, Gabriel said, "I'm sorry. I should have told you earlier. I shouldn't have just run off and left you worrying. I was stupid not to say anything."

"I trusted you not to tell," Crispin said. "I thought I'd upset you. God knows it's happened before." He felt heat rise in his cheeks, and he hurriedly looked at the worn blue carpet.

"It was still wrong of me."

Crispin looked up then. "You were scared. So was I. Let's leave it there."

Meyer got up and shoved his hands into his pockets. "You have the kindest heart I've ever met, Crispin."

"I'm afraid of a lot of things, but I'm not afraid to admit when I'm scared."

"And now?"

Crispin grinned shakily. "I'm only scared that you'll refuse me."

Meyer came closer. "I would have told you at once, not come all this way." He drew his hands from his pockets and unbuttoned Crispin's coat. He pulled it open only far enough to insinuate his arms beneath and wrap them around Crispin's waist.

Crispin couldn't get his breath again. He returned the embrace, tentatively at first, then held on more tightly when Gabriel relaxed against him. He bent his head, rubbing his nose against Gabriel's neck, which smelled of his familiar shaving lotion.

"Mmm," said Gabriel.

Crispin felt, for a few moments, as if time had stopped. He closed his eyes and shifted even closer. His feet were still cold, and he desperately wanted to wash off the filth of weeks, but he never wanted to let go of Gabriel, who was giving him the one thing he needed most in the world. He let go and stepped away. He said, "We can do that again, without all these damn clothes."

Gabriel pushed his specs up his nose and grinned. "I like the way you think."

Perhaps Gabriel wouldn't like what Crispin had in mind. He was prepared for disappointment, of course. He would take whatever Gabriel offered, but he couldn't quite shake the desire to have Gabriel inside him, closer than he could be in any other way.

Crispin shed his scarf and coat. "We can wash and then soak."

"Sounds lovely."

It was the single most painful shower he'd ever had. He was lucky he didn't bring himself off with his hand without even trying. One day, Crispin reflected, he would like to have Gabriel in his own house, in his own bathroom, not a hotel bathroom with other people's rooms on either side. He'd be able to watch every shift of his muscles as he bent to wash himself, his long toes curling against tile, his back arching in the way that it might arch over Crispin's. They'd be able to share a tub, and fondle each other beneath the water and above its surface. For now, he admired the hairy calf that dangled over the tub's edge while he squeezed water from his curls. "We could go out," he said. "Have some supper."

"Or we could have bread and cheese and wine later this evening. Do you want some wine, first?"

Crispin shook his head and met Gabriel's eyes. "No."

Back in their room, Crispin stripped off his towel as soon as the door was closed, yanked down the coverlet and turned on the lamp. The corridor had been icy, but now that he was warm, he couldn't bear to hide himself anymore. He was already erect, his cock nearly reaching his belly. Gabriel dropped his towel, as well, and met him halfway in a close, warm embrace that made him shiver with lust more than he had from cold. Crispin traced his hands up and down Gabriel's back, entranced by the softness of his skin over the powerful muscles in his shoulders, and by the individual bumps of his spine. Gabriel stroked him in return, his touch tentative at first, then he bent his head to Crispin's throat and gently bit.

Crispin laughed, even as he arched his neck into Gabriel's mouth, rubbing his skin against the bristles of his mustache, the smooth hardness of his teeth. "Oh, right there," he said, grinning when Gabriel scraped his teeth down the length of a tendon. He buried his fingers in Gabriel's thick golden hair, not so much to direct him as to simply hold on.

Gabriel worked his way down Crispin's chest, nipping at his pectorals through the curls on his chest, moving inexorably downward. Crispin said between gasps, "What do you like?"

"This," Gabriel said, gently closing his teeth on a nipple and sucking, hard.

"Fuck," Crispin said, his fingers working against Gabriel's scalp.

"Yes," Gabriel murmured. "I like it when someone's at my mercy." Abruptly, he lifted his head, his eyes wide. "I didn't mean that the way it sounded."

Crispin grinned. "It's not bad when someone wants to be at your mercy." He dragged Gabriel's head to him and kissed him, openmouthed and rough, then pressed their bodies close together. "Let me tell you what I want. I've had lots of time to think about it. I want our clothes off, and the lamp lit, and you looking at me and me looking at you." He leaned back, just enough to thoroughly study Gabriel's face, and his shoulders, and his chest, and his belly, and his circumcised cock in its astonishing veined smoothness. Later, he wanted Gabriel's cock over his tongue and jammed against his palate. He put his hand to Gabriel's cheek and rubbed with his thumb, then kissed him slowly, humming in his throat when Gabriel kissed him back. He pulled away and said, "I want you to fuck me, and I want it to be all right that I want to be fucked." He paused. "Is it?"

Gabriel's throat moved as he swallowed. "Yes. If it's what you want."

Crispin nodded sharply. "Yes. I want to be fucked by you, and I want us to remember, later, that it happened. And tomorrow, I want to do it all again."

"It doesn't sound like much," Gabriel said in a slow and thoughtful tone. "You already have most of it, and we'll get to the rest shortly."

"Exactly," Crispin said. "Except this is the first time I— not like that—but in the light. Do you know what I mean?"

Gabriel flushed. "I don't know, I haven't always done the right thing by you—"

"When it counts, you have," Crispin said. "You're here now. I trust you, you know. I have since we met. I know you won't think less of me because I want to be fucked."

Gabriel met his gaze again. "How could I, when I've done it myself?"

"You'd be surprised," Crispin said, and kissed him again.

Gabriel drew back first, but not too far. He spent a few moments staring into Crispin's eyes. Crispin felt another smile stretch his face. He leaned forward and nudged his nose against Gabriel's. Not coincidentally, his cock bumped into Gabriel's. "Well?"

Gabriel's eyes had gone hot. He asked, "Do you have anything we can use?"

"In my coat pocket."

"Why don't you fetch it, then?" Gabriel sat on the bed.

Crispin got the tin and tossed it to him. Gabriel caught it one-handed and examined the wrappings. After a moment, lounging back on the bed, one knee drawn up, he picked apart the knotted string with teeth and fingers. Crispin's cock twitched as he imagined those teeth on him.

Crispin sat next to him. He wanted to touch Gabriel's softly furred legs, so he did, stroking their length, feeling the hair beneath his palms as well as hard muscle. He remarked, "I used that kind once before." He pictured the slickness on him, in him, and shivered. He wanted Gabriel in him so badly that he physically ached. He swallowed, his throat suddenly dry. "Put some on your cock. I want to watch."

"Kiss me first."

"I've never kissed anyone as much as I've kissed you,"

Crispin said, stretching out beside him, fitting their bodies together. When his cock slid against Gabriel's, he closed his eyes for a moment, catching his breath. He was going to make this last.

"I like kissing," Gabriel said, cupping his hand over Crispin's buttock. "I'm going to kiss you all over."

Crispin slipped his tongue between Gabriel's parted lips. Soon they were clutching each other and panting.

"I have to stop," Crispin said, his chest heaving against Gabriel's. "I wanted to make it last."

"Next time," Gabriel promised. His hand circled gently on Crispin's arse. "Do you want me to bring you off first?" When Crispin shook his head, he said, "Turn over for me, then."

Crispin lay on his belly for Gabriel and felt safer than he had in months. He rested his head on his folded arms and closed his eyes as Gabriel kissed him between his shoulder blades, leaving a warm spot behind.

"Let's try this pillow," Gabriel said, arranging it beneath Crispin, then stroking the backs of his thighs. Crispin heard the metallic scrape of the tin's lid being twisted off, then felt a warm, wet kiss pressed to the small of his back. Oiled hands stroked from there to the backs of his thighs, then eased into the crease of his arse.

Velvety sensation rushed up his spine; he shuddered, sighed and relaxed into Gabriel's gently probing, stretching fingers until his skin thrummed like a plucked string. "That's good," he said. "Put some on your cock."

"Do you want to turn over and watch?"

"Just hurry," Crispin said, grinning into the sheet. He suddenly wanted to laugh. He did laugh when the head of Gabriel's cock pressed inside him, until he ran out of breath.

"Deeper," he said, breathing in, then out, relaxing himself to accommodate more.

Gabriel groaned as he slid farther inside. "Oh, Crispin, that's lovely."

"A little more."

"There?"

A blast of focused pleasure shot through his nerves. "Yes. There. Please."

Gabriel gripped his hips, bracing himself. "Hold on."

Crispin didn't have to fear discovery or rejection. He submerged his conscious mind in a sea of pleasure as Gabriel steadily rocked in and out of his body, inexorable as the tide. The pleasure surged and receded and slapped him to a near peak and receded again, with no pattern except that he never slid too far away to feel every fraction of Gabriel's skin rubbing against his, inside and out.

Crispin dug his fingers into the mattress, trying to hold back the climax that jolted nearer with every thrust. Gabriel's hand, slick with sweat and salve, landed on his back and massaged and scratched there, an added pleasure far enough from his cock and his arse that he felt stretched between the two, attenuated like metal being drawn into wire, the whole of him quivering, shuddering, desperate to snap.

He dug his hands into the mattress and shoved backward, in rough counterrhythm to Gabriel's thrusts, once, twice, then he came so hard he thought his spine would break.

In the aftermath, Gabriel's trembling arm locked around his belly. His cock was still hard, still buried deep inside. "All right?" he said huskily.

"Finish it," Crispin gasped, pressing his hand over Gabriel's and closing his eyes to savor every short, sharp thrust. It didn't take long for Gabriel to come with a hoarse cry, his arm nearly crushing Crispin in the process.

Afterward, they lay on their backs, holding hands even though the bed forced their bodies to press together from shoulders to knees. Crispin was sweaty, sticky, sore and utterly happy. He said, "The best part is, we can have another bath."

19

LUCILLA DROPPED TO THE GROUND AND CLOSED
the lorry's door behind her. She instantly missed the cab's stuffy
warmth. The woman driver, who spoke nothing but Flemish,
gave her a cheery wave and roared away into the night.

However deserted, this was enemy territory. Shells burst
some miles away, brief flashes swallowed by the vast dark. The
ground shuddered, but it wasn't as bad as they'd felt at the
hospital. Lucilla tugged her farmer's cap lower over her eyes
and walked to a half-collapsed shed, where another of Pascal's
agents had left certain items for her use.

A canine corpse, meant to be exchanged for one of the
werewolves, was the heaviest item, and luckily was fresh
enough not to smell too much. It looked nothing like a wolf,
but hopefully it would pass initial inspection after most of the
flesh had been burned off. The blanket-wrapped corpse
rested in, ironically, a dogcart, which also held a can of petrol,
a prybar, a canteen, clothing and blankets. She already carried
a filled match safe, buttoned safely into her trouser pocket,
and a medical kit inside a shabby rucksack.

Pascal had also given her a pistol, and shown her how to load and fire, but she had little confidence that she would actually hit anything in the heat of the moment, not to mention that any shots fired would bring guards running. She touched the pistol's smooth, cold surface inside the rucksack, remembering his arms around her, his front pressed to her back, his mustache brushing her ear as he murmured, "Relax, grip firmly but not tightly, and squeeze the trigger." He'd sounded as if he was speaking of another activity entirely.

She shook off the memory. "All prepared for a life of crime," she muttered. After checking her direction with a compass, she wrestled open the shed's poorly hung door and hauled the dogcart outside. The stars provided little light, and the air was crystalline with cold.

"I'll soon warm with exercise," she told herself, and set out. The road roughly paralleled a set of unused train tracks for some distance. She would know Kauz's secret laboratory by the configuration of its buildings; it ought to be the only such structure for miles. She only hoped she could recognize their layout in the dark, and find where the werewolves were being held. She couldn't do anything about that now, so she restricted herself to putting one foot in front of the other and not stepping into any holes.

About a mile along, she heard the roar of a motor. She crouched low by the roadside, concealing her shape behind the bulk of the dogcart as the vehicle, an unmarked ambulance, drove by, too fast for the rutted road. As soon as its headlights were lost in the distance, she hurried in the direction from which the ambulance had come. She'd gotten a decent look, but that likely wouldn't help her identify it later; ambulances, even motor ambulances, were as common near the front as fleas on a dog. She could only hope the closed rear of the ambulance hadn't concealed a pair of werewolves.

She needn't have worried about finding the laboratory. A half mile farther down the road, an electric spotlight beaming down from a pole nearly blinded her. It shone directly onto the muddy ruts left by a heavy vehicle, recently departed.

The dogcart would leave ruts, as well, easily seen. "Bugger," she muttered, and wrestled the canine corpse to the ground, still wrapped in its blanket. She would have to drag it that way, and hope the blanket blurred the tracks. For now, she took only the pry bar, which could double as a weapon.

Skirting the edges of the bright light, she soon spied a path of footprints, several layers of them beaten into the mud. The path led nowhere. "Not much of a secret entrance," she murmured, and cautiously approached. From the right angle, she could see a wooden trapdoor that presumably led to an underground area. The trapdoor looked heavy and awkward, possibly a problem for her strength alone and single pry bar. Also, the underground was more likely guarded, by humans or dogs or mechanical traps. She would scout out the aboveground facilities first so she would be able to report on them to Pascal.

The central of the three buildings had once been a station building for the defunct rail line. The windows were boarded, the door blocked by hammered-in strips of plywood. An open shed to one side smelled strongly of petrol and oil; greasy rags lay heaped on the ground near more ruts from tires. Lucilla took note of these, as potential additions to the fire she planned to set.

A walled toolshed stood behind, and in front of it, a bearded man with a rifle. A chill of fear and excitement flushed her spine. Carefully, she stepped back into the shed's darkness and looked around for other guards. When she saw none, she focused on the man she'd spotted. The guard leaned back against the shed's door, his shoulders slumped, his arms cradling the rifle against his belly. His head wasn't quite upright. After some minutes, Lucilla concluded gleefully that he was dozing.

Quietly, she snuck back to her supplies. She'd had plenty of experience lately in emergency anesthetization. A bottle of ether and a cloth would serve. She took a slightly different path back toward the open shed where she'd hidden before. Once concealed in the darkness, she worked out the ether bottle's cork with her teeth and poured a measured amount onto a folded cloth. She felt as calm as if she stood in an operating theater, with the same heightened awareness of all that surrounded her. When the cloth was soaked, she walked quickly to the guard and clamped the cloth firmly over his nose and mouth.

He didn't wake fast enough to struggle, and soon his muscles went slack. Lucilla caught his weight, staggered, then dragged him a distance away before returning to the shed. She considered claiming his rifle, then decided against the extra weight and instead heaved it as far away as she could.

The toolshed's door was held closed by a length of chain and a newish padlock. "Oh, ho," she breathed, inching closer then, when she caught a whiff of familiar scent, even closer. It was hard to mistake the smell of ether, much more than she had just used. The whole shed must have been pumped full of it, which explained the rags stuffed into the gap between the door and the dirt.

The chain resisted her pry bar, until it occurred to her to attack the door's hinges instead. Cheap and rusted, they yielded almost immediately, and she had to suppress a crow of triumph. She danced back out of the way as the door hung balanced for a moment, then fell to the mud with a soft *thump*.

The shed was dark inside, but she could make out a bulky shadow on the dirt floor. Tucking the pry bar into her belt, she went closer. A wolf. Its bound feet twitched, reassuring her that it was alive. Ashby, or Miss Claes?

It didn't matter which, she couldn't leave the wolf here. Even from here she could smell blood as well as ether. Also, given that the wolf captive was in a surface shed instead of safely below, it would not surprise her if the wolf had been left here for pickup by another ambulance, or perhaps the same one when it returned.

She needed to act quickly. First the wolf out of the shed and into the dogcart, ready for escape. Then the canine corpse into the shed, and the fire. If she had time, she would go below and see if she could locate the other wolf; if the ambulance, or any other vehicle, returned, then she would flee, and leave finding the other wolf to Pascal.

Once she'd dragged the wolf, whose reddish fur looked like Ashby's, into the dogcart, she hurried back to the shed, dragging the blanket with the decoy corpse. The ether still in the air inside the shed would catch fire more effectively than petrol, and make the fire seem accidental, she hoped. She dug out her match safe and struck three matches on its rough surface before cautiously tossing them through the shed's fallen door. The ether caught with a gusty noise, and she hurtled backward, laughing a little in shock, which soon turned to urgency as she realized the ongoing noise was an approaching motor.

"Bugger," she gasped, and sprinted for the dogcart. She had to get Ashby to safety, and quickly.

★ ★ ★

Hot wires of pain stabbed Lucilla's wrists and shoulders as she dragged the dogcart down a pitted farm path, her heels sinking deeply into the mud with every step and having to be wrenched free. Despite her gloves, her hands were blistered, and she'd no energy for cursing. She'd run through all her adrenaline from earlier. All she had left was endurance and fear that she and her burden wouldn't reach the abandoned barn before dark.

Twenty steps more. Ten. Five. The barn's door was barred. She dropped the dogcart's poles and shook her hands, trying to return feeling. In the cart's bed, the wolf stirred and whimpered, perhaps returning to consciousness. She couldn't soothe him yet. She grasped the wide wooden bar and heaved. She had to throw her weight against the door to shove it open. Wincing, she seized the poles again, dragged the cart inside, and struggled with the door until it was firmly closed. A bar hung on the inside. She didn't dare risk leaving the door alone. Nearly sobbing in frustration, she hoisted the bar into place and pounded it down with the heels of her hands. When she'd finished, she leaned against it for long moments, trembling from exertion. Assuming she had not just locked them into the wrong barn, all she had left to do was care for Ashby's injuries and await rescue. She could surely manage those two simple things.

When she turned, the wolf was on his feet, head hanging low, his body swaying gently from side to side. His brushlike tail drooped. "Lie down," she said. "You're injured."

She wasn't sure if he hadn't heard or if he ignored her. Dark streaks of dried blood looked like mud in his rufous pelage. More blood smeared his muzzle. He took one step, then another, his nails skidding on the wood when he began to slide down toward the open end of the dogcart. Lucilla broke his fall, throwing them both sideways to avoid the poles. She landed panting in stale, dusty straw, pinned down by a weighty mass of fur. Though she felt his breathing, she could not help but be reminded of the canine corpse she had dumped in Kauz's laboratory shed, in place of Ashby, before setting it alight.

After a brief inspection of his limbs, the best she could manage from flat on her back, she shoved at his shoulder. "Off, you idiot," she said. "You might have hurt yourself far worse doing that. Just like a man." He rolled limply to the floor and she rose, brushing straw and fur from her coat and trousers with feeble hands. The wolf whimpered, then pinned his muzzle beneath his bloody paws, a bizarre parody of a man covering his face with his hands.

"Stay there," she instructed. She staggered back to the dogcart and opened her rucksack of supplies.

She found her battery torch first. She set it to hand, as the barn, with its sparse, high windows, would grow dark more quickly than the outdoors. She needed to be able to see what she was doing. Next, she extracted a bottle of carbolic solution, some of the powder she used for wound dressings, salve and bandages. She hadn't thought to bring a razor, which had been very foolish, as she'd known she might be treating an animal. Perhaps her surgical scissors would be enough. He'd scraped off some of his fur through struggling in his bonds, and that seemed to be the source of most of his injuries. She wasn't sure about his mouth. He had likely been muzzled, but she also suspected he'd been struck.

She heard a sharp rustle behind her, then thrashing. "Stay still!" she commanded, and turned. The wolf spasmed, whimpered and abruptly began to change, his body twisting in the straw. "Damn it!" She fell to her knees beside him, but could do nothing, even while he whimpered continually and writhed. "Ashby, stop it! Stop! You're hurting yourself!"

With a last tortured growl, his spine arched, and there in the straw lay a naked human man, his pale freckled skin scraped raw at the throat, wrists and ankles. His mustache didn't hide that his mouth looked as if someone had repeatedly hit him. He coughed, a painful, ripping sound.

"Christ," he said, his voice like broken glass. "Oh, Christ, that hurt." He closed his eyes and turned his face away, his mouth working.

"Idiot," Lucilla said, running her hands over him, ignoring his flinches. The wolf's foreleg had been injured, she was sure, but Ashby's looked less painful. Gently, she probed the bruising that remained. "Did you heal already?" When he didn't answer, she gripped his shoulder. His skin felt cool. Shock wasn't a surprising outcome. She'd been distracted by the miraculous change of wolf to man. She returned to the dogcart for the blankets. By the time she came back, he was shivering. "Ashby!" she said, chafing his hands. "Talk to me."

"Changing helped," he said. "Except you pay. Christ. Hurts. Thank you. Thank you. Thought I'd die there. Thank you." He curled in on himself, his arms protecting his stomach.

"You're welcome," she said. "Hold still. I'd like to wrap up these scrapes. We're safe here."

"Where—"

"We're waiting for rescue. Mr. Fournier is sending a motor—"

"Miss Claes," Ashby said. "Is she—"

Lucilla said, "She wasn't with you, but we were prepared for that possibility, we're sure we know where she is. Major Fournier will find her and get her out."

"She's not dead," Ashby said.

"No, not dead," Lucilla reassured him. She wasn't sure, but it was pointless to worry him just now, when they could do nothing. "Hold still," she said. "This will sting."

"You have no idea—ouch!—how funny that is."

An hour later, Lucilla sat in the dogcart, arms wrapping her updrawn knees, while Ashby, in the clothing she'd brought, paced and swung his arms, occasionally stopping to bounce on the balls of his feet and stretch his neck. Though dressed as a farmer in trousers, loose shirt, vest and soft cap, he did not resemble a farmer in the least; he looked entirely too predatory for that. She said, "It will be some time yet, I think."

"I can't stand this," he said. "The door being closed."

"We could open it a bit. It was closed when we arrived."

He shook his head. "Best not." He trotted to the rear of the barn and rapidly climbed the ladder leading up into the hayloft. He came down again almost as swiftly. "Thought I smelled mice. They've been at the seed corn."

"Perhaps you could hunt them," Lucilla said, knowing if he didn't occupy himself soon, she would go mad.

He shook his head. "Too tired to change again." He turned away suddenly.

She was sorry she'd said it. She knew what had likely happened to him. She ought to have been more forgiving of his nerves, but she was nervous, too. As when she and Pascal had stolen the motor, she hadn't been frightened or worried at all during the rescue. She'd been cool and casual as she hacked off the lock to Ashby's cell. She'd been exhilarated when she'd got safely away, Ashby in the cart behind her. Now, as she waited, she felt cold and nauseated and a bit shaky. She wanted Pascal to arrive and put his arms around her.

Ashby came back to the dogcart and held out his hands to her. "Battle nerves?" he asked.

He sounded matter-of-fact, which gave Lucilla the courage to place her cold hands in his warm ones. He pulled her to her feet then wrapped her in his arms, briskly massaging her back with his knuckles. She said, "Is this the cure for your men's nerves?"

He rubbed his cheek over her hair. "I might be fraternizing a bit with you. You did rescue me, after all."

Gradually, she stopped shaking. When she moved away from Ashby, he looked momentarily helpless, then shoved his hands into his pockets. "How long until our rescue arrives?"

"I'm not sure," she said. "It wasn't easy to find a motor to secretly commandeer. The owners—the driver couldn't leave except at certain times."

"We could set off on our own," Ashby suggested.

"Too far," she said. "Besides, I didn't fetch you out just so you could be picked right back up again."

"As if we'll be any safer in the motor of a complete stranger," he said, then closed his eyes. "I'm sorry. I'm a bit nervous."

"If it helps, the motor belongs to a nunnery," she said.

Ashby began to laugh. "Oh, good. Perhaps I'll have them send a postcard to Mater. She'll be thrilled imagining that I finally went to mass." Then he sobered. "I'll ask her to pray for Miss Claes."

Tanneken strained, struggled, twisted. The metal mesh only grew tighter. At least the others were gone, leaving behind a fug of chemicals and anger and cowardice. None could now see how humiliatingly she was trapped, wire slicing deeply, only her thick undercoat preventing the grid from cutting her skin.

She whuffed out an exhausted breath and collapsed to the cold floor, panting. She could no longer smell Captain Ashby at all. He must be similarly confined, far enough away that she would not smell him. Dense walls would prevent her from hearing his howls. Or he might be dead.

Enraged, she again writhed, trying to bite the wire, succeeding only in cutting her gums and smearing her muzzle with blood. The pain brought her back to herself for a moment. It was unwise to care what happened to her fellow captive. Apparently, it was too late to remind herself of that fact. It did matter to her, if Ashby lived or died. There were not so many werewolves in the world that she could afford to scorn one, especially one who was not her enemy. One who did not curse her sharp human tongue.

One whom she liked.

To run with another through starlit darkness would be the kind of joy she hadn't felt since before her mother first fell ill. He could not be dead. Their kind did not die easily. She knew that more than most. She might be able to—

Was this hope?

She heard a rustling in the corridor outside her cell and she tensed, bracing to leap should the grid be removed. The door was too thick for her to discern how many enemies there might be. She heard scratching like mice in the walls, distant clicks, then a pop and wheeze as the door eased open. She inhaled and then froze. Even without the familiar sharpness of lime shaving lotion, she recognized Pascal Fournier.

Her lips slid slowly back over her teeth. She smelled no one other than Fournier and, without her willing it, she fell momentarily limp. A soft whine escaped her throat.

"Ah, *merde*," he whispered, hurrying to her. "Hold very still, Madame Claes—Tanneken—"

The shock of hearing her own name while in wolf form kept her from moving as he reached into his coat pocket and emerged with a pair of cutters. His execrable accent as he murmured to her was reassuringly real. Carefully, he insinuated a blade into one of the squares pressing into her bloodied muzzle and, after a moment's painful pressure, snipped the wire. It sprang free. His breath eased out with hers. "We are very lucky we thought to search here. I must cut a few more." He brushed his hand over her head before beginning, once again, to cut.

Freed from the wire cage, Tanneken's limbs throbbed with the pain of returning blood flow. She rocked unsteadily onto the concrete floor, then nearly yelped when Fournier scooped her into his arms, a dizzying swoop high into the air. She thumped her jaw against his chest in protest, but he made no answer, ducking out the door and hurrying through a dusty corridor she did not remember having traversed before. She must have been carried through it before, unconscious. He shoved through another door with his hip—this one bore a flapping, cut chain—ran up a short flight of wooden stairs and used the back of his shoulder to fling open a trapdoor above their heads.

She smelled musty wet leaves, cold ground, burnt petrol. Fournier did not stop to set her down. Within moments she was sprawled across the rumble seat of an auto, which smelled intriguingly not only of Fournier but of an unknown woman.

Perhaps the auto belonged to someone else. Fournier dumped a blanket over Tanneken and said, "Stay hidden." The auto's motor growled to life, vibrating the leather seat cushion beneath her. She panted out pain and worked at stretching her muscles as Fournier drove them to what she hoped was safety, traveling much faster than her own feet would have taken her. She could see nothing, and smelled little beyond the interior of the vehicle and the blanket over her head. It was so anticlimactic and dull, she could not help but believe that she truly was free.

After not much longer, she fell asleep.

She woke when Fournier whisked off the blanket. He eyed her for a moment. "Please don't bite me when I lift you out."

She lifted a brow, then yawned. Freedom was sweet, but she was too exhausted to fight anyone, and she would have to change form if she wished to ask what had become of Ashby.

Fournier lifted her out. "Shall I set you on your feet?" he asked with grave courtesy.

After a moment's thought on how to communicate, she awkwardly bobbed her head.

Tanneken didn't recognize the house to which he led her, and it smelled of long emptiness. No other house was in sight, though there was a stable, also empty and stale, and a fenced paddock. The inhabitants had no doubt fled during the Boche onslaught. After thoroughly sniffing the front doorway, she followed Fournier inside, aware that she hadn't the strength to go much farther.

Her nails snagged on a threadbare runner in the front hall. She hurried through, not liking the narrow space, and hesitated at the foot of the staircase. She preferred to climb stairs as a human, but the idea of changing shook her with revulsion. She padded cautiously up the carpeted steps after Fournier, who waited for her at the top. He said, "I have clothing for you, if you'd like, and I brought you some food."

She saw an open door and darted inside. She chose a corner facing the door and settled into it, wrapping the brush of her tail around herself and resting her muzzle on her front paws. When he stepped into the room, she growled, and he backed away.

"Very well. I'll leave you alone for now. Come down to the kitchen when you're hungry."

20

NOEL LIFTED HIS HEAD AS THE LORRY APPROACHED the house. Tanneken was there. Relief swamped him, and he sagged in his seat.

"Yes, Sister Claudette, this is the house," Lucilla said to the driver. "I recognize the trees Monsieur Fournier described."

Noel barely listened. As soon as the lorry squeaked to a stop, he thrust aside the tarp, vaulted over the side and ran for the house's door. Inside, he immediately heard claws on wood. The sound came from upstairs. Without waiting for Lucilla, or for Fournier to appear, he leaped up the stairs, three at a time. He turned right and flung open a door. Tanneken, in wolf form, stared up at him. Noel closed the door, dropped to one knee and bared his throat. She flew at him and gripped his neck in her powerful jaws.

He didn't move, inhaling hot wolfy breath as she panted against his throat. Her teeth dented his skin but didn't break it, the pressure only enough to let him know she *could* bite if she desired. He would let her. If she needed that, to feel safe, he would give it to her.

Slowly, he lifted his right hand and let it descend to her ruff, closing his fingers among the stiff guard hairs without quite gripping.

He heard voices downstairs: Lucilla and a male voice he assumed was Fournier's. Their conversation was relaxed, intimate; there was nothing to fear here. He lifted his other arm and looped it about Tanneken's neck.

A moment later, he lay on his back on the dusty wooden floor, Tanneken's front paws planted on either side of his head, her tongue lolling in his face. The hard floor felt good beneath his back, perhaps because he had the freedom to stretch out to his full length, free of physical pain and restraint. Noel grinned up at her. "I'm pleased to see you, as well."

Tanneken nuzzled his neck with her cold nose, then licked from his Adam's apple to his jawline. He said, "I'd let you lick me if you changed, as well."

She bumped her nose beneath his chin, forcing it up. She growled, not quite a warning.

"Or you can bite my neck again. I'm perfectly satisfied for you to be on top." Though his palms itched with his need to embrace her, woman or wolf, he resisted, curling his fingers into his trouser legs, instead. "I'll understand if you'd rather not be human at the moment, but…" He swallowed. "I'd take it as a great favor if you would change. Just for a little. Please?" Slowly, he rolled his head to the side, exposing his throat again. "Or I'll change, if you like. I'm a bit tired, but I can manage."

Tanneken's ears lost a fraction of their alertness. Then she changed, her body writhing and convulsing atop his, the intimacy so shocking he could hardly bear it. He looped his arms around her loosely, while her skin and muscles rippled and transformed.

She was panting when she'd finished, but her change had been fairly swift and without undue pain. He tightened his arms around her, breathing in her complex human scent and relaxing for the first time in days. He had never embraced her before, not when they were both two-legged. The skin along her spine felt soft as flower petals beneath his fingertips. "You're all right," he said.

Tanneken withdrew almost immediately, sitting up and straddling his waist. "I will not be all right until I've licked Kauz's lifeblood from my jaws." Expanding on this theme, she burst into a spate of Flemish profanity.

Noel, forced to wait, rested his hands just above her knees and spent the interval admiring her naked form, particularly her breasts, while enjoying the pressure of her sleek bottom against his cock. After she ran out of words, he said, "I can report the location of Kauz's laboratory. The artillery can shell it into dust."

"Not good enough," she said. "What if he learns of this attack, and flees? What if your artillery is not accurate?"

He decided defending the honor of his nation's army would not be apropos. "What if you walk into his den and someone rips you open with a machine gun? He'll be on his guard against us now. He knows what we can survive, and can guess what we can't, even if his tame wolves haven't betrayed what it takes."

"He is your country's enemy," Tanneken pointed out. "For that reason alone, you should want to kill him."

"For what he did to you, I want to kill him," Noel said, tightening his fingers on her thighs.

"You will not take my revenge from me," she said, her voice low and cold.

"No. You'd never forgive me. And I hope to remain in your good graces."

Impatiently, she pushed her hair back from her face. "You still harbor delusions. I haven't the time for such as you."

"After Kauz is dead, you might," Noel said. "After he's dead, what will you do then? If you still want a child, I'd be happy to give one to you. We could marry and have a child with our wolf natures, Tanneken. Isn't that what you wanted, before all this began?"

"I should not have told you." She shoved his hands away from her and rose, standing over him.

To stop himself from reaching for her, Noel wrapped his arms around himself. It helped with the stabbing ache in his chest. He said, "It's hardly an uncommon desire, especially for our kind. That's why you married Edel."

"And you? Have you done something foolish in the hope of a child?"

"All manner of things, and I seem to be doing it again now," Noel said. He closed his eyes. "You could just tell me *no* and be done with it."

Long moments passed. She murmured, "I don't know that I can bring a child into this war. And I am no longer fit to be mother to a helpless creature."

His heart twisted. "Don't be ridiculous."

"I will be a murderer once I kill him. And I do not care. I will kill him and rejoice that he is dead."

Noel opened his eyes and sat up. "Do you know how many men I've killed?"

"No." She eyed him belligerently.

"Neither do I, but the numbers have gone up steadily since I came to France. Would you say I'm not fit to have a child?"

Tanneken said nothing. Noel said, "I'm not put off by that sort of thing. Quite the contrary. If you don't want to try with me, just say it." Again, she said nothing.

Someone knocked on the door. "We're fine," Noel said.

"Are you hungry?" Lucilla said.

Mentally, Noel cursed the interruption even as Tanneken's stomach growled.

Tanneken seized the robe that had been left for her and belted it on. She opened the door wide. "Take me to the food."

Lucilla glanced quizzically at Noel, who still sat on the floor.

He said, "A cup of tea wouldn't go amiss."

If he hadn't been so distracted by Tanneken, he would have heard Lucilla's approach, and smelled the mouthwatering bouquet of onions sizzling in butter. Halfway down the stairs, his stomach awoke and he was ravenous. He should have expected his appetite; he'd changed several times in various states of injury while sleeping minimally and eating less. Right now, presented with a fresh deer's carcass, he would have eaten the lot, or tried.

Fournier waited for them in the huge farm kitchen, a tall and lanky man who looked close to Noel's own age. His blue uniform jacket and kepi were draped over the arm of a chair, and he'd rolled up his shirtsleeves to cook. Noel sniffed. Fournier wasn't a wolf, but he was related to one, and not too distantly, either. Apparently oblivious to this fact, Tanneken daintily cut the folded crepe he'd just slid before her. Of course, she'd met him before. It was no surprise to her. Her lack of interest in Fournier as a possible mate gave Noel hope.

He said, "Thank you, Major. For finding us and bringing us out. And also for the food."

Fournier looked uncomfortable. He said abruptly, "Sit.

Mademoiselle Daglish is making tea in the English way for you. Here is bread until I can cook more crepes. Madame Claes is eating the one I had hoped to share between you."

Noel tore into the baguette, the first fresh bread he'd tasted in weeks. He moaned in pleasure as the yeasty flavor hit his tongue. "How did you find us?" he asked around a mouthful. He swallowed. "And what are your plans for Kauz and his merry band?"

Fournier said, "I had hoped you would help us with that, as well as Madame Claes. Kauz must be stopped, but I don't think it wise to reveal his work to the world."

"I can agree with that," Noel said.

"We should burn it all," Tanneken said, forking more crepe into her mouth.

Momentarily distracted, Noel watched her chew. She was visibly enjoying her food. He said, "I'd prefer to be well out of range when that happens. A delayed fuse would be better."

Lucilla set a folded towel on the table, then set a teapot atop it. "I think it will require more than a spy and a nurse and two werewolves."

Fournier said, "There is the added problem that the underground laboratory where Madame Claes and Captain Ashby were being held is some distance from the official laboratory. It is the official laboratory where experimentation with chemical weapons is taking place, and that is what my government wishes destroyed. Of course, it must be destroyed, but not at the expense of leaving the secret underground facility. Perhaps, Mademoiselle Daglish, you could travel with me to the official laboratory, while Captain Ashby and Madame Claes destroy the underground chambers."

"I have a better idea," Lucilla said. "We enlist my brother,

Crispin, for the official laboratory, and let the army take care of it. He'll be glad to know you're alive, Ashby."

Crispin Daglish seemed to belong to another life, one he'd almost forgotten in recent days. Noel said, "Then we'll need Gabriel Meyer, as well. He already knows that I'm a werewolf, and is no mean hand with tactics, and best of all, he can speak German pretty well. Bob Hailey would help, as well. They're trained for raids like that. I would send them to the official laboratory, where they won't see anything untoward. The rest of us should go to the secret facility, and make sure that no records or samples survive from werewolf captives."

Tanneken said, "So long as these soldiers stay well clear of me, I do not care how many helpers you have." She looked sharply at Fournier. "You will do this for me. I do not wish to have imbeciles from your government trying to attack in taxicabs and the like."

She referred to an incident in early September, in which French troops had been transported in taxicabs and anything else, to protect Paris. Noel might have assured her nothing like that would happen again, but in truth, he had little confidence in the higher levels of command when it came to acting quickly and effectively.

Fournier set a crepe and silverware in front of Noel and said, "I begin to understand why others dislike working with me."

After their meal, Noel felt almost drugged. He'd passed through the shaky stage back in the barn, and then the jittery stage. Now came the exhaustion; he could barely remember what Fournier and Lucilla had been discussing. He braced both hands on the table and shoved himself to his feet. "I'm for bed. Madame Claes? Shall I escort you?"

Abruptly, she pushed away the tea she'd been nursing and rose. "We are safe here for the night?"

"We are," Fournier said. "I will be on guard." He exchanged a look with Lucilla that might have been apology.

"Then I, too, would prefer to rest," Tanneken said.

Noel suddenly felt much more alert. He offered her his arm and, after a suspicious glance, she laid her hand lightly on it, as if they were parading into the supper room at a regimental ball. Halfway up the stairs, he asked her, "Are you going to change?"

She didn't mistake his meaning. "It's safer to have teeth. Fournier has a pistol, but he is not dangerous enough."

"May I stay with you?"

"You intend to seduce me," she said flatly. She turned left and went into the second room, the one farthest from the kitchen below.

"It's hardly seduction if you know what I'm about," he said reasonably. She hadn't stopped him from following her into the room. Noel closed the door behind them. The room held a substantial iron bed, a wardrobe, a washstand and two shabby armchairs before a fireplace. Wood bristled from a pail on the hearth, with some crumpled newspaper shoved in on top. He knelt, his back to Tanneken, and began to lay a fire.

"What do you want?" she asked.

Noel reached up and felt around on the mantel until he found a tin of matches. As he lit the tinder, he said, "I want you to want to live, for one thing."

"I don't want to die," she snapped.

"You don't particularly seem to want to live, either," he said. "You'd go for Kauz's throat even if he had a gun in his hand, wouldn't you?"

"That's different," she said. When he glanced at her, she stood with her arms crossed over her chest.

"Since I've been in France, I've seen how it goes when men don't care anymore. I make it my business to keep them alive, as best I can. And you—well, I want you to live."

"I would be happy to live, if it can be managed."

He sat cross-legged on the hearth, relaxing as heat licked up his back. "All right, then. If we get out of this alive, will you consider marrying me?"

"To have a child," she said.

"Yes." His heart tried to pound its way out of his chest. He didn't dare say more. He was normally glib, but this could so easily go wrong.

She turned away, paced a few steps, then returned to face him. The fire crackled; he breathed in wood smoke and ash. "The Boche have overrun my estate."

"Would you come to England? I am the only son."

"You have siblings?"

"Two sisters, much older than I, one married to a human, with human children. And my parents are still living, and three of my grandparents. We would have a house of our own, I promise."

"I might have no money, even if the war ends and the Boche are beaten." She sounded as bland as if she were selling turnips.

He rose to his knees and held out his hands. When she hesitantly clasped them, he said, "I have money. I'll give it to you outright if you want. None of that matters anymore. What matters is that I'll be a good husband to you. I would never betray you. If anything happened to me, my family would care for you, and not grudgingly, either."

"You English do things differently," she said.

"Not really. *I* do things differently." He raised her hands to his mouth and kissed them. "Will you think on it?"

She drew her hands out of his grip. "After I have killed Kauz, I will consider it. Stand up. There is one more thing I must know before I consent to marry you."

Noel couldn't stop himself from grinning. "I was hoping you would get to that."

She shed her robe, letting it fall to the floor. "Take off those clothes."

She was beautiful, sleek and muscular beneath clear, smooth skin, which his palms already itched to caress again. "In any particular order?" he asked. She'd already seen him naked, so he should try to make it interesting.

A hint of a smile flickered at the corner of her mouth. He hadn't realized she had a dimple. Suddenly, he wanted to lick it. She said, "The quickest order."

He stripped off his woolen vest and shoved the braces off his shoulders, then lifted his foot and worked off his heavy shoes and woolen socks. "It's a bloody good thing I'm not in uniform," he said. "Those damn puttees would be killing me about now. Though these shoes don't fit, and I'll be glad to be rid of them."

She said, her smile briefly appearing again, "Turn around as you do that."

"I like you," Noel said, doing as she asked. She would have a fine view of his arse while he stood on one foot to remove his other boot. He unbuttoned his trousers and shucked out of them. He hadn't bothered with the drawers Lucilla had given him, but Tanneken might not have noticed that yet, as his shirt hung nearly to his knees. He turned back to her. "Would you like to remove this yourself?"

"You're playful," she said. "Even now."

"Is there anything wrong with that?"

She was silent for a long time, then she beckoned him forward. "No. No."

Noel looked down at her, nose to lips to breasts, and said, "I recall you like *stimulating conflicts*."

"I will tell you what I want." She flicked open the button at his throat, then two more, and pushed the open collar over his shoulder.

Noel obligingly undid another button, so his shirt slid down his torso. "Good. And you want?"

Tanneken watched his shirt catch on his erection. She lifted it with one finger and let it flutter down his legs to the floor. He shivered at the phantom touch, and at the rising scent of her arousal, fed by his own scent, he was sure. "You have freckles all over," she noted.

"Do you have any objection to freckles?" It was growing difficult to concentrate on his words.

"I've not previously considered them," she said. She rose on her toes and mouthed his throat, then slid her open mouth over his, sucking at his lower lip. Noel caught her in his arms, remembering at the last moment not to grasp her too tightly. Instead, he let his hands roam over her smoothly muscled back while they kissed. She was aggressive, frequently nipping at his lips, his chin, the soft spot beneath his jawline, while her nails dug into his chest, each sharp little pressure like a spark of electricity prickling over his skin.

His cock throbbed against her soft skin, and she squirmed against it, forcing him backward until his knees smacked into the edge of a mattress.

Tanneken was sucking on the thin skin over his collarbone,

and he could barely speak for shuddering in pleasure. "We've a…bed…right here."

Without removing her mouth from him, Tanneken bore him down, squirming atop him before she rose to her knees. Straddling his hips, she pinned his shoulder to the mattress with one hand. Noel reached up and thumbed her nipples, which tightened instantly. When he rubbed them, she threw her head back and gasped, rolling her shoulders, before pushing his hands away. "I want you from behind," she said.

"I thought you'd want to keep an eye on me."

"I don't fear you," she said, and kissed him again, her tongue lubriciously mapping the interior of his mouth until he couldn't breathe. She withdrew and squeezed his shoulder muscles, then his arms.

"I'm glad," he said. "Are you sure you don't want to just take me like this?" His stamina had deserted him. One more kiss like that, one more roll of her body over his cock, and he was sure he would come like an explosion.

"You can go deeper from behind," she said, and he moaned, imagining it.

"Right," he said, or thought he said, as they shifted positions. He was practically blind with lust, deaf with it. He felt as if he floated in her scent as it rose about them in a cloud, spicing the air and settling on his skin like a million tiny touches. He licked up the length of her bare spine, sucking on each vertebrae, inhaling her with his mouth and nose, and almost didn't notice her reaching hand on his cock until he bumped against the slick lips of her cunt. "Oh, Christ," he said. "Tanneken. Let go." Her fingers loosened and he breathed a sigh of relief.

"I want you now," she said.

"Christ, I want you, too," he said, easing the head of his cock between her lips. Her scent changed, grew richer, and her cunt grasped at him, slick and hot. He stopped, tears of pleasure knotting his throat, and tried to regain control.

Tanneken wriggled backward, taking him a bit more. He gasped and dug his hands into the sheet. "Do you want this to last more than five minutes?" he asked. It had been far too long since he'd had sex of any kind.

"Deeper," she demanded. "Fuck me." She thrust her hips back, and suddenly he was engulfed head to base in heat, in wetness, in her rich scent.

He couldn't think. He thrust raggedly, with none of his usual finesse; Tanneken thrust back against him, her round arse thumping into him even as his balls slapped into her, both of them grabbing at the sheets, the blankets, each other. He hooked one arm around her waist and found her clit by moving his hand until she cried out, and stroked her there softly in counterpoint to their rough intercourse. It was fast, messy, glorious.

Tanneken growled when she came, her cunt squeezing him over and over as hot cream spilled over his hand. He sank his teeth into her shoulder and she shuddered against his belly again, this time moaning and burying her face against the pillow.

Noel's arm shook from holding his weight. "All right?" he asked. He was barely able to get the words out.

"Yes," she said, low and sultry. "I want to be on top now."

She was going to kill him. Noel clenched his jaw and shifted onto his back. Normally, he loved this position and the gorgeous view it provided, but now he was beyond anything but craving, his skin on fire, his cock ready to pulse out of his skin. "Fuck me, damn it," he said.

Tanneken grinned and licked her lips. She had two dimples. Dazed, he watched her shove her long hair behind her shoulders and cup her breasts from beneath, lightly grazing her thumbs over her engorged nipples. She rolled her hips and he cried out.

"Mine," she said. She bent over and set her teeth in his neck. She swiped with her tongue, pinched up a layer of skin, then let it go and licked again. Her hard nipples rubbed his chest like hot brands.

"Yours," he agreed, surging up with his hips.

She muttered in Flemish and began to ride him much more slowly than he would have liked. Her heady scent fluttered into his nostrils with each shaky inhale. Restlessly, he ran his hands up and down her sides, at last finding a grip on her arse. She didn't seem to mind if he dug in his fingers, so he held on there to restrain himself from moving his hips.

When she began to speed up her riding, he closed his eyes. She squeezed him from within, until he felt his whole body was clenched in wet heat. Shudders rippled over his skin and he thrashed beneath her, losing control of his muscles almost as if he were shifting forms. She rode him harder, leaning over so her nipples brushed his chest, grinding herself against him. When she came this time, he rushed after her, muffling his cries in her shoulder as his cock jolted deep inside her, each separate convulsion rippling more pleasure from his head to his heels. Then his exhaustion caught up to him, and he drifted, barely aware of her surreptitious touch on his cheek. "Yes, I will marry you, if you make the process of getting children so entertaining," she whispered, and he smiled before he fell asleep.

21

LUCILLA COULD NOT IMMEDIATELY LOCATE CRISPIN, which was frustrating in the extreme, as she knew that if Kauz had the slightest inkling of danger, he would pick up his secret laboratory and move somewhere else, probably deeper within German territory, and they might never find him again.

Kauz would not have been fooled long by the canine corpses that had been left for him, if there had been enough left of them for Kauz to examine; the decoys were only a delaying tactic. Kauz would be suspicious because his two captives had escaped so close together in time, even though they were being held miles apart. He would know his captives could not have escaped without help; but would he expect them to return? Would he consider the wolves or their rescuers enough of a threat that he would have to find a new location for his experiments with captives? If so, their only hope was the difficulty of moving a facility that possessed such complex needs.

Lucilla was also counting on Kauz's arrogance to keep him

in place. Finally, once Crispin and his colleagues attacked Kauz's larger, official laboratory, the one the German government knew about, Kauz's lines of communication would be kept so busy he would, hopefully, become distracted. In the best case, some of his men from the secret facility would be sent to the official laboratory, and Lucilla and her group would have fewer opponents to overcome as they set about acquiring Kauz's research and destroying whatever they could.

The courier Pascal lent to her returned quickly, but with the news that her brother had journeyed to Paris on leave.

Lieutenant Meyer was also on leave, while their battalion was engaged in helping to lay a railway to the rear of the line of battle. In the midst of her annoyance at their absence, she felt a niggling curiosity—were the two men on leave together? Had Crispin gotten his wish? Or was he even now sitting, alone, at a darkened table in a smoky café, lost in regret?

It was an odd feeling, to worry about her little brother's romantic life. She had never done so before because there had never been any romance for him, or not any she'd known of; even knowing what she now knew about him, it was difficult to imagine him in that light, though now that the idea was in her mind, she had a strong intellectual curiosity concerning what two men might be like together. She had always been so busy with her studies, and later with her work, that she had never had enough time for Crispin, for either his joys or his griefs. Now, as she wondered what he was doing, she keenly felt the lack.

Private Hailey arrived at the hospital late that same evening, bearing a large rucksack over her shoulder. Lucilla stared at her, nonplussed at her appearance in the ward, but quickly surmised she'd read the message intended for her officers.

Acting as if Hailey had been expected, she said, "If you can take a seat over there, I'll show you where you can sleep when my shift ends."

Her shift lasted well beyond its allotted time, and when she returned to find Hailey, she found her deeply involved in a game of cards with three of the patients, one of whom hastily stubbed out a cigarette as she approached.

"Come along, Hailey," she said.

Hailey apologetically discarded her cards and shoved a pile of coins into her pocket. "Yes, Sister."

Lucilla led her to the kitchen, which, fortunately, was deserted, and put on the kettle for tea. "Do you know where my brother is? Did Lieutenant Meyer go with him? It's urgent that I find both of them."

Hailey, who was still standing near the door, rocked uneasily from heel to toe and back again. "Why?"

Lucilla's gaze snapped to her face, which was a study in blankness. Tea-colored eyes stared back at her, but gave away nothing. Lucilla said, "I know what my brother is, Hailey. He told me himself. And he told me what his hopes were. So tell me, can you find them?"

"Paris," Hailey said. "I'll need a ride."

The road to Paris was in awful shape. Bob clung desperately to the Zouave piloting the motorbike and tried to ignore the fragments of cold mud whipping her cheek and splatting on her goggles. Periodically, the rear wheel would skid in a puddle and the bike would be knocked askew, sometimes careening far enough to one side that the Zouave's boot would scrape through mud; he would shout in French, right the machine with a disconcerting jerk, and off they would speed again, weaving in and out of various ambulances, lorries and the occasional horse-drawn wagon. Aside from trains, she had never traveled so fast in her life, especially not balanced half on a seat and half on a saddlebag.

Traffic grew heavier as they approached Paris, necessitating that the Zouave slow down. Bob fumbled the envelope from her jacket pocket with gloved hands and checked the hotel's address once again. Inside was a scribbled note from Captain Ashby, dated a mere two days before, with details of their irregular mission for the French. It definitely beat being back with the battalion, laying a railway in the rain.

The Zouave left her at the Hotel Lutetia with a cheery salute and more incomprehensible attempts at English, then rattled off, his scarlet trousers flapping in the wind. She found her handkerchief and wiped most of the mud off her face before swathing it in her muffler, hunching her shoulders against the cold and trudging across the hotel's cobblestoned courtyard.

Inside wasn't much warmer than outside. The concierge was also wrapped in a muffler, and the end of his nose looked distinctly red. He at least spoke some English. Hailey was able to make herself understood once she unbuttoned her coat to display her uniform and pointed out the names she wanted in the register.

Meyer came down to meet her, closely followed by Daglish. They looked clean and warm and well fed, and she was startled by her stab of jealousy. They in turn looked startled to see her. She dug out the letter, bundled in with the other papers she'd brought. "Got some important news."

Meyer and Daglish exchanged a glance. Meyer said, "You look chilled to the bone. Come on up to our room."

Once climbing the staircase, it became evident to her that

the two officers were clean and she was not. It wasn't the mud so much as the fact that she hadn't had so much as a wash since she'd left Sister Daglish, and before that, it had been weeks since she'd had a real bath. She'd been hoping for one on leave, when she could get some privacy; maybe there'd be a chance of one before they had to leave Paris. Though there might not be time. She'd likely need to scrape the dirt off herself with a knife. Twice.

The door of their small room had barely closed behind them when Meyer asked, "What is it?"

She couldn't stop herself from smiling. "Ashby's alive!"

She wasn't prepared for Meyer's knees to go. Daglish grabbed him before he could hit the floor and eased him onto the bed, where he sat staring at her as if he was about to weep, but grinning, too. Daglish looked at the neatly printed list she held and said, puzzled, "Is that my sister's handwriting?"

Explanations took rather longer than she had expected. Unlike her, the two officers easily accepted that Ashby had been found by a French spy, and had seconded them to help destroy a German laboratory, while Ashby and the French were to destroy another. Until she'd met the Zouave courier, who'd appeared in record time to carry her to Paris, she'd had her doubts; she'd believed Ashby was alive, she'd recognized his handwriting, but had thought the rest of it an elaborate joke.

Meyer was confused as to how Lucilla Daglish had become involved, but her brother said that she knew a man with the French army. He left it unspoken exactly how she knew him, but his implication was clear. Hailey confirmed that he meant the mysterious Major Fournier, and stored this new information away.

She produced the map drawn by Major Fournier and the

list of supplies that she and Sister Daglish had arrived at together. The fabric and notions were for Bob to make camouflage clothing and masks like those used by snipers, to enable them to pass as closely as possible before beginning their bombardment, which would involve as many jam-tin grenades as the three of them could manufacture in the time available. Major Fournier had promised tobacco tins, guncotton and fuses for those, with apologies that he could offer nothing better; the French had no more proper grenades than the British.

By this time, she was sitting on the floor, not wanting to dirty any of the furniture or, worse, get lice in the sheets; Meyer had the bed, and Daglish the chair. Daglish said, "I played cricket. I should be the one heaving the grenades."

"I'll keep a pipe going for you and light the fuses," Bob said. She still felt filthy, but at least she was pleasantly warm in the steam-heated room. The wine Meyer had poured for her didn't hurt, either.

Meyer said, "Perhaps you should stay behind, Hailey. We could get into serious trouble if we're caught."

"No. Sir."

"We're officers. We'd be much better off if captured. And—"

"No. Sir." She rose and shrugged out of her coat. She knew why Meyer was trying to keep her out of it. He didn't want to risk a woman. But Lucilla Daglish was going to risk her life, and so was the Belgian woman spy. Hailey wasn't about to be left out. "Is there a proper bath in this place?"

"And a shower bath," Daglish confirmed with a sly grin, acknowledging his own delight in this luxury. "Want my soap? I've got some cresol soap, too, if you want it."

"Do I!" she said, grateful to her toes. Cresol soap killed lice.

Meyer started to speak, then stopped. Daglish glanced at him. "Something wrong?"

She stared him down.

"No," Meyer said. "Nothing. Take my towel, Hailey."

The bath was heaven. She locked the door and showered first, three times, before having a lovely soak in the tub. Then she changed into her clean uniform, shoved the other into a laundry bag and hurried downstairs to see about getting a room for herself. Sleeping in privacy was the greatest luxury she could think of at the moment, and that way, Meyer and Daglish would have one final night of privacy, as well. They might never have another chance, poor buggers.

She wasn't sure what to do about Daglish. His sister knew her secret, as did Ashby and Meyer. And she knew that Daglish was a sodomite. He wouldn't be likely to tell, for fear she would expose his secret. They neither of them could throw stones. But she'd grown used to keeping her mouth shut tight about herself, and it wasn't as if there was a real need for him to know. If he knew, he might start to treat her differently, as Meyer had just tried to do. It didn't matter if he did it out of kindness, it was still hard to take when she'd been in battle just as much as they had. Maybe more, because usually she was running through fire without any protection.

Maybe it was Meyer with whom she needed to have a talk. She remembered him once admitting that his inevitable fate at cricket was to be chosen last, so it wasn't as if he could take her place in grenade throwing. Aside from that, it didn't look like this war was going to end anytime soon, and if that was true, she would be working with him for a long time to come. She wouldn't be able to stand it if he treated her like a china plate.

She bolted her door securely before daring to crawl naked between the clean bed linens. The well-worn cotton caressed her scrubbed skin with heavenly softness. She lay in luxurious abandon for a long time, listening to the occasional traffic on the street below, and thought on the future. Sister Daglish had a lover, or at least a potential lover, as well as her work. Sister Daglish was not as self-sufficient as Bob had thought. Or, rather, she was, but she also had a man. Could Bob manage the same, while still keeping her independence and her career?

There was always leave. Daglish and Meyer had managed quite nicely. Only time would tell if they could maintain the necessary separation between duty and sex. She'd never had an inkling, until he'd told her, that Meyer and Ashby had been lovers, so perhaps Meyer would be good at that. Daglish, she wasn't sure. It had been clear to her that he pined for Meyer at all sorts of inopportune moments. Maybe it would be easier for him, now that he'd gotten what he desired. She'd fucked Meyer, and enjoyed it quite a lot, but she hadn't felt the urge to shag him silly every time she saw him. Perhaps that sort of thing could work out.

Except she had the added problem of not being what she seemed. It was bad enough to be thought a sodomite. If she were discovered to be a woman, she would be out of the army in a heartbeat, with no pension and probably criminal charges levied. For all she knew, it might be treason to offer your weak womanly body to protect the shores of Britain, or some such rot. Compared to that, sneaking off on one's leave to help destroy an enemy laboratory was small potatoes.

The following morning, she did her necessary shopping, then took the train with her two officers out to the countryside. She rode in a carriage full of enlisted men, of course, and won a couple of guineas and a packet of cigarettes at cards before Daglish poked his head in the door to fetch her for their stop.

As promised, a lorry awaited them, driven by a French nun, small and round and wrinkled like a dried apple, who waited patiently beside the cab with her hands steadily counting off a rosary.

Bob remembered the rosary she'd found in Ashby's things, adorned with an enameled circular seal of a wolf lying down with a lamb. So far as she knew, he'd never taken it out of its velvet pouch. She was suddenly glad she hadn't yet had time to send it to his mother. He was still officially listed as *missing,* not *killed,* and for once it was the truth. When they saw him again, she would give him the rosary.

She wished Ashby were here now, to tell her what to do. He'd always had a dab hand with advice; not as comforting as Meyer usually was, but getting right to the point and re-minding her that things weren't as bad as they looked. He'd probably tell her to forget about what she'd done with Meyer, and he'd be right. So when the nun dropped them off at a spacious billet in a little hamlet half-destroyed by shelling, she immediately took her sewing supplies and carried them into the dining room.

Daglish went to check on the grenade supplies that were supposed to be in the gardening shed. Meyer hurried after her, his arms loaded with yards of fabric wrapped in brown paper. "Where would you like me to put this?" he asked.

"Table."

"Do you need any help?"

She unrolled her housewife and plucked out a pencil and a tailor's crayon. "You can't draw patterns."

"Well, no." She could still hear him breathing, and finally he said, "You're angry with me."

She shrugged.

"Because of Crispin?"

She shook her head. Men could be so slow. Anger bubbled through her veins.

"I won't say I'm sorry for trying to keep you out of this."

"Why not?" She turned to face him. Her anger boiled over and she said, "Bloody hell, I even got shot in the line of duty."

He paused, looked away, then looked back at her. "And if you were...Pittfield, say...yes. You're right. I am sorry."

As usual, he was genuine, but she was still a bit angry. "Get me some newspapers, will you? Or butcher paper."

"I really am sorry."

"Go on, now. Sir. We'll talk about it later."

22

TANNEKEN INSISTED ON TRAVELING TO KAUZ'S
laboratory as a wolf. She wanted to have every sense available
to her at its utmost capacity. If she needed to communicate
with the humans, Ashby would be able to interpret her body
language well enough. He intended to stay in his human
form so he might use a pistol and be able to manipulate small
objects. Tanneken felt Mademoiselle Daglish ought to be able
to fill this role, except that Ashby was undoubtedly more
skilled in the use of guns. Monsieur Fournier would be too
busy attempting to extract Kauz's foul scientific records before
they destroyed the buildings.

She rode in the back of the open motorcar with Ashby and
an Enfield rifle reeking of oil and metal beneath its wrappings; Mademoiselle Daglish drove, and Fournier spoke to her
in low tones, oddly enough about mathematics, and occasionally passed around a flask of hot coffee. All of them were well
wrapped against the bitter wind, which, Tanneken thought
smugly, was nothing to her fine pelage.

After a few miles, Ashby took his glove off, rested his hand atop Tanneken's skull, and scratched with his nails. Of course, he knew the places most rewarded by scratching, and also knew when to shift his attentions to her jawline, and then her chin. Tanneken allowed the familiarity. She had agreed to marry him, after all, and it felt astonishingly pleasant. She remembered with a pang that the last—and only—person to caress her in wolf form had been her mother. Her mother's touch had not, however, been the same. Not at all. She shifted in the small space available to her and let her chin fall heavily on Ashby's thigh. She knew he had not worn underthings, to enable him to quickly shed his clothing should he need to change. Quirking her brows, she licked him between his legs, laughing to herself when he jolted in his seat and then laughed, himself.

"What's so funny?" Mademoiselle Daglish called over her shoulder.

"Just blowing off steam," Ashby replied, fondling Tanneken's ears. She huffed out a breath and had the pleasure of feeling him shift in his seat.

Mademoiselle Daglish drove to a railway siding and braked in the shadow of a bullet-riddled freight car. "We walk from here," Fournier said, rewrapping his scarf and carefully buttoning his dark overcoat over his lighter-colored uniform. He'd earlier exchanged his kepi for a knit wool seaman's cap. One like it covered Ashby's bright hair, and another confined Mademoiselle Daglish's longer locks. The humans quickly shouldered rucksacks, the two men carrying weapons, as well.

A few hundred feet away, it was easy to see why walking was required; the rails had been wrenched from the ground, some twisted from the force of explosions. Great ruts from lorries scarred the earth. Feeling as if she hadn't been free for months, Tanneken ranged freely through the dead grass, sniffing out rodents and listening to their tiny rustles as her three companions hiked along the remnants of the railway. She could see why Kauz would have chosen his location now. He would have wanted to take advantage of the railway, for delivering such items as heavy fencing and wire cages.

She took a moment to roll in the crackling grass, scrubbing the remembered scent of confinement from her nose. When she arose, she felt cleaner, and when the others caught up with her, she trotted next to Ashby for a time. She found his scent comforting, a reminder of sex and, even more, a clear sign that she was not alone. She would not be alone when she approached the laboratory buildings that masked the entrance to Kauz's underground corridors, for the first time seeing them from the outside, while conscious. She would not be alone when she entered the rooms that stank of chemicals and pain and fear.

She lifted her head and deeply tasted the chill wind, concentrating on the tangled ropes of scent it brought her. It was easier to submerge beneath the wolf as she did that, and the rest of the night passed in a succession of moments, each filled with dead grass and live earth flashing beneath her paws. When she suddenly smelled danger, she nearly spun on her haunches and fled. She'd almost forgotten her purpose.

Ashby's gloved hand burrowed into her ruff and stayed there as he crouched beside her. "Tanneken," he said softly.

It was enough. She swished her tail once and lifted her brows, knowing he would be able to make out her expression in the nimbus of light thrown by the laboratory's electric flood lamps. She could not, however, disguise the faint trembling in her muscles. She was unsure if it sprang from anger or fear. She decided it was a combination of both.

Ashby rubbed his face against hers. She huffed out a surprised breath and licked his nose.

Mademoiselle Daglish turned her back on the fenced buildings and set down her rucksack. "The entrance is on the other side," she remarked. "The shed I burned, when I brought out Ashby, is to this side."

Tanneken lifted her head. Yes, she could still smell the taint of petrol and ash, and even the scent of wolf, oddly fresh to have been a reminder of Ashby's presence. The other wolves, she realized. They were here.

Bob didn't smell any dangerous chemicals outside the laboratory, but perhaps they didn't have any smell. She crawled back across the stretch of bare ground and squirmed down into the scratch trench Daglish had dug for cover, between the two men. Daglish lay on his belly, his head turned toward Meyer, though she couldn't see the direction of his gaze through the camouflaged sniper's hood he wore. Meyer had the deeper side of the shallow trench; he crouched over their grenades, inspecting the tobacco tins for leaks or damage from the trip here.

They'd had a ride first with a slender, pretty Belgian woman named Miss Wuytack, who was one of Monsieur Fournier's spies. She'd been a little taken aback that neither Daglish nor Bob had spared her a second glance. She'd made a valiant attempt to flirt with Meyer, until he skillfully let slip that he was a Jew, and then he spent the rest of the ride staring out at the countryside while the spy drove on in resolute silence.

After Miss Wuytack let them out, they'd loaded their

grenades onto a hand-operated railway cart, which took them as far as a deserted hamlet, recently abandoned by the troops of both sides. Past that hamlet was enemy territory, though it didn't look any different to Bob than what had gone before, until they began to spot small groups of patrolling soldiers. So far, they'd successfully avoided contact with the enemy, but that wouldn't last long, now that they were dug in near a semi-official government-funded German laboratory.

It was time for action. "Half a dozen guards," she reported, her breath fogging in the cold air. "Couple smoking, out by the latrines." She stopped and wiggled a hand beneath her camouflage overshirt to extract a rock that was poking into her belly.

"Fancy uniforms. Every one with a shiny prick on his hat."

Daglish choked on a laugh. Meyer cast her a look she couldn't decipher through the sniper's hood he wore, but she could tell it wasn't appreciative of her humor. She added, "No machine gun."

Meyer carefully laid out rows of jam-tin grenades. They had twenty-one. "Seven each," he said.

"Ten for me and eleven for Daglish," Bob corrected.

"I thought you were holding the pipe."

Daglish said, "I can't carry them all. Hailey will hand them over as they're needed. What we've got should be plenty."

Meyer said, "I seem to recall that I should be in command."

"We're on leave," Bob said. She rolled onto her back, tugged off one glove with her teeth and began checking through her webbing equipment, making sure she had multiple tins of safety matches. She dug out the cheap pipe and pouch of tobacco she'd bought in Paris and set about the delicate process of getting it lit. Hopefully, the smell wouldn't be strong enough to carry all the way to the Germans standing guard.

"I'd still like it if you would be careful," he said.

"Us, too," Daglish said. "Try not to shoot us, will you?" He patted the butt of the rifle they'd brought.

Meyer snorted. "I think the camouflage will help me identify you, even from back here." He fidgeted with the grenades again, but plainly it was just from nervousness, not anything that needed doing, so Bob laid her gloved hand atop his.

She said, "Ashby'll be terribly disappointed if he doesn't get to see you, after all this."

"I don't think he'd be all that happy if one of you was killed, either." Meyer pulled away and ran his hand over the rifle barrel. "Cold as ice," he remarked. "I wonder if it shoots frozen bullets?"

It would have been better to have grenades thrown from all directions, but it hadn't been practical with only the three of them. Meyer had insisted that one of them be armed with a more accurate and long-range weapon, much as the infantry were protected by artillery. Of them all, he was the best shot with a rifle, though he wasn't as good as Southey or anywhere near as good as Mason, back at the regiment. Hailey reminded herself that accuracy like Mason's or even Southey's wasn't required here. All Meyer had to do was plug someone until he couldn't attack anymore. Even the worst shot in the regiment could usually manage that.

Meyer interrupted her thoughts. "Be careful. Both of you."

Daglish said, "I, for one, don't intend to be killed. Hailey, you ready?"

"Yes," she said.

After that it was the usual sort of running and dodging and flinging oneself into cover, except the sniper gear was uncomfortable and she had to do everything more carefully because of the grenades, and normally, she wouldn't be given grenades, even jam tins, because her job was to carry messages. In front of Meyer, she'd pretended she didn't mind, but in truth the grenades made her nervous enough that her palms were sweating inside her gloves. She was good at staying concealed, though.

Daglish had taken platoons out on raids, so he knew what he was about. When they reached the stand of trees that was their midpoint, he settled in among the leaf litter and silently began to lay out his grenades in an arc around his feet. Bob did the same, then slipped the lit pipe from its loop on her webbing. She could still see a red-orange glow within the pipe's bowl. She stirred up the embers just a bit with a stick and murmured, "Ready."

Daglish rose slowly, stretching his arm and rotating it to make sure his sleeves—uniform beneath, sniper tunic above—wouldn't catch and land a grenade on top of them. He scooped up a tin in each gloved hand and held them out to Bob, who held the pipe bowl to the fuses until they caught. Together, they counted, then Daglish threw, strong clean arcs that nearly made her whistle in admiration.

He'd easily cleared the tall fence. She counted another second, then two explosions ripped the air, one after the other. Sound rushed in on her, and she realized she hadn't been breathing, but she was already lighting the next grenade, holding the fuse steady in the bowl of the pipe until sparks crackled, slowly eating their way up the fuse toward the tight-packed guncotton. The explosion would fling free the nails and other bits of metal rubbish they'd packed into the tin. The sharp odor of gunpowder singed her nostrils, or was it smoke from the laboratory compound? She held the grenade up to

Daglish without looking at him, shook burning ash off her leather glove, then began to light the next fuse.

Daglish had thrown perhaps half the grenades before she heard the gate rattle open and the *pop-pop* of rifle shots. "Run?" she asked. She risked a glance; three guards had ventured out, staying close to the fence.

"Two more," Daglish said, heaving the grenades he held. They landed on a roof, and the resulting explosion resulted in a tower of flame as dry wood caught fire. He hissed with satisfaction as the flame leaped to another roof, which caught fire with a roar. "Meyer's killed one." He unbuttoned his holster and yanked out his pistol. "Take this, in case."

Bob shoved the pistol through her webbing and lit the next grenade. Daglish threw it toward the open gate. The two remaining guards scrambled to be out of range before it exploded, and Meyer picked off another. "Here," she said, shoving another lit grenade into Daglish's hand.

The last guard retreated into the laboratory complex, scrambling over the rubble of the gate. Daglish tossed a last grenade after him. "Now we go," he said. "He'll no doubt be calling for reinforcements."

"Got to collect Meyer," Bob said.

Daglish faltered for a moment, then patted her shoulder and together they retraced their steps. An hour later, they were on their way back to Paris.

Lucilla felt like laughing as she hurried through the laboratory's deserted underground corridors, a rucksack of chemicals on her back and a wolf trotting at her side like a gundog. The situation wasn't funny, not in the least—the stinking room full of cages had dispersed that notion immediately—

but she felt the same euphoria as when she and Pascal had stolen Kauz's motor. Her vision was unnaturally clear, her heart pumping blood until her fingers and toes tingled, and her thoughts were sharp as needles.

She stopped at a crossroads in the corridors and shoved one of her bottles into a convenient spot made by the junction of two crossbeams, feeling a distinct satisfaction as the bottle fit snugly into the narrow space. She didn't bother digging into the corridor's dirt wall, as she doubted it was flammable.

Miss Claes stalked up the left corridor, head lifted to catch any scent of Kauz. Having grown used to this, Lucilla ignored her while she fixed a new rubber cap to the bottle, one she precisely pierced to allow a slow but steady drip onto the wood. Eventually, the acid would eat through the rubber and the remains would spill out, but by then discretion wouldn't matter. She placed one more bottle, stuffed guncotton at several key points, wound in fuses and hurried after Miss Claes. She'd prepared every one of the corridor branchings for collapse; now all that remained was to set the fires and hope Pascal had calculated correctly, and the flames would follow the path they'd set instead of flickering into nothing for lack of air.

This area was silent but for her booted footsteps and the faint click of Miss Claes's claws on the roughly laid wood floor; it smelled dank and dusty. She'd left Pascal waiting at the underground room they'd identified as Kauz's office, hurriedly sorting through messy piles of laboratory notebooks while Ashby stood guard with both rifle and pistol. Ashby had assured them, his voice uncharacteristically flat, that he would smell Kauz arriving. Though Miss Claes couldn't speak in her current form, Lucilla had the distinct sense that she'd agreed vehemently.

She had a clear idea that Miss Claes wasn't entirely happy with what they'd found in the facility. Anger and anxiety both seemed to boil off the wolf and into the stuffy air. Without really intending it, Lucilla's footsteps sped up. Within a few moments, she was nearly running to keep up with the wolf's steady lope. At times, she lost sight of the blond brush of tail and knew which direction the wolf had passed only by the fresh scratches on the flooring, made by claws skidding around a corner.

Surely she would know if something had gone wrong. She would have heard guns, shouts—

Growls.

Many growls, more than Miss Claes could produce alone. Lucilla hesitated only a moment before shifting her rucksack onto the floor. Bracing her back against a dirt wall, she extracted two bottles, one for each hand. If she threw them with enough force, they would break. Pulse pounding, she edged around the corner.

The door to Kauz's office stood open, and guarding the door were four wolves, fully as large as Miss Claes, their pelages dark and unkempt over cruelly tight collars, their lips threateningly curled. Two faced outward, and two inward. Lucilla lifted her arm, then lowered it. Miss Claes was too close. Lucilla wouldn't risk harming her and perhaps damaging her ability to fight. She eased to the side, hoping to remain unnoticed as well as see inside the office. When she did, her heart began to race and the blood sang in her ears. Kauz was there, his back to what must have been a hidden door, for she could think of no other way he might have bypassed Ashby, who blocked the open door into the corridor.

Kauz held a shotgun to Pascal's shoulder, the sort used for

hunting birds, but with the end of the barrel crudely sawn off. One twitch of his bony finger to the trigger could easily blow Pascal's head from his shoulders, or rip open his jugular, or pulp a mass of flesh including major blood vessels and nerves. Clear images of what would remain after such a close shotgun blast flashed through her head like lantern slides. Only a lack of air caused by horror kept her from screaming aloud.

"Who is there?" Kauz said in German.

Lucilla drew a steadying breath. "Miss Daglish," she said.

"Are you the Frenchman's whore, or the wolf's?"

"Neither," she said. "Who are these wolves?"

"My children," he said with patent falseness.

Ashby growled, "They're not yours."

"On the contrary, creature. I have raised them to be mine. You will see, when they tear you limb from limb. But not the bitch. I have need of her. My lads are lacking a mate, you see."

"I'll shoot them first," Ashby said.

"You won't, you know," Kauz said. "You forget, creature, that I have observed you carefully. You will not slaughter your own kind." He raised his voice, commanding, "Kurt! Immanuel! A step closer."

Ashby did not retreat when the wolves paced closer. Lucilla weighed the bottles of acid in her hand, wondering if she could be accurate enough to break the bottles on the door frame itself. Though now, she would only damage two of the enemy wolves.

Pascal said, "If you kill me, Kauz, these others will kill you. I imagine you wish to live, to see the end of your experiments."

Kauz said, "The creature will not be able to shoot me, for Kurt and Immanuel will take him down like a deer, and I will be free to leave here. Emil and Friedrich will easily defeat your bitch, and the whore is of no consequence."

"Would you like to eat one of these bottles?" Lucilla inquired. She wondered if she could fit one between Kauz's jaws.

Kauz ignored her. "Kill him! You know what will happen if you don't!"

Lucilla couldn't take her eyes off Pascal. His expression burned with rage and frustration. His pistol still rested at his hip, but both of his hands were full of notebooks.

A frenzy of growls yanked her gaze to a tangle of bodies on the floor: two, no, three of Kauz's wolves, and Ashby, whose naked flesh flashed as he attempted to get out of his clothing and change form.

Miss Claes grappled with the fourth wolf and, a moment later, pinned him to the floor, her teeth flashing at his throat in warning. The wolf fell limp, and she hurdled his body, toward Kauz.

The shotgun roared and Lucilla screamed.

She ran forward, her legs tangling with the fourth wolf, who had bounded to his feet and blocked her advance. She staggered, grabbed for the wall and fell. "No!" Pascal shouted.

Lucilla scrambled to her knees and saw Pascal, sprawled on the floor, his hand lifted, seemingly unhurt. Her breath exploded outward and, unbidden, tears of relief flooded her cheeks.

Tanneken crouched over Kauz's fallen form, her teeth buried in the shredded remains of his throat, a geyser of blood spattering her face.

Ashby lay naked on the floor in a pool of blood, one leg twisted unnaturally beneath him, and three wolves slowly shrinking back from his weak but steady cursing.

The fourth wolf licked Lucilla's arm and then, before her eyes, shifted into the form of a barely adolescent boy, wearing a collar.

23

THE HOTEL'S LOBBY WAS COLD AS THE GRAVE AND was giving him the shakes. Gabriel wrapped his arms around himself and shifted from foot to foot. Hailey, damn her, was sprawled at her ease in a once-plush red armchair and flipping through an abandoned fashion magazine, studying the drawings.

"No word yet," Crispin said, rehanging the telephone receiver and stepping out of the booth. He pulled the folding glass doors shut behind him. "Mrs. Vlyminck said to call again in a few hours. She doubted she would have news before suppertime, and she informed me there were more important matters afoot than Major Fournier's little mission."

"If Noel's gotten himself killed, I'll fucking kill him again," Gabriel said under his breath. He winced away from the memory that he had in fact killed someone else, several someones, only hours before.

"Upstairs," Hailey suggested.

"A good plan," Crispin said. "I don't know what I did without a batman. Come along, Meyer."

On the stairs, Gabriel said, "Wouldn't the two of you rather go out? We could see the sights."

"Sleeting," Hailey reminded him.

"I'm for another bath," Crispin said. "It's too bad I can't wash enough to last me through the next few months on the front."

Gabriel's mind presented him with the image of Crispin's sturdy, nude body, slick with soap, bubbles clinging enticingly to the curls on his chest. He remembered the tight clench of Crispin's arse on his cock. His body's surge of desire resonated with his desperate fear for Noel's safety and his usual post-battle shakiness. He had to stop climbing, and press his hands against the flocked wallpaper to prevent himself from seizing Crispin then and there. "Good idea," he said, then had to swallow, his throat felt so thick.

Hailey pushed past him, and he closed his eyes at her accidental brush against his chest. He wouldn't mind her soft warmth curled around him, either. He wanted to burrow deep in her heat and sweet womanly smell.

He wanted both of them pressed to his bare skin, their mouths and hands roaming over him until he forgot even his own name.

He was a cad and a lecher and half a dozen other shameful things. Ashby had been with two women at one time, he knew, but this was different. Neither one of his companions had invited him to do anything like what he was imagining. Well, Crispin likely would, once he'd had his bath, but Hailey—he'd not pleased Hailey, by treating her too much as a woman and not a soldier. And he hadn't mentioned their tryst to Crispin, and it would likely horrify him; it would likely horrify him even more if he knew Hailey was a woman.

If Hailey wasn't interested, that would be all right. He supposed. She could stay alone in her room, and—

"You coming?" she asked.

Hailey and Crispin both were standing in the corridor, while he still stood a couple of stairs below them. He moved toward them, mentally shaking himself. "I need a drink," he said, striving for lightness.

"Could do with one," Hailey said, peering at him from beneath the brim of her cap.

"Brandy," Crispin said with satisfaction.

The room he shared with Crispin felt cozy and safe. The three of them took off their boots, sat on the rug and drank the brandy from coffee cups. Gabriel edged closer to the radiator and felt his inner trembling diminish with the warmth of it, and of the brandy, and of Crispin's shoulder so near his own. Though he'd only drunk two swallows of the alcohol, he must have drifted, for the next he knew, Hailey was shaking him by the knee. "Sir?" she asked.

He set down his cup before he could spill it. "Not tonight with all that rot," he said. "Just my name, if you can do that for me."

Crispin eased closer but didn't embrace him as Gabriel wished he would. Of course he wouldn't do such a thing in front of anyone else. Gabriel shouldn't be melancholy about it. It wasn't as if this room wasn't rife with secrets. His entire life had been like that. First his heritage, which he'd tried to conceal until he learned he couldn't; then Ashby's inhuman abilities; then their sexual relationship; and finally, the fact that as many women as he desired, there were just as many men. He had been hiding that knowledge even from himself. If he hadn't been struck here and now with both desires at once, he might be hiding that knowledge from himself still.

Crispin said, "Do you want us to leave? So you can get some sleep?"

"I've a deck of cards in my room," Hailey remarked.

Don't leave me. The words didn't make it past his throat. Instead, Gabriel grabbed Crispin's wrist, and Hailey's, as well.

Crispin turned his hand over and tangled his fingers with Gabriel's. His smile was crooked. "Ashby will be fine," he said. "He's gotten himself out of worse scrapes than this, hasn't he? Remember when Evans found that grenade that hadn't gone off, and—"

Gabriel was shaking his head. "I wasn't thinking of him," he admitted. "I was thinking of myself."

Hailey gently slipped her wrist free of Gabriel's grip and poured a little more brandy into his cup. "You're fine, sir."

"No. No, not really." *I'm not normal.* Though if he thought about it a little more, Crispin wasn't normal, either, nor Hailey. Isobel. Even now, knowing what he did, he could scarcely put her true name together in his mind with the person he knew. Perhaps for that reason alone they belonged together. Perhaps for that reason, they would not reject him. He said, "Will you stay here with me? Both of you?"

"Long as you like," Hailey said. She gave him a second, sharp look. "Sir, did you mean—"

Gabriel flinched, unsure if her tone was meant to be censorious. He shouldn't have suggested it. He wasn't asking only for sex. If she accepted him, one way or another, Crispin would also know her secret.

Crispin let go of Gabriel's hand. "What did you two get up to?" he asked suspiciously. "Hailey, I never would have guessed it of you. And you, Gabriel—he's under your command—"

"It was only the once," she said. "I asked him. When we thought Ashby was dead. And it's not like you think, Daglish."

"I think I've been an idiot," he said.

Gabriel grabbed his shoulder and kissed him, rather uncomfortably because his spectacles dug into his face. Crispin made a sound in his throat, and Gabriel kissed him again, just under his jawline, until he felt Crispin's hands gripping his shoulders. Only then did he pull back. "What do you think now?"

Crispin looked befuddled.

Hailey scooted closer and sat up on her knees. "Daglish," she said in her soft, husky voice. "I like you, and I want it to be all right between us."

"It's fine," he said. He looked at Gabriel. "You didn't make me any promises, not really. Nor did I. I was only—I haven't had the best luck with, with…"

"Lovers," Hailey supplied.

Gabriel said, "Is it all right with both of you? If we—" He swallowed the pleading words he wanted to say.

Hailey turned to Crispin and said, "I've never done it before, with two other people. But I think I'd like to."

Crispin looked indecisive, but said, "I'll give it a try."

Hailey touched his hand. "One more thing."

"It's all right, Hailey," Crispin said gently.

"No—you might not like this." She looked down at her lap, then into his face. "I'm a woman, Daglish. My real name's Isobel, a friend just called me *Bobs* and *Bob* as a joke. I wear men's clothes so I can be in the army, and—well, everything else you know about me is the truth. Except I don't have a cock. Meyer might not think it matters, but I guess it matters to you."

"You're not joking."

"No."

"Definitely not," Gabriel said, finding his voice.

Slowly, Crispin grinned. "I'll be buggered."

Hailey grinned back. "I'd give it a try, but I'd need one of those wooden cocks first."

"Maybe some other time," Crispin said. "It's odd but, you know, you don't seem like a woman to me."

"That's the idea."

"No, you—" Crispin grinned again, then sobered. "It's still all right with you? I mean, with me being—"

Hailey smiled, a gentler smile than Gabriel was used to. Then she leaned forward, braced her hand on Crispin's shoulder and gently kissed him on the mouth. "That's not so bad, is it?"

When she drew back, Crispin was smiling sweetly, too, a smile that pierced Gabriel to the heart. "Hmm. That felt all right, but I'm not sure yet. Maybe you could—"

Gabriel had begun to feel left out, and the longer he sat alone, the more he craved contact. "There's a nice warm bed right here," he said.

Crispin and Hailey—Isobel—exchanged a look. Each pushed one of his shoulders. Startled, he didn't resist, and landed on his back on the coverlet. Isobel—no, Bob—said, "We should help him get his clothes off. Daglish, you distract him."

Crispin stripped off his uniform tunic and tossed it on the chair. Loosening his tie, he crawled onto the bed, then bent over Gabriel, removed his spectacles and kissed him deeply, wet and hungry and tasting of brandy.

Distantly, Gabriel felt Bob's fingers at his waist, unbuttoning his braces from his trousers. He jerked when her fingers brushed his cock while unfastening his fly. Crispin pinned his shoulders and kissed him again before moving on to biting his neck.

He tried to help Bob by lifting up, but didn't manage very well because his arms had tightly wrapped around Crispin's torso and he couldn't concentrate on anything but broad, sleek muscles shifting beneath his hands. He would have pulled himself inside of Crispin's strong body if he could. As soon as his trousers and drawers were off, he hooked one bare leg over Crispin's and tumbled him onto his side.

Crispin's shirt was still tucked in; Gabriel couldn't get his hand onto skin that way. Frustrated, he growled, and Crispin rolled him onto his back. "The tie's not de rigueur," he commented, working at the knot, while Gabriel traced fingers over his belly; the muscles trembled, just a little, which mollified him.

Bob reached around Crispin and deftly undid his tie, as well, whipping it off with a flourish. Gabriel watched her fingers travel down Crispin's chest, swiftly unbuttoning, until her hands collided with his at Crispin's waist.

He grabbed her fingers and gently squeezed. "Who gets to undress you?"

"Oh, we'll manage," she said. She moved their joined hands down, over the bulge in Crispin's trousers. Crispin gasped and closed his eyes.

"You'll manage all sorts of things if you keep that up," he said breathlessly.

Gabriel gave Bob's hands, and Crispin's cock, a hard squeeze, craving that pressure all over his own body. Inside his body. He looked up into Crispin's face. The skin around his mouth was reddened from Gabriel's mustache. "Are you willing? To try all sorts of things?"

"What sorts of things?" Crispin asked.

"I know you like being fucked," Gabriel said. "Would you be willing to fuck me?"

"I've never done it," Crispin said in a rush, then looked down and returned to unbuttoning Gabriel's shirt.

Bob had Crispin's braces off his shoulders. Gabriel slipped his hands beneath the open lapels of Crispin's shirt and soothingly rubbed his chest. When Bob finished unbuttoning Crispin's fly, he slid his hands lower and rubbed there, too. "Do you want to?"

"I might hurt you," he said softly, still focused on Gabriel's shirt, though his hands had stopped moving.

"I'll let you know," Gabriel said. "Will you? I want both of you."

The tone of his voice must have given him away, because Crispin leaned down and kissed him sweetly. "If that's what you want. The tin's not empty." He looked over his shoulder. "You've got too many clothes on, Bob."

Gabriel agreed. She hadn't even removed her tunic yet.

Bob stripped efficiently, at least as far down as her drawers and chest wrappings. Then she stopped, Crispin's fingers just brushing her arm. He said, "You should come up here with us."

For the first time since Gabriel had known her, she looked uncertain. "You want to help me get this off?" she asked.

After a glance at Gabriel, Crispin sat on the edge of the bed. "Come here." He set to work. Bob watched his hands, her own loose at her sides.

Gabriel took the opportunity to sit up, strip his shirt over his head, and reach to the head of the bed where he found the tin of salve. He sat behind Crispin and put his arms around him, resting his chin on Crispin's shoulder, watching him unwrap Bob's chest.

When the bindings were gone, she rubbed her nipples with her palms. "Bit sore," she confessed.

Crispin touched the red marks above and below, but shied away from her breasts. His hands went to her waist. "These, too?"

"Go on," she said. After Crispin had shoved her drawers down, she stepped tidily out of them, and forward. "You still all right, Daglish?"

"It's Crispin," he remarked absently, studying her with interest. "May I touch—"

"You don't have to," she said. "I guess Meyer'll take care of that."

"No, I want to, if you don't mind."

"I'm here, aren't I?"

Gabriel said, "I *will* want my turn later." He turned his head and kissed Crispin's neck, then used his chin to dig into his shoulder while he passed his hands over the soft fur of Crispin's chest. From the side of his vision, he saw Crispin's hands tentatively cupping Bob's breasts and testing their weight in his hands. The sight aroused him. The allure of the forbidden? The piquancy of trying something for the first time? Or—he flushed, thinking this was probably true, though embarrassing—did he just like to watch?

"They're soft like...I don't know what." Crispin rubbed his palms over her nipples. "Does that feel good? I'm not hurting you, am I?" After a moment, he grinned. "No, I guess I'm not hurting you."

She grinned back. "You've got the hang of it already." She rested one hand on his curls. "Maybe a bit harder. Or you could suck on them. If you wanted."

"I'll be careful," Crispin said earnestly. Suppressing laughter, Gabriel nuzzled the back of his neck while Crispin did just that, his head bumping into Bob's hands, her fingers stroking through his hair as well as Crispin's. After a while, Crispin drew back and touched Bob's flushed cheek. "You do like that. It doesn't matter that it's me."

She tunneled her fingers through his curls. "I like that it's you. You're a good fellow. You even share your nut-milk choc."

"I'm guessing Gabriel will make a better job of it." He twisted his neck, so his lips brushed Gabriel's cheek. "You're being awfully patient."

"Just enjoying the show." And, he realized, he was also a bit relieved that the two of them hadn't demonstrated over-whelming passion for one another. He wasn't ready to share his partners quite that much, not yet. Gabriel squeezed Crispin's waist. "Bob, why don't you join us. I think Crispin should have a demonstration of what you like. Ladies first, and all that."

Crispin took Bob's head in his lap while Gabriel kissed first her mouth, then her breasts, then, after she kicked him firmly in the calf, her cunt. When Gabriel dared a glance now and then, Crispin was watching him, his cheeks flushed, his eyes hot. Crispin stroked Bob's hair tenderly from her forehead, traced the shape of her lips and smoothed his hands over her shoulders. After Gabriel had licked and suckled her into climax, Crispin eased free. Before snuggling behind Gabriel, he kissed her mouth.

Spooned between the two of them, Gabriel closed his eyes, luxuriating in the hot press of skin all over his. Knots in his shoulders, ones he hadn't even noticed, loosened. He nuzzled into the velvety softness that hid at the base of Bob's neck while his hands toyed with her nipples; her hands lazily guided his in the pressure she wanted. Crispin had one leg thrown over Gabriel's hip, one hand stroking his ribs and the other teasing the very top of the cleft between his buttocks. Gabriel could feel Crispin's cock hardening against him. If he shifted even slightly, his own cock rubbed against the feathery hair at the base of Bob's spine. He pressed his lips to Bob's ear. "I'm sorry," he said. "Do you forgive me? You did a good job today."

She turned her face so his lips brushed her cheek. He could see her smile. "Couple more fucks like that and I suppose I could forgive you."

"I'll do my best." Gabriel closed his eyes, luxuriating.

After a time, Crispin said, "This is lovely. But a bit awkward if we move too much."

Bob said, "Maybe I could help you. With that tin. I want to see how it works."

Gabriel snorted a laugh into her hair. "Perhaps I should hire out for demonstrations."

"Your idea," Bob pointed out. She extracted herself from his embrace and clambered over him, with a great deal of unnecessary fondling that made him laugh again. "Show me how it's done, Crispin." Firmly, she patted Gabriel's arse. "Don't worry, sir. We'll take proper care of you."

Bob had never imagined she'd be naked with Crispin Daglish, much less having his hands guide hers over Gabriel Meyer's naked back while Gabriel made soft noises of pleasure, for once not trying to direct the action. It didn't feel so much like sex to her as it might have with someone else. This was more relaxed, more like playing. She liked it. It felt lovely and safe, a feeling that was in all too short supply in recent days. She asked, "Do you always have to do this first?"

"No, I just like to touch him," Crispin said, sharing a

sideways grin with her. She could tell that he did; his cock was nearly up to his belly with interest. She wouldn't mind getting her hands on it, or her mouth, but she supposed she ought to let him save it for Gabriel; he'd like that a lot better.

She slipped her hands from under Crispin's and pressed the heels of her hands along Gabriel's spine, all the way up to his neck, before wiggling her fingers into his fine blond hair and scratching his scalp. "Mmm," he said. "You could keep on doing that."

She ran her fingers over his ears, dipping inside, then tugging on his lobes. "What about that demonstration?" she asked. She squirmed until she faced Crispin, who straddled Gabriel's legs.

He said, sounding doubtful, "You really want to see?"

"Sure." She was desperately curious to know what could be so wonderful that it caused men to risk prison.

"Most people wouldn't want to see. They'd rather not know."

"*You* like it," she pointed out.

Crispin flushed all the way to his hairline and he looked away, shy as a boy. His voice muffled by the bedding, Gabriel noted, "You could be fucking me right now."

Taking pity on Crispin's nervousness, Bob said, "Give me the tin." Once she'd opened it, she gathered thick salve on her fingers and dropped the tin on the bed. "Hold out your hands."

Crispin grinned shakily and extended his hands to her, palms up. "Use a lot," he said.

She rubbed his hands between hers to warm them. His hands were tense, so she squeezed and manipulated them a bit as she applied the salve, as she might do for her own hands after a long day's sewing. Crispin looked both startled and grateful for the extra attention, and she felt a rush of affection for him. She leaned forward and rubbed her cheek against his. "That good?"

He nodded, briefly kissed her, and without further comment, set to work. It wasn't, Bob reflected, much different than she'd experienced with her first lover, except it was the other side of course, and she thought it was taking longer. That seemed to be more Crispin worrying about hurting Gabriel than anything really necessary, given how Gabriel made pleased sounds and pushed up against Crispin's twisting fingers.

After a while, she asked if she could try. Her smaller fingers eased in without any trouble; Meyer's muscles gripped her snugly, and for a moment she almost forgot what she was doing, as she imagined tightening her cunt on his cock in the same way. She remembered what she was about and stroked upward, feeling for the smoother spot Crispin told her to find. Everything felt tight and hot and smooth to her, or at least she thought it did, until his skin texture changed under the pad of her index finger and Gabriel stiffened and groaned deeply.

She wanted to do that again. And again, while he writhed at her touch; her eyes were glazing over, she liked it so much. Lord, that probably made her a sodomite, too. She rubbed the spot once more, gently, and licked her lips when Gabriel made the same sound, only more pitifully this time, since she hadn't given him as much as he wanted. She said a bit shakily, "Could he come like that?"

"Like a grenade," Crispin said hoarsely, while Gabriel made a noise between a curse and a laugh.

"You'd better fuck him right now, then," she said, reluctantly exchanging places. She wiped her hands on a bit of sheet. "What's the best way?"

Gabriel and Crispin finally settled on Crispin's standing and Gabriel facedown on the bed, his legs hanging over the side. This left room for Bob to hold Gabriel in her lap, as Crispin had done with her earlier. This felt good, too. She was in the mood to be the one holding, instead of being held. Especially once Crispin gripped Gabriel's hips and got started, and Gabriel made more delicious groans into her thigh, his fingers clenching at her helplessly while a haze of sweat and sex rose around them. She held him as tightly as she could, her fingers digging into his muscles, and stared while Crispin's nervous incredulity faded into absorption, then into such single-minded intensity that she wanted to grab him and sink her teeth into him. His stocky frame was beautiful in motion, his powerful shoulders and upper arms and pecs, even his belly flexing with each push from his muscular arse, each thrust ending in a twist as if to shove himself harder inside, deeper inside.

Each impact flung Gabriel's weight into her and throbbed inside her cunt, like she was the one getting fucked. It was more than enough to keep her hungry and wet. She felt as if she was right in the middle of a sexy dream, all this show just for her eyes. Maybe it could really be just for her. Hoarsely, she said, "Stop."

Crispin made a strangled sound and slammed his hips into Gabriel, holding there for a long moment. "Why?"

"I want you to," she said, licking her lips.

"Fucking get on with it!" Gabriel growled.

"Pull out a bit," she whispered, and Crispin did as she asked, his face twisted with agonized pleasure. Her belly contracted at the sight. She'd done that.

Gabriel groaned. "Don't stop."

"Do it slow," she said, the words falling out of her mouth

as if they traveled straight from her cunt. "Make him feel it. Every inch."

Gabriel's startled cursing strangled into moans and uncontrolled twitching as Crispin slowly, slowly entered him, and just as slowly withdrew. Crispin cursed steadily, too, his eyes fixed on hers, his pupils wide and black as the Thames at night. She could barely breathe for lust. When she felt Gabriel's muscles tremoring beneath her hands, she murmured, "Fuck him hard," then a bit louder, "faster."

A few thrusts and Crispin was jerking uncontrollably, coming so hard she could almost see the contractions rippling through his body. He collapsed onto Gabriel's back and gasped for breath, his weight shoving her deeper into the mattress.

Gabriel's hands dug painfully into her. "I want to fuck you," he said. "Isobel, please. I need you *right now*."

She licked her lips. "Turn over," she said. "You all right, Crispin?"

He grunted and helped shove Gabriel's legs onto the bed before collapsing up near his shoulder. He looked dazed and satisfied, a little smile playing around his lips. Bob gave him a quick kiss before she responded to Gabriel's urgent hands and voice, mounting him in one long slide that made both of them moan.

Gabriel's pale cheekbones blazed with blood. His hair was dark with sweat, even his mustache, and his eyes seemed huge, his pupils almost hiding their blue irises. She rocked back and forth on his cock, gently, and stroked his chest with her hands. She wasn't calming him, not really. He opened his mouth a couple of times, but nothing came out; in the end he licked his lips and panted, staring into her face, his hot, callused hands like manacles on her wrists.

When she couldn't stand it anymore, she rocked harder,

rubbing her clit against him with each forward motion, and squeezing him with her inner muscles, until she swore she could feel him swelling even more with each clench.

"More," he said.

"Not yet."

Crispin was petting Gabriel's hair, watching his face more than he watched her. It was a strange kind of intimacy, each of them in their own world but also together, all focused on the same end, all of them wanting to touch someone and not to be alone, and to reach that place where for a few moments nothing else mattered.

She rode Gabriel harder, keeping him inside her and bending low enough that her nipples brushed against his chest. They were so sensitive it was almost agony, while at the same time it felt as if electric shocks were shooting all over her body. She closed her eyes, searching for climax. Gabriel grabbed her, his forearms sliding in the sweat on her back, his neck arching to touch his head to hers. She could hear him moaning softly, rhythmically, or maybe it was her, or both of them. He squeezed her with his arms and his hips jerked; she shot abruptly to a higher level of agonized passion, crying out with it, but she was wound too tight, and couldn't make herself come.

She felt Crispin's arm wrap around her hips and then his hand, big and square, nudging between her body and Gabriel's, finding where they were joined. His thumb slid over her swollen clit, and she ground down on his hand, just the extra bit of friction she needed to fall over the edge. She trembled helplessly in wave after wave of orgasm until she had to pull loose of Gabriel's cock, her cunt too tender to bear any more pleasure.

Crispin took over then, patting her softly with one hand before engulfing Gabriel's cock in his mouth, his cheeks hollowing with the force of his sucking. Gabriel's hands clenched in his curls, his hips pumping, Crispin riding the motion and not once letting go; then, all at once, he took a breath and Gabriel's cock seemed to disappear down his throat. Gabriel arched and froze; it was only after a moment or two that she realized his cock was twitching in Crispin's mouth, spurting his seed straight down the other man's throat.

After, they lay in a sprawled, awkward pile. Gabriel, whose idea it had all been, was deeply asleep. Bob snuggled up to his back and Crispin to his front; then Crispin reached over and rested his hand on her back, stroking a little. "Thanks," he said.

"Show me that trick sometime?" she asked.

"Trick?"

"Did you really swallow—"

"I did. Takes practice."

"Sexiest thing I ever saw," she said sleepily. Then, "Fuck, we're due back. In another day."

Crispin sighed, and squeezed her shoulder. "We'll get leave again."

"We will?"

"All of us. Together."

LUCILLA CRAMMED ANOTHER WAD OF CLOTH onto the wound in Ashby's side and prayed that he remained unconscious. The boy, Friedrich, crouched beside her, pressing more bandages against Ashby's mangled thigh and flinching each time he moaned. He hadn't said a word since he'd changed form. Miss Claes, still in wolf form, paced and warily swung her head between them and the three other wolves, who huddled together against the wall, as far as possible from Kauz's torn body. It was clear she did not trust the boy, but Lucilla needed another pair of hands, and Miss Claes did not seem about to provide any.

Pascal ran back into the room, carrying an armful of cloth and wooden poles, which she soon identified as a disassembled stretcher. "Can he be moved?"

Lucilla had seen men wounded worse who suffered days of exposure with no dressings, and some of them had survived. Ashby's inhuman constitution would no doubt aid in his survival, as well. And it wasn't as if they had any choice.

Quickly, she began to bind on the pads of fabric. "How will we get him up the stairs?"

Pascal spoke to Friedrich in rapid German, requesting his aid. Cringing a little, the boy crept forward. Pascal gentled his tone and gave the boy instructions concerning opening doors and holding a lantern, then pointed to the other wolves, commanding them to change form.

Miss Claes stalked over to them, lowered her head and growled. Lucilla glanced up in time to see the wolves writhing into human shape. They were older than Friedrich, but not by much, perhaps fifteen or sixteen at the most. At Miss Claes's significant growl, they stumbled forward. Two of them helped Pascal to assemble the stretcher. The third knelt next to Lucilla, uncaring of his nakedness, his overlong dark hair hanging in his eyes, which were an odd pale green, hooded beneath full lids.

"I will lift," he said in a voice barely above a whisper.

"What's your name?" she asked.

"Immanuel," he said. He wrenched at his collar. Lucilla stopped him, made him turn around and unbuckled it from his throat. He seized it from her hand and flung it, hard, into the corner, onto Kauz's body. Then he helped her lift Ashby's supine form onto the stretcher.

The route by which Kauz had entered the room was a narrow tunnel that presumably led to the surface; after she opened the door, Immanuel whispered, "It stinks." She gathered this was a chemical stink, specifically chosen to repel the young wolves from attempting escape by that route.

Pascal said, "We'll retreat as we entered. We will discard the stretcher if it becomes too cumbersome, and carry Ashby in some other manner."

"Let's hope he's as hardy as I think he is," Lucilla commented. She turned to Immanuel. "Come along. And you— what's your name?"

The tallest boy's lips moved, but no sound emerged. He swallowed and looked embarrassed. Immanuel said, "He is Emil." He pointed to the other boy, who now crouched next to Friedrich. "That is Kurt."

"I'll need two of you to help me," Lucilla said.

Immanuel shook his head. "We cannot leave."

"We must leave now," Pascal said. "We have set explosions. These corridors will collapse."

"No! We must find Bruno and Franz."

You might have mentioned them before, Lucilla thought irritably. "Could they be in the surface structure?"

Pascal growled in frustration, sounding uncannily like Miss Claes. "The ground will collapse, as well. Do you have any idea where they might be?"

Kurt spoke for the first time. His voice was surprisingly deep for his apparent age. "We know their scent. I will change."

Pascal glanced at Lucilla. She said, "We must get Ashby to safety. Perhaps Miss Claes—"

Pascal dropped to his knees. "Tanneken. Will you accompany this boy?"

Drying blood spiked her blond fur, and Lucilla could have sworn her fangs had grown, or perhaps it was that her lips had drawn so high on her gums as to expose every wicked inch of shining tooth. Her eyes had a mad gleam. For a moment, it seemed as if she might not understand Pascal's words, but then she abandoned her scrutiny of the boys, licked Ashby's cheek and nipped at Kurt's leg, obviously encouraging him to get on with it.

Lucilla turned away as Kurt shifted form, unable to watch what seemed to be a much more painful process than Ashby's normal transformations. Perhaps he trained his muscles in some way. She knelt beside the stretcher and checked his pulse until Miss Claes and Kurt trotted from the room. Pascal was marshaling the rest of the young werewolves, and soon the two older boys had lifted the stretcher. Pascal led the way down the tunnel, his own pistol in hand and Ashby's tucked into his clothing. Friedrich carried the lantern just behind him, and Lucilla kept an eye on the rise and fall of Ashby's torso, also making sure no more blood soaked through his dressings.

The shotgun blast was bad enough. She hated to think of what bacteria might live in the mouths of werewolves, particularly ones who looked half-feral and bore an unwashed odor even she could smell with no trouble whatsoever. If she'd had carbolic, she would have doused his wounds in a gallon of it. Add the risk of bacteria to Ashby's having attempted to shift while he'd been attacked, and she couldn't even hazard a guess as to what damage had been done to his muscles. It worried her that his wounds had not shown any signs of healing when he'd become human again. She could not care for him on her own. He needed a hospital, and soon; his wounds needed disinfecting and irrigating and likely some delicate surgery.

Of course, all that would be moot if her carefully placed explosions completed before they had escaped the tunnels. She couldn't stop it, not in the time allotted, and with no supplies to do so.

Immanuel said, "I know a shorter way out."

Pascal whirled, causing Friedrich to jump. The lantern light flared wildly. Lucilla saw Pascal's nostrils flare as he asked, "Where," and she wondered if he was actually scenting the air, trying to determine if the boy spoke truth or lie.

"From the big cage room," Immanuel said. "I saw."

"You didn't," said Emil. His voice was hoarse, unused.

"Did. I woke up one time." He looked to Pascal. "There's a box, with a rope." He shuddered. "Small box. But it goes up."

"A dumbwaiter," Lucilla surmised. "It'll be rough on Ashby, but so will an explosion."

Immanuel had not lied. She and Emil went first, holding Ashby between them. He roused enough to whimper, then passed out again when she had to bend his leg to make him fit. Inside the wooden cabinet, Emil dragged on the rope. Lucilla chewed the inside of her cheek, trying not to choke or gag on the mingled stenches of blood and old sweat and horrid chemicals, not sulfur or acid but something infinitely worse that stung the soft membranes of her nose. It was like the powder she'd tested, though less potent. Whatever it was, it would soon go up in flames with everything else Kauz had created.

Once outside under the clean stars, she expected Emil to run, but he did not. He sent the dumbwaiter to fetch Friedrich and Immanuel. Pascal had decided to go last. In the meantime, Lucilla showed Emil how to go about a chair-carry. The two of them hauled Ashby's unconscious form slowly but steadily out of danger. Given the choice, she would rather have been hauling him in the dogcart, and she cursed freely every time she had to readjust her grip.

She did not see Immanuel and Friedrich emerge, as she was too busy hurrying in the other direction, but the two boys caught them up almost immediately, Friedrich still tightly gripping his lantern. Immanuel took her place carrying Ashby, so she turned to look for Pascal.

He wasn't there.

Perhaps it had not been as long as it seemed. She crossed her arms over her chest, aware of the cutting wind as it whipped across her face and throat, now bare thanks to Ashby's excessive need for bandages. Perhaps she had missed seeing him in the dark.

She would have heard his boots thumping on the hard ground, as she could now clearly hear the soft murmur of Friedrich speaking to the older boys. Where was Pascal? How long did it take to lift one's self out of a hole when a perfectly good dumbwaiter was provided? She reached for the watch she habitually wore pinned to her apron only to find, of course, that she wore a now-bloody overcoat over men's clothing. She dug for her watch in her waistcoat before finding it in an inner pocket of her jacket. By the time she had it in her hand, and realized she wouldn't be able to see the face without Friedrich's lantern, a bloodcurdling series of howls tore the air, swiftly followed by a flood of fur running at full tilt across the frozen ground. Following them, though necessarily slower, was Pascal.

Lucilla yelled and waved. She immediately felt like an idiot, but at least the yelling had dispersed some of the terrible tightness in her chest. The wolves shot by her—three, pursued by the larger Miss Claes—and Pascal came next. She grabbed his arm and they ran together, while behind them the ground shuddered and erupted in dust and flame.

An hour later, Lucilla crouched next to Ashby and waited for Pascal to return with a lorry. Miss Claes, who never had changed back into a human, lay by Ashby, her chin resting on his knees and her eyes closed. Blood was drying on her muzzle; not hers, but Kauz's. The two smallest wolves, Bruno and Franz, lay curled together a short distance away under the protection of Friedrich. The four older boys had accompanied Pascal, primarily to keep them out of range of Miss Claes's protective instincts toward Ashby, whom they had wounded grievously.

Lucilla tugged off her glove and checked the pulse at his throat. It beat strongly, if a little too shallowly. A human would have succumbed to shock already, she suspected. The skin on his cheek wasn't warm, but neither did it hold a deathly chill. As she drew her hand away, he made a small sound of protest. Miss Claes lifted her head.

"Got a Blighty wound," he whispered. She could hear the smile in his voice.

"Yes, you're going home," Lucilla said. "If you don't heal too quickly."

"Won't." He sighed. "Too much. S'all right. Tanneken'll come with me. She said." He closed his eyes. Miss Claes crept forward and licked his cheek.

Lucilla hugged Crispin one last time, then shoved him gently toward Ashby's hospital bed. She'd managed to obtain one of the unused isolation rooms, so none of his current visitors had been chased out after shift change.

Hailey fussed over the new uniform she'd brought to replace the one lost when Ashby had first been captured. Miss Claes sat quietly and elegantly in the corner, her feet drawn up onto a brocaded armchair that she made into a throne. Her greetings to her future husband's friends had been equally regal; her eyes flicked warily from one person to the next. Gabriel Meyer, whom Lucilla had been relieved to find she liked, sat next to the bed in a more utilitarian chair, bent close to Ashby and conversing with him in a low voice. He had quite enough visitors for now.

"I'm going outside for a while," she said.

She shed her cape and apron in the changing room, opting for an overcoat instead, then wandered out to the terrace. A couple score of the ambulatory patients sat there, listening to a makeshift orchestra play whatever all of the musicians knew, or partially knew. Presently, it was some semblance of a waltz. She didn't see Pascal. She circumnavigated the building until she found him on the path leading to X-ray and her quarters.

"Looking for me?" she asked.

He turned to her and bowed, sweeping off his kepi. "*Mademoiselle* wishes to dance?"

"My card isn't quite full," she said, and allowed him to sweep her into his arms. She slipped her arms beneath his greatcoat and held him tightly as they danced atop frozen mud. After a few minutes, she commented, "You're a terrible dancer."

Pascal bent and kissed her ear. "I am brilliant instead. Also, I know where you prefer to be licked."

Lucilla wrestled him to a stop and kissed him. When she pulled away, she held on to his arms and studied his face in the harsh electric light from a pole nearby. "You will be careful, won't you?"

"Always."

"I would hate for you to come to any harm," she said, her fingers plucking the sleeve of his greatcoat.

"I plan to stay well out of danger from now on. As much as I can do so." He paused. "And you? Will you come to see me, at Rue Deuxième?"

"Pascal," she said in a rush, "I'll understand if it's not possible, but do you think I could work with the boys, if they agree? Examine their blood, and look at their cells? Nothing invasive, I promise." She looked at the ground. "I can't help it. I'm so curious I think I'll burst."

He laughed and kissed her lingeringly. "I'll ask. They are eager to please. And one of them, Immanuel—he asked about you already." He paused. He said very quietly, "I don't think they yet understand I will not leave them to fend for themselves, no matter how I try to convince them otherwise. They believe that I will find other werewolves to be their families, but not that I do so for their good and not mine." He looked away, then back at her. "They were not so lucky as to have a Grand-Oncle Erard."

"Perhaps that's one good thing to come out of this war," Lucilla said. "There are people from all over in France just now. It might make the task easier."

Pascal said, "And after this war ends? Will you stay here then, and study werewolves? With me?" He paused. "I could go to England, if you prefer. The food is abominable, but for you, I would endure it."

Lucilla laughed. She slipped her arms around his waist again and squeezed. "Either. Yes. I'd like that more than anything."

ACKNOWLEDGMENTS

Ann, John and Judith made this book a thousand times better with their poolside critique of the opening chapters, and I cannot thank them enough for their insights at that crucial time. Thank you to my agent, Lori Perkins, who found my work a home at Spice Books. I'd also like to thank Susan Swinwood; my editor, Lara Hyde, for her swift, friendly and honest responses to whatever I needed; and all the staff at Harlequin Books who produced such a beautiful book. Finally, thanks to Diana for reading the revised manuscript and to Kat for the title.